MW01516669

# The Rite Place

## by
## Susan Cutsforth-Freitas

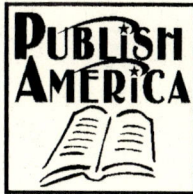

PublishAmerica
Baltimore

First printing

ISBN: 1-4137-5641-7
PUBLISHED BY PUBLISHAMERICA, LLLP
www.publishamerica.com
Baltimore

Printed in the United States of America

# Dedication

My family, who has supported and encouraged me. To my girls,
Sadie, Emily and Carrie, who made sure I was always appreciated;
my mom, who kept me on task; and especially my husband, Ernie,
who believed in me when I didn't believe in myself.

# Acknowledgments

Karen, my sister and technical advisor, whose help over the years made it possible for this manuscript to be printed instead of floundering in the Never-Never Land of computer hard drives.

# Prologue

The small country town was especially quiet; missing was the early evening bustle. Townspeople making last minute preparations for a quiet spring weekend were missing.

The slowly setting sun cast shadows throughout town, giving the impression of sudden abandonment. Perhaps it was an old ghost town, the spirits of the residents lurking in the ensuing darkness.

A lone figure scurried silently across the town square, throwing grotesque shadows in the waning sunlight. Startled by the bark of an angry dog, the figure hesitated, holding its breath, to assure its anonymity.

Stopping in the shadow of an ancient fir tree, hunching to appear smaller, the huddled form darted across the last street to safety. Peering right and left as it approached a small cottage, it paused slightly at the front door for one last quick look.

Opening and closing the door quickly, denying as little light from inside an escape, the figure leaned against the door to catch its breath. When it's breathing returned to normal it lifted the heavy curtain covering the small living room window while a smile of satisfaction spread over the dull features. It's smile broadened at the warm glow growing in the distant sky.

Swaggering to the adjoining room, it carelessly threw its shoes and coat into the corner. The figure collapsed into the nearby rocker. Sitting quietly for several minutes, it rocked slowly back and forth, waiting for the return of regular heartbeats. The hollow silence of the room was broken by the creaking of the old wooden rocker and an occasional raspy chuckle.

The replica of a small Tiffany lamp sat on a table next to the chair, casting an eerie light throughout the small room. The glow illuminated a polished silver frame filled with the photograph of a young woman dressed in an old-fashioned wedding dress. The photograph, torn in half, had aged. It was fading to the comforting brown of antique family portraits. Yellowed, curling flowers, long ago cut from a magazine, were haphazardly glued to the ragged edge.

"As soon as I get my breath I'll tell you what happened today," the figure finally spoke, breaking the silence. Looking blankly into the dark recess of the room, it added, "I'm a hero, Momma, sort of." It became silent once again as it replayed the events of the day in its mind.

The room was filled with the clutter of clothing thrown in mindless disarray to cover the bed and floor. Clips of newspapers and magazines were strewn about the room, mixing with the clutter of clothing. The room was a virtual library of paperback books. Some new, some old, all were in various stages of being read; a vast display of mystery authors.

"I'm thirsty, Momma. How about you?"

It leaped from the chair and scurried out of the bedroom into a larger living area, no longer mesmerized but suddenly full of nervous energy. Immediately the difference between the two rooms was apparent.

The stark neatness of the room stood in comparison with the messy, drab bedroom. The large room was bare except for an old gray sofa and two faded, flowered armchairs that gave the room it's only color.

A few pictures, absently hung, were dwarfed by the hollow expanse of wall. A fireplace, the only thing in the room used with any regularity, was directly across from the chairs. Next to the fireplace sat a box filled with wood topped by a well-honed hatchet.

The figure walked across the room, pulling back a heavy curtain that hid a small kitchenette. The kitchenette, neater then the bedroom and more inviting then the living room, was obviously rarely used.

Opening the small refrigerator and taking out a cola, the only contents besides a few old containers of Chinese take-out, the figure grabbed an old "Coke" church key to open the cola. Extra care was given to diligently wash and dry the church key before returning it to its resting place.

Returning to the bedroom, the picture of the young bride was grabbed before collapsing on the bed with the cola. The swipe of an empty arm cleared the night stand and the photo was set on the table beside the cola.

"Boy! What a day, Momma! Miss Marples or Miss Silvers couldn't have done better!"

Plopping gracelessly onto the bed, it punched the pillows mercilessly to make a comfortable sleeping area. Twisting and patting, fluffing and plumping, it arranged the bed like a little nest.

Draining the cola in one gulp, a smile of satisfaction filled the dull features. "Well, Momma, there was a murder today...that's right, a real murder... right here in this little dump of a town. Soon all of the stupid people will be stalking each other!"

Relaxing in the little nest, picking up the silver frame, the words began to slur.

"What fun it'll be watching them look over their shoulders...wondering who did it. I was so clever...clever as any of those books you read...smarter than Agatha or any of them."

The smile slowly disappeared, replaced by a grimace of anxiety. Sleep slowly overcame the exhausted figure...amidst black secrets and dark dreams.

# Chapter One

Jessie, with her arms crossed stiffly over her chest, stared out the window. Wondering where Roger could be was becoming a habit. Somewhere in the midst of her thoughts the hum of the endless bickering between her kids slipped into her thoughts.

"I've had enough. This is it!" Jessie mumbled out loud, more to herself than anyone. She spun around to leave and was startled by the question in the eyes so like Roger's.

"Enough of what?" questioned Jordan.

"Enough of your bickering!" she said brightly, trying to mask the truth behind her anger. She crossed the room in several quick strides to grab her purse. Pulling the keys to her new BMW she absently tossed them to Cristal, she was already planning her next move.

"You're not going to let her drive the new Beamer, are you?" Jordan croaked. "She doesn't even have her license!" He whined with a petulant look so like his father's that it fanned the anger growing within Jessie.

Trying to stem the irritation threatening to spill onto the children, she said, through clenched teeth, "Jordan, you had better hurry, or you will miss your ride!" She gave Jordan the look that stemmed further argument.

"Aren't you coming?" he asked, already knowing the answer. Turning to leave, unnoticed by the preoccupied woman, he gave her one last imploring look. He walked slowly to the door, pausing before quietly closing the door.

Jessie was so involved in her thoughts she didn't hear the toot of the horn as Cristal and Jordan pulled out of the driveway. She reflected on the first time she and her father had driven to the ranch on that same driveway...

*****

"Hurry up Jessie." Jake was hollering at her. "We don't want to get there in the middle of the night." Jake was in a hurry to leave; the memories of the last year were more than he could bear. They were the kind no one wants to remember—or forget!

His wife, Pearl, had been the reason for his being. Before he met her he was nothing more than a glorified hot walker, drinking to make him forget the failure he had become, spending what little cash he made on poorly placed bets at the racetrack where he worked.

In the beginning he was going to be Jake Johnson—owner, breeder and trainer of the best racehorses in the U.S.A.! Unfortunately things hadn't worked out as he had planned.

Then he met Pearl Mason. She was as beautiful inside as she was outside. Her physical frailty hid an inner strength unlike anyone Jake had ever known. They would talk for hours about the future; she made him believe in himself again. He started thinking about someone besides himself; quit feeling sorry for the way things had turned out, and suddenly wonderful things began to happen.

He came to work one day to find he was in charge of training a three-year-old mare. Her bloodlines were nonexistent, but she had real potential. She won several major races, and his reputation catapulted. The support from Pearl had set his life on an even keel; marriage and children were the next step for Jake.

He was surprised at his difficulty in making Pearl say yes to his proposal of marriage. She insisted he was too good for her. Imagine that, he was good for her!

Pearl found once Jake Johnson made up his mind nothing stopped him. Six months later they were married, and Jessica Pearl Johnson was on the way.

He gained his reputation, stable and breeding stock. He realized dreams were fine but the real miracles of life weren't money or fame. Pearl and Jessica were the true inspirations of his life.

His little Jessica was born in the image of Pearl, sweet and beautiful, but she had a strong will of her own. Jack proudly boasted his genes contributed to her independence. Life was wonderful and Jake questioned what he had done to deserve so many wonderful things.

Unfortunately, Jake's question was answered. Suddenly Pearl began losing strength. Her frailty compounded the illness she was unable to shake.

The day Pearl went to the hospital was the last truly content day he lived. He made the doctors try everything. They tried new procedures, new drugs, anything to possibly save her. He planned a trip to Mexico to a homeopathic clinic as a last resort; before they could leave Pearl was so exhausted she begged him to let her go.

Holding Pearl as the last labored breath escaped her body, he dropped the facade of hope and wept for the loss of his love. The illness had come quickly and Pearl was gone so suddenly he wasn't prepared for the desolation of life without her.

He would sit for hours staring at nothing, ignoring his surroundings and his daughter. Jake sold every one of his horses to pay for Pearl's hospital cost, leaving him with nothing but an empty horse ranch and a bright-eyed youngster. Misery filled him; the prospect of a life without Pearl was unbearable. Jumping back into the bottle, looking for peace, Jake lost the reputation he had built with Pearl at his side.

Jessie's independence was put to the test trying to get the father she had once known to return to her. She had the wisdom of someone beyond her years; she instinctively knew Jake needed time to heal the gaping wounds left by her mother's death. The little girl took over where mother had left off; she cleaned house, did laundry and made her limited variety of meals. It was as if she was the parent and Jake the spoiled child. Coaxing her father to go on, she found herself exhausted by the end of the day. She protected him from bill collectors as long as she could and when she thought she had come to the end of her rope, she was saved by an unknown source.

One night after Jessie had gone to bed an old nemesis of Jake's came to him with a proposal. Roger Rite II offered him the opportunity to work with his horses. Roger wouldn't take no for an answer. Late at night, over gallons of black coffee, Roger explained this was the chance to keep the promises he had made to Pearl. As the fog in Jake's brain began to lift, he mulled over the offer. There was a chance with enough work he could forget the loneliness of life without Pearl. Sobering up, he let loose of his stubborn pride and accepted the opportunity.

Packing what little they had left into his old beater, Jake wasted no time heading for their new life. Jessie begged him to stay. She didn't want to leave the place filled with memories of her mother, the only home she had ever known. Fearful she would lose the memories she had of her mother if they left the ranch, she threw one of the few temper tantrums of her life in the hopes of changing Jake's mind. Jake, in the hopes of putting Jessie's fears to rest, promised Jessie he would never let the memories of her mother disappear.

Jake had to hurry, before he could change his mind, and quickly they were packed and on their way.

"Jessica Pearl, if you don't shake a leg I'm leaving without you." Jake smiled, thinking she could make it on her own better than he ever could. He headed back to the house ready to haul her out bodily if it was necessary.

"I'm coming, Jake. I just had to make sure you weren't forgetting anything," Jessie called. Looking over her shoulder, she took one last look at the only home she had ever known; Jessica squeezed her eyes tightly, hoping to imprint the memory on her brain.

Watching her leave the house and waiting to be boosted up into the cab, Jake saw in the little girl a miniature of his Pearl. He hadn't lost Pearl, here was the copy of her sitting beside him. He would always have her with him.

Jessie turned for one last look at the place where she had grown up, praying she would always remember her life here. She wiped away the tears falling down her softly rounded cheeks. She remembered the last time she saw her mother and the promise she made to take care of Jake.

"Jessica Pearl, I love you and always will. You take care of yourself and your father. I'll watch from heaven. Let me see you take care of him. You be my big girl. I love you more than I can say." She told her mother she would take care of him because if anyone needed taking care of it was Jake!

Jessie found it hard to keep from asking questions about where they were going. She could tell by the black look on Jake's face she should just sit back and enjoy the scenery. She was about to ask if they would ever get there when before her hung a sign that read "Circle R Ranch," proclaiming they had reached their destination. Jessie was relieved to have the trip over until she noticed the signs on each side telling people to "Keep Out."

"Boy, Jake, did you ever find a friendly place for us to go," Jessie said.

What little excitement she had left was draining out of her; she should have stayed at the old place! There were no mean signs there keeping people out.

"Don't worry, Jess," Jake said softly. "We will make it. We have each other."

Looking past the Circle R Ranch sign, Jessie saw, for the first time, her new home. Out of a cloud of dust rode a man on the biggest chestnut stallion Jessie had ever seen. Behind him flapped a little boy, holding on for dear life. She didn't know it at the time, but here was the person who would change her life, not for the better but for the worse!

Jake slowed the grumbling beater down to ask the man where he should park. Jessie was intrigued by the slow smile spreading across the man's face as he looked at her.

"Just park outside the main house, Jake," the man said, still staring at Jessie. "Well, I don't have to be introduced to this little lady," the man drawled. "This has to be Pearl's little girl."

Jessie was surprised to find the man knew her mother but refused to say anything to the tall stranger. She just stared at the small boy clinging to the saddle straps, trying to keep his seat. She gave him a wide smile and was saddened by the look of terror in the small boy's eyes. Jessie could tell the small boy was a couple of years younger and an immediate overwhelming sense of protection overtook her.

"Well, what do you think of Big Roger?" Jake asked as the headed for the large ranch house.

"I thought he had lots of money," Jessie answered.

"He sure has. He practically owns the entire state!" he said as he parked in front of the large ranch house.

"Well, if he has so much money why doesn't he buy that boy his own horse?" Jessie was filled with confusing emotions.

Jake bellowed, surprising Jessie. She had not heard him laugh since Momma had died. She found she liked the sound, but refused to drop the interrogation. She just stared at him with eyes he thought were too solemn for a 10-year-old. Jake finally answered, "Big Roger likes to control things."

"Well, he can't control me," Jessie stated flatly.

"No, I'm sure he will find that out soon enough," Jake added with a wide smile. He thanked God for this small wonder; she was a true replica of his beloved Pearl.

Jessica was soon to find out she alone had a way of handling Big Roger. As the years went by the only way she exploited it was to try to show Big Roger he was making a mistake with Little Roger. Even for her tender years she knew it was one mistake he would one day regret.

She found she genuinely liked these people, everyone except Little Roger's mother, Glynis. She knew she would never have the closeness she had with her own mother. She couldn't figure out Glynis; one minute she was fawning all over Little Roger, the next she looked at him with such vile contempt Jessie was surprised it didn't melt the sterling silver!

Glynis was always complaining about Jessie not being enough of a lady, but then Glynis complained about everything Jessie did. Little Roger's habit of following Jessie like a puppy and repeating word for word everything she said was enough to insure Glynis's loathing. Glynis didn't want Little Roger to love anyone but her. When Little Roger informed Glynis that Jessie was his friend forever, it cemented Glynis's hatred.

Jessie got used to helping Jake when it came to training the racehorses. She went from stable girl to hot walker to exerciser in a matter of years. Jake felt although Jessie was his daughter he wouldn't give her any advantage. She would have to prove herself just like anyone else. Of course, it didn't stop him from swelling with pride when she outshined every handler they ever hired!

As the years passed, Jessica learned how expansive Big Roger's holdings were. She talked easily with Big Roger, and he would listen to her, never belittling her dreams the way he did Little Roger's.

The day Jessie began calling Little Roger "Roj" it seemed natural for everyone to follow suit, much to Glynis's horror! Glynis refused to call him by Jessie's nickname until one day Roj stopped answering to "Little Roger," giving Glynis one more reason to dislike Jessie.

The day she tried to send "that girl" to finishing school was the day she found the last vestiges of her authority had vanished.

"Roger, she needs finishing school. You all act like it is respectable for a teenage girl to go around smelling like a cowhand," Glynis said in her sweetest "I'm just trying to do what is right" tone.

"She is going to want to get married some day, and I'm sure her husband won't want to sleep with a girl smelling from horse dung."

"You know, Glynis, I could never figure what it is you dislike about 'that girl' as you so politely put it. Now I have finally figured it out; you are jealous!" Roger said. "I won't hear any more of this nonsense." He said this with a finality that made the hair on the back of Glynis's neck stand up!

"Well, next year Little Roger is going to the academy. She will be so lonely without him toddling behind her. I was only thinking of her," Glynis sniffed.

"That won't work this time, Glynis. I've made up my mind." Roger started out the door. "I've decided to keep Roj here to see if some of her spunk won't rub off on him!" He walked out with the slam of the door, to cut off Glynis's scream of outrage.

The explosion of a crystal bottle of expensive perfume was the last thing Roger heard as he stalked down the wide expanse of stairs. "Well, if I'm lucky that's all this little episode will cost me," he grumbled. Glynis filled the hours left by Roj's abandonment by plotting her revenge on Jessie.

Jessie and Roj slipped from the familiar camaraderie of adolescence to the intimacy of young love. Jessie had always felt an overwhelming responsibility to Roj because of Big Roger's treatment of his son. The more he showered Jessie with praise, the farther away he drove Roj. Over the years Jessie had developed an understanding of Glynis's treatment of the men in her life. Glynis was not capable of loving relationships. Her life's goal was centered upon herself; ultimately her only concern was the glorification and satisfaction of herself.

Roj and Jessie's relationship was filled with rocky roads, but they usually ended the same way: heads together, giggles filling the air.

Roj was jealous of Jessie's friends when Jessie entered high school. He was used to being the center of attention in her life, and he was afraid she would find someone to replace him. He reacted with a spite and vindictiveness to make Glynis proud. As he turned from an adolescent into a teenager the space between the two widened. During his high school years he was known as quite a Don Juan. His reputation as a heartbreaker spread throughout the county, giving his father one more thing to upset him.

Jessie's decision to go away to college instead of commuting was based on Roj's behavior. She was unable to decide the true extent of her feelings. She would flip-flop; one minute she felt overwhelming love for the young man, then she would feel hate. She felt they needed some space to straighten out their emotions. Jessie and Roj grew distant when Jessie went to college. When she would come home for summer vacation she found a petulant young man she didn't recognize. Gone was the sensitive young man of her childhood. The abyss between Roj and Jessie had grown, making life around the ranch difficult when Roj was around. Jessie put all of her energy into learning about the running of the ranch.

When Jessie returned from college, instead of a gangly teenager she was a beautiful young woman who stole the heart of the young man. It was Roj's turn to go away to college, putting credence to the theory "absence makes the heart grow fonder." After Roj's first year at school they found the closeness they had lost in the last few years. Roj's tender love letters made Jessie's heart yearn for him to return. The lengthy letters she sent back were filled with news of the ranch and her loneliness without him.

To Glynis's horror, Roj and Jessica were becoming close in a way she had always feared. This was not puppy love! They found common ground as young adults. They were inseparable during the summer months, keeping in constant touch while Roj was away.

To fill her hours with Roj away at college, she spent her time learning the intricacies of the Rite fortune. Jake and she still worked together with the training of the racehorses, but the rest of her time was her time, and it was spent learning the vastness of the Rite holdings. By the time Roj graduated from college it was obvious to everyone that marriage between the two wasn't far away.

Glynis produced a graduation party which surpassed anything the county had ever seen. Glynis was on the constant lookout for a young lady of "proper breeding" for Roj to wed. Glynis was horrified when Roj took the opportunity to announce their engagement when every important person in the state, including the governor, was on hand.

Glynis and Jessie reached an armed truce, but she was less than fond of the idea of her and Roj being married. Glynis took every opportunity she could find to introduce Roj to every beautiful, eligible girl in the state. Jessie was amused by Glynis's antics, but Roj was overwhelmed with anger and during the meetings treated his mother with so much animosity it made Jessie feel sorry for the woman.

On Jessica's wedding day she stood at Jake's arm at the top of the stairs filled with the strangest feelings. This was the same stairwell she and Roj had slid down as often as they could get away with it! She thought about throwing her leg over and riding it down, just for the fun of it! She felt a chill run down her back as Glynis turned to give her the sickly smile that had been pasted on her face since learning of the engagement.

Jessie whispered, "My God, she can read my mind!"

"Don't worry, Pearlie, just wedding-day jitters. You and Roj are going to have a great marriage," Jake said, looking down at her lovingly. Jake said a silent prayer, From my mouth to God's ear, to insure what he said came true.

Big Roger insisted it was his duty to send them on a honeymoon so grand it would leave the townspeople reeling for years, a honeymoon so fantastic they would be more than ready to take over when they returned. Big Roger's pride at the way his son had turned out was beaming from his usually sour continence. He felt as if the two could take over and bring the Rite holdings to an even higher plain. Unbeknownst to everyone, Big Roger was looking forward to retirement; at last he was ready to fulfill his dreams of travel.

The honeymoon included a grand tour of Europe, Greece and, last but not least, Arabia (to check into some breeding stock that interested Jake. As Big Roger said, "Why waste a perfectly good business opportunity?").

The honeymoon was everything she hoped it would be and more. In Paris she had carte blanche in all the top design houses, dinners at the Ritz, and strolls through the Louvre Museum. Their stay in Ireland afforded them a chance to ride to the hounds on the most beautiful Irish warm-blood jumpers Jessie had ever encountered, giving her the idea of increasing their stock to include jumping stock. During the day they walked hand in hand down the boulevards; everyone that saw them knew they were young lovers.

She was surprised when Roj decided to take a side trip to Monaco. Although Roj lost a bundle at faro she was still thrilled at the sights of royalty passing nightly. They giggled like teenagers at the thought of Glynis sitting on the throne, waving her specter like the Queen of Hearts, ranting "Off with their heads"! They knew Glynis would feel right at home! They roared until their sides hurt at the thought of Jake running around in red tights, announcing the queen's arrival, and Big Roger dressed as the March hare, hollering, "I'm late! I'm late, for a very important date!"

Their trip to Arabia was fantastic. They were shown horses of royal breeding that dated back hundreds of years. There were banquets of unique but delicious foods of every descriptions and dancers clad in golden baubles and silken outfits.

They traveled by camel to isolated oases which beheld the mystery of the ages. Spring water bubbled forth with the coolness of a mountain spring. They marveled at the agelessness of the people they met. They had expected to be treated as amiable strangers, but were accepted with warmth they would remember forever.

Big Roger had given them an open-ended account in case they found stock to buy. They found the perfect Arabian pair to add to their already large breeding herd. Everywhere they went they found animals that would increase their breeding stock. Jessie found mares and stallions the likes of which she had only dreamt. She found herself anticipating the results of introducing the bloodlines of these animals.

Roger's fascination with the Middle East wasn't as strong as Jessie's. She found him being impatient at her suggestions to see more of the area. He was tired of the heat, what he found to be bland food, and the accommodations that he found to be less than satisfactory.

To Jessie's consternation they had their first fight as honeymooners and tried to do whatever she could to lighten Roj's mood. Roj decided they had enough stock and made plans to head home without even consulting Jessie. Jessie saw for the first time in their marriage, but not the last, how arbitrary Roj could be.

Once back home, Roj's attitude seemed to change daily. Gone was the carefree, fun-loving man she had fallen in love with and married. He was replaced by a quarrelsome, distant boy Jessica hadn't seen in years. Everyone at the ranch had been pleased with the change the four years at Harvard had made in Roj. Jessie always blamed herself for the change in Roj. If she had been a better wife, maybe he wouldn't have lost interest.

When she became pregnant she thought Roj would be as happy as she was. The pregnancy only seemed to put more distance between them, although they rarely talked anyway. One day she caught him before he left on his daily business, shyly broaching the subject of names for the baby. He surprised her when he told her he had already chosen a name. Jessie didn't understand why, but the name irritated his father and put the foundation to a wall which grew over the years, a wall which never came down.

She liked the name, but when she asked Roj what made him decide on this name he looked blankly at her and refused to answer. Again Jessie wondered what she had done to raise his anger, and then she realized another wedge was placed between them, ever widening the gap which was never bridged.

After the birth of their son, Jordan James Rite, Roj seemed satisfied with life, surprising everyone by his willingness to work with his father. When Jessie found herself pregnant again she was delighted there would be a little brother or sister for Jordan.

She soon found Roj didn't share her jubilation. Roj seemed to resent her pregnancy as if it were an intrusion. She felt just the opposite; she was convinced that if Glynis had only had someone else besides Roj to love, she wouldn't have been so possessive of Roj.

Ultimately, Jessica lost interest in questioning Glynis and Roj's attitudes because soon she would have someone else to shower with her bottled-up love.

The day their little Cristal was born the sun broke over the horizon, glimmering in the freshly fallen snow. The ranch looked like a crystal fairyland. It had to be an omen: early snow, an early birth, perhaps an early end to all their strife.

As she had predicted, Roj was suddenly agreeable to everything. This was to be their little Cristal! Perhaps she could "read" them a new future. Life fell into a satisfactory routine. Roj went off to take care of his daily business. Occasionally he graced them with his presence. He made it home for holidays and special occasions, but his outside activities became the talk of the county. Talk Jessie chose to ignore for as long as possible.

Estralita Mandez had been hired to take care of Roj when he was a baby. As he outgrew the need of a nanny she became their housekeeper and most trusted employee. She was the mother Jessie lost and the one person Big Roger listened to where Roj was concerned. When the kids were born she pampered Jordan and Cristal where she had left off with Jessie and Roj. With Estralita keeping a spotless house and making the meals, little was left for Jessie to do. She turned to Jake or Big Roger to fill her days with odd jobs.

The more Roj seemed to abandon her, the more love she gave to Jordan and Cristal. She felt she had to give the kids more love as the gulf between Roj and his family grew. Roj either ignored them or showered them with "things" to salve his guilty conscience. She was heartbroken when Glynis ignored them. She acted as if they had the plague, or more aptly, defective genes!

Jessie felt Jordan and Cristal were her greatest achievements. She loved them so much, maybe too much! It seemed as if she had nothing left to give Roj. Things between her and Roj were insignificant when she saw them putting their heads together to make some kind of mischief; she knew her life would always be special.

When the occasional need for discipline arose, Jake and Big Roger made her feel the ogre! Two more doting old men you couldn't find! Big Roger, who's battle call had been "Spare the rod and spoil the child" when Roj was a child, treated his grandchildren as if they were perfect angels incapable of wrong doing. Jake, on the other hand, followed the teachings of Pearl, who said, "With enough love, children will outgrow any bad behavior."

It made the rejection of Glynis and Roj more acceptable for her, but she had a problem explaining it to the children. She could ignore the rejection, but she was never able to find the words to explain it to the kids.

"We'll just have to learn to love him all the more. The more love you give the more you get," she told them. She could tell by the looks on the children's faces that they were too young to understand. With time they would learn what she meant.

When the rumors started about Roj's "flirtations" Jessie just worked harder trying to ignore them. The day Jordan came home with stories about Roj and other women was the day Jessie decided to put an end to her marriage. Her kids wouldn't have to live with the disgrace Roj made them live under. She'd had all the sly looks and snickers behind her back she could take. Everyone liked Jessie, mind you, but it is so easy to take glee in the fact that, when "high society" falls, they all have a long way to fall! Even nice people find satisfaction in the problems of people as wealthy as the Rites.

Before Jessie could begin divorce proceedings, Big Roger's plane was lost on their annual vacation to the Jamaican islands. When the authorities gave up, Roj and Jessie went to oversee their own search.

"Little hope of survival," "Lost over the Atlantic," "No physical evidence." These were the phrases Roj wouldn't accept. Two months of searching passed before Roj agreed to give up and go home.

When they returned to the ranch Roj made it clear he would no longer be referred to as "Roj." He was now "Big Roger." He made it very clear he would do what he wanted, when he wanted, how he wanted. He gave very little heed to anything Jake or Jessie told him.

Jessie hoped with the resolution of Big Roger and Glynis's death Roj would turn to his family to help get over his grief. Surely they would get back the intimacy they had known.

Jessie's hopes of a return to their early marriage weren't to be. Returning home late from a business meeting one night, driving past The Lanes, a longtime teenage party spot, Jessie spotted Roger's Cadillac resting against one of the large firs. Horrible visions leapt through her mind. Roj had been drinking heavily lately and anything was possible. When she shined her flashlight in the window, the last thing she expected to see was Roger and another woman.

Her anger flared, and she began to open the door, but she was stopped cold by Roger's look of contempt, one to rival Glynis, even on her blackest day! Returning to her car she knew her marriage had come to an end. Somehow she had to get the courage to tell the children. Deciding that they needed to start on a new life, she began formulating a plan to get Roger out of their lives.

Jessie tried to count how many times their plans had been ruined by Roger's little "indiscretions."

"This really is the last straw!" Jessie exclaimed, surprised by the echo of her voice in the empty house.

Looking around, full of anxiety, the walls seemed to be closing in, making her claustrophobic. *I have to get out of here*! her brain screamed. She ran out of the house, the thought of flying across the valley on the bare back of Tiger Lil' seemed the immediate solution to the turmoil of her mind.

"No problems, just the wind in my face." It was the solution she used as a child when she felt alone or forgotten. Slipping the hackamore on the suddenly edgy animal, she didn't waste time with a saddle but jumped on and flew from the barn.

Her isolation grew as she flew across the meadow. The anger she had hoped would flow out of her increased with every stride of the mare. Jessie was pulled back to reality by a sudden flash of light and a bellowing explosion.

Jessie fought to calm the frightened animal and out of the corner of her eye she caught a movement and the flames lapping at a nearby stand of trees, making her thoughts flash through the events of the day. She lost the struggle to control Tiger Lil; flying through the air, Jessie was reminded of a slow-mo segment in a movie: Cut scene. Fade to darkness…

# Chapter Two

Sam had tried to quit smoking hundreds of times. He stood mesmerized by the pack of Camels in his hand, a conflict growing inside of him. "Sam Ellison you're a big boy now. If you want a cigarette, have one!" he berated himself. He stepped onto the porch to have his cigarette, smoking outside, and the one consolation to his conscience when he saw Jessie Rite fly by on one of the many thoroughbreds raised at the Circle R Ranch.

Jessie, involved with her thoughts as she and the mare galloped across the terrain, wasn't aware of the solitary figure watching her from the porch of the old farmhouse. The ensuing dusk hid the scowl marring handsome features illuminated by the glow of his cigarette.

"Damn fool woman! I guess she can afford to ruin fine horseflesh," he reasoned as he watched the two fly into the distance. "Didn't even bother to saddle the animal properly," he mumbled to himself. As he watched the rider and horse fly into the distance he was reminded of the last run-in he had with the Rites.

\*\*\*

Sam found himself drawn to the movements of the remarkable animal in his holding corral. Sam had been amazed to find the stallion loose, grazing beside his favorite (well, truthfully, only) mare. Sam knew the reputation of the stallion and had heard many stories about the exorbitant price charged for the stud fee.

Tired of speculation, he contacted Roger Rite to see if what he had heard was correct. He chuckled to himself, imagining the expression on his face when Rite told him the figure. Sam would have had to sell the farm to afford the stud fee, and he decided it would be counterproductive.

Sam would have loved to be a fly on the wall at the Circle R Ranch when they received the call telling them he had their stallion. He felt sorry for the poor soul that allowed the animal to get loose. Any horse of this value was insured, but you never recover the true cost of an animal of his caliber.

He watched the horse cantering around the small corral, pawing the ground in anger, kicking the air as he passed where Sam was standing. An occasional whinny from inside the barn brought the stallion to a screeching halt. The sun glistened on the flawless dark coat of the stallion reflecting the subtle trembling of muscles. His gently sculptured nose flared as he held his head high trying to catch the scent of the mare. The stallion, enraged by the mare kicking the sides of her stall in an attempt to break her confinements, bucked and stomped around the corral, searching escape.

The two horses were different sides of the coin: the stallion was flawlessly built and dark as a winter night, his shining black coat glowed a midnight blue in the bright sunlight. The mare was white as snow. Her perfectly sculptured body was covered by a silken coat as soft to the touch as a Persian kitten. The fullness of her wave-leaden mane and tail reminded one of the pictures of fairytale unicorns.

Watching the massive animal pace the small corral it seemed impossible an animal as large and strong could be tempered by the gentleness evident in the large black eyes.

Sam watched in awe, considering the outcome of a match between his mare and the one in the corral. The two horses were as different as night and day. The stallion was as dark as night and the mare as white as a winter wonderland. However, the mare stood as tall as the stallion, and her broad chest and muscle-covered legs conveyed strength to match the stallion.

The mare's disposition was one of solitary devotion. She had one master and withheld her affection for him alone. Sam was often reminded of the day he first saw the frisky filly. Many people tried to coax the beautiful little animal to their side of the arena.

Sam pushed his way through the spectators to get a glimpse of the action. He quietly leaned against the rail, absorbed in thought. He knew from his first sight of the filly he had to have her. To the amazement of everyone present the filly slid to a halt, turning, listening to an unspoken call. She shyly whinnied at Sam, and he slowly held out his hand. The filly lost her earlier nervousness and brazenly cantered over to where the young man stood. She nuzzled the outstretched hand, thrilling Sam and forging a lifelong bond.

Sam was grateful for their bond. He would have never been able to control the stallion enough to corral him if not for the help of the mare. When Sam had found the two of them grazing side by side in the lush meadow along the winding brook, he knew to whom the stallion belonged. By keeping his distance from the stallion and making sure the mare was in constant view of the stallion, he was able to lure the tense animal into the holding corral.

Sam had split feelings about the possibility of his mare being serviced by the elegant animal. He knew the exorbitant fee the Rites got for this particular animal, but on the other hand could he be held responsible for the actions of a stallion which had come on to his property?

Sam's thoughts were interrupted by the sound of a truck screeching to a halt in the loose gravel of his driveway. He flinched at the look of anger on the face of the man vaulting from the barely settled vehicle.

"What's the big idea, Ellison?" Roger Rite "The Third" obviously figured a good defense was a strong offense.

"Good day to you too, Rite," Sam said through gritted teeth, trying to be patient with the arrogant man. Sam got a look through the open door of the truck at the sullen form of what Sam assumed was Roger Rite's son.

The young man was on one hand contrite, looking around for something to focus his attention on, and on the other hand, anger oozed from every pore of his body. Sam could tell all wasn't good between the father and son.

Roger watched the stallion prance around the corral, agitated by the increasing crowd. "He is a magnificent specimen, isn't he?" Sam watched as Roger's chest swelled with pride.

"He certainly is."

The stallion caught Roger's scent and swerved to avoid any close proximity to his owner. The horse stopped, reared and pawed the air as if to warn Roger to keep his distance. They all heard an anxious knicker from the barn as the stallion screeched a warning to Roger.

Roger looked in the direction of the barn, remembering what he had heard about the mare's reputation. He had wanted a chance to buy the animal from Sam since he heard about its breeding and conformation. Roger smiled, thinking perhaps Jordan's incompetence could work to his advantage.

"I hear you have a mare worthy of my horse. Mind if I get a look at her?" Roger looked toward the barn. "I'm willing to make you an offer you won't match anywhere."

"I'd be happy to show her off." Sam was proud of the mare, but he had no intention of even listening to any offers. "Maybe your son would like to see her." Sam watched as the direction they were heading seemed to interest the young man.

Roger paused, sensing Sam's interest in the young man. "Sure, why not?" He held no particular interest in the activities of his son, but noticed Sam was interested in meeting the boy and considered he might be able to use it to his advantage.

Roger waved Jordan to follow them. He glared a silent warning, making Jordan shift uncomfortably. "Sam Ellison, this is my son, Jordan. We can thank him for almost losing Gallant Man." Jordan recoiled from the remark as if he had been physically assaulted.

Sam reached out to shake Jordan's hand and was rewarded with a look of appreciation. Sam's smile was returned by a shy look of thanks and a barely audible, "Nice to meet you, Mr. Ellison."

Sam showed the two where to wait as he brought out the mare. Sam put an arm over the neck of the agitated animal to quiet her and spoke soothingly in her ear as he put the halter on her.

Being a natural entertainer, the mare perked her ears and began to prance provocatively for the small audience. Sam paraded her around the two so they could get the full impact of her perfect proportions.

Jordan looked at the mare without letting out so much as a breath, afraid he would spoil the image if he said anything. Roger didn't think it was possible to find as fine an animal as Gallant Man, and he didn't like the idea that this was perhaps a superior animal to his stallion. He knew he had to have her, no matter what the cost.

"What's your price, Ellison?" All sense of propriety gone, Roger was all business now. He wouldn't leave until he had this mare. Jordan felt sorry for Sam Ellison. He knew the look on his father's face, and he had never seen anyone since Granddad Rite overcome his father's will. Not even Grandpa Jake.

"Sorry. She's not for sale," Sam said as he turned to lead her back to her stall. This was nothing new to him; Sam was used to everyone who saw her wanting her.

Roger's anger flared as he watched Ellison slowly dismiss him. He wasn't used to being denied what he wanted. "Look, Ellison, I can tell you could use the money." The edge of Roger's lip turned in a distasteful snarl as he looked around the clean but shabby buildings.

Sam smiled ruefully and turned as he caught the nervous movements of the young boy. "Well, what do you think of her?" Sam tried to get some sort of conversation out of the young man, but all he was rewarded with was a casual shrug of shoulders.

Roger could tell further talk at this time was worthless. He barked at Jordan to get in the truck, and Sam watched as the boy jumped nervously and quickly headed for the truck looking slyly at Sam before hopping in.

"This isn't over yet." Roger didn't even try to hide the fact he was upset with Sam's denial. "I'll send someone over to pick up the horse. You know, Ellison, you should just sell her now while you can get what she's worth. I intend on having that animal." Roger didn't wait for a reply; he spun on his heel and jumped in the truck, barely getting the door closed before ripping down the dirt road. Sam shook his head as he watched the gravel fly and the dust roll behind the roaring truck.

Sam wasn't surprised when word got around about his mare being bred with the famous Gallant Man. The talk had finally died down about Sam's capture and return of the famous stallion when Sam had Dr. Chuck Smith, the local veterinarian, confirmed the mare was pregnant.

What did surprise Sam was the breeding bill he received from Roger. Sam gave the bill all the thought it deserved before tossing it in the garbage. The entire county knew the story about Jordan leaving the barn open and the stallion escaping. Still, Sam was surprised when he received, several months later, the papers saying he was being sued for breech of contract.

Roger wasn't aware of Sam's background in law, hoping to intimidate him with a law firm known for getting results for their clients. Sam wasn't easily intimidated, which Roger was about to find out.

When the judge threw the case out with cause, Sam's estimation around the county went up considerably. Roger was soon to become the talk of the county; talk he didn't like. Talk around the county was centered on a name for the offspring. Many thought it should be "Rite's Folly." Roger's anger flamed every time he heard mention of Sam Ellison; his hatred grew as he tried to find a way to pay Ellison back for the embarrassment he had caused him!

\*\*\*

Sam threw the butt of the cigarette away, the memory of Roger Rite sapping the enjoyment he'd expected. Closing the door he promised himself the next time he saw Jake he was going to ask him about the "bright young woman." Was she used to riding hell-bent-for-leather with dark so close at hand? She showed no concern for her own safety, let alone the safety of her horse.

He had never met Jessica Rite but the talk around town made her seem like a saint. While she was putting up with a worthless husband, she was also running one of the most successful breeding ranches in the country. People probably weren't aware of her nocturnal habits.

"You would think she knows she could get her neck broke." Still grumbling to himself, Sam pulled out his ledgers to get started on his monthly juggling act. A boom sounded, rocking the light fixtures that hung above the table, settling dust on the papers scattered around him.

"What in the Sam Hill?" he asked No One In Particular, the cat he had taken in for companionship. Looking at the cat (who was roused solely by the sound of a can opener or the chirp of the parakeet Sam had bought for added company), he shook his head as he stepped over the slumbering animal to open the door.

The sky was lit by a warm glow as if a bonfire gone awry. Sam grabbed his shovel and ran to the old jeep, happy it turned over without its usual coaxing. Driving toward the glow, he wondered if he should have called the ranger station before leaving the ranch. He could use his new CB when he got to the scene if necessary. "I knew this CB would come in handy," Sam congratulated himself as he rumbled over the dusty gravel road.

Sam was surprised to see so many cars ahead of him, but what caught his attention was the cause of the fire.

# Chapter Three

The strobing of the lights on the sheriff's car was lost in the glow from the growing blaze. The sheriff was edgy because of the amount of people already packing the accident scene. When he rolled to a stop his attention was captured by the grisly scene facing him.

The large white Cadillac gave little doubt to the identity of its occupant. Although it was obvious by the scorched automobile there had been an explosion. Perhaps the result of an accident, it was common knowledge Roger Rite was not opposed to driving while under the influence of alcohol.

To the sheriff's knowledge he had never been apprehended, but he wasn't naive enough to think Roger was opposed to spreading his considerable wealth to keep his record clean.

Sheriff Boatwright allowed the firefighters to do their job unhindered. He spent the time surveying the scene from a discreet distance. The explosion was not extensive enough to completely destroy the Cadillac. The sheriff figured he had plenty of work to do after the firefighters gained control of the spreading fire that was probably a result of the explosion.

The smoke-covered windows indicated the inside of the car had been involved in some sort of fire. The smoke billowing out of the driver's window dwindled to a slight fog, showing a pair of boots projecting from the window.

The Cadillac was wedged against a now-scorched fir, obviously the start of the fire that was threatening to engulf the entire area. Flames were licking the ground spreading from one small stand of trees to the next.

Sheriff Boatwright was relieved to see the firefighters gaining the upper hand with the fire. They were lucky the accident hadn't happened higher in the mountains where the timber was thicker and would have allowed the fire to take hold and cause immense damage.

The fire around the car had burnt itself out, leaving smoldering ashes and the acrid scent of burnt flesh. Sheriff Boatwright shivered at the grisly sight; no amount of experience hardened a person to a sight like this.

Sheriff Boatwright surveyed the growing crowd. *Keeping these people out of the way isn't going to be easy*, he thought to himself. All he had to work with were three reserve deputies. Suddenly it seemed as if people were coming out of the woodwork.

He hated what his gut was telling him about this "accident." Since becoming the sheriff of Delaney County he hadn't seen anything close to what had happened tonight. One of the reasons he had resigned the DEA was the growing disregard for life he had to deal with day in and day out. He came to Delaney County expecting to see nothing more than a few domestic quarrels or perhaps some stolen cattle.

This was far out of that league. He had enough years in the DEA to recognize an accident when he saw one. This was more than a simple drunk driving accident, this much he was sure of.

He noticed Sam Ellison arrive in his old jeep and motioned for Sam to join him. "Over here, Sam." Now this is the kind of help he needed!

When Sam arrived in the small community he was surprised to find old friends from the DEA, Sheriff "Boat" Boatwright and his wife, Marsha. Sam and Boat had worked together at the DEA, but had lost touch over the years.

"Glad to see you, Sam," Sheriff Boatwright greeted his friend. "Do you mind helping me check things out?" The sheriff needed to gather as much information as quickly as possible.

Surveying the area, he noticed the local volunteers had gained control over the slow-spreading fire. He thought to himself, *There mustn't be a person left in town*. He recognized almost every vehicle present. Just a few weeks later in the year and this fire could have quickly gotten out of hand.

Sam used his shovel to police the area, looking for hot spots waiting to re-ignite as the rest of the volunteer firemen worked the main fire. The sheriff had been too occupied to notice the people arriving were carrying firefighting equipment. Quickly the group was working in junction with the firefighters, making progress against the quickly burning fire.

When the area around the car was deemed safe by the fire marshal, Sheriff Boatwright and Sam headed to the accident scene. The sheriff and Sam walked around the car silently, looking at the ground. They both said at the same time, "Too many footprints."

The sheriff mumbled to himself, "Reserves!"

Roger Rite III's white Cadillac was up against a large fir tree blocking entrance by way of the passenger side. The smoke-blackened windows made seeing inside the car difficult. Walking around the car they saw the driver's window had probably been kicked out by a pair of blackened boots, which still protruded from the inside.

Sam noticed something had been drug along the ground. Backtracking to its origin, Sam noticed several cigarette butts thrown about. "Hey, Boat, it looks like we might have a good print over here," Sam said, looking at the ground and at the gas tank. "I am sure this is where the explosion started."

"Mark it and we'll get to it later," yelled Boat. "It looks like the fire's under control. We need to get this area cordoned off before everything is ruined."

The sheriff had the reserves round up all the non-critical volunteers to keep them out of the area until he and Sam were finished. A buzz of excitement hummed subtly from the people as they noticed the charred remains of the Cadillac. The crowd waited impatiently for more information about what had happened. The group was abuzz with speculation about just what had happened. Several theories were being bantered about already.

Boat's instincts were becoming a reality as he realized the car's explosion and ensuing fire seemed to be caused by a gas can set under the car and ignited. Boat wondered how the inside of the car had gotten so involved. He didn't like what he was thinking already.

"This is from the Flying A," he said. It was an obvious deduction because there was only one service station in the area and as he kicked the can over part of the Flying A logo showed on the burned remains of the can. There was only one Flying A station left in the state. Boat, looking at the area, kept thinking how well-staged everything seemed to be. "Looks like someone went to a lot of trouble to set this up," he added.

"Have you called the state boys yet?" Sam asked.

"No. I need some more time to get a handle on what happened. I don't want them getting on their high horses. They'll try to leave me out of this one, you know, the 'dumb county sheriff.'"

Sheriff Boatwright called to one of the reserve deputies, "Get my forensic kit out of the trunk of my car, will you, Billy?" Turning to another reserve he said, "Hey, George, get some tape and get this area marked off. We don't need to damage any more of the evidence."

"Feels like the good old days," Boat said to Sam with a sheepish grin on his face. He knew Sam didn't like to be reminded of the days they spent together in the DEA.

Giving Boat a grim look, Sam thought, *I wonder how Boat is going to get his little samples tested if the state takes over the investigation.*

It was as if Boat heard the unasked question. "I've been here long enough to meet some very interesting people. I bet you didn't know the science teacher at the high school used to work for the state coroner's office? He got burned-out just like we did. He likes teaching and enjoys working with the kids, but he does miss the excitement. Besides, he owes me a favor or two," Boat said with a wink.

Looking from Sam to the car, Boat said, "Shall we?"

Sam opened the back door, carefully testing for heat, unsure if the residual smoke wouldn't burst into flames.

Sam leaned carefully into the vehicle, quickly surveying what had happened. "Don't you find it interesting? This guy put his foot through the window with all the doors unlocked?" Sam said more to himself than to Boat. Sam was concentrating on a way to get a better look at the front seat without disturbing any more of the clues than necessary when he spotted glass lying around the floor and on the front seat.

When the sheriff got his first chance to look at the front seat he felt his stomach roll. Although he wasn't used to seeing corpses with their pants at half-mast, he was assured of the identity of the driver. With Roger's reputation it hadn't surprised him. Roger was literally caught with his pants down. The real shock came when he noticed there was a second corpse!

Boat felt his heart flop at the sight of the second body. He was terrified it could be Roger's wife, although the word around the county was that Jessie and Roger were having marital problems and had been for years. Boat didn't like the idea of Roger's infidelities but the alternative was more dreadful.

"I guess he parked here one time too many." Boat sighed. The more he looked the situation over, the more it seemed a little too contrite.

Sam and Boat were too involved in their work to notice the new group of cars pull into the clearing. Sam was finishing his search when he caught a glimpse of the coroner's car.

"Hey, who's in charge here?" the potbellied coroner bellowed. "I'm here to do a job, and I don't need any amateurs screwing up my work!"

"I'm in charge here," Boat replied. "I'm sure no amateurs will have to screw up your work!" He added sarcastically.

"What do you mean?" the coroner said, puffing up like a fighting cock ready to go at it. He had never liked this pushy Easterner and was irritated when he was able to be elected county sheriff. *These Easterners are worse than foreigners taking over the country*, he thought.

Sergeant Garza of the state police walked over. "Hey, Corny, don't you know who you are talking to?" Garza snarled. "These two are ex-DEA agents. Real big shots! Their specialty is screwing up drug busts!" Smacking the coroner on the back, he gave a donkey-like guffaw. Sam silently stepped up, ready to intervene in case of a fight.

"I'm here now, Sheriff," Sgt. Garza said to Boat. "Step back and see how a real pro handles things. Maybe you'll learn a thing or two."

Sam stepped between the two just in time to save the sergeant another broken nose. Boat didn't need another letter of reprimand from the state attorney. "It's not worth it, Boat. We are finished here anyway."

The fire was out and the state boys were busy throwing their weight around. The exasperated locals decided to call it a night; there wasn't any more information to be had anyway, so they headed back to town.

"Wait a second, Boat," Sam called to the sheriff as he climbed into his patrol car. "Let me buy you a drink at Gloria's. I'll meet you there in 15 minutes." Then he jumped into his jeep so the sheriff couldn't say no.

Boat waved an acknowledgment and said, "Make it an hour; I need to let Jessie know what has happened. I don't want "Garbanzo Bean" to be the one to break the news," Boat said, getting a perverse satisfaction out of the use of the childish nickname. It was a short drive to the Rite place, and he wasn't looking forward to this conversation.

Boat noticed the house was dark and no one seemed to be about. He knocked on the door but didn't wait long for an answer. He could tell no one was around. Even though when Roger was around things at the Rite household were subdued, this was one of the happiest households he had ever known. He left a quick note for Jessie and realized the one thing he could use now was a drink.

# Chapter Four

When Sam arrived at Gloria's he ordered a boilermaker and moved to a quiet booth in the corner, trying to piece together what had happened. Sam's attention was drawn to the usually placid Rob Roy Ritter. Instead of the wide smile pasted on the mostly dull features, tonight he was agitated, almost angry.

Boat walked in as Sam was about to ask Rob Roy what was the matter. Sam caught Boat's eye as he ordered a shot then said, "I'll take one with me, Gloria." Grabbing the drink, Boat headed to the corner to join Sam.

"That was quick," Sam observed.

"I forgot tonight is Bible study for the ladies, but I left a note to call me as soon as Jessie gets home."

"Do you think you will have any trouble with Garza?" Sam queried

"No, he's nothing but a candy ass. He likes to throw his weight around, but I can handle him," Boat said, downing the second straight shot.

Gloria sashayed over to where they sat and asked, "Can I get you another one, honey?"

"No thanks, Gloria. I've had enough. Just bring me some coffee. Sam, too." Boat sighed heavily as the bawdy woman swished away to get their order.

Sam decided not to make an issue of the fact that Boat hadn't asked his preference but instead made a general observation. "He's still pissed you ousted him as sheriff."

Sam noticed some color rise in the sheriff's face.

"Naw, he's just a piss ant!" They both laughed, the first time since finding the smoking Caddie.

"What's all of the excitement, Sheriff?" Gloria asked as she set down their coffee, the sound of breaking glass emanating from the back of the tavern. "What's that clumsy oaf done now?" Gloria mused, hurrying to the back.

Both men expected the usual, "Yes, Momma." They were surprised by Rob's angry, "Oh, shut up, Momma. You're so stupid!" followed by Rob's quick exit through the front door, and Gloria's unsuccessful attempt to stop him.

"You get back here, you idiot. Don't you run out on me again!" Gloria screeched as Rob Roy slammed the door in her face.

The men looked at each other in disbelief, Sam being the first to recover. "Did you think the day would come when you would hear Robbie talk like that to Gloria?

"No, but it's about time," Boat answered. Everyone in town had a soft spot in their hearts for Rob Roy. He was a sweet natured young man with mental capabilities of an eight-year-old. Rob Roy was stricken with a high fever when he was a baby that left him mentally limited.

The townspeople were used to seeing his sunny smile as he rode his three-wheeled bicycle around town, retrieving bottles to recycle. He was the town's unpaid "litter patrol." Under the tutelage of Jessica Rite he learned what things he could recycle and what things he needed to discard.

Everywhere he went he was greeted like a family member. Many of the older people in town were like surrogate grandparents to the young man. His father was unknown, but once they dealt with his sweet nature and pure innocence they were unable to resist his charm.

Turning their attention back to the matter at hand, Sam asked, "What do you think the state boys will make of this mess?"

"Knowing Garza, he'll probably call it a double suicide!" he said, making them laugh for the second time. "Sgt. Garza is the biggest a-hole I've ever met," the sheriff added, leaving out several unflattering expletives for courtesy's sake.

Boat smiled at the thought of Garza filing a double suicide report. He turned to Sam and said, "I think we've got our first double homicide in Delaney County."

Sam nodded his head as he flagged Gloria over for more coffee. "Figuring that out doesn't take a genius. Was I the only one to notice things just weren't right out there? I noticed Roger was keeping up his reputation. The other victim curled under the dash was completely nude. I never found any clothes, did you?" Sam said, hoping to establish he wasn't losing his touch.

Boat paused to think about what Sam had seen. "You're right, none of this makes any sense. I never saw Roger drink anything but bourbon. The front seat was littered with beer bottles but not one bottle of the hard stuff. There wasn't anything in the back seat, just the front seat. It's crazy, I tell you. Someone tried to stage this little play."

Sam reached into his pocket and pulled out several plastic bags.

"Look at these," he said, tossing the bags to Boat. "What do you make of these cigarettes? They are fresh and they were all over the place, but I didn't think Roger smoked. Either he or the other victim was on The Lanes all day or our murderer had quite a habit."

Shaking his head, Boat said, "The explosion was no accident. The gas can was placed under the car and lit. Doesn't make sense, the whole thing should have gone up like an inferno. Maybe the explosion from the gas tank blew everything out."

Neither wanted to vocalize how farfetched a theory it was. Each wondered why someone would go to all the trouble scattering clues around the murder site.

The murderer wanted it to look as if these two were having quite a party. "If they were going to have a party you would think they'd have found a more private place than The Lanes. You never know who might end up there on a Friday night," Boat said.

"I would have liked a better look at the girl," Sam said. "Do you think this could have belonged to her?" he asked, showing Boat a necklace he found beside the car.

"Let me see that," Boat said, reaching for the necklace. "That's Jessie Rites. I'd recognize it anywhere; she wore it all the time." Boat was angry he didn't take a closer look with the other victim. He wasn't concerned it may have been Jessie. He knew Jessie was ready to file for divorce.

Boat waved Gloria over for the bill just as Marge rushed into the bar searching for Boat. Finally she spotted him in the corner with Sam. "I'd think twice before I ordered another drink, Herman Boatwright!"

The chorus of "Herrman!" by the other customers was stilled by a black look from Boat. Before Boat could say anything, Marge said, "I got an urgent call from the Rite kids, something about their mom and dad missing."

"Let me take care of the bill while you and Marge head for the Rites'," Sam said, reaching for his wallet.

"Why don't you come with me, Sam?" Boat said with a pleading glance.

"I think I'd better get home," Sam said with a wink to Marge. "I'm sure you're in good hands now. Besides, I have a mare about to foal. I need to check on her."

Slipping an arm through Boat's, Marge asked, "So you and Sam are Friday night drinking buddies now?"

Opening the door for Marge, Boat decided he needed to get Marge on a different track. "My, aren't we in a huffy mood tonight? What's the matter, you the big loser at Bible study tonight?" Boat asked with a charming smile, quickly changing the subject. "You'd better tell me about the call."

"There was no game tonight, almost everybody called and canceled. Besides, you know I hate it when you call our poker game Bible study!" Marge said, trying to keep the argument going. How she did love making up! One look at Boat told her he was in no mood for bantering.

"Gee, honey, you look so tired tonight. Why not let me drive you to the Rite place," Marge said, smiling sweetly. The only answer she got from Boat was a glare as he gave her an ultra-gallant bow, opening the driver's door for her.

"You can drive, Marge, but no prattling on about me and Sam drinking." Boat had learned long ago it was impossible to argue with Marge and win. Boat settled back to unravel the latest development in this case.

Marge looked at Boat out of the corner of her eye and tried to get him into a conversation with her. "The kids seemed really upset because their mom wasn't home. Something about a mare that was missing. They were so excited I couldn't get anything concrete out of them. I told them to calm down. We would be there in no time."

Marge could tell something was going on inside Boat's head, but he just sat staring into the night. "Herman Boatwright, what is going through your head tonight?" Marge was trying to keep her temper under control. When she and Boat left the DEA she thought Boat was through with these dark moments. He could be so exasperating when he was like this!

"You know how it turns me on when you use my full name, Maggie, but I don't have time for that now. We have some bad news for those kids," Boat sighed as he glanced back out the window.

"What happened tonight?" Marge asked, immediately concerned. "I can't even pick a fight with you. Come on, hon. what's got you so upset?" Marge slowed the car to get a safer look at Boat.

"There was a double murder out at The Lanes. Roger Rite was killed,"

Boat said. "I didn't get that good a look at the other victim, but if what I hear is true it could be anyone." The churning feeling in his stomach was telling Boat this would get messier before the night was out. He was relieved to have it out in the open. It amazed him how much easier life was just sharing things with Marge.

"I wonder why Jessie never showed up for the game tonight," Marge said quietly to herself.

"What did you say?" Boat said loudly, startling Marge. "Jessie never showed? Where is she? I went up to the house earlier and no one was there." The nervous churning was erupting into a full-blown case of indigestion; everything about this evening was affecting his stomach. First a blown-up caddy, a missing woman, and now the kids calling, raving about a missing mare.

Trying to take his mind off his problems, Marge said, "You promised to keep our little secret about the poker game. Can you imagine what would happen if the whole town found out about our gambling? Poor Andrew would have a holy cow!" Glancing at each other they broke into a nervous laughter, momentarily breaking the tension of the ride.

"Well, Boat, here we are. What are you going to tell those poor children?" Marge said, shaking her mane of red hair as if to deny what they were about to share with the teenagers.

"I'm not sure yet, Maggie. Just keep them as busy as you can."

Cristal, ran to the car, jerking the car door open for Marge.

"What's happened?" she asked almost hysterically. "Dad should be home by now, and Mom's not anywhere! We saw the fire by "The Lanes." Has something happened to our folks?" Marge looked from Cristal to Jordan and back. Wiping the tears that were streaming down Cristal's face, she put her arm around Cristal's shoulders. "Let's see what Boat has to say."

Jordan stood apart from the trio with his arms crossed defiantly across his chest. Marge and Cristal walked around the car, following Boat to where Jordan stood.

Boat reached to put an arm around Jordan's shoulder, but Jordan shrugged it off and took a step backward. "I need to ask you some hard questions, kids." Boat looked sadly back and forth between the two children; the closest thing to their own that he and Marge would ever have.

"Do you know where your mom and dad are?"

"How am I supposed to know where my old man went today, or any day for that matter," Jordan snarled. "Cristal and I went to get a bite to eat before we went to the drive-in alone. Mom was here waiting and wondering where Dad was, as usual." Boat noticed a strange light glint in Jordan's eye for just a second and then it was gone.

"When we got home we saw the barn door wide open. We thought Mom might be with Pretty Gale since she's about to foal.

"Tiger Lil's stall was empty, and Mom wasn't around." Then Jordan seemed to remember something, but he quickly changed the subject. "Has something happened to our folks?"

Boat looked first to Marge, then to Cristal, and said, "We can go into that later. Do you know where Jake is this weekend?"

"He took a bunch of the racers to Waverly Farms to get them in shape for the sweepstakes. We've got the number in the office if you need to get in touch with him.

Boat looked at Marge and said, "You'd better give it to Marge so she can get in touch with him." Boat took Marge aside and explained that they needed to get in touch with the authorities to start a search for Jessie. He gave her a list of people to call, letting Marge know that she was in charge of keeping the kids busy.

"Come on, Cristal, you and Jordan can help me get some sandwiches and coffee going. It's going to be a long night."

"Marge, do you know what happened to Dad? I know something awful has happened to both of them," Cristal said, following Marge into the kitchen. Luckily Marge didn't have to lie to Cristal. "We don't know if something has happened to both of your parents."

"Cristal, I have to use the phone now. Can you get started with the sandwiches?" Marge said. "I need to call your grandfather about Jessie and Tiger Lil. I'll be in to help in a few minutes."

Cristal started the coffee and sandwiches, trying to remember how the evening had turned out so terribly.

***

Jordan, as usual, was complaining about Dad having to be gone so much. *Jordan, why do you always try to make him mad?* Cristal thought. I don't mind, I just don't listen to him. *If Mom wasn't always so upset...*, Cristal thought, looking forward to opening weekend at the drive-in.

"Oh, little miss goody-two-shoes, you don't even have a clue as to what's going on here," Jordan said, exasperated as usual with Cristal's sunny disposition. "The world could stop spinning and you would think how great it was, everything was floating."

"What do you know?" Cristal said, doubling up her fist, the urge to fight building. "I could knock your block off and then you'd be floating!" As Cristal started to take a step toward Jordan she remembered the look on her mother's face when she said, "I've had enough and this is it!"

When her mother hurried across the room, digging in her purse, it surprised her, but she was dumbfounded when Jessie threw the keys for the Beamer at her! Not wanting her mother to change her mind, she grabbed her purse and ran out to the car. "I'll get her warmed up," she called merrily over her shoulder.

Cristal nervously awaited her mother and Jordan. She said out loud, "She probably was just kidding me." When Jordan stomped down the stairs, she was doubly surprised to see Jordan come down the stairs without their mother. "Where is Mom?" she asked Jordan.

"I guess little princess wins again. You get to drive tonight," Jordan fumed.

"Well, I don't care if you are going to be grumpy, Jordan. I'm not going to let you spoil my evening." With a happy toot of the horn she drove off, heading for town.

Jordan slouched as low as he could and still stay buckled in the seat. Jordan figured it didn't matter what happened now, he'd just die of embarrassment if anyone saw him with his little sister driving! *It's all Dad's fault! If he would come home once in a while maybe Mom wouldn't be so upset all the time.* As if the only thing bothering her was the fact he wasn't ever at home.

"I hate him; I hope his dick falls off!" Jordan said, slamming his fist into the soft dash.

"You shouldn't talk that way about Dad," Cristal said softly, embarrassed by the vulgarity.

"What do you know? You're still his little princess. You wait you'll find out what a jerk he is. Your friends don't tease you about his screwing every woman in town!"

"I don't want to argue about this anymore." Cristal paused, hoping Jordan would cool off. "What are we going to do now? It's too early to go to the drive-in."

"Oh, geez, I don't care," Jordan said with a sigh, turning to look out the window so Cristal wouldn't see his teary eyes.

"Jordan, you want to drive?" Cristal asked. She was hoping to see if it would make him smile again.

"Just leave me alone," Jordan answered.

Cristal was pulled back to the present by the conversation she heard coming from the office. "Hi, Sam, this is Marge. Boat asked me to call you." Cristal was surprised by Marge calling their neighbor Sam Ellison.

Sam interrupted, "I'm glad you called. It dawned on me I saw Jessie ride by on one of her horses earlier tonight. I knew something was going to happen. Tell Boat I'll be right over and we'll use the "Willie" to look for Jessie." Sam hung up without waiting for an answer. Cristal walked to the office door and was surprised by the concerned look on Marge's face as she slowly replaced the receiver.

# Chapter Five

It sounded like a million flies buzzing around her head. Jessie tried to shoo them away with arms so leaden they felt as if they were tied to her sides. Steadily the buzzing increased, making Jessie fear her head would burst.

She heard her name called over and over. Far in the distance, voices coming in different directions. She felt as if she was in a game of blind man's bluff.

"Leave me alone, I just want to sleep!" Jessie tried to say, but back came the buzzing. "Just leave me alone," Jessie mumbled. Slowly her eyes opened, against her will, to bright lights and a strange room.

"Nurse, she is coming to," called a familiar voice.

Slowly turning her head she saw her father standing by her bed. "Jake, what's happened? Where am I?" Jessie asked as she covered her eyes to shield the blinding light.

Jake was about to answer, but the nurse stopped him short. "You'll have to leave while I take a few tests for the doctor."

"Where is my husband?" Jessie asked the nurse. She tried to sit up making her head spin. "Just lie back, Mrs. Rite, the doctor will be in to answer your questions in a minute."

While Jessie waited for the doctor she tried to piece together what happened. She could remember getting Jake ready for the trip. She checked Pretty Gale and was getting ready for the poker game. She wanted to remember something else, something that flew away just as she was about to grasp it. The memory was so foggy. Shaking her head to remember only made it throb. An image would fade in and fade out like a pair of binoculars unable to keep in focus.

Dr. Waldron walked into the room trying to decide how much information was safe to tell Jessie. "Hi, Jessie," the doctor said a little too gaily. "How's that head of yours doing?"

"You're the doctor, you tell me," Jessie retorted testily. "Right now I feel like I need some questions answered."

"No, Jessie, you let me ask the questions." The doctor took his time with Jessie's exam. "What's the last thing you remember, Jessie?" the doctor said, looking into her eyes with a pen light that sent lightning bolts through her brain.

"Not much. Everything seems to be a blur." Jessie was becoming more impatient.

"Do you feel any nausea or pain?" asked the doctor.

"Just a gigantic headache. Do you mind? Your light is killing me," Jessie said, waving him away.

"Well, that's normal. I think you are a very lucky gal. I want to keep you here one more day just to make sure everything is a-Okay," the doctor said brightly as he turned to leave. "I'll send Jake and Boat in now. They need to talk to you."

"Why is Boat here?" Jessie asked, sensing something was really wrong. She felt like a different person. She didn't know why but everyone and everything irritated her.

"Boat will answer your questions. You need to stay calm," the doctor said, letting Jake and Boat into the room.

"Jake, where is Roger? Why isn't he here?" Jessie asked. Something was very wrong.

Jake looked at Boat, trying to find the right words. Jessie looked from one to the other, waiting for an answer. "Jessie, I'm sorry. Roger is dead. He was killed out at The Lanes." Slowly Boat stepped to the bed. He waited for Jessie to absorb what he had told her.

"Jessie, there are some questions I have to ask you." Boat hated asking the questions now, but if he didn't do it, Garza would. He was sure Garza wouldn't be concerned with Jessie's health. "Do you remember what happened to put you in the hospital?"

"Not really," Jessie replied, adding dryly, "What happened to Roger?" She found something interesting at the foot of her bed.

Boat took a deep breathe, "There was an explosion at The Lanes, the teenage hangout by your place."

Jessie jerked her head up, sending shock waves down her neck. "Really, Boat, I know all there is to know about The Lanes." She fixed Boat with the stare for which she was famous for in bargaining circles. The look made Boat check out the floor while adding, "Roger's body was found in the Caddy. We aren't sure if it was an accident yet or not."

Jessie laid back and closed her eyes. "I suppose since he was at The Lanes he wasn't alone. Oh, never mind. I know the answer!"

Jake stepped in front of Boat and took Jessie's hand. "Pearlie, don't concern you with that now. The kids are with Marge and they're doing fine. You just rest up, and we'll sort out this mess after you come home." What Jake said had a familiar ring to it. She had heard it many times in the last 17 years.

The nurse came in, hustling the two men out. "Mrs. Rite needs her rest. No more questions tonight. You can come back in the morning." The nurse felt a pang of sympathy for the older man and added, "We'll take good care of our patient." Jessie turned her head to the wall as Jake and Boat left the room so they wouldn't see the tears fall silently down her cheeks.

***

"Come on, Jordan, Marge made our favorites. You don't have to be so rude," Cristal said in an attempt to get Jordan to eat.

"Oh, shut up, you twerp," Jordan said, trying unsuccessfully to ignore Cristal, muttering, "What a jerk. Even dead he embarrasses us."

Marge, not about to win any "mother of the year" awards, was having trouble keeping her patience. "Get off it, Jordan. Your Dad didn't get himself killed just to embarrass you. Eat your dinner before you wear it to bed."

Jordan was too surprised to speak. When he looked at Cristal she was staring at her dinner to keep from laughing. "Marge, do you think everyone is laughing at us?" Cristal asked quietly after she was sober enough to not break out laughing.

Glaring at Jordan to make sure he had the good sense to keep quiet, Marge said, "No, Chrissy, honey. Everyone feels terrible about what has happened to your family." Still glaring at the top of Jordan's head, she said, "Everybody realizes how terrible this is for you." She was challenging Jordan with her tone to keep his opinions to himself.

When Boat entered, Jordan and Cristal jumped up from the table. "How's Mom?" they chorused.

"Fine," Boat replied, a little out of sorts. He was not used to having teenagers around either. The looks of trust on their faces made him ashamed of himself. "Really, kids," he said softly, "she'll be just fine. Doc says just one more day and she can come home."

"See, kids, I told you she would be fine," Marge said, a sigh of relief flowing from her lips. Neither she nor Boat missed the look of relief that passed between the kids. "Okay, kids, get the sheriff a plate so he can help us eat all this food."

They said a quick grace to assure Jessie's recovery and dug in with a fervor missing before Boat brought the good news. They all sat back after emptying the dishes and gave a sigh of contentment.

They were happy Jessie would soon be home. The void of their father's death was temporarily filled by the imminent return of their mother.

"Help me clean up and then we are off to the Big Boy for banana splits to celebrate!" Marge said as she hustling the two into the kitchen to get them started.

Returning to the table she said, "I feel sorry for these kids. All these years putting up with that so and so…"

Halting her expletives, Boat said, "Now, Maggie, he was their father."

"At least now they can get on with their lives," Marge said, looking at Boat out of the corner of her eye. "Maybe Sam could run over and check on them for us once and awhile."

"Marge Boatwright!" Boat growled, recognizing the look in Marge's eye.

"Okay, okay. It was just a suggestion; after all, he is a lot closer then we are." Marge recanted for the moment, but was not giving up on her future plans for Jessie and Sam.

"Maggie!" Boat threatened with his tone.

"We're finished, Mrs. Boatwright!" the kids shouted in unison as they tore into the room, interrupting the argument before Boat could put his foot down.

"Can we go now?" For the first time since this mess began Jordan was showing some animation. They all ran out the door, and Boat watched them, thinking how big they had gotten since he had first seen them,

\*\*\*

He and Marge had just moved to town, and they had just started unloading the moving van when Jessie showed up with two little towheaded kids in one hand and dinner for them in the other. The two children looked enough alike to be twins.

Cristal was the perfect name for her. She had eyes as blue as the waters of Crystal Lake. When she smiled, she sparkled like pure mountain quartz. Hiding behind her brash, almost obnoxious brother, people had a tendency to miss her.

But Jordan, no one could miss him! He had a way of capturing everyone's attention. He stood ramrod straight and asked questions as straightforward as his posture. He had an insatiable appetite when it came to people; he wanted to know everything about them, no matter how personal.

He asked why there weren't any kids to play with. Boat cringed, waiting for one of Maggie's famous biting replies but from the onset she and Jordan had an immediate harmony. Standing toe to toe, this Amazon-like woman and this little blonde tike took to each other immediately.

"Why, that's none of your business," Marge said, smiling at Jessie to ease her anxiety.

"Why are you so tall?" Jordan wanted an answer to his questions, and Marge realized he would keep asking until satisfied.

"Because my Dad was tall," Marge answered.

"How old are you? Are you ever going to have any kids? I think I like your house. It's smaller then ours, you know. But I like it. You want to come to our house? Boy, is your hair red. How come?" Jordan fired the questions so quickly it was impossible to answer any of them.

Before Marge could answer, Cristal pushed Jordan out of her way. "I love red hair, and when I grow up I'm going to have red hair and be tall and beautiful just like you," she said, ending the inquisition. She stared Jordan into submission. People were always amazed when the petite girl was able to stop the precocious young man with a dark glare.

Jordan lost interest in Marge when he noticed Boat. He headed to where Boat was standing and introduced himself. Boat looked at the small boy and was amazed at the quickness of his mind. He was as articulate as many grownups Boat had known, and was just as vocal.

"My mom says you used to be a G-man. Did you ever kill anyone? My Dad has a lot of guns, you know. Do you ever let anyone shoot your gun? Boy, isn't it big?" Jordan looked at the gun in awe. "I have to go to school next year, you know." And off the two went. The small one jabbering like a magpie, the older patiently answering each question.

Cristal looked curiously at the many figurines Marge had been unpacking.

Marge had been collecting them for years, and they were the first things packed whenever she and Boat had to relocate and the first ones set up upon arrival.

"Well, you've met the Rite kids. I'd like to say they're not always this forward, but it's just not true. They seem to say what's on their minds no mater how hard I try to stop them," Jessie apologized.

"You don't have to apologize, Jessie," Marge said. "Boat and I like to know where we stand…whether with adults or kids," Marge said, winking at Boat when he gave her a pleading glance to save him.

"I hope you'll come to the ranch for dinner as soon as you are settled. I know Roger is looking forward to meeting you, Boat," Jessie said. "Glad you're back, Mags!" Jessie said as she was pulled out of the house by the two precocious children.

***

The sound of car doors slamming brought Boat to the present. All three walked through the door, carrying a bag of goodies. Boat was once again struck by the changes in the "twins" as he remembered them from their first meeting.

It seemed as if Cristal had grown into a woman before his eyes. Jordan now was as tall as Marge and no longer the towheaded scamp, but a tall chestnut haired man-boy. The only thing unchanged was his insatiable hunger for knowledge. Questions are something he was always asking. No easy answers for that lad. He was both sides of the coin. On one hand he was sober and thoughtful and on the other a happy-go-lucky jokester.

"Who ordered the dessert, Maggie?" Boat asked with a smile touching his lips. "Not Jordan!" The two girls said in unison.

"Well, then, it's safe to dig in! Bring on the splits!" He bellowed.

The next day when Jordan and Boat went to check on Pretty Gale, Jordan turned to Boat and said, "Sheriff, can I ask you a question?"

"Sure, Jordan," Boat replied, dreading the answers he would have to give Jordan about his father.

"Why didn't you and Mrs. Boatwright have any kids?" Jordan asked nonchalantly.

Boat was dumbfounded for a minute by the question. He was trying to figure out a way to tell Jordan about the murder but this question was the last one he expected.

"Well, Jordan, sometimes people just can't have kids. Working for the DEA, Marge and I knew there was a possibility we would leave kids alone. After quitting, well—it just never seemed to happen."

Jordan thought for a minute and then said, "Too bad." This seemed to satisfy him, and he didn't pursue anything else.

Boat had to get some information about what happened. He knew if he didn't get the answers someone would have to, and he didn't want that person to be Sgt. Garza.

"Jordan, I'm going to have to ask you some questions. You don't mind, do you?' Boat figured now was as good a time to get the questioning over. "Can you tell me what happened Friday night at your place? What happened before you and Cristal left for the movies?

Stiffening, Jordan looked straight ahead out the windshield and said, "Same thing as usual. Dad was supposed to take Cristal and me to the movies. It was Mom's poker night, but Dad never showed up. She was watching for him out the window and then all of a sudden she sent Cristal and me to the movies. She was real worried. She let Cristal drive the Beamer, for crying out loud!" He was suddenly humiliated again at the thought of his little sister being able to drive the car. When he couldn't continue explaining, he asked, "Why did Dad always have to ruin everything? We could have all gone to dinner, then Dad, Cristal and I could have gone to the drive-in. If only he would have come home!"

"What time was that?" Boat asked.

Jordan looked at Boat quickly. He remembered what his mother said about she had "had it" and wondered what she had meant. "It was about 5 p.m."

"Kind of early to go to the drive-in, wasn't it?" Boat said, watching Jordan stiffen again.

"Well, Mom wanted us to get something to eat first. We were all going out, but Dad was, you know, busy."

Boat could tell by the stubborn set of Jordan's jaw he was finished answering questions. It didn't matter because he got the one answer he didn't want. Jessie had been alone all evening from 5 p.m. until Sam and he found her unconscious in the pasture well after midnight.

He hated to think what Garza would do with this little piece of information. Why couldn't Roger keep his pecker in his pants, then maybe this wouldn't have happened! Somehow he had to protect this family. He considered them his own, and he didn't want to see them hurt anymore because of the spoiled jerk. *I guess the only way is to find the murderer*, Boat thought.

# Chapter Six

Jessie felt like a fool as she was wheeled down the hall. "I'm perfectly able to walk," she said crankily as the nurse pushed her toward the exit.

"Now, Jessie, just let the lady do her job," Jake said a little too sweetly. Jake was trying to be patient with his daughter but after the last few days his patience was running thin.

"I wish everyone would quit treating me like an invalid," Jessie said, her temper flaring. She glanced around to see if there was anyone else she could pick a fight with to release her pent up energy.

"Look, Jessica Pearl, we are just trying to get you home. We don't need you stirring up trouble. Just sit there and act like a lady, and then maybe we can get you home without everyone in town thinking you're a spoiled brat!" Jake said, matching Jessie's irritation.

Jessie started to reply when the nurse said, "Well, here we are. All set to go home!" She was offering her hand to help Jessie stand up. "You take it easy, Jessie, and call if you have any problems." Then she hurried down the hall before either one could start an argument.

"How are the kids, Jake?" Jessie said casually, hoping her irritation didn't show. She thought to herself, *If I had just gone to the drive-in with the kids none of this would have happened. Why did Roger have to treat us the way he did? Many times this year I wished he was dead instead of Big Roger and Glynis. Could I have killed him? If only I could remember!*

"Jessie, are you listening to me?" Jake said, "The kids are fine. I thought it was better to leave them with the Boatwrights. I figured it would be easier for Marge to bring them over while I was getting you."

Swinging into the front driveway, Jessie noticed Marge's car hadn't arrived. She would have a few more minutes before she had to face them. If only she could remember more of that evening, maybe she wouldn't be so nervous.

"Jessie?" Jake asked for the second time. "If you need to talk maybe we should do it now before the kids get home."

"Thanks, Jake, but I really can't seem to remember much of what went on in the last few days. I wish I could but things seem to be lost in fog. My memory just won't focus."

"Well, you know I'll do anything to help," Jake patted her shoulder, reminding her of when she was young. He would want to help her, but never quite knew what to do. Jake sat her suitcase down as he noticed a box with a note on top of it:

> *Dear Rites,*
> *I was sorry to hear of your tragedy. I didn't want to intrude on your privacy, but thought you might like some of my famous cookies. You will be in my prayers tonight.*
> *Your friend,*
> *Sarah Hart.*

Jake, about to tell Jessie about the gift, was sidetracked when the slamming car doors announced the arrival of his grandchildren. He set the box down and the generosity was forgotten in the shuffle.

First Cristal came flying in to embrace her mother. She was happy to see she really was okay. With the realization, the sobbing began as a release of the tensions of the last few days.

Jessie comforted Cristal, but she was confused by the glare from a distant Jordan. She gave him a hesitant smile, but she was more confused when he stomped into the living room and fell into the first chair he came to.

"Go ahead and cry, Cristal. Just get it all out, you will feel better. We'll get through this together," Jessie said over the lump in her throat. "Jordan, are you going to give me a hug?" Jessie asked.

Jordan chose to ignore the question. She turned to Marge and asked, "How can I ever repay you and Boat?"

"You don't have to thank us," Marge said, looking at Jordan. "Everyone got along just fine. We always have a good time with the kids."

"Mom, do you know what happened to Dad?" Cristal asked when she was able to speak without hiccupping.

"Yes, honey. Boat told me when he came to see me in the hospital," Jessie said, with a wary eye on Jordan. "It is horrible, but I'm sure Sheriff Boatwright will find out what happened."

"Oh, brother," Jordan said as he jumped up and hurried to his room.

"I've just about had it with that kid," Jake said, starting after him.

"That's okay, Dad," Jessie said, surprising everyone with the uncustomary title. "Just give me a few minutes to get settled, and I'll go talk to him."

"Well, I don't see why everyone is pussyfooting around him," Jake said. "I think I should go out and see about Gale Storm. She still hasn't foaled, and I'm starting to worry about her."

"Thanks, Jake. Call me if there is anything I can do to help," Jessie said. "Let's get some coffee, Marge."

"No thanks, I have to get home and rest. I'm not as young as I used to be," Marge said with a smile.

"Thanks for everything, Mrs. Boatwright," Cristal said, starting to Jordan's room. "I'll go get Jordan. I know he wants to thank you, too."

"That's all right, Cristal. Boat worked the devil out of him while he stayed with us. He needs some rest," Marge said as she winked at Jessie. "I'll just run along. Tell him to call us later."

Cristal watched as Marge headed out the door. "You know, Mom, Mrs. Boatwright would have made a great mother. Jordan was a real jerk when we first got there, but Mrs. Boatwright had him eating out of her hand in no time."

"This has been very hard on Jordan, Cristal," Jessie said. "You know men have a harder time handling these things than women do. We'll just have to give Jordan a little more time. We'll get through this. It'll be hard, but we will. Remember how hard it was when your grandparents were lost."

"Mom, Dad really isn't ever going to come back, is he?" Jessie wiped a tear that ran in a perfect line down Cristal's cheek. "Was he really as bad as Jordan says?" Cristal hiccupped.

"Your father did the best he could," Jessie said, trying to keep the anger out of her voice. "Jordan loved your father, it was just very difficult for them to get along. The men in this family seem to have a history of that sort of thing."

"Jordan will stop that history. He is really neat when he's not trying to be a jerk," Cristal said.

"Well, let's see if he is ready to talk yet." Jessie smiled at Cristal.

"Not me. I think I'll see what Gramps is doing." Cristal was happy to get a little space from the moody young man. Jessie felt she was on her way to recovery.

"No time like the present," Jessie said, bearing herself up. "I may as well get this over now; it's never going to get any easier."

Jessie knocked on Jordan's door. She almost hoped he wouldn't answer; at least she would have had a short reprieve.

"It's not locked," Jordan said. "No one is stopping you." As Jessie sat down on Jordan's bed she noticed Jordan was looking very intently at a magic book she had gotten him for his 13th birthday.

*He's not ready*, she thought to herself.

"You want to talk, Jordan?" Jessie said as she pushed back the lock of hair always falling across his eyes.

"What's to talk about?" Jordan said, throwing the book down. "The jerk finally got himself done-in. At least we don't have to be embarrassed by him anymore!"

"Jordan, don't you ever say that about your father again," Jessie said as she made him look at her by putting her hands on both sides of his face. "He did the best he could, and you'll respect your father or else..."

"Or else what, I'll end up...?" Jordan said, jerking out of her grasp but still looking at her. "What do you care? He made a laughing stock out of all of us. Even in the end he was able to leave us without any respect in this town."

"Jordan, what are you talking about?" Jessie was appalled by the resemblance between Roger and Jordan. "You are wrong, Jordan. Your father did the best he could. He gave you a home and a pretty nice one at that," Jessie said calmly, amazed the anger was slowly flowing out of her.

"Big deal, Granddad kept it running while Dad screwed everything up," Jordan said with a steely look in his eyes so like his father's it made Jessie shiver with its intensity.

"Jordan, some day when you're grown up and you have a little more distance from this, you'll see you are being very hard on your father. You know he didn't get himself killed just to embarrass you." Jessie got up to leave. "Don't be so hard on your dad, Jordan. In time we'll get through this, together." By the time Jessie was through Jordan was absorbed in his book again, or pretending to be.

Jessie quietly shut the door. As she walked away she heard what she thought was the book hitting the wall and Jordan sobbing. It tore at her heart, but she knew Jordan would have to deal with it in his own way. Maybe after the funeral he would be ready to talk about his feelings.

Jessie felt as if she had been through the ringer. Every muscle in her body ached. The pain pill the nurse had given her at the hospital was wearing off, and her head was beginning to pound.

She thought about going to the foaling barn, but couldn't find the energy. "Jake will call me if he needs me," she promised herself. "I'll just lie down for a few minutes."

Jordan felt bad about the way he treated his mother, but he needed someone to blame. Deep inside he felt it was his fault. If he hadn't said so many bad things abut his father maybe he would be alive.

He was tired of sulking alone and decided to look for more pleasant company. He passed his mother's room and noticed she was asleep. He immediately felt bad because he hadn't even asked how she was feeling. He wasn't interested in seeing another one of their horses have a baby, but he didn't feel like being alone. He decided to see what was going on in the foaling barn.

\*\*\*

Jessie woke with a start. She couldn't remember what day it was. She felt as if she had slept for days and it took her a moment to gain her bearings. The medicine she had taken before laying down had made her throat dry. When she realized she had only slept for a few minutes, she felt the need for some normalcy in her life. She wanted to join Cristal and Jake at the barns. Perhaps Jordan would be ready to join them.

She looked in on Jordan and found his room empty. She was sure she knew where to find him. She thought, after a cool glass of water, she would go see how Gale Storm was faring.

Jessie started out the door and noticed a cloud in the distance. She started down to the foaling barn to see if Jake needed any help when she noticed it was a police car. Thinking it might be Boat with some information, she decided to wait on the porch.

As the car came closer she realized it was a state car. "Oh brother, now what has happened?" Jessie moaned. As usual, Jessie opted to take the bull by the horns and go on the offensive. She had found it was easier if you confronted all your problems head on.

"Hello, officer," Jessie said, holding out her hand. "I'm Jessie Rite. Can I help you with something?" Sweaty hands. *Boy what a jerk*, she thought, unconsciously wiping her hands on her denim pants.

"Sergeant Garza, ma'am," the officer said in his best *Dragnet* voice. "I'm here to ask you a few questions about your husband's accident." He noted the surprise that was on Jessie's face.

Jessie tried to control her surprise at the officer calling it an accident. Jessie said, "I'll do anything I can to help. Please come into the house where we can be more comfortable." The last thing Jessie wanted was for the kids to be bothered now.

"Can I get you some coffee?" Jessie asked, hoping for more time to calm her jagged nerves. "Perhaps something else cold to drink?"

"No, ma'am, on duty," the officer said, taking out his notebook and flipping through it until he came to his notes on the homicide.

Jessie motioned for him to sit on the sofa. She took a chair opposite him. Now she realized why Boat and Marge were always calling this guy "Garbanzo Bean." When he took off his hat his head had a definite bean shape to it.

Jessie waited for him to get settled. She noticed his skin was very light for someone spending time outdoors. The most distinctive thing about him, though, was his watery blue eyes. They had a cruel look about them, indicating the small-minded vindictiveness he was noted for. She couldn't decide if circumstances made him hide his feelings or if he was just emotionally bankrupt.

He was smaller than Jessie expected. Policemen don't seem as big as they once were. Pasting a smile on her face, Jessie decided to let the sergeant make the first move.

"Well, ma'am, I guess you are anxious to get this over with?" Garza said with a mealy smile on his face.

"Well, yes, I'm interested to find out what happened to my husband," Jessie said. "This has been very difficult for all of us."

"Well, ma'am, first I'd like to know how well you knew Robyn Smith."

"I know she works at the Ramble Inn," Jessie said flatly, knowing instantly she was the girl found with Roger. "I'm afraid I don't know her very well."

"Where was your husband Friday?" the Sergeant asked.

"He had business out of town. Working, as far as I know," Jessie said, rubbing her eyes.

"Where were you Friday afternoon?" Garza asked.

"I was home all afternoon and evening," Jessie said.

"I see, well, just a few more questions, ma'am," the sergeant said patronizingly. "Just how was your relationship with your husband?

Jessie looked him squarely in the eye and said, "Not the greatest. Things hadn't been going well for several years."

Jessie could tell by the look on Garza's face that this wasn't much of a revelation. Except perhaps the fact she freely admitted it.

"Where were your children Friday afternoon?" Garza asked begrudgingly.

"They waited for their father to come home from work and when they didn't hear from him, they left for their outing," Jessie said, hoping he would be satisfied. "They left a little early to get something to eat," Jessie added, hoping to cut off any more questions from the policeman.

"Why didn't you go with them?" Garza asked gruffly. This wasn't going the way he had hoped. She was not nervous enough for him. He liked intimidating his suspects, getting them to blurt out more information than intended. Almost gleefully he noted this question got her attention.

Jessie looked at the window, hoping to catch the memory whirling away every time she got close to remembering. "We…ah…we have a mare about to foal. We are concerned she might have trouble. I stayed home to make sure she was okay." Jessie was afraid Garza could tell she was lying. She wasn't even sure why she did lie. She didn't have anything to hide…or did she?

"I hear you were thrown from one of your horses and ended up in the hospital." He searched through his notebook. "Let's see. This happened the night of your husband's murder. Why were you riding so late if you had a mare foaling?" Garza knew he had her.

Jessie could almost see him rubbing his hands together in glee. "I was so nervous waiting I thought a ride would clear my mind." It could have been the truth—it should have been the truth.

Garza decided to go for the jugular. Maybe he could throw her off. "Did you know about your husband taking women to The Lanes for fun?" Before Jessie could answer, he added, "Did he take all his girls there?"

"I don't know about all his girls," Jessie said quietly. "But for as long as anyone can remember it was the party place for lots of teenagers."

"So your husband acted like a teenager?" Garza threw in. Before Jessie could answer, Garza changed tactics. "Do you know of anyone that Roger was having trouble with?" Garza added.

Jessie gave Garza a small smile. "Trouble?" Let him do his own legwork.

"Would you mind if I talked to your kids, ma'am," Garza asked politely.

"I would rather you didn't, Sergeant Garza. I'm sure you can understand this is a very difficult time for them," Jessie said, trying to match the officer's politeness, but actually losing patience with him.

"Just one more question then. Does your husband drink any particular brand of beer?" Garza asked.

"Well, actually, he doesn't drink beer at all. He drinks Jack Daniels and water," Jessie said, standing to put an end to the interview.

Jessie led the policeman out, and she and the policeman stood almost eye to eye, each testing the other's mettle. Jessie was too tired to spar any further, and Garza decided to wait for more information from the coroner. They said polite goodbyes as Jordan came running up the walk. "Mom, Jake needs your help. The mare is in real trouble."

"Well, Sergeant Garza, if you will excuse us," Jessie said, thanking her guardian angel for perfect timing.

"If you don't mind, ma'am, maybe I can help," the policeman said, thinking he would get some useful information.

Jessie tried to find a way to refuse him, but in the end had to agree. "That's very kind of you, Sergeant Garza."

When they arrived at the barn, Jake was washing up to help the poor mare. "Pearlie, get at her head, will you? She doesn't have the strength to do this on her own."

Jessie moved to calm the tired animal. The mare tried to lift her head and nickered as Jessie stroked the failing animal. "It's all right baby, we'll help," Jessie said soothingly. Jessie looked at the faces begging for good news and shook her head as the tears rolled down her cheeks.

Garza surveyed the area, noticing the barn was nicer than most people's homes. The floor was clean enough to eat off of. Everything was in its place, shiny as new. *I wish my wife was this neat.* Garza sighed. "Crazy rich people," he said to himself, shaking his head.

While Jake and Jessie were preoccupied with the mare, Garza noticed the only thing out of place in the barn was a baseball bat standing in the corner by the cleaning equipment.

"Oh no," he heard the teenage boy groan. "I'm sorry, Mom." As he turned around he saw a young girl sobbing quietly by herself. Jessie was holding her son and comforting him, while looking at the mare which obviously didn't make it. He noticed the old man rubbing a pretty little colt.

"Well, Jake, is he going to make it?" Jessie asked solemnly.

"If we can get him on his feet he has a good chance," Jack said hopefully.

Soon everyone in the barn was rooting for the little fella. "Come on, boy, get up. You can do it!"

Even Garza was crossing his fingers; something about the vulnerability of the small orphaned animal touched him in an unusual manner. Soon the small gathering let out a "whoopee" as the small colt stood on wobbly legs, giving a triumphant whinny. Soon it was trying out its legs and nickering for something to eat. The group looked sadly on as the little animal smelled its mother and nickered questioningly.

"Jordan, run and get some nursing formula for this little guy," Jake said, winking at Jessie. "Cristal, help me get the heat lamp set up for him."

"Well, ma'am, I'd better get going. Hope the little fella does okay." Garza left, forgetting about the bat in the excitement of the moment.

"Thanks, officer," Jessie replied, surprised by the vulnerability he had shown.

"What did he want, Pearlie?" Jake asked as Cristal headed for the warming lamp.

"Oh, it's nothing much, Jake. He just had to ask some questions about Roger," Jessie said, looking sadly at the mare who gave her life for the colt.

"You know, Jake, life really does have a way of going on and on. I hope the kids can adjust to their new lives as easy as this little guy seems to be."

As Jordan brought the bottle of formula, Jake reached for it. "Can I, Grandpa?" Jordan asked. The shock of Jordan's request made everyone speechless. Jordan never wanted anything to do with the horses. "Please?" Jake nodded his head. The colt wobbled over to Jordan and nuzzled his leg. The colt ate hungrily, causing Jordan to smile through tear-filled eyes.

"Well, kids, I guess you have a summer project. I'm turning complete care of this little guy over to the two of you," Jessie said, relieved when they looked at each other and smiled. "Have you decided what you are going to name him?"

"Not yet!" The two said in unison.

"Well, I'm sure you'll have plenty of time to consider," Jessie said, relieved to have her two children involved in life instead of mired in grief and death.

# Chapter Seven

Sarah Hart watched the people of Silverton arrive for the most controversial event to hit town for decades. Shaking her head, she thought, *I should have figured Rite would get a big sendoff!*

Sarah liked sitting in the back. She found it the best place to view everyone entering. She had found long ago it was easier to tell what people thought of the "poor deceased" before the services started. It looked as if everyone was happy to see the last of this guy.

Sarah felt a flush of pleasure as she watched David Cumming's arrival. Some of the joy dissipated because his mother was with him, making her feel immediate irritation.

She hated it when David hunched, which he usually did when he was with his mother. She thought he was a handsome man. He was tall, the way she like her men. His brown hair was thick and wavy, definitely his best feature. He was a little thin, but she would remedy that one day soon. If it weren't for his thick glasses everyone could see his lovely dark brown eyes.

Watching David greet people solemnly, she noted David didn't smile much, probably because his teeth were in need of some good dentistry. When he didn't have his nose stuck in a horticulture book or messing in his greenhouse, he was actually quite interesting and very well educated. She liked people who used their heads more than their mouths. She would take care of his few little flaws after they were married.

There was his mother to deal with and, of course, her flea-bitten mutt. How this whiny, mousy little woman ever produced such a remarkable man was beyond her. "I wonder if she knows how ridiculous she looks, with her gaudily dyed black hair and the way she dresses! I bet she hasn't bought a new outfit in the last 30 years," Sarah hissed.

One thing was for certain, she understood Agnes. Yes, this was one person she understood. She wanted David to herself. She undermined his self-esteem every chance she got. She tried to make him look like an incompetent to anyone listening. That was all right; she would take care of Agnes. When the time came she would start on the remake of David. Starting with his teeth and ending with those ridiculous glasses. Everyone would see she was the one to find the potential no one else could see in him.

"Yoo-hoo, David," Sarah said, waving at David and his mother, "come and sit with me. I've been saving you a place." She gushed, "Agnes, what a lovely dress. Is it new? Here, sit by be, I've been saving you a spot."

Sarah felt her pulse race; she was excited to see David. Almost better then seeing David, she could revel in another's misery with someone who depended on her insight. Agnes was that perfect person. She had been in Silverton for several more years then Sarah. How she knew so much abut everyone when she hadn't been out of her home since she went blind was a miracle to Sarah.

"Agnes, where is your adorable little guide dog?" Sarah knew the answer, but she couldn't miss the opportunity to show David what an ingrate his mother was.

"I feel self-conscious bringing him in here with all these people," Agnes replied with the whine that made David recoil in disgust. "What if he started barking right in the middle of the service or if he had an accident? Why, I'd be so embarrassed I'd die!"

David pulled away from his mother's cloying grip. "I have to go talk to Charlie about some business." David hurried away before his mother could make further demands on him.

Walking quickly away, David let a pent-up sigh escape. *Can't I go anywhere without that woman turning up?* he thought.

"Don't worry, David, I'll take care of Agnes," Sarah said to his retreating back. "I wonder what business he could have with Charlie."

David cringed at the syrupy quality of Sarah's voice and thought to himself, *Those two make a perfect pair. Sometimes I don't know which one is the most aggravating.*

Sneaking a quick look back at the two women, he couldn't resist the image of two vultures deciding which body to pick clean. Sarah was such a small woman, even his mother looked large sitting next to her. It surprised him she was able to throw cases of books around as if they weighed nothing. She had a deceptive strength about her that went beyond the force of her dubious personality. She could use a good haircut, and an update in her wardrobe, but one thing which always surprised him was her large gray eyes. He had learned from experience that the only way to gauge her true emotional state was to watch them turn from a steely gray to coal black with her impending anger.

"Okay, Sarah, you be my eyes. Now don't you leave out a thing," Agnes said, minus the usual whine she reserved when talking to David. She rubbed her hands together trying to warm their usual iciness. Agnes was ready for some fresh dirt!

Sarah noticed, not for the first time, when David wasn't around Agnes showed remarkable independence. "Well, everyone that's anyone is here today. You would think it's a national holiday. I would be surprised if there was one business open in the whole county."

"Jessie and the kids seem to be holding up rather well," Sarah said rather shortly. "You would think she would at least show a little remorse." Everyone in town had heard the rumors she was missing when they found her poor husband and the girl murdered.

"What do you mean?" Agnes asked, sidling closer. She didn't want to breach a confidence. "I thought an accident caused poor Roger's death."

"Well, the scuttlebutt is, it was no accident. The tramp got exactly what she deserved," Sarah said flatly.

Sarah remembered the first time she met Robyn. David brought her into the library. She was dressed like a prostitute. David never did see what kind of a girl she was, but Sarah knew. All she wanted was to ruin David's reputation. Poor David; men are always such fools when it involves a large pair of breasts.

Looking over at Winnie and Andrew, Sarah said to Agnes, "Did you ever notice Winnie always seemed to get flustered whenever she was around the Rites?"

"She is so shy; she is probably intimidated by their wealth. You know a lot of people are," Agnes replied. Thinking she had real reasons to be flustered, she always acted real shy, but Agnes knew a thing or two about acting.

Sarah noticed Winnie going over to comfort Jessie. "It takes a lot of gall to go to your lover's wife and comfort her when you've been messing around with her husband for years!" When Sarah wasn't working in the library she spent her free time walking. She had found Roger Rite at his favorite parking spot more than once. The day she caught Winnie and Roger was the last day she showed mousy little Winnie any regard.

"Well, here come Bill and Sharon Marshall." Sarah wondered why they would possibly want to console the Rites. Roger got their daughter pregnant. He did everything but put the bottle of pills in her hand.

"I'm surprised they could show their faces here after the way they raised their daughter," Agnes said, putting her hanky to her nose. She had sensed a foul odor and was trying to protect her sensibilities.

"Sorry for your problems, Jessie, but I can't say I'll miss your husband," Bill Marshall said to Jessie.

"Bill, please, this is not the time or place," Sharon said, nodding to Jessie. She took Bill's arm possessively and pulled him to a pew near the back.

"Really, Sharon, do you think Jessie is going to miss that no-good S.O.B.?" Bill asked his wife, staring into space and remembering a better time.

*\*\*\**

"Mom, Dad, guess what?" Elizabeth Marshall said, hurrying into the back door of the drug store. Not waiting for an answer, she replied, "I've been nominated for Spring Queen!"

"Gee, honey, that's great," Sharon said, smiling at her daughter. She thought it was better if she didn't run. Everyone knows who wins these things and it's not a slightly pudgy bookworm. Oh well, we all have to learn to handle disappointments. "I know you'll win," she said crossing her fingers and saying a silent prayer for luck.

"Hey, what's all the commotion?" Bill said, carrying supplies out of the storeroom. He smiled at his little girl. He acted as if he hadn't heard her news so she could have the pleasure of telling him herself.

"I'm going to be the next Spring Queen!" Elizabeth said with glee.

"Just think, I'll be related to royalty!" Bill said, smiling at his daughter.

*\*\*\**

If only things had turned out different. Old money thinks it can do anything to anyone and not pay for it. When they found the note and the cold body of their only daughter, Bill and Sharon wanted to kill Roger Rite. They tried to have him arrested but the police said they couldn't do anything. It was suicide, and there was no proof Roger was the person who got Elizabeth pregnant. As usual, money buys everything, even freedom. Well, Roger had gotten his in the end. Good riddance to bad rubbish.

\*\*\*

Sarah fell silent as Gloria and Rob Roy Ritter walked in bold as brass. It took several seconds to find her voice. "I don't believe it! Gloria Ritter and her retarded boy just showed up. Everyone knows how Roger felt about her!"

"Mind you, I'm not one to criticize, but you think a business owner, even if it is a saloon, would dress with more decorum," Sarah whispered to Agnes, "She insists on dressing like a teenager as if anyone would be deceived by her clothes. I suppose we should be grateful they are at least black. I wonder if she ever washes her face or just layers on more makeup." Sarah giggled nervously.

Gloria walked down the aisle. *I still turned every head in the room, just like when I was a teenager*, she thought. "I guess when you got it, you never lose it," she informed anyone willing to listen. "Hurry up, you dummy," she chastised Rob Roy. "Do you have to drag you feet? No wonder everyone thinks you are an idiot!" she slurred.

Rob Roy kept the same pace. "You can make me come, Momma, but I don't care what happened to Roger. He deserved it. He always made Miss Jessie cry!" Rob Roy plopped down in the nearest pew.

"Shush, you idiot," Gloria hissed, "You want everyone in the county to hear you?" She was trying to keep suspicion away from them. If anyone found out about her and Big Roger's arrangement she could jump right to the top of the suspect list.

"Well, well, well, here come the Reynolds sisters," Sarah said with a conspiratorial smile on her lips. "You know what they are saying about them, don't you?"

"Who's saying what?" Agnes whined. "I never hear anything. David never takes me anywhere; I'm always the last to hear all the news."

"They're not really sisters, you know!" Sarah lisped secretly. "They are living like a married couple!"

Agnes gasped, causing a coughing fit that showed no sign of stopping. Even in Agnes's warped imagination she couldn't understand what could cause two women to do those things with each other!

Turning to view the commotion, David saw the source of the noise. He quickly turned back to Charlie before Sarah noticed his interest.

"So, my boy," Charlie said, slapping David on the back in greeting. "How are you doing?"

"Okay, Charlie. I just wanted to thank you for taking care of Robyn's arrangements."

"That's fine, David, I knew she had no family or friends except you and me. I never realized her grave is almost next door to Roger's." Charlie found a bit of irony in the fact.

Charlie had run the only hotel and restaurant in Silverton by himself since his wife died. No one new exactly how old he was, but he had gained a reputation as the grumpiest man in Silverton years ago.

He had to run the hotel and restaurant practically single-handed because he was such an ogre to work with. When Robyn and her boyfriend roared into Silverton on his motorcycle, he was struck by the similarity between Robyn and his late wife. It wasn't so much a physical resemblance as one of character.

David was the only other person besides Charlie to notice Robyn was capable of incredible loyalty. When she made you her friend she would go to unbelievable lengths to defend you. She was brokenhearted when her biker boyfriend chose to listen to the rumors going around the bar about her and the other men.

She accepted beating after beating from him to show him her love. But she was left high and dry after one unusually damaging beating that left her hospitalized for several days. Her boyfriend didn't mind her hooking for him when the men were of his choosing, but if she thought she was going to go out on her own she had another thing coming!

Charlie took her in, paid for her hospital bill, and let her work it off with room and board thrown in. She proved to be invaluable to him. He wasn't as young as he used to be. He needed the extra help to keep the hired hands in line. It was an added bonus to find Robyn had a good head on her shoulder. She learned quickly and had a way with people, unlike Charlie.

He promoted David's cause every way possible. He understood her attraction to Roger, but he didn't like it. He had come to think of her as the daughter he and Myra never had. He knew David wasn't the most exciting man in town, but he would take care of her the way she deserved.

Her life had been one of constant upheaval. After her father left her mother a parade of men came and went through the house. His departure sent her mother to the bottom of a bottle. When her mother was rational, she blamed Robyn for her husband's abandonment and when she was drunk she took her anger out on Robyn with physical violence.

Robyn finally decided life on her own couldn't be worse than life with her drunken mother and her parade of abusive boyfriends. She was surprised when Charlie and David didn't blame her for everything going wrong in her life.

When she told Charlie her background she fully expected him to throw her out, but he just told her she could stay as long as she wanted, hoping she would recognize David's strong points and some day agree to marry him. David was head over heals in love with Robyn and would have gone to any lengths to make sure she was happy.

He tried to warn her of the danger getting involved with Roger Rite could cause. He could only hope when Roger tired of her he would leave her with enough dignity to stay with David under his protection. He wouldn't have the chance to find out because once again he was burying someone he loved.

"I'll stop and say goodbye after the service today," David said sadly. It upset him Roger would rest anywhere within a 100 miles of Robyn but there was nothing to be done about it now.

"Isn't your mother's friend waving at you to join them?" Charlie said with a twinkle in his eye. "I never knew her very well; I felt there was something very different about her."

"She's been a real friend to my mother—and me, too, of course," David added quickly. David shivered at the thought of Sarah and him being anything more than co-workers.

People stopped milling around and sat down as Pastor Andrew walked up on the podium. While the hushed whispers wound down, in walked Selma Billings on the arm of Dr. Chuck Smith. Chuck was trying to comfort his obviously upset assistant.

Everyone in town was aware of the feeling of unrequited love of Dr. Smith. Selma wasn't one of the town's favorites. Everyone saw her as a fortune hunter. She had gone through every available wealthy man the county had to offer, to no avail. Luckily for them she ended up showing her real intent sooner then later.

It never deterred the way Dr. Smith felt about Selma. The love he felt for her was evident to all who saw them together. He would take her back, let her lick her wounds after each disastrous affair, and be her lover until she found a new paramour. She quickly tired of the quiet, sensitive man and would soon be on the prowl to find another victim.

The crowd settled down and awaited the last rights of its neighbor. Each person had his or her own reason for attending. Some were here to make sure Roger was really gone, others to celebrate his passing, and even a few were here to mourn his passing. Everyone was curious to hear what Pastor Andrew could find good to say about Roger Rite III.

Pastor Andrew took a deep breath and walked to the podium, fighting for the right words for the service.

"Friends, we meet here today to lend our support and love to members of our community in their hour of need. Let's bow our heads in silent prayer." Andrew bowed his and tried to concentrate but ugly visions kept appearing no matter how hard he tried to banish them!

Winifred and Roger. She vowed it was only once, but how could he believe her. She was a healthy young woman, at times too healthy! Administering to his congregation was a drain on his strength. He tried to satisfy her, but she could be so demanding. He often wondered if Satan was directing her. These thoughts would lead him to trouble and confusion!

"Today we mourn the loss of this family. We join our hearts and prayers to help them remain ever faithful in their devotion.

"This man, Roger Randal Rite, the third, was a young man. Some thought his death was untimely, but who are we to question God's time? Andrew thought to himself, *This is going well, keep the subject simple, and get through it.*

"Roger Rite came from a family that made this county their home for generations. A family that has known happiness and prosperity as well as sadness. A family of righteous, God-fearing people and a family of rogues. He leaves a loving wife and two children who will miss him greatly.

"Give them your support in this, their hour of need. Pray they will not mourn forever but will find peace in the grace of our Lord. This sadness will pass and their lives will go on. Our Lord tells us we are all his children, and he forgives our sins. Love the sinner and not the sin."

Andrew started sweating; he was having trouble remembering his text. How could he go on? "Now let us pray." Andrew scanned the first pew for Winnie, wondering how she was taking the passing of this adulterer. When he spotted her he noticed a small frown around her eyes. *Is she mourning him*? Andrew thought, then he noticed a small smile of encouragement from her and he knew he could do it.

"Father, help your children. They have a difficult time ahead of them now. Let them grieve their loss and find solace in the fact their loved one is resting in peace, if the unholy can find peace. They may some day meet him again. As we all wait for redemption, our Lord Jesus Christ waits to welcome all his loving servants to life everlasting. Amen."

The sermon ended with many of the people looking at each other, questions in their eyes. A small murmur broke out around the congregation. Many people wondered why the usually unflappable Pastor Andrew was acting so strangely.

People shuffled out of the parlor, and Jessie couldn't figure out if her nervousness made the sermon hard to follow or did Pastor Andrew seem to ramble? She had dreaded coming today; she figured everyone would be distantly polite, curious and even outright rude. She never would have thought everyone would ignore them as if they had the plague.

"Jessica," Jake said and turned to Jessie, "I'm taking the kids on ahead. I see someone coming I'd rather they not have to deal with."

Jessie groaned as she saw who was coming full speed ahead.

"Jessica Rite, wait!" Over scurried Theda Reams, publisher, editor and reporter for the *Silverton Gazette*. "Can I have a minute of your time?"

"I'd rather not…" Jessie tried to avoid her, but once old "beagle nose" got the scent there was no stopping her.

"Have the police found any suspects?" Theda decided to get right to the point since these people seldom gave answers worth printing.

"No comment." Jessie said, trying to push pass Theda.

"Who was the woman found with your husband?"

"No comment." Jessie decided if she gave enough non-answers Theda would leave her alone. Wrong.

"Are you being investigated by the state police?"

"No comment," Jessie barked.

"Is it true your husband was cheating on you since you got back from your honeymoon?" Noticing a murderous glint in Jessie's eye, Theda tried to get several questions out. "Is Sheriff Boatwright vouching for you so you can stay out of jail? I hear your children moved out because they thought you killed your husband. Are all your holdings, including the ranch, being held in probate because your husband didn't make a will?"

"Look, you vulture, if you don't get away from these people, I'm going to do something you'll regret!" Sam said, coming up behind Theda.

"So, this is your new beau?" Any comments, Mr. Ellison, isn't it?" Theda said as she backed away from Jessie.

"Not one you can print. Now let these people bury their dead," Sam said melodramatically for effect.

Theda decided the dark rage forming on Jessie's face was not worth staying for. She had more than enough for a great story. It might get picked up by one of the big papers upstate. She tried one more passing shot as she backed away from the obviously angry man.

"Mr. Ellison, didn't you and Roger Rite have a civil suit pending something about misappropriated stud rights?" Theda was grateful to get the sentence out before beating a hasty retreat.

"Thank you, Mr. Ellison," Jessie said, relieved to have Theda Reams out of her face. "You've been a great help to us lately. I don't know how I can repay you.

"No problem," he said matter-of-factly as he turned to go to his old jeep.

"I wonder why Roger never liked him," Jessie murmured as she got into the waiting limo. Jessie sat in the limo with an arm around each child. "You know, Jake, I don't believe how cruel people can be. I don't think *that* woman knows the meaning of the word respect.

"It's better to ignore the likes of Theda Reams, Jessie," Jake said thoughtfully. "Everyone knows she never bothers to get her facts straight."

"Maybe, but it doesn't hurt any less that we will be the main topic of conversation when that trash is passed all over the county," Jessie said. "Will this ever get over?"

She looked at the kids who were holding up so well. It made her feel like a baby whining about every little thing happening.

"Jordan are you okay?" Jessie asked. "Cristal?"

Both kids shook their heads at the same time, afraid if they said anything they would start crying. When their mother looked back out the window they looked at each other, then quickly away.

Jake had a good look at what was left of his family. He decided they were definitely Pearl's kin. They had her quiet strength. This kind of thing made them stronger. *Not like me*, he thought. *All I want is a bottle of booze and a quiet place to get drunk!*

"Jake, how are holding up?" Jessie finally thought to ask. It had been so long since she had seen her father in anything except cowboy boots and Levis; she had forgotten how handsome Jake was.

This must be hard on him. He always tried to get Big Roger to give credit to Roj for his accomplishments. Big Roger never could see the point. He always said, "He'll just turn into the sissy his mother wants if we don't keep him in line."

Maybe Big Roger would be proud of the way Roj took over after the accident. Blood runs true, but Jake believed him when Big Roger told him he would always have a place on the ranch. After Big Roger and Glynis were lost he was almost relived when Roj told him Big Roger left control of the ranch and holdings to him. Finally Roj was given the acknowledgment he had always craved from his father. "Oh well, getting too old for this baloney anyway!" Jake said out loud.

"What did you say, Jake?" Jessie asked absentmindedly.

"Nothing, Pearlie," Jake answered.

Noticing the kids stiffen brought Jessie back to the present. "Not much longer and we can go home and relax." It sounded lame but it was the only thing she would think of to say.

They walked up to the gravesite slowly. This was the last place they wanted to be. But they were too proud to let old "beagle nose" catch them showing it!

The cemetery was full of thrill seekers, friends of Jessie and the children, and many just plain curious people. What did they think, that Roger was going to get up and do a jig for an exit? Jessie found herself getting angry with the people that followed.

"Here, my friends, sits a grieving wife," Andrew started. "Ah, for the love of a faithful woman."

Jessie wiped her nose, and she looked at Jake out of the corner of her eye. The only response she got was the slight shrug of his shoulders. *What is going on here*? Jessie thought a question that echoed throughout the gathering.

"As we bury our neighbor and friend…" Andrew paused as if trying to gather his next thoughts. "If you can call an adulterer a friend, if you call a man who defiles women a friend." Andrew paused as he drew in a deep breath.

Andrew started to speak, but everyone had to strain to hear him. He was speaking in such a low voice. "The evil deeds of a wicked man ensnare him. But a man who commits adultery lacks judgment." He increased in volume as he glanced at his wife. "The tenth commandment tells us thou shall not covet your neighbor's wife. But a man who lacks judgment derides his neighbor."

The murmurs broke out in the crowd, drowned out by Andrew's increased vehemence. "But be sure of this: the wicked will not go unpunished!" Andrew paused, holding his Bible aloft, a startled look on his face.

Looking around the crowd, he said. "As he has injured others, so he is to be injured!" Screeching as if in pain, his Bible still aloft, he ended, "Show no pity, life for life, eye for eye, tooth for tooth, hand for hand, foot for foot!"

Andrew stood, an avenging angel peering down at the closed coffin. This was a man who had caused much pain. The crowd was shocked into silence, the only person capable of motion was Andrew's wife, Winnie.

Winnie walked by Jessie and the children, giving them a pleading look of apology. "Come, Andrew, it's time to leave." Just a few people heard Winnie's apology to her husband as she led him off. "I'm so sorry, Andrew; I didn't know you still felt betrayed."

Jessie and Jake watched as Winnie helped Andrew into their car and drove away. "Well, what do you think that was all about? I had no idea he hated Roger so much. What do you think caused it?" Jake asked Jessie. Jessie didn't answer the question because there was no need for any answer. The gathering was full of speculation, all of it true! "I didn't think Roger had any particular dealings with Andrew accept an occasional Sunday in church."

Boat and Marge approached Jessie, wanting to ignore Andrew's bizarre behavior. Catching the tail end of their conversation, Boat added his own question. "Well, if he didn't have any dealings with Andrew, maybe he had an association with Winnie?"

"If I'm catching your meaning right, Boat, you're inferring the minister's wife isn't any better than a common-uh-waitress, if you get my drift." Marge broke in, "This is no place to go into such matters, and we'll meet you at your place, Jessie."

Jessie didn't know whether to be angry or relieved no one was offering his or her condolences. "I had no idea we would be treated this way; at least you know who your real friends are."

"Let's get the kids home, Jessie. It's been a long day, and I'm anxious to get these fancy duds off," Jake said, changing the subject.

Walking with Cristal behind Jake and Jordan, Jessie was struck by how Jordan had grown. He was almost a head taller than Jake.

"Do you know why Pastor Andrew acted so funny, Mom?" Cristal asked after they had gotten into the limo for the ride home. "Naw, Cris. This is just another chapter in the 'Rite place saga.'" Jordan sniped.

"Not now, Jordan," Jessie said, ending all conversation on the ride home. Jessie felt an unnatural relief that her husband was finally laid to rest. She could find no forgiveness in her heart. The pent-up anger flowed from her body as she turned to give the coffin one last look.

There was a solitary figure left standing before a recently covered gave. Jessie knew without asking it was the grave of the second murder victim. David knelt at the grave and placed a small bouquet of orchids on it. Jessie felt more sadness at the fact Robyn had died because she had become embroiled with Roger.

Pulling into the drive, Jessie noted, with relief, there were no cars around but Boat and Marge's. The children made a mad dash to the barn to see their colt. Before Jessie could tell them to change their clothes, she heard the phone ring, causing instant irritation. They were receiving a long list of prank calls since Roger's death. She had hoped she could be spared today.

"Hello," she said more sharply than intended did.

"Jessie, this is Winnie. I called to explain about this afternoon."

"It's all right," Jessie said. "Everyone has been upset by what's happened to Roger."

"I am to blame, so please let me explain," Winnie begged.

"Really, I don't think I'm up to this right now." Jessie tried to back out gracefully, afraid of what Winnie was going to say.

"Andrew thought he could go through with the service, but the stress he has been under lately was too much for him," Winnie stammered. "It's my fault. I didn't mean for it to happen. It just did," she sobbed.

"How could it be your fault? Andrew should have had someone else perform the service if he felt he couldn't," Jessie said, ignoring the implication. Quickly this conversation was making her feel strange.

"I know you probably won't forgive me, but I have to tell you what happened," Winnie sighed. "Last summer I was bringing Cristal and Jordan home from youth group. Do you remember when you and your Dad went to Kentucky for the horse sale?"

"Yes." Jessie definitely didn't like the way this conversation was going.

"Andrew and I were having problems. We were arguing about trying to adopt, we were arguing about everything. We had an unusually bad argument before the children arrived. Andrew can be so cruel and hurtful sometimes. I know its no excuse for what I did, but when I dropped the kids off, Roger was home." Winnie took a deep breath, trying to calm down. "I did something evil with Roger. We, I mean, I was an emotional wreck; all I could think of was a way to hurt Andrew as badly as he had hurt me.

"Roger was more kindhearted than I had ever known him to be. He could see I was upset and wanted to know if there was anything he could do. I told him no, I had to be going. I got a few miles away from the ranch, and I couldn't stand it anymore. I pulled over to the side of the road and began to cry. Suddenly Roger was there... holding me, comforting me. I just didn't realize what was happening. He promised me no one would ever know. The worst part of it is, I can't believe it, it happened where they were killed." Winnie was quietly sobbing by this time. "I'm sorry, Jessie, but Roger and I committed adultery."

Jessie hadn't wanted Winnie to confirm her suspicions. "I don't need to hear this now."

"I don't understand why Roger had to tell Andrew. He made a special trip to the rectory to discuss all the vile details. He relished the idea of hurting Andrew and me. Why, I couldn't understand. I made Andrew promise to keep what happened to us, but the pressure just got to him." Winnie was quietly sobbing as she waited for a response from Jessie.

"I'm hanging up. Don't call back." Jessie had trouble catching her breath as if she had just finished a marathon. The doorbell rang just as she slammed the phone into its cradle.

\*\*\*

"Jessie, please don't hang up!" Winnie knew she was talking to a dead line, but she had to try to make Jessie understand.

"Winnie, please come here," Andrew said softly. "I have to tell you something."

Winnie needed to think for a minute. "Maybe I should just leave? Yes, I could start over somewhere fresh!" Being the sensible woman she was, she knew the inevitable would only be postponed. "Coming, Andrew." Saying a short prayer, she joined Andrew.

Winnie entered the bedroom and was stunned by Andrew's angry glare. He was beckoning her to come closer. She was afraid of what would happen if she got within Andrew's grasp.

"Now, Winifred, don't be afraid. The Lord has spoken to me. He knows you have a good heart. The devil is after you, and I have to help you avoid his clutches." Andrew had removed all of his clothes except his boxer shorts. He was holding his old-fashioned razor strap limply at his side.

"Please, Andrew. I beg of you." Winnie began unbuttoning her dress, knowing if she didn't do what Andrew wanted, without argument, it would be worse. "Please, Andrew!"

# Chapter Eight

"Jessie," Marge repeated, "who was on the phone?"

"No one," Jessie said, trying to hold back the hysteria.

"Well, for no one you are shaking like a leaf," Marge said.

"Please, Marge, can we just drop it for now?"

"Sure, Jessie," Marge said as she put her arm around the smaller woman. "But you know I'm here for you, don't you?"

Jessie looked at her longtime friend with glistening eyes and nodded her head.

"Oh, hell, let's get something to eat. I got rid of the entire bunch of curiosity seekers, but I was wise enough to keep the spoils!" Marge said, waving her arm at the food laid out on the table. One thing she was sure of; Jessie always had a hearty appetite. Marge still marveled that this small woman could put away more food than most football players could.

"Well, maybe a bite," Jessie agreed. "Boat, did you get a chance to see the new foal?" Jessie asked absently as she entered the living room with a platter full of food.

"No, Jess. Sam and I will go down and get the kids," Boat said, looking at his uncomfortable friend.

"Hello, Mr. Ellison, I didn't see you," Jessie said, putting her hand out to greet Sam. "Thanks for the help today. Please stay and help us eat some of this food."

"Well, I'd be glad to, Mrs. Rite," Sam said formally. "If there's any left." Sam smiled sheepishly, blushing at the quip.

Everyone watched Jessie as she studied her plate. They broke into laughter at the same time, momentarily breaking the tension of the day.

"Between Jessie and Cristal, you'd better make a run for it if you want to get anything more than crumbs!" Boat said, wiping his eyes on his sleeve.

Jake and the kids walked in as if on cue. "What are all the tears about?" Jake asked as he watched the threesome wiping their eyes.

The group turned their attentions to Jessie, who was just taking a king-size bite out of a chicken leg. They burst out laughing again which only seemed to cause more confusion. "What?" Jessie mumbled, oblivious to everything happening around her. She was intent on staving off her sudden hunger.

"Must be a private joke," Jessie said with a mouthful of chicken.

"Cristal, look at all the food!" Jordan said, causing more peals of laughter.

"Oh no!" Boat and Marge said in unison, making a mad dash for the table.

"Crazy," Jake and the kids agreed, missing the point. They decided food was more important at this point than figuring out the joke.

Suddenly everyone was hungry!

The group ate in an easy silence until no one could force another morsel. Clearing the table was easy because for a small amount of people they had hearty appetites.

The evening passed in easy comfort, stories were passed from one subject to another. Sam was given an insight to a family full of love and disappointment. The stories were filled with sadness because of Roger's self-imposed omission.

Sam listened to the stories, thinking that this was what he had missed all these years. There was a familiarity about these people, a comfort easily passed to anyone willing to accept it. Sam thought once again that if Roger had only looked to his family for companionship, things would have turned out differently.

"Kids, it's late. One last check on the foal and it's off to bed for you," Jessie said.

"Jeez, Mom," Jordan argued, "You treat me like a little kid."

"Jordan, mind your mother," Jake said. "It's back to school tomorrow, and you have chores to do before the bus comes."

Jordan started to say something, but the look on Jake's face told him he had pushed his luck as far as he should. He decided it was just as easy to hear the conversation, well almost as easy, through the heat vents in his room. He knew his family, and he knew they would talk more freely with Cristal and him "in bed."

"Jordan, are you in bed?" Cristal hissed at the door. "Let me in!" she said a little louder.

"Come in before you get us both in trouble," Jordan said as he grabbed her hand and pulled her into his room. "What do you want?" he said, glancing at the vent, wondering what he was missing.

"Why do you think Pastor Andrew said all those weird things today?" Cristal said, her eyes wide with innocence. "I always thought he and Miss Winnie liked Daddy."

"Jeez, Cristal, you are such a baby! They like Dad's money, that's all!" Jordan said with exasperation. "Besides, I told you a long time ago, Dad was a jerk. Everyone hated him."

Cristal motioned for him to come closer. "You know what I think?" she whispered in his ear. As soon as he got close she hollered, "I think *you're* the jerk!" She stomped out the door.

Jordan flopped on his bed, trying to decide whether to be mad or insulted. "Oh, what the heck," he said with a smile on his face. He looked at the vent and decided he didn't care what they were talking about. He just didn't care! It had been a long day, and he was going to bed!

***

"How are you and the kids doing?" Marge asked as she put the last of the food in the refrigerator.

"Just fine!" Jessie barked

Marge took her friend by the shoulders, forcing her to look up at the taller woman. "What's the matter? I know the call earlier today upset you." Forcing Jessie to look her in the eye, she coaxed her, "Why don't you tell me about it. You'll feel better once you get it off your chest."

Jessie slumped against the sink for support. "It was Winnie. She had something to get off her chest," Jessie chuckled humorlessly. "I can't believe I'm this upset." She was taking a deep breath to keep tears threatening to spill over at bay. "It's only more of Roger's little indiscretions that he had."

"Not Winnie!" Marge said. "I can't believe it. When did this happen?"

"It doesn't matter, you know. I figured I wouldn't be humiliated by Roger any more, but he seems to be reaching out from his grave to ruin my life," Jessie said, the tears finally pouring down her cheeks. "Now not only will we have to put up with rumors about the murder, we'll have to put up with more grist for the rumor mill because of Andrew's behavior."

Jessie took the towel she used to dry her hands and wiped her face. "I've decided to get to the bottom of this. If I wait for the police to do their job it'll never get done," realizing what she said, she tried to smooth over the implication. "Boat's so busy and those state police are so stupid they'll never get any answers. I know by the way Garza questioned me that I'm their prime suspect."

Marge spotted the chocolate cake and decided it was time to put her plan into action. "I say we get the guys in her and knock off this cake. We can decide the best way to go from here."

Not waiting for Jessie to object, she called to the men, "Okay, boys, last chance to get dessert!" She stepped back to avoid being trampled by the stampede.

"Is that your famous double chocolate, Marge?" Boat asked. He was afraid to look at Marge. He could feel her brain churning from the living room.

"Double chocolate with chocolate ice cream!"

"Look out, guys, they're up to no good. Chocolate ice cream too!" Jake said, winking at Sam.

"Well, I have to get home," Sam said, trying to back out the door.

"Oh, no you don't, Sam," Boat said, grabbing his friend by the coat sleeve "One for all and all for one. If we get led to the slaughter house, we go together!" Boat said, halting Sam's exit.

"Okay, I give up!" Sam said, slipping out of his coat.

They were seated around the table, each with a heaping portion of cake and ice cream in front of them. Jessie turned to Boat and said, "Now we are alone, what have you come up with on Roger's murder?"

"I'm not in on the investigation," Boat said, keeping his eyes on his plate. "All I have is basic preliminary information."

Everyone stopped eating to wait for Boat to give them the details. Boat looked first to Jake, then to Marge, then to Jessie. He didn't see how he could get out of giving Jessie what she wanted, even though he was sure it would probably cause her more pain.

"The state has decided to put the case in the active file under 'death by murder, persons unknown.'"

"Just what does that mean?"

"They are waiting for more information from the coroner. The preliminary investigation tells us little more than we expected."

"Just what did 'we' expect?" Jake asked, leaning closer as if he was afraid he might miss some important part.

"The female victim was killed somewhere else and put in the car. She was identified as Robyn Smith." Looking directly at Jessie, he went on, "It is certain she and Roger had sexual relations before they were killed."

Jessie looked at the table for a long time before she said, "Is there anything to prove it?" As she finished the question she lifted her eyes to meet Boat's, hoping the answer would be different then the one she saw.

"Yes, Jessie. The DNA tests prove it." Boat went on and got all the information out in the open to cause as little pain as necessary. "The coroner put the time of death sometime between 4 p.m. and 7 p.m. The bodies were damaged enough by the fire to make it impossible to pin the time of death down any closer.

"We know the girl was killed and moved, while Roger was killed on the site. Roger had two wounds on his head; they are assuming he was hit at the same place Robyn was killed, then moved to the murder scene and hit again with a blunt wooden object. Roger had carbon monoxide in his lungs, so there is no doubt he died at the scene after the explosion.

"Robyn was beaten and strangled. Roger had a large blood loss, so the coroner is certain one of the blows occurred before they were transported.

"The evidence doesn't point to any one person or persons. There is a lot of leg work and sorting of evidence to see what is real and what is manipulated." Boat let out a long sigh with the final piece of information. He said it all in one breath.

"Well, I guess this makes me the most likely suspect," Jessie said bluntly. "I was afraid of that. I figured as much the way Sgt. Garza was interrogating me," Jessie said. "Well, I'm not going to let them put this in a file somewhere and forget about it."

"Let it lay, Jessie," Jake said with exasperation. "Things will quiet down and then we can get on with our lives."

Jessie glared at Jake and then looked around the table to get the other's reaction to what he had said.

"No, it won't, Jake," Sam said with such vehemence it surprised everyone at the table. "I saw the way everyone looked at Jessie and the kids. It will hang over all your heads until the real murderer is found."

Everyone was silenced by Sam's remark.

"Sam's right. Unless something is done to find the real culprit, Jessie will be suspected of this forever," Marge said flatly, turning attention to Boat.

"My hands are tied," Boat said, shaking his head. "If I get involved, people will say I got my friend off the hook. I've already gotten a letter expressing the view I should turn my notes over to the investigating team."

"Did you?" Sam asked, giving Boat a knowing glance.

"Hell no. I was told to stay out of the investigation, wasn't I? How could I have any notes?"

"Okay, Boat, what do we do next?" Marge asked, excited at the thought of working with Boat on the investigation.

"We go home. Jessie has had a long day. She needs some rest. The next few days getting the estate settled will be very grueling," Boat said, standing and retrieving his plate to clear the table,

"Just leave them, Boat. I'll take care of them later. I am awfully tired," Jessie said, stifling a yawn.

Jake waved everyone away from the mess. "Jess and I can take care of the dishes. Thanks for everything."

"Give us a call if you need anything," Marge called as Boat led her to the car.

"Boy, I'm beat!" Jessie sighed.

"Go to bed, Pearlie. I'll take care of straightening up this mess," Jake said, pushing her toward her bedroom.

"Thanks, Dad," Jessie said, feeling like a little girl again. "I love you."

"I know," Jake said over the lump in his throat.

Watching Jessie go into her room, Jake turned to find Sam still sitting at the table. "Hey, Sam, I thought you had left with the others."

Jake thought this guy was like the invisible man sometimes. It was probably what made him so good at his job.

"I needed to talk to you for a minute," Sam said, getting up from the table. "I don't want to interfere. I know what a hard time this has been for all of you. If there is anything I can do, you let me know."

Jake was surprised by the offer. Sam wasn't known for involving himself in other people's problems. "That's real nice of you, Sam," Jake said, putting out his hand to shake the younger man's. "Right now we just want to get through the legalities and get on with our lives."

"You tell Jessie I'm ready to settle this lawsuit any way she sees fit," Sam said. "I never wanted a fight in the first place, but Roger seemed determined to have a go-around."

"I'll let Jessie know what you said," Jake said as he led Sam toward the door. "By the way, how is your mare doing?

# Chapter Nine

Jessie woke to the sound of rain pounding on her window. Stretching, she tried to guess the time, but the darkness of the storm camouflaged the hour.

Groaning, she rolled over and looked at the clock. "Oh no, look how late it is!" She rolled out of bed, chastising herself. "Late! What a great way to start the last week of school!" Throwing back the covers and bounding from the bed, she called to the kids, "Jordan! Cristal! It's time to get up!"

She pulled her robe on as she ran out the door.

"Jeez, Mom, what are you hollering about?" Jordan asked as he collided with his mother in the hallway.

"You guys are going to be late if you don't get the lead out!"

"What's going on?" Cristal asked as she came out of the bathroom. "What is Mom raving about?"

"She thinks we need to get the lead out," he answered, shrugging his shoulders. "We already have all our chores done. We are leaving to catch the bus now," he said with the exaggerated slowness one would use with a small child.

"I guess I was more tired than I realized," Jessie said as she moved to make coffee.

"We made fresh coffee for you, Mom," Cristal said, mimicking Jordan. "Kids!" she added, smiling at Jordan.

"Get out of here before I whip both of you," Jessie threatened lightheartedly, looking for something to scare them with, settling on an oven mitt she picked off the counter and waved it menacingly.

"OOOOHH!" they said in unison as they grabbed their books and sped out the door.

"Ingrates." Jessie smiled after them.

"Are you threatening those poor orphaned children with violence?" Jake quipped lightly, noticing the happy mood everyone was in this morning.

"Violence is too good for the little ingrates!" She liked the way "ingrates" rolled off her tongue.

"Nice to see things getting back to normal," Jake noted.

"Yeah, I wasn't looking forward to today, but I think things are going to be fine," she said thoughtfully. "The kids made fresh coffee for us. Those two never cease to amaze me. One minute they fight like cats and dogs and the next they're working together like Siamese twins."

"That's kids for you. I figure it's a conspiracy. They try to drive you slowly around the bend and then they act innocent. Kids are little barbarians in disguise." Jake paused as if caught in a daydream. "I remember when you and Roger were little, the two of you kept Glynis on a tight rope," Jake said, catching the hurt in Jessie's eyes. "Sorry."

"That's all right, Jake," Jessie said, rubbing her forehead. "I can't expect Roger's name never to come up in conversations again."

"Yeah, but we don't have to turn the day to a sour note," Jake replied as he poured himself a cup of coffee. "Who made this coffee, Cristal or Jordan? Let's hope we don't find anything lying at the bottom of the pot!" Jake laughed as he quickly changed the subject.

"You know, I would look forward to one of his goofy jokes! I miss them. It's been so long since he's been any fun. Even one of his practical jokes would be welcome," Jessie said, looking into her cup as she feared something might crawl out of it.

"Remember, look out what you ask for!" Jake said as he rose to leave. "I'd better get to work. Things haven't been running too smoothly lately. It's time for us to get things back on track."

Watching her dad head down to the barns, the vision of Roger standing at the foot of her bed waving for her to follow was so strong it startled her, making her spill coffee all over the table.

She had the image of Roger at the foot of the bed, telling her to meet him at the playhouse. She hadn't thought of the playhouse for years.

When Roger and she were little and they wanted to get away from Glynis, they would go to an old tree house built in one of the oaks "Old Dolly" had planted. The tree house had been built years before by Big Roger's dad, Grandpa Rite, for Big Roger.

Roger's Grandpa Rite had seemed a thousand years old as he had sat in the shade provided by the stately oaks. Jessie and Roj had loved to sit and listen to the stories about the old Rite homestead. It was like living in a piece of history. Roger Rite, the first, had made his way west after listening to a speech by Horacio Alger telling all the young men to "Go West." His imagination was fired by the account given, telling of the abundance to be found in the wild west of the 1800s.

Even though her husband had an active imagination and a flair for writing, the stories associated with the ranch never attracted him. He seemed to be looking to other subjects for inspiration.

The old oak had a hiding place in the belly where they would keep their "valuables." Roger, a journal in which he wrote daily, well, as daily as a 12-year-old would. Jessie had kept her favorite ribbons and medals in the box. "I wonder what happened to Roger's old journal," Jessie mused aimlessly.

Those were the good old days. The most important thing on her mind was keeping her thoroughbred in shape for the many horse shows in which Big Roger continually entered her. Roger loved going through her ribbons and medals asking all kinds of questions about this particular show, or what it felt like when she lost. To bad Big Roger didn't appreciate Roj's sensitivity.

"That is enough stalling! Those papers aren't going to take care of themselves." Jessie smiled to herself. "I'll jump into a hot shower first and then to work!"

Jessie got out of the shower to the ringing of the phone. She didn't make it in time. "They'll call back."

Looking at the dreary day outside made Jessie crave a nice warm fire. It would probably be her last chance to hear the crackle of a fire all summer. It would be her last chance to watch the flames dance. It was one thing she could count on to calm her nerves. Maybe it would help today. Jessie watched as the fire quickly began to roar, and she began feeling relaxed, until the ringing of the phone brought an end to her reverie.

"Hello?"

A low, muffled voice asked to speak to Jessica Rite.

"This is Jessica Rite."

The voice in whispered tones asked, "How does it feel to get away with murder?" A click at the other end told her the line was dead.

"Creep!" Jessie yelled into the phone. "That's a great comeback, Jessie," she said as she slammed down the phone. "I suppose I should get use to this if everyone thinks I did it. Even the look in Jordan's eyes accuses me. Great, now I'm carrying on a conversation with myself!" With a quick look around the room to make sure no one had heard her; she headed to Roger's office to work on the business papers.

It was creepy going through Roger's things. In the last few years he had become so secretive about business matters. In fact, the secrecy began after his parent's accident. He hadn't been interested in any of the corporate businesses until then; suddenly he was "Mr. Business."

"Well, let's see what kind of shape things are in." Jessie started with what she thought would be the simplest job, straightening the desk. She got things a little neater, and she started reading the transactions Roger had been in the midst of completing. She became so engrossed in what she was reading that she lost track of time. She didn't hear the kids calling when they came into the house.

"Mom, are you here?" Cristal hollered.

"Jeez, Cristal, where do you think she would be? The Beamer is outside, isn't it?" Jordan headed for the fridge. "I hope there is some chocolate cake left."

"Me, too," Cristal agreed, salivating at the thought of the cake.

They sat at the table with half of the cake in front of them; they were trying to decide if they should split it down the middle or just grab a fork and dive in.

Cristal said to Jordan. "Jordan, do you think things will change now that Dad is gone?"

Jordan looked at the wide-eyed innocence in his sister's eyes and decided to forgo the smart remark. "Dad wasn't here much anyway. We'll get used to him being gone."

Cristal looked at her big brother for a long time to see if he was kidding or not. "I thought I was the only one who felt that way."

In Cristal's matter-of-fact way of dealing with things, she was already on to the next order of business. "I say we eat the whole thing before Jake or Mom can get any more!" She grabbed a fork and dove in.

Although he didn't admit it, Jordan had always felt awed by his sister. She always saw through to the heart of a problem, even when she was little. Once she made up her mind, things were settled, and she went onto the next item on the agenda, never looking back or regretting a decision.

"Sisters!" Jordan said. Then he decided he'd better get his fork or she'd eat the whole thing. Like her mother, Cristal's little figure belied her hardy appetite.

When they finished up the last of the crumbs, they heard Jake stomping the mud off his boots. They made a mad dash to hide the cake platter. They were innocently working on their homework when he came into the kitchen.

"Any chocolate cake left?" Jake didn't know what to make of the two "angels" doing their homework.

"Well, I think I'll go check on the colt," Cristal said, jumping up and heading out the door.

"Me too." Jordan followed.

Jake found the cake plate and thought to himself, *Jessie is right—ingrates!*

As if called by magic, Jessie strolled into the kitchen. "Boy, what a pig, Jake." Jessie smiled as she pointed at the platter.

"Hey, I didn't even get a morsel!" Jake growled.

"I suppose the mice ate it all?" Jessie said, smiling and clicking her tongue as if Jake were an errant little boy in which she was disappointed.

Setting the platter in the sink, Jake said, "Real funny, Pearlie!"

Jake turned to leave when Jessie stopped him. "Hey, Jake, did you see this copy of Big Roger's will?"

"No, Roger took care of all the paperwork," Jake said. All the humor was gone from his face. "I was allowed to keep my job as trainer if I didn't get in Roger's way."

"This doesn't look right to me. Roger was always telling me his problem was Big Roger didn't trust him. I can't figure why he left everything in Roger's care. I was too upset at the time to check things over. I just hoped Big Roger was making up for all the years of neglect," Jessie said, heading back to the office without waiting for a reply

"Women!" Jake said, shaking his head as he decided to join the kids in the barn.

Jessie was trying to make some kind of sense out of what she was finding in the office when the phone rang. "Hello?" she hollered into the phone with little patience.

"Is that you, Mrs. Rite?" Sam asked tentatively.

She recognized Sam Ellison's voice. "Sorry, Mr. Ellison, isn't it?" she told herself the excited flutter in her stomach was because of the earlier call not because she was attracted to the man on the other end of the line.

"What can I do for you?"

"Well, my mare's foaling. It seems to be taking a long time." Sam didn't like to ask for help, but he swallowed his pride. This was too important to let pride stand in the way.

"Jake and I will be right over," she said, slamming down the phone without waiting for a reply. "One mare lost is enough."

Jake was coming out of the barn with the kids when Jessie came bounding down the walk. "Sam Ellison's mare is in trouble."

"Let me get the kit. You get the truck, Jessie."

By the time they had driven the short distance to Sam's he was waiting for them. "She seems pretty wore out," Sam said to Jake, giving Jessie a grateful smile.

*How can she look so great?* Sam tried to keep his mind on his problem at hand, but it wasn't easy. A woman hadn't affected him this way for years. He was resigned to the fact he would spend the rest of his life keeping the bird safe from his no good cat, but...

Jessie was oblivious to the scrutiny Sam was giving her. She watched as Jake gave the mare a quick examination. Jake could tell more about a horse by running his hands over it than most trained veterinarians could with all their fancy equipment.

"Well, Sam, I think you're about to become the owner of a great runner!" The mare raised her head and gave a wild-eyed look at Jake. "It's all right girl, I'm just here to help," Jake said soothingly.

"Jessie, get down by her head," Jake asked without looking, intent on his job. "I think this little fella is going to need a little help."

Jessie remembered the last time she and Jake had to do this and said a quick prayer. She could tell by the look on Sam's face this mare meant a lot to him. The mare gave weak knickers and tried to stand as Jake pulled on the reluctant foal. Sam felt as if time had stopped. He held his breath, awaiting the final outcome of Jake's ministrations. His patience was rewarded with a long-legged filly.

The filly stood almost immediately on wobbly legs and nudged her mother instinctively. The mare had enough energy to rise to a sitting position and began licking the filly vigorously. The filly curiously wobbled around the stall for a few minutes, making the mare nervous.

The mare got to her feet and gave a great shake as if to say, "Thanks for the help, but I can take over from here." The mare positioned herself between the little filly and the humans.

Jake and Jessie backed out of the stall as she nervously stomped. "They are both going to be fine," Jake said, pumping Sam's hand up and down furiously. He was grateful his help had meant a happy outcome this time.

The filly wobbled on ever-stronger legs. She walked instinctively to the back of the mare to get some nourishment from her mother. This had been one trying day!

Sam shook Jake's hand up and down as if it was a well handle. "Thanks, Jake, I don't know how I'll ever repay you. Turning to Jessie, he grabbed her in a big bear hug and swung her around until she was dizzy.

Abruptly he stopped, holding her for a minute and looking into the greenest eyes he had ever encountered.

"Maybe you should put me down," Jessie suggested.

"Sorry, Mrs. Rite," Sam apologized.

"No problem, Sam. I think by now we can be on a first name basis, though." Jessie was having trouble slowing her racing heart.

"Okay, Jessie. You have a deal," Sam said, still intrigued by her dark green eyes.

"Looks like you have a fine filly here, Sam. Your mare is going to be fine. Keep her and the filly in for a few days to make sure everything is okay." Jake seemed more interested in the mare and filly than what was transpiring between his daughter and his friend.

"I guess we need to head home now," Jessie said with a feeling of loneliness enveloping her at the thought of leaving. "Come on, Jake, I might even let you drive."

The quiet of the ride home was broken by Jessie. "Jake, what do you think of Sam Ellison?"

Jake wasn't surprised by the question. "I think he's as fine a man as you will find anywhere. Hardworking (this being as high a compliment as Jake gave anyone), honest and not afraid to lend a helping hand when necessary is how I would sum him up."

Jessie thought to herself, "You wouldn't find him running around on his wife, I bet."

"You know, Jessie, not all men are cads," Jake said as if he was reading her mind.

"I was just curious, Jake. I think I want to drop this stupid lawsuit. Roger only wanted to get his hands on the mare, anyway," Jessie said, not bothering to defend her late husband. "After seeing her I see why Roger became so obsessed with her. She is gorgeous!"

"Now, Pearlie, you'll have to forgive him some day. If not for yourself, you have to for the sake of the kids. It's not healthy for you to harbor hostility," Jake preached. Then, to break the tension building, he added, "Vintage Oprah. See, I don't spend all of my time in the horse barns."

They both laughed. Changing the subject, Jessie said, "Going through Roger's office, things seem to be very wrong."

"I have thought so since Big Roger left the entire estate to Roger."

"What do I do now, Jake? Somehow "Old Beagle Nose" got her information right this time. Roger left no will I can find. Did he ever think of anyone besides himself?"

"When we get home I'll help you go through things. Don't worry, we will find the answers," Jake said matter-of-factly, purposely ignoring the question.

Cristal came tearing out of the house as Jake and Jessie drove in. "Mom, guess what?" she said, hopping from one foot to the other. "We decided on a name for the colt."

"Slow down, Cristal," Jessie said, slinging her arm around the younger girl's shoulder. "Let me guess." Closing her eyes and frowning, she rubbed her chin in a perfect mimic of Jake when he was confronted with an overwhelming problem.

"I know," she said as if struck by inspiration, "Flicka."

"Jeez, Mom," Jordan said, rolling his eyes with exasperation. "That's a girl's name."

Everyone stopped walking to look at Jordan as he dropped this pearl of wisdom. "Is that right, Jordan?" Jessie asked as if overwhelmed by this information.

"Really, don't you remem…"Jordan decided to ignore everyone as they started to giggle. "I don't think you guys are funny," Jordan said soberly.

Then the whole group started laughing. "Sorry, Jordan," Jessie said, trying to stifle her laughter. "But you left yourself wide open!" Then she glared at everyone to keep them from laughing. "So, what did you come up with?"

"Our Gale's Hope," Cristal said proudly. "We are going to call him 'Hoppy' for short.

"That was Cristal's idea, not mine," Jordan said, rolling his eyes skyward.

"Well, I think it is a great name," Jessie said, putting her arm across the shoulders of both her children. "How is the little fella doing?"

"He's doing great. He comes running up to me every time I come into the barn, even if I don't have food!" Jordan beams.

"He's really strong, Mom," Cristal cut in. "Grandpa thinks we have a real winner on our hands. He said we could train him ourselves."

Jessie looked at Jake and sent him a silent thank you.

"Well, it's about time these kids did something besides decorate the place," Jake said, rubbing each one on the head.

"Jeez, Grandpa, my hair," Jordan said, embarrassed by the familiarity. "I just got it cut."

"I'm ready for food," Jessie said, breaking into a run. "Last one there makes dinner!" she challenged, looking over her shoulder. The race was on!

# Chapter Ten

Jessie found she had trouble sleeping. She tried to remember what had awoken her as she drank her coffee. The coffee tasted bitter, causing the throb in Jessie's head to increase. There was something gnawing at her, something she should remember. Ever since her accident, a vision kept blurring and forming, forming and blurring, never clear enough to make out. It was like a name on the tip of her tongue.

Jessie got up and dumped her breakfast down the disposal. Even the sunny brightness of the kitchen seemed an irritation.

She loved her kitchen. She had remodeled the old-fashioned utilitarian-style kitchen into a bright, homey area. Glynis would turn over in her grave if she knew Jessie was teaching Cristal and Jordan to cook. Glynis complained the only thing Jessie was good at was cleaning stalls and now she was teaching the children the drudgery of cooking!

Even Jake was a little leery of the improvements Jessie had insisted upon. After she had the skylights installed and the old pantry turned into a walk-in refrigerator, he had to admit things were coming together very nicely.

Roger, on the other hand, had sided with Glynis. He had said they had a perfectly good housekeeper to do all the cooking. He was satisfied with the old kitchen. When she gave him a guided tour of the refurbished kitchen the closest thing to a compliment he gave her was a nod of his head. She never did get Glynis to come into the kitchen to see the improvements.

"Real ladies don't take the chance of getting grease on their clothing," Glynis sniffed arrogantly.

Cooking had become an artistic outlet. Some of her creations were renowned countywide for their "ingenuity." Several cooking classes and many cookbooks later, she had become an excellent cook.

Today all she wanted to do was get the distasteful task ahead of her accomplished. Roger's will had to be here somewhere. She wanted to find it and soon. No more interruptions until it was accomplished. Jessie knew once she set her mind to it that she would do it. For some reason her enthusiasm was hard to find.

"Okay, Jessica Rite, enough procrastination on your part! Get on with it. The sooner started, the sooner finished."

*This little pep talk always works,* Jessie thought. Heading for the office, Jessie was interrupted by the ringing phone.

"Hello?"

"Mrs. Rite?"

"Yes," Jessie said nervously after all the prank phone calls she had been receiving.

"This is Fred Ames of Johnsford Mutual Insurance."

"Look, Mr. Ames, I really don't need any insurance right now," Jessie snapped at the man.

"I just need to talk to you about the policies Mr. Rite bought for the two of you last year."

"I think you have me mixed up with someone else," Jessie said nervously.

"You are Jessica Pearl Rite, aren't you?" the man said jovially.

"Yes." Now Jessie was starting to become nervous.

"Why don't I come over and I can go through the policies with you. You'll have a better understanding of what I'm talking about."

"That will be fine. Can you come at 2:00?" Jessie asked the man, impatiently looking at her watch.

"You might want to have a lawyer there, Mrs. Rite. Some of these policies can be confusing," the agent said.

"Thank you, Mr. Ames, wasn't it?"

"Yes, and I'll see you at 2 p.m. this afternoon."

Jessie put the phone down and headed to the office. The feeling things were getting out of hand wouldn't go away.

Jessie stated to give Jake a call when she remembered he had gone to the Wasco auction. "Like we need any more horses around here!" she said, irritation welling within her. Everything seemed to get to her these days. Maybe it was the whack on her head. "Excuses, excuses, excuses. You need to get to work!" Jessie berated herself. The feelings of inadequacy Roger had instilled in her didn't evaporate just because he had been murdered; if anything they seemed to multiply with each new surprise.

Roger's death had shown her she would need to learn to depend on herself. Jake wouldn't be here to solve every problem she encountered forever. Jessie grabbed a cup of coffee and headed into the office when the phone interrupted her again.

"Yes?" Jessie said impatiently.

"Did I call at a bad time?" Sam asked tentatively.

"Just more details to be handled." Suddenly Jessie felt refreshed just hearing his voice.

"Can I do anything to help?" Sam asked. "I'm really not just a land baron, you know. I have some knowledge of the law."

Jessie's chuckle sounded hollow. "That's okay; it's just some mix-up about insurance policies. How can I help you?" Jessie hoped he didn't want anything pressing; she was at the end of her rope.

"No, nothing. I just called to thank you for the other night and lend a hand if I could." Sam was disappointed he wouldn't get a chance to see her.

"No thanks are necessary, but I appreciate the offer. I hope you'll leave the offer open. You never know when a good land baron slash lawyer might come in handy." Jessie tried to keep her voice light. "Maybe the kids and I could come and see the new filly after school. They are in charge of our new colt and doing a great job. I'm sure they would be full of advice." This time she was laughing with real humor at the thought of Jordan telling Sam how to handle his filly.

Hanging up the phone, Jessie felt her stomach flutter at the thought of seeing Sam this afternoon. "I'd better get to work," she said, shaking any more thought of Sam out of her head.

Jessie took a deep breath, squared her shoulders, and decided to dive right in straightening the papers. "I never realized Roger was such a pig." She found drinking glasses sitting around the room. Some of them were filled with an odd assortment of growing compounds in them. As usual, Jessie got so engrossed in her work that she lost track of time.

"Jessie, are you in here?" Jake asked from the kitchen. "Hey, Jessie, there is a gentleman here to see you. He says he has an appointment."

Jessie was startled. "I'll be right out." Looking around the once-cluttered office, Jessie decided she had not accomplished as much as she had wanted. As usual she was still cleaning up after Roger. Smoothing her unruly mass of curls, she walked to where the two men were waiting for her.

"Mr. Ames, isn't it?" she asked, reaching to shake his hand. "I'm sorry I didn't hear you knocking on the door." As she turned to Jake she noticed a confused look on his face. "Dad, this is Mr. Ames. He has some insurance matters to discuss with me."

Motioning for Mr. Ames to follow her to the office, she turned to Jake and asked, "How's Hoppy doing, Dad?"

"He is just fine," Jake answered, confusion increasing the line between his eyes.

"Don't worry, Jake; I can handle this," Jessie said, dismissing Jake much in the same way he remembered Pearl doing when she had something puzzling on her mind.

Jake thought to argue but decided his little girl had to grow up some day. She wouldn't have him around to straighten out her problems forever. "It was nice to meet you, Mr. Ames. If you need me I'll be in the training barn, Jessie."

Easing into Roger's overstuffed chair, Jessie nodded to a chair across the desk from her. Jessie stared at him without saying anything, making him very uncomfortable.

Jessie had taken an instant dislike to him although she couldn't pinpoint why. He was dressed in a well-cut suit, expensive, but not too expensive. His hair and hands had the look of someone with a long-standing appointment with his cosmetologist. Hooded eyes scrutinized you intently. He was an attractive man; the only problem was that he worked very hard to be ordinary.

*Well, Freddie boy, you've fallen into it this time. This could be your lucky day. This one looks like the perfect gal to take home to Mom,* thought the agent, smiling broadly He noticed Jessie Rite didn't look much like a widow.

She was a tall woman with just the right amount of leg. Her thick head of hair was streaked silver at the temples, making a lie of her willow-thin figure and youthful features. Although she obviously spent lots of time outside, her peaches and cream complexion bore the healthy glow of a 16-year-old.

She was dressed casually in Levis and a designer t-shirt that perfectly matched her emerald green eyes. His imagination taking over, he fantasized her lying on a bearskin rug wearing a Frederick's of Hollywood teddy and black spiked heels. He was afraid to let his imagination go any further or "things" might grow out of control.

"Well, Mrs. Rite, are we ready to go over these policies?" he said with a too-charming glint of capped teeth. "You seemed somewhat surprised by my call."

"Mr. Ames, I still haven't a clue to what you are talking about," Jessie said, not even trying to hide her impatience.

"That is why I'm here, Jessie," he said, pulling his chair closer to the desk, looking around conspiratorially.

"I'm rather busy, *Mr. Ames*, why don't you get to the point," Jessie said, emphasizing the "Mr. Ames."

The charming smile slowly disappeared from his face, and he straightened in his chair. "Mr. Rite got in touch with us last year to write several policies for him." He paused for effect, hoping to find a chink in this woman's armor. "These policies are written for very substantial amounts of money. If you'll just get your copies, we can go over them and finish the paperwork." Suddenly he was as impatient as Jessie.

Jessie searched her memory of last year. She couldn't recall Roger making any plans with her for insurance changes. Ames noticed the frown on Jessie's face increase and thought, *These rich bitches; they marry rich and then think they are above everybody else.* Putting the smile back on his face, he could tell something was bothering her.

"Well, Mr. Ames, as you can see, I'm still trying to sort out all of Roger's papers. This is a substantial estate and quite frankly these policies come as a shock to me." Jessie decided the direct approach was the best one to take with this guy.

Ames saw a chance to turn this to his advantage and decided maybe she wasn't as strong as she appeared. His ability to capitalize on the smallest weakness and not be afraid to use it to his advantage made him the best policy writer in the office. He wasn't bothered by the fact he pushed through policies other companies wouldn't handle. In his mind he was the greatest writer since Lloyds of London!

Rising from his chair he headed around the desk to lay the policies in front of Jessie. "See, we started these policies in 1993. Your husband wanted to insure you would always be cared for since he was covered by corporate policies that were automatically in force at his birth. But he wanted you protected for the kids' sake," he said, puffing up like a rooster about to crow. "It was my idea to cover both of you instead of him alone. You know we can't be too careful these days."

Jessie pushed back her chair to gain as much distance as she could. "I haven't found any policies in his papers. Are you sure he received them?" Jessie asked. The dull ache in her head was building to a thundering pulse.

"You know, Jessie," Ames said, putting his hand comfortingly on her shoulder. "I think you need some help sorting out this mess. I could call my office and tell them I won't be in this afternoon," he said, starting to rub her shoulder. "I know how difficult it can be for the little woman when they lose their man."

Jumping out of the chair quickly, as if hit with an electric shock, she turned to face him. Jessie said, "To begin with, I'm not a little woman. If I need help, I'll ask my family and friends, not a complete stranger. Now, unless you want me to call your company and tell them you are harassing me, I suggest you get out and leave all my husband's papers." Ames, retreating back around the desk, gathered his papers and headed out the door.

"Also, I want all the papers pertaining to my husband's policies." Jessie could tell Ames was good at keeping notes.

He stopped for a second as if he was ready to deny her request. As Jessie reached for the phone, he opened his briefcase and pulled out the file, flinging it across the desk. "You know, lady, I'll never write another policy for this family, and I'll tell all my friends about you, too!"

Jessie opened her eyes as wide as she could and put a hand across her mouth in mock horror. All she saw of Ames was his retreating back.

"Are all guys jerks, or what?" Jessie said, glancing over the first policy. Once again Jessie lost track of time. Going over and over the policies was tedious, and she got more confused each time she read them. She heard the mantle clock strike five, and she realized she had missed the kids coming home from school. It was time to fix dinner. Her head was throbbing and her eyes felt like hot coals. "I'm finished for the night."

Shutting the door to the office, hoping to shut it out of her mind at the same time, she headed to the foaling barn where she knew the kids would be playing with the colt.

"Mom, guess what?" Cristal said enthusiastically. "Hoppy knows his name. He comes every time we call him. He's so smart he is going to be one of our best jumpers, I just know it."

"I told you, Cristal, he's going to be a racer. Gramps says he's got the legs for it," Jordan broke in.

"Well, I think it's a little early to decide what to do with him," Jessie said, trying to soothe both their ruffled feathers.

"Jeez, Mom, you always stick up for Cristal," Jordan pouted.

"Leave your Mom alone, Jordan. Besides, she is right. It's a little early to decide what to do with Hoppy," Jake said, putting his arm around his grandson's neck and giving him a friendly noogie.

"Who's going to help me with dinner?" Jessie said, looking around pleadingly.

"Please, no more casseroles!" Jake begged. "I'd rather be baked in the oven myself."

"Jake is right! No more casseroles!" The two kids joined in unison with Jake. "I say No-more- casseroles, no-more-casseroles!"

"Okay, okay," Jessie said, raising her hands in surrender. "I think I'm ready for some Moo goo gai pan!"

"Yeah!" they said as the kids sprinted to the Blazer.

"On this auspicious occasion I think we should let Jake drive, after all, it was his idea for no-more-casseroles!" Jessie wasn't ready for a dispute over who would drive.

The chant "No-more-casseroles!" Was replaced by "Moo-goo-gai-pan!" This was chanted all the way to the Dragon House. Luckily they didn't have far to drive. For the first time in two weeks their nervousness at going to town was forgotten.

Sam noticed the Rite family as he walked into the Dragon House. They seemed to be a likable family. If you didn't know better you'd believe they didn't have a worry in the world. He returned Jake's wave and headed to their table.

"Hey, Sam, join us for dinner. We just ordered," Jake said as he approached their table.

"I'll sit for a minute; I called an order in already." Sam smiled at Jessie, for the first time noticing she could easily be the older sister rather than the mother. "Hi, how'd your meeting go this afternoon?" he asked.

Jessie just waved her hand and shook her head; she didn't want to talk about it. "Just more papers to deal with," she said, settling the matter.

Sam could tell when to leave well enough alone. He turned to the kids. "Did Jake tell you about my new filly?" The kids shook their heads, so he continued. "I hear you two are the experts in case I need someone to help me with her," he said, giving each one of them a crooked smile. Jordan just shrugged his shoulders, but Cristal was won over immediately by its charm. "Maybe you could come over this weekend and take a look at her, if you're not too busy."

Cristal jumped in before Jordan could say anything. "That would be great. We have a new colt, you know. His name is Hoppy, and he's an orphan, but Jordan and I and are taking real great care of him, aren't we, Jake? We could come over after we get our chores done." Jordan shrugged his shoulders and dug into his food so he wouldn't have to say anything.

"Well, there's my food. I guess I'd better get home before it gets cold. See you this weekend, kids," he said over his shoulder as he left to pay for the meal.

"Jeez, Cristal, why can't you keep your big mouth shut?" Jordan said as he flushed a brilliant red. "I don't care if the guy has 20 fillies, I say he is a jerk!" he said, looking for his mother's reaction. He didn't like the way Sam looked at her.

"You know you want to see the filly. Just the other day you were wondering when his mare would foal!" Cristal said defensively, adding, "I like him. I think he is real nice."

"Jeez, Cristal, you're such a baby," Jordan said, exasperated.

"Okay you two, enough!" Jessie said, thinking to herself maybe she would take him up on his offer. She was getting headache thinking about going over the insurance papers again.

***

"Oh, Momma, quit being so whiney!" it said, rifling through the pile of junk on the bedroom floor. "Ah, there you are." The figure acted as if the shovel were alive, an old friend not seen for many years.

"You know, Momma, I thought the stupid police would have that witch, Jessie Rite, behind bars by now. I suppose you can't put the poor widow in jail because she had the bad taste to kill her husband!" it said through gritted teeth. "I don't care if you like her! She is nothing but a witch with a capital "B." I know I said I was going to give the shovel to Winnie Andrews. Lucky for me her husband got everyone looking at the both of them," it snickered while remembering Jessie's reaction at the memorial service.

"I think we should get people wondering about Selma Jackson. Yeah, she is always going around with her nose in the air when she is nothing more than a glorified dog washer!" It tore off the tattered robe and jumped into the middle of the messy bed, continually turning and fussing, fussing and scrunching, making the little nest perfect. It folded itself into a small ball as it angrily released a deep sigh and settled into a fretful sleep.

# Chapter Eleven

"Come on, Jordan, I've got all the chores done," Cristal said impatiently to her brother, who was taking his own sweet time to finish his breakfast. "You never eat this much in the morning," she added to get his attention.

"You go without me, Cristal; I have plans for the day," Jordan said, studying his bowl, looking for the last remaining morsels.

"You promised you would go to see his filly!" Cristal said, stomping her foot for punctuation.

"Jeez, I never said I'd go. That was your great idea," he said, slipping his thumbs through his belt loops and leaning back on his chair.

"What's going on in there?" Jessie called, giving the two kids a minute to get their story straight. "I thought you were going over to Sam's to help him with his colt today?" Jessie asked as she entered the kitchen.

Jordan righted the chair before his mother had a chance to say anything. "Jeez, Mom! You're as bad as Cristal. I never said I was going. It was all her big idea."

"Come on, Jordan. You know you are as curious as Cristal," Jessie said as she ruffled his hair.

"Okay, I'm going, but this is the last time. If that guy can't take care of his stock, maybe he shouldn't have any," Jordan said, smoothing his hair into place as he gave his mother a hooded glance.

"Good," Cristal said, hopping up and down. "I have the horses waiting." She took off, pulling a reluctant Jordan with her.

Jessie decided to use the quiet of the early morning to get started on

Roger's papers. She knew if she didn't get to them she would just end up with another anxiety-filled night, and she needed some rest. She warned herself she had to get the papers correlated, hopefully in this century.

She decided to use a new tack. If she put the papers into categories she could go through them more efficiently. So for the next several hours she categorized over and over until she saw a trend developing. There were several time blocks missing out of each category, the same time blocks, in fact. She was about to start on the least controversial category, the ranch bills, when Jake appeared at the door.

"Hey, Pearlie, looks like you are finally getting a handle on all these papers," Jake said.

"You know, Dad, these papers aren't just in confusion, and there are blocks of them missing. Roger was up to something, and I'm afraid to find out what it was." Jessie sighed.

"Look, Jessie, Roger wasn't my kind of businessman, but I don't think he would do anything to jeopardize you, the kids, or the ranch. He had more brains then that," Jake said, feeling concern for his family and the only home he had known for 30 years.

The ranch papers were the only records in order, Jessie noticed, after she got them organized. "How much control did Roger have over dealings connected with the ranch?" Jessie asked.

"I pretty much had free reign. You know how he hated getting his boots dirty."

Putting the file away, Jessie sighed. "Maybe he just trusted you."

"Bull," Jake added sadly.

"Look at these, Jake," she said, holding up the file of insurance policies. "All these policies, but nowhere can I find the originals to the ones Ames brought."

"Let me take a look at those," Jake said, reaching for the file. As he shuffled through the papers he noted there were several policies missing. "Let me have a look at the other policy files.

"That is all the files," Jessie said, getting a sick feeling in the pit of her stomach.

"No, I mean the file of full life policies," Jake said slowly.

"Look, Jake, I'm not a simpleton. I'm telling you this is the only file," Jessie said, starting to lose her patience. "Maybe he did something with them, because these are the only policies."

"They have to be here someplace, Jessie," Jake said, still missing the point; there were no more files. "I remember the day Big Roger got the policies for everyone. He couldn't wait to let me know you would be set no matter what. They were seven figures, if I remember correctly. They were ours when they came to term."

Jake sat back in the chair, releasing a long sigh. The resentment he had felt for his daughter's husband was returning in spades!

"That's fine, Jake, but I tell you there are no more files."

"Let's have a look at the other files," Jake said as he suddenly remembered her saying blocks of papers were missing. He wanted to know just exactly what papers were missing.

"Well, here are the wills." Jessie handed the file to Jake, hoping he would find them in order.

Jake put the files on his lap and scanned them one at a time, repeating the process before he spoke. "This isn't right. I was with Big Roger the day he made the change to this will. I don't remember him making the one dated two months before the plane crash. As you can see, I was his witness on every will or codicil except the last one. I never heard of these lawyers," Jake added, looking at the latest codicil of Big Roger's and Glynis's will.

Jessie had gathered the stack of corporate files and was looking at them. She was confused. Many of the accounting ledgers were missing. "Jake, can you remember when Big Roger had his will updated?" Jessie asked.

"It was about 6 months before the plane was lost," Jake said, picking up each file Jessie put down. "You remember the time Big Roger got so mad at Roj, because he was dragging his name through the mud, and threatened to cut him out of the will."

Jessie thought for a minute then added, "Yes, when Roj decided to move into Silverton I thought it was just another one of Roj's temper tantrums. He quit talking about it almost as soon as he brought up the idea."

"I tried to get Big Roger to tell me what all the fuss was about, figuring it was Roj's behavior behind it. We talked often about his "activities." Big Roger hated the way he treated you and the kids," Jake said, glancing at Jessie to get her reaction.

"They must have solved the problem, because they got along fine before Big Roger and Glynis left," Jessie said quietly. She was tired of letting Roj's affairs hurt her.

"Roger quit working for the corporation for a while, didn't he?" Jake questioned Jessie.

"Well, he did seem to take some time off before the plane was lost," Jessie said, remembering with mixed feelings one of the more pleasant times in the marriage. It was the last time she thought there was a chance to salvage their marriage.

When the plane was reported missing, everything had changed. She had been fooled by Roj over and over. Jessie angrily brushed away the tear rolling down her cheek. No more tears, she was tired of crying over Roger Rite III. She was going to find out what had happened, and then she would be free to start all over again. Roger was gone now and if she could rid her life of the questions maybe she could get on with the life she dreamed of having.

"You know, Jake, I've had all the misery I'm willing to take from him. I don't know how, but I'm going to clear up this mess once and for all. It doesn't matter what it takes, or who I have to ask for help; I'm getting to the bottom of this."

"What can I do to help?" Jake asked his daughter, feeling proud of the strength of character she showed no matter what the obstacles.

"I need to go through these papers with a lawyer, and I don't trust anyone around here," she said, then thought of Boat. "I'm going to go over and talk with Marge and Boat." She straightened the piles of papers, rose from the desk and headed out the door without waiting for any reply from Jake.

Jake watched his daughter stride out the door, smiled wryly, and after a minute he shook his head and went out to the barns. The quiet strength emanating from her wiped away any worries he had about her taking care of her and his grandchildren after he was gone.

# Chapter Twelve

Marge was removing the clothes she had hung from the line in the fresh spring breeze as Jessie walked toward her. Marge had her arms full of sheets and a mouthful of clothespins, but she flapped an elbow at her friend in recognition.

"If you are getting ready to take flight I suggest you put down all those sheets!" Jessie teased.

Dropping the clothespins into the basket, she greeted the other woman.

"Jessie, glad to see you. Grab the rest of the sheets, and I'll make us a pot of coffee," Marge said, ignoring the barb.

They giggled and reveled in memories of when they were younger. Keeping her hands busy folding the sheets, Jessie waited for Marge to pour the freshly brewed coffee.

"Thanks for the coffee, Marge."

Marge watched her friend stir her coffee, although she hadn't added anything to it, and decided not to beat around the bush. "So, Jess, what can I do for you?"

Jessie considered backing out, but changed her mind. "I need some help going over Roger's papers," she added bluntly.

Both of the women jumped as they heard the front door slam. "Hey, Jess, how you doing?" Boat said, putting his hand on Jessie's shoulder and squeezing it comfortingly.

"Well, Boat, I think I need some help, and I don't know where to start," Jessie said with her usual directness. "Roger's papers are all screwed up and half of them are missing. I think I may have some real problems. I need legal help. I'm not sure I can trust anyone in town with the information.

"You know, Jess, I can't get involved in an official way. It wouldn't take more than a day to get around the county I was helping, causing more problems for you."

"Boat is right. Jessie, you need help, but maybe not legal," Marge said, getting a look in her eyes that made Boat uncomfortable.

"What are you driving at, Marge?" Boat asked, shifting uncomfortably in his chair. Boat knew he was in trouble when he saw the twinkle grow in Marge's eyes.

"I know how you feel about me intruding, but I think Sam is the one to help, Jessie." Marge kept going before Boat could say anything. "He's the perfect one. He has a legal degree in this state and investigative skills…"

"I agree with Marge," Boat broke in before Marge could finish.

"Now, Boat, don't interrupt. I also know we can trust him to keep the information to himself… Wait, you agree?" Marge said, speechless for the moment.

"You'll catch flies, Maggie," Boat said warmly to his wife. Turning to Jessie, he added, "Do you want me to call him for you?"

"No, Boat, he has already offered to help. I guess I will take him up on his offer."

"When are you going to talk to him?" Marge asked curiously.

"Maggie."

"I was just curious; I thought she might want some moral support," Marge replied, wounded by the judgmental tone in Boat's voice.

It's all right, Boat. I appreciate all your concern," Jessie said, trying to smooth Marge's ruffled feathers. Turning to Boat she said with her usual good humor, "I'm sure Marge realizes it's a little early for matchmaking."

"Walk me out to the car, will you, Boat?" Jessie asked, ending the conversation and dismissing Marge but soothing her feelings with a hug. She promised to get together for lunch at the earliest possible date. Turning to Boat, she asked, "Do you have anything new on the case?" She tried to give her problems a generic sound.

"Nothing concrete. I'll try to get you some information before Monday," Boat said, hoping the weekend would make it easier for him to weasel information out of his buddies at the state office. "Jessie, I have a question for you." Boat paused trying to find words which wouldn't accuse her. "Do you know what happened to your locket?"

Jessie instinctively reached around her neck. "No, I just assumed I lost it when Lil' threw me," Jessie answered, feeling guilty for a reason she couldn't explain. "Why do you ask, Boat?"

"Hold on, Jess," Boat said as he opened the door to the cruiser and retrieved something out of the glove box. "Sam found this by the Caddy after the explosion."

He grabbed for Jessie as she seemed about to fall. Jessie closed her eyes for a second; an image flitted across her memory as she tried to hone in on the picture.

"Jess, you okay?" Boat was afraid of what her reaction meant.

Quickly opening her eyes and righting herself, she said, "I'm fine, I just don't understand. If I could only remember." she squeezed her eyes tightly. If only she could conjure up the image permanently. "Something is on the edge, like the name of someone from the past on the tip of your tongue, and then it's gone.

"Have you been back to the doctor yet?"

"I have an appointment Monday. Maybe he can explain what's going on." Jessie got into her car, rolled the window down and gave Boat a smile of encouragement.

"Doncha be a-worrin' yorself, shariff, I'll hang around this har town so you won't have to come-a looking fur me!" Jessie said jokingly, hoping to ease the tension around Boat's eyes.

She gave a quick wave and pulled away, not waiting for Boat's reply. When she looked in the rearview mirror she noticed Boat had already headed into the house without waiting to see her destination.

"I need a drink!" Jessie said to herself, heading to the nearest spot she could think of.

Jessie walked into the dimly lit bar. Shielding her eyes against the stark difference between the bright spring afternoon and the grim lighting of the bar, Jessie decided, "Maybe this isn't such a great idea." It was too late. Gloria recognized her and made a beeline over before Jessie could escape.

"Imagine, it's the famous Jessica Rite? I think you need to sit right down here at the bar and let me buy you a drink. What'll you have?" Gloria said, not letting Jessie get a word in edgewise. "I suppose you drink the same thing your husband does. I mean, your late husband?"

Jessie looked at the woman she had gone to school with, not amused. Jessie said, "Rrrarrrrrow! Aren't we a little catty today? No thanks, Gloria, I'll just have a glass of white wine." Turning to go to a table, she saw Rob Roy sweeping the bar. She was once again struck by the feeling of familiarity about the boy. She gave him a warm smile when he shouted, "Miss Jessie!" and hurried over.

"Rob Roy, how have you been?" she asked, genuinely concerned for the young man. "You promised to come and help me with my garden. It's about to take over the rest of the farm."

"Oh, Miss Jessie, I'm sorry. Mama hasn't let me go out since the terrible thing happened to Robyn and Mr." He slapped a hand over his mouth as if to stop what was coming out. "I'm sorry, I didn't mean anything, really, Miss Jessie, really!" he said as the tears began to stream down his rough cheeks.

"Its okay, Robbie," Jessie said soothingly. "I know you wouldn't hurt me for anything." Jessie wondered why the mention of Roger would upset the young man so thoroughly.

She reached for his hand to comfort him. Gloria walked over and growled, "Leave the customers alone, you dummy. They don't want you blubbering all over them." Rob Roy turned and ran to the back.

Before Jessie could say anything, Gloria blurted, "Leave my boy alone. You rich people think you can run everyone's lives. We'll see who comes out ahead on this one, lady." Gloria turned on her heel after slamming down the glass of wine so hard that Jessie was surprised it didn't shatter the glass.

Jessie sat for a minute, trying to figure out what Gloria was talking about. Giving up, she drained the glass and headed for home. Approaching the door Jessie decided she didn't want to be indebted to this woman for anything. She walked back to the table and threw a five-dollar bill down on the table. "That should cover the cost of the cheap wine and the tip," Jessie threw over her shoulder.

Jessie was angry she allowed herself to be drawn to Gloria's level. It seemed there was something about the woman that brought out the worst in her.

Jessie was surprised to find herself suddenly pulling into her driveway. Lately she had trouble keeping her mind from wandering. It felt like blocks of time would disappear.

The kids came tearing out to greet their mother, brightening her world immediately.

"Mom, Sam said we could come over any time and help him with the filly—she is so cute—she looks like Hoppy—I don't think she is as smart as Hoppy—but you never know," Cristal said in one long sentence without taking a breath.

"Jeez, Cristal, you would think you had never seen a horse before," Jordan said, rolling his eyes for emphasis. "I guess that guy isn't so bad," he added.

Jessie smiled at her children, marveling at their ease in picking up the pieces of their broken lives. "What does everyone want for dinner?"

"I think Jake is making his famous chili," Jordan said, shuddering. "I hope you stopped for milk. We are going to need it."

"Jordan, you haven't been helping with the cayenne pepper again?" Jessie demanded.

"No, I swear Mom, he did it himself."

Jessie and Cristal laughed at the stark terror on Jordan's face. They all remembered the three days he spent on the stool the last time he helped spice Jake's chili.

"I feel brave. Let's go chow down," Jessie said.

"Jake, I smell chili. Jordan didn't help, did he?" she said as they entered the kitchen, winking at the kids.

"I'm taking the cornbread out of the oven now. Get washed up and get out here. I'm waiting for you like one pig waits for another," Jake bellowed.

Jake said a quick grace, and Jessie decided it was time to let the kids and Jake in on her plans to get Sam's help. "I was over at the Boatwright's today. We decided I need help straightening out the mess I'm in." Everyone stopped eating, looking at the young woman blushing a bright red. It was difficult to tell if it was embarrassment or the chili, so everyone just waited for her to go on.

"Boat and Marge think I need some help. The state is dragging their feet in this investigation. Until they find the real murderer I'm still the prime suspect." Jessie looked at each person at the table, taking plenty of time to let her statements sink in.

"People like to think the worst and the worst is that I'm the one who killed your father and Ro…Robyn." Jessie had trouble saying her name. "I know this is difficult, but we have to decide what to do."

"Your father's papers are a mess and quite frankly there are legal questions to be answered." She hated bringing this up, but they would have to be told sooner or later.

Everyone at the table was quiet for a few minutes, and Jessie let them consider what she said. "I have decided to take Sam Ellison up on his offer to help," she finally said softly.

"Jeez, Mom, why would you want him to help? I think you should get a real lawyer," Jordan said angrily.

"Mr. Ellison *is* a real attorney, Jordan," Jake cut in, "In fact, he is probably the perfect person to help your mother." Jake saw the stubborn set of Jordan's jaw. *A trait inherited from his mother*, Jake thought with exasperation. He decided now was as good a time as any to relate Sam's history.

"You know, Jordan, Sam's family has been around these parts almost as long as the Rites. Did you ever wonder why his place is surrounded by Rite property?" Jake asked, looking at each person at the table for a minute, giving them a chance to digest the question.

"Why is it, Grandpa?" Cristal asked, obviously very interested in the topic of conversation.

"He comes from a very proud family. They never wanted a big spread like your Great-Grandfather. They just wanted to live peacefully, content with what the farm could produce." Jake told them of the first time he and Sam met.

"He was a young man full of ambition and out to rid the world of corruption and evil. Such an arrogant young guy." Jake chuckled at the memory. "He was the kind of man that demanded attention from everyone.

"He was oblivious to his effect on women. Men found in him a friend always ready to lend a hand when needed. Always ready for a good time, he knew how to hold his liquor and played a fair hand of poker."

Jake met the young man when he was going to college and helping out on his uncle's ranch in the summer. Jake wasn't surprised when he heard he had gone to Florida to become a DEA agent, but Jake was surprised the day Sam showed up to lay claim on the family ranch years later.

Jake went on. "He was an ambitious young man, and he did well as an agent; he got his law degree and went directly to work for the DEA. He was one of their best agents but the death and corruption he dealt with daily finally burned him out. His last case cost him the life of his second partner and gave him the limp you see. He was married once but the long hours and the constant danger was more than she could take. After the divorce he put all his energy into his favorite hobby, martial arts. He got his black belt and was entering tournaments, doing very well for an amateur. He had entered a national tournament, but right before the tournament he got shot.

"He hasn't done any competing since. When his uncle died, leaving him the farm, he decided to come back to Delaney County."

"I *bet* he was a big shot DEA agent. He probably never got out of the office and just made up all these stories," Jordan snapped.

"Well, Jordan, I never heard Sam talk about those days at all. It was Boat who told me," Jake said patiently.

Everyone was pushing the food around on their plates more than eating and finally Cristal was the first one to speak. "You know, Mom, whatever you do is fine with me."

"Yeah, Mom, whatever you say," Jordan added, angered by his little sister's easy acceptance of the situation, but not wanting to make any more waves about it.

"Well, Pearlie, whatever you decide is fine with us. All you have to do is ask, whatever you need is yours," Jake added.

Jessie smiled gratefully at her family. She decided it was fortunate that Jake and Big Roger were around when the children were little. She shuddered to think what would have happened without their strength. Family problems like hers and Roger's are what made problem children. She was indeed a very lucky woman.

Suddenly her appetite returned with a vengeance. She was ready for mounds of fried potatoes, cornbread and chili, the hotter the better!

"I'll clean up the mess. After this wonderful dinner Jake made he deserves the night off and you kids need to get your homework finished. School's not over yet," Jessie said, sending everyone away.

Jessie needed a light job that would leave her mind clear but keep her hands busy. Something kept nagging at the back of her mind. Maybe some light mess duty would help it break loose.

Finishing up the few dishes, she wondered where Jake had learned to be such an efficient cook. She needed some fresh air, and a short walk might clear out the cobwebs. Then she could get back to organizing the corporate papers. If Sam agreed to help she wanted the papers as orderly as possible.

She always loved the garden behind the house. Living in high desert country made you appreciate the subtleties of the seasons. It took a practiced eye to catch the changes in seasons, but once you got used to them they seemed all the more precious.

As she wrapped her arms around the large trunk, Jesse said, "There you are, old friend!" to the old elm tree she and Roger played in when they were small.

Admiring the budding leaves and leaning her face comfortingly against the gnarled bark, she was transported back to a simpler time. A time when the hardest thing she had to do was be nice to Glynis.

"Yes, old fella, it's been a long time since I've been to see you." The melancholy she felt made tears well up in her eyes. She remembered the last time she and Roger had played in the tree house. She saw the image of the sweet young boy as real as if he were in front of her now.

\*\*\*\*

"Aw, come on Jess, you never play with me anymore," Roger said, pouting. Jessie was never able to resist the petulant look forming around Roger's lips when he wanted his way."

"Okay, Roj, but not for long. I promised Jake I'd work out the new jumper today," Jessie said, smoothing the lock of hair falling across Roj's forehead.

"I wrote a poem for you," Roger beamed proudly. "Ya want to hear it?"

"That would be great, Roj," Jessie said. She was very proud of the stories and poems Roger wrote. She knew in her heart that some day he would be world famous. Unfortunately, Glynis and Big Roger didn't take the time to see how talented their son was.

"It's not very good, Jessie. The other day when I watched you riding it popped into my head. I could hardly write fast enough to get it down. Here goes:"

> *Riding the Brazen Wind*
> *By Roger Randall Rite III*
>
> *As the wind blows through her auburn hair,*
> *I stop and look, and I see her there,*
> *Riding the brazen wind.*
> *The girl and the horse they are but one,*
> *As they jump and they run toward the setting sun,*
> *Chasing the brazen wind.*
> *When I'm old and tired, and my eyes grow weak*
> *The image of the horse and girl I will seek,*
> *To challenge the brazen wind.*
> *As the memories fade and get jumbled about,*
> *The young man I was will rise and shout*
> *Into the brazen wind.*

Jessie read the poem over several times, amazed at the way it touched her. "Roj, did you really write this?" she asked as she wiped tears from her eyes. Through the poem she was able to see herself now, and Roj, old and gray.

The young boy seemed years beyond what she knew him to be. He held his breath and slowly nodded his head, afraid if he said anything she would change her mind.

"Roj, it's so beautiful it makes my heart sore," Jessie said, clutching the poem to her chest.

"I'm sorry, Jessie; I didn't mean to make you sad," Roj said, lifting his chin in the air to stop the quivering.

"Don't be sorry. It's beautiful. I love it," Jessie said, handing him the journal.

"No, Jessie, I wrote the poem for you. It's yours to keep so you can remember me forever," he said, proudly tearing out the paper to give to Jessie.

\*\*\*

Jessie remembered, with a heart-wrenching sadness, the day as if it were yesterday. She tried to remember what she had done with the poem. It had been so long ago!

Jessie was chilled by a strong breeze blowing from the mountains as happened often in the spring. The tears streaming down her eyes were chilled by the evening breeze. "Oh, Roger, what happened to the sensitive boy?"

She turned to go into the house, and she wondered…but it couldn't be possible. She returned to the tree and looked in the cavern of its trunk to see if by some miracle the journal was still there. She chuckled hollowly, no journal…but a small box caught her eye.

"Now what could this be." Reaching down, she touched the box, causing her to shiver but not from the cold. Jessie, ever practical, thought, *The kids probably put this here and forgot all about it.* She tried to open it but was surprised to find it locked.

She trotted up the kitchen steps and flung the door open. "Kids, look what I found!" Cristal and Jordan looked at each other with confused looks on their faces.

"Jeez, Mom, what's with the old rusty box?" Jordan asked soberly.

"It's neat, Mom, whose is it?" Cristal said, looking over Jordan's shoulder curiously.

"It's not yours?" Jessie asked. "It can't be anything important. Who would leave it in a tree?" She was getting a rolling feeling in her stomach she tried to attribute to Jake's chili.

She felt very tired suddenly. Laying the box on the counter, she said, "I'm tired. I think I'll take a hot shower and go to bed." She shivered, not from the cold, but from the eerie feeling she got looking at the locked box.

The kids watched as their mother took one last look at the rusty box before heading to her room. Jordan walked over to the box and gave it a quick shake. He had never seen it before and couldn't find anything interesting about it.

Sometimes he felt like the fall from her horse had done permanent damage to his mother. She had been acting strangely every since she fell. He hoped it was the fall causing the change in his mother. He didn't want to believe she had anything to do with his father's death.

Cristal watched the play of emotions over Jordan's face but was afraid to ask what was bothering him. Lately he got mad at everything she did or said. She looked quickly at the box and decided it wasn't of interest to her. She liked the idea of a soft bed. She seemed to have lost all of her energy lately. She had trouble keeping her mind on school and often she thought about how it must have been for her father.

"Well, I'm going to bed. We have to get up early tomorrow. I suggest you do the same." Cristal left Jordan looking at her as she headed for bed.

"Women!" Jordan exclaimed.

# Chapter Thirteen

The day broke with the cheery brightness of early summer. The sunny morning promised warmth waited for after the long cold winter. Jessie felt like a teenager, bold but intimidated, excited yet nervous, as she dialed Sam's phone number. The thought of hearing his voice made her heart race. Jessie felt almost relieved when she realized Sam wasn't going to answer. More than once she scolded herself for the feelings she was having. The guilt would surface; after all, her husband was dead, his murderer not found. She should be grieving longer, but she found she couldn't deny her feelings.

"Yeah," Sam answered the phone. The curt answer was a lingering habit after the many years working for the DEA. Jessie almost hung up the phone, deciding he wasn't going to pick up.

"Is anyone there?" Sam started to get mad, because he made a mad dash into the house, tripping over the cat and sending it screeching out of his way, straining his own weak leg in the process.

"Hi, Sam, it's Jessie," she said, letting out a nervous laugh.

"Sorry, I didn't mean to yell at you. I just about broke my neck and killed my cur of a cat, trying to answer the phone," he chuckled.

"I'm sorry; I hope you're okay. And your cat, too," Jessie apologized nervously.

Sam's curiosity was peaked by the tone of Jessie's voice. He felt very protective of her; he hadn't felt this way about a woman in a long time. "What's the matter, Jessie?" he asked, suddenly serious.

"Well, Sam, I need to take advantage of your offer. I've been going through Roger's papers, and they are a real mess. I don't know what I should do. I don't trust Roger's lawyers, and I don't know who else to turn to. I need someone who will help me and keep this information to themselves. Marge and Boat suggested you. I hope this isn't an imposition. You did offer, and I need someone I can trust."

"And all in one breath," Sam quipped.

Jessie's apprehension was suddenly gone. She needed help, not some Smart Alec. "Oh, never mind, I didn't mean to interrupt your morning," she said huffily.

"Hey, I was just kidding. Don't get so mad," Sam told her, realizing this was no kidding matter. "I'm glad to help any way I can. I made the offer because I meant it, not because I felt obligated. Jessie, when should I come over?" he said, suddenly businesslike.

Back on the terms Jessie was comfortable with, she told him to come after lunch. She hoped it wouldn't take long. She didn't know how long she could be in the same room with him and still keep her feelings to herself.

Jessie decided to spend the morning being lazy. She would pamper herself by reading while she soaked in a bubble bath, a luxury she hadn't afforded herself for a long time. Grabbing one of her favorite romance novels, she stopped at the linen closet to pull out a bath sheet to wrap herself in after her bath.

"Hey, Mom, Cristal and I are going to work with Hoppy. Grandpa said he wanted us to go into town with him to look at halters. He said we can start training him pretty soon."

"Okay, have a nice time," Jessie said, thinking she wouldn't know what to do without her Dad. It was almost as if he could read her mind from the garden house. He knew when she needed to be alone and when she needed the support of his presence.

Jessie decided she would need substance while reading. She headed for the kitchen. Looking through the cupboard for something to snack on, she noticed the box she found in the tree trunk.

"You leave me alone today. I'm just going to relax and read," she said stubbornly to the rusty box.

Jessie gathered her snacks and headed for the bathroom. While the water was running she decided to turn on the answering machine and perhaps some soothing music; she didn't want to be interrupted.

Removing her clothes and slipping into the hot bubbles, she felt the tension leave her body. "Yes, this was terrific idea," she congratulated herself. She reached for her book and tray of goodies and tried to get lost in the gothic theme of the book.

Twenty minutes passed, and her mind continued to wander to the rusty box sitting on the counter. She shook her head to get her mind back on the story but it was as if the box was calling her. "Jessie, Jessie, I'm waiting for you."

"Oh, nuts," Jessie swore. "Now I'm swearing at inanimate objects," Jessie said. "I'm not going to be satisfied till I find out what is in that box."

Angry about her impatience, Jessie grabbed her robe and put it on without drying off. Heading for the kitchen, she promised herself she would get into the tub and finish her book as soon as she opened that darn box!

She grabbed the box angrily and tried to open the lid before she remembered it was locked. "Let's see, I think an ice pick." Going to the utensil drawer, she began rifling through it, finally spying the ice pick. Looking back she decided it wouldn't have hurt to have a butcher knife too, just in case.

Jessie was so intent on her job she didn't notice someone was watching her work on the box. Sam decided to come and apologize in person. He wasn't used to civilized company. You could hardly call his cat civilized. He realized after the contact with this family how much he had missed people, the one thing he hadn't thought would ever happen.

He finally decided to knock on the door. Jessie swung around, hiding the pick behind her as if she was a child caught in some mischief. When she realized how she must look, she was immediately embarrassed. She pulled the pick out from behind her, put it on the counter, and walked to open the door for her surprise guest.

Trying to smooth her wild hair, she was once again embarrassed by her pleasure at finding Sam at her door.

"Sorry, I guess I caught you unaware!" Sam said. Involuntarily his eyes roamed her half-dressed state. He was feeling things he knew were best to be ignored but with her auburn tresses, damp from an obviously recent bath, curling charmingly around her soft features, and her damp robe clinging provocatively to her ample curves; he was having trouble remembering why he had come.

Jessie was unsettled by the way he looked at her. This was something that hadn't happened in years. "Help yourself to some coffee, and I'll go put on some clothes," she said, turning the most enchanting pink Sam had seen in years.

Sam was unable to speak, so he just headed to the pot of coffee and poured a cup. He sat down and stared into the cup of rich, black coffee, thinking of how much it reminded him of her dark hair. "Get a grip," he said, trying to keep his mind on business.

"Sorry you got such a strange reception, Sam. I wasn't expecting anyone here until later. Jake took the kids into town to do some shopping for Hoppy. If I know Jordan and Cristal they will plague him to buy them some pizza at the Pizza Barn," Jessie said, pouring herself some coffee.

The two were as nervous as a pair of cats in a living room full of rockers. As they sipped their coffee they sneaked looks at each other, hoping to stay nonchalant. They were obviously very attracted to one another.

Sam was the first to break the silence. "Well, I know something is bothering you. I figured I would come over and take a look at the papers, if you don't mind."

"Oh, I don't want to ruin your Sunday, Sam," Jessie said.

"You're not ruining anything, Jessie. I was watching No One in Particular suspiciously eyeing the poor parakeet," Sam replied.

Jessie gave a look of confusion.

"That's my cat," Sam answered the unasked question.

"Would you care for more coffee?" Jessie asked, considering what a strange name it was for a cat. Sam raised a hand and shook his head for his answer. Sam rose to follow Jessie. She liked the fact he didn't waste time with a lot of words. She seemed to be able to read his thoughts sometimes and the realization made her flush a pleasant peachy color.

Following in her wake, Sam noticed she seemed to walk in a cloud of floral scent. He wanted to reach out and devour her. Once again he pulled back to reality; he needed to keep his mind clear if he was going to help her.

She stopped so suddenly he almost ran her down. "What the heck?" Sam said, a little more gruffly then he intended. "Sorry, my leg is still a little sore."

"I'm going to open that darn box," she said, almost pushing him out of the way to get by. "I just have to see what's inside."

Sam just shrugged his shoulders and made himself at home in the office until she returned. Sam locked up as Jessie entered with the rusty box in one hand and a large butcher knife in the other. "I said I was sorry, Jessie. You're not going to come at me with that thing are you?"

Jessie looked from the box to the knife and to Sam. She couldn't help but smile at the funny picture it must have presented.

"That's more like it," Sam said. "I've missed that smile. You have been way too serious of late, young lady," he chastised her.

She raised the knife in a threatening manner and said, "It's not to late, Mr. Ellison. You'd better behave yourself."

"I'm at your mercy, ma'am," Sam said humbly.

They both laughed nervously. Jessie thought how good it felt to laugh again. How long had it been since she had had fun with someone her own age? Too long! She decided to enjoy the day, no matter what it brought.

She laid the box on the desk and whacked at it with the large knife. She raised the knife to hit it again when Sam grabbed her arm. "I don't think that is going to work, Jess. Here, let me." He took the knife and gently laid it on the desk. Then he looked around the desk for the perfect tool, grabbed the letter opener, and within a minute the box was open.

"That's amazing. I've been working on that lock forever, it seems. Where did you learn such a strange skill?" Jessie wondered.

Sam raised an eyebrow and gave Jessie a shrug. "All in the line of duty." He laid the box in Jessie's outstretched hand. "All of the sudden I'm very nervous," Jessie said.

"It's probably a box of souvenirs left from years ago." Sam comforted Jessie. A sigh of relief escaped Jessie's lips as she saw what was inside. It was just a couple of old keys.

"Just some old keys," she said, closing the lid.

"Let me have a look at those," Sam said, concern showing on his face. "These are safety deposit box keys. Do you recognize them?"

The familiar rolling feeling in her stomach had become her constant companion in the days since Roger's death. "I knew it, I just knew it," Jessie said, plopping into the nearest chair and putting her head in her hands. "This is never going to end."

"It's all right, Jessie, it'll end. We just have to work on it," he said, taking her into his arms to comfort her. Sam thought to himself that he could kill the guy. Luckily, someone had already beaten him to it. Why didn't he see the jewel he had in this woman? What was it Jake was always calling her? Pearlie, yes, that was it, this girl was the perfect pearl.

Jessie felt warm and secure in his arms. Something she hadn't felt in— well, she couldn't remember ever feeling this secure. She had always taken care of Roger. Later he went off on his own, leaving her to handle the raising and care of the kids. It felt good to just rest, to forget everything happening to her, and to enjoy being held in the arms of a man.

Neither of them heard the front door slam or the kids calling their mother.

Suddenly the office door swung open and framed in the doorway stood two startled children.

"*Jeez, Mom!*" Jordan hollered.

The two jumped apart as if they were stung. "Jordan, wait," Jessie called. "Cristal, this means nothing. Mr. Ellison was just comforting me," Jessie pleaded hollowly.

"*Mr. Ellison?*" Cristal accused with her question. Cristal couldn't believe her ears. What had happened to "Sam"? All of a sudden her mother was calling him Mr. Ellison, like that would make it all right.

Sam placed a calming hand on Jessie's shoulder. "Let them alone for a while, Jess. I'm going to leave now. We didn't do anything wrong."

Jessie looked up at him with eyes so green he could imagine himself falling into the emerald green of the Loch Ness. His heart was wrenched by the sadness and confusion in them. He was angry with himself, as if he could somehow be the cause of that sadness.

"I'll be back tomorrow after the kids leave for school. We'll get this mess straightened out and settle the problems with the kids.

Jessie just nodded and led him to the door. "Thanks," she said solemnly as she opened the door for him. She watched his retreating back, wanting not to feel guilty. The kids meant the world to her, but her feelings for this man went very deep too. Men were always trying to seduce her; after all, she was wealthy, attractive and she was a woman. Sam was the first man she felt at ease with. There was something very special about him; she wanted to know him better.

\*\*\*

While lying on her bed, Cristal stared at the ribbons and awards displayed on the wall. It took her back to the time when as a child her mother would let her look at the many ribbons she had won as a child. Cristal's plans had been set as a child. She wanted to be the best horsewoman Delaney County had ever had. Her fifteenth summer would be the first year she was allowed to go away on her own to gain the skills to become the horsewoman she had always dreamt she was destined to be. Cristal didn't know why but it hurt that any man could replace her father. She wasn't sure why she felt so empty, but she couldn't even cry. It had started when Grandpa Rite and Glynis's plane had disappeared. Now this guy was trying to take Daddy's place.

She was full of anger at her mother and her father. Why did he have to leave her? She just wanted life to be the way it was when her grandparents were alive.

She had her plans set for the summer. She would rest for a couple of weeks and then spend the rest of the month at the Greensford Academy. Then she would come home for the Fourth of July, then go back for another three weeks at Greensford. It would be almost two glorious months of freedom. Searching for an outlet for her anger, she grabbed her lamp and hurled it at the wall filled with ribbons and certificates.

Jordan heard the commotion and ran to find out what had happened. "Cris, you all right?" He saw her crumpled in a pile on her floor, her body wracked with silent sobs. He felt sorry for her.

"Jeez, Cristal," he said, bending to help her up. "You shouldn't let this upset you so much."

"Why don't you leave me alone? You don't care, you always hated Daddy!"

"That's not true," Jordan said, surprising himself with the confession. "I just wanted him to treat Mom and the two of us better. He shouldn't have acted the way he did, but I miss him too."

"Is Mom going to marry Mr. Ellison? How could she do that to Daddy?" she asked, the dam bursting and the tears flowing down her face.

"It'll be okay. Mom is smarter than that; she couldn't be fooled by that guy's smooth talk."

"I'm not spending one minute longer than I have to in this house watching the two of them together," Cristal said with a finality Jordan recognized.

"I've decided to go to camp like I planned. I thought Mom would need us but it looks like she has all the company she needs," she said with a feeling of sadness she never felt before.

Tapping lightly on Cristal's closed door, Jessie asked, "Cristal, are you okay?"

Jessie, worried at the sound of the lamp hitting the wall, arrived in time to see Jordan go into the room. "Let me come in."

Cristal wiped at the tears streaming down her face and gave Jordan a questioning look. Jordan got up from the bed and went to open the door. Jessie looked from one child to the other, hoping to find some weak spot in their anger, but was disappointed. "Are you kids willing to let me explain?" she questioned them.

Neither child was willing to say anything, so Jessie opted to take it as an affirmative answer. "Mr. Ellison," she started, but seeing the anger flare in

Cristal's eyes, she quickly changed tack, "Sam, was just trying to comfort me." She decided to go on quickly to avert any interruption before she got everything out. "This hasn't been easy. You know things weren't good between your father and I for a long time."

The two kids looked from their mother to a spot at their feet. The resignation was apparent as their shoulders drooped. "I got the box open." When they lifted their heads the confusion was obvious. "The old rusty one I found in the old tree house. There are a couple of old keys in it. One is for a safety deposit box. I'm sure it is your father's." The kids gave her a look that said, "So?"

Jessie decided to take the direct route with the kids. They were going to find out sooner or later. "Your father's papers are a mess. Jake thinks some of the insurance policies your Grandpa Rite bought are missing and most of the corporate accounts are also missing. When I got the old box open I found keys in that box and the implications of what it meant was one blow too many. Sam felt sorry for me. He just wants to help."

Jordan looked at Cristal and then to his mother. "We understand *perfectly,* Mom." Jessie wanted to be relieved by the sentence, but the lack of feeling in Jordan's eyes made her nervous.

"Cristal and I have changed our minds about staying home this summer. We want to stick to our original plans."

Looking from one child to the other, Jessie knew now wasn't the right time to try and explain. Things were happening so fast in her life; her life was out of control.

"If that is what you want, I guess I agree."

# Chapter Fourteen

Jessie was roused by the ringing of the doorbell. "What the…" Jessie didn't have time to finish the sentence because the two kids burst into her bedroom, squealing in excitement.

"Mom, get up, Nana's here!" Cristal pounded on Jessie's door as she flew to get her hugs from the woman that was like a grandmother to her when she grew up.

Jessie didn't take time to put on her robe, she just ran out to greet the old woman. "Nana, what are you doing here? We didn't expect you back from your vacation for another month!" Jessie sobbed as she ran to embrace the small woman.

"Now, now, Pearlie." She was the only other person besides Jake to use the endearment. "Nana's here, everything will be all right."

Since the accident, Jake had trouble sleeping through the night. Many times he spent the early morning hours staring out the kitchen window, wondering what he could have done to change the events of the last month.

The approach of the strange car piqued Jake's curiosity. Who in the world would pick the middle of the night to visit the Circle R? The darkly clad figure could only have been one person, but she wasn't expected for several more weeks.

Jake only took time to put on his boots before he hurried to greet the housekeeper. He was heartened to see the four people he loved most in the world in a football huddle. "Estralita, is that you?"

The huddle broke and out stepped the spry little woman. "Yes, Señor Jake,

I am here." She beamed proudly, having kept her return a secret from everyone but old Gramps down at the train station. Passenger trains don't stop in Silverton anymore. The only way for her to get here was by bus. She wanted to be driven straight out to the ranch, so she had him make the arrangements for her.

"Come, let me make us some coffee. I need to hear all about my poor boy." The sadness etched small lines around her eyes, the only lines in the Spanish woman's face.

"We tried to get in touch with you but when we called your sister's house she said you had gone to visit your great-niece and wouldn't return for weeks," Jessie started, sad at the reason for her Nana's return, but grateful she had returned nonetheless.

"It's been awful, Nana," Cristal sobbed, looking at her mother with accusing eyes before kneeling at the little woman's feet and putting her head in her lap.

Jordan walked over to her and put his arm across her shoulder and looked at his sister strangely. "Nana, Dad's gone. Somebody killed him. No one is blaming Mom—out loud—but you can see they think she was the one."

Everyone was shocked by Jordan blurting out the facts. It had been easier to ignore what everyone was saying than to acknowledge it,

"Isn't it time for you two to get ready for school?" Jake asked.

"Jeez, Jake, there are only two more days of school. Why do we have to go today?" Jordan whined. "We haven't seen Nana for months."

"Because it's your job," Jake said with an unaccustomed edge to his voice. Cristal looked up at her grandfather, then at her brother, thinking this was the start of one of their wars. She was surprised when Jordan turned to leave. She quietly got up and joined him at the hallway.

"Don't worry, my dear ones; I'll be here when you get home with your favorite snack ready."

The little housekeeper got up to start breakfast, but was stopped short by Jake and Jessie.

"You are still on vacation, Nana," Jessie said. "Jake and I will make breakfast. You just sit back; we are going to treat you like a queen."

It was so wonderful just having her home that Jessie was afraid it was all a dream and she would wake up to find Estralita gone. The little woman was the force behind the ranch running smoothly. She kept the house spotless, running the house with an efficiency born of many years of experience. She had a knack of knowing when to offer advice and when to let the person work the problem out on their own. With Roger gone, she was the one that had been at the ranch the longest.

Jessie called the kids to breakfast and, putting the last of the plates on the table, she was able to get a good look at the older woman. "Oh, Nana, how did we ever get along without you?" she said, hugging the small woman. Estralita was the closest thing to a mother Jessie had known since her mother had died. She found strength just in knowing Nana was here to lend support.

Nana, as usual, pooh-poohed Jessie's remarks and went about eating her food. The kids asked questions about the people they only knew by Nana's stories. They were regaled with the funny stories Nana brought home like souvenirs.

"Some day I'm going with you, Nana, so I can meet all these people," Cristal said, reveling in the joy their "Nana" spread wherever she went.

"Time to catch the bus," Jake noted as he headed off to work.

"Remember to get home on time or no treats!" Nana threatened as usual.

"Okay, Pearlie, tell me what's been going on since I left," Nana said, all humor gone from her eyes.

Jessie leaned her elbows on the table and rested her head in her hands as if the weight of it would break her slim neck. "I don't know, Nana. Roger just kept his antics up until it finally got him into trouble, permanently," Jessie said, tired of talking about Roger and his problems.

"My poor Little Roger," Estralita said in her quaint Mexican lisp. "All he ever wanted was love. Too bad the only ones to give him real love were pushed away."

Jessie jerked her head up to look at the little Mexican woman. A strange thought popped into Jessie's head. "How old are you, Nana?" She gazed intently at the woman as if she could read her mind.

Jessie couldn't remember the woman looking much different than she did now. She was very small, almost doll-like, with raven black hair and eyes, and the smoothest caramel colored skin Jessie had ever seen. Her forceful personality made sure no one ever questioned her authority. She watched, time after time, as Glynis backed down from this fiery little woman. When Glynis complained and demanded Big Roger fire the woman, he just laughed and told her, "You go ahead and fire her yourself!" She was never fired.

Nana just ignored the question and asked once again, "What happened to my boy?"

"He was found out by The Lanes. The Caddy was blown up and there was a girl with him. It was that waitress at the hotel, Robyn something." Jessie knew her name, but she just found having the name in her mouth distasteful. Besides, what difference did it make? It could have been any one of a dozen women, if what Jessie heard was correct.

"What is Sheriff Boat doing about it?"

"Nothing he can do. He has been warned by the state boys to stay out of it."

"Well, then, what are the Federalies doing about it?"

"Nana, we don't call them Federalies in the United States."

"Don't change the subject. What are they doing about this mess?"

They have the information in the open case files under 'suspects unknown.'"

"Those...why aren't they doing something to find the murderer?"

"They think they have the murderer. They are just waiting for enough information to file charges."

"Who do they want to file charges against?"

Jessie just looked at the woman for a minute and then said solemnly, "Jordan was right on that count."

"Not you? Don't they know you couldn't harm a fly?"

Jessie was saved from answering by the front door bell. "Oh no, I forgot Sam was coming over." Jessie jumped up and reached to smooth her unruly hair.

"Sam?" Estralita asked.

"He's a neighbor who is going to help me go over Roger's papers."

Estralita was like a family member, therefore she was never afraid to give her opinion on any subject. The way she made sure her authority never wavered was to choose the battles she could win. She knew which battles were best left unchallenged.

"Good morning, Sa..." Jessie was cut off by a surprise visitor.

"Jessie, a good morning to you." Gloria Ritter hadn't been to the ranch since the fateful night she and Big Roger had their last confrontation about their short-term affair.

Gloria was surprised returning to the place that had ruined her life wasn't more emotional. "The old homestead hasn't changed much over the years, has it?" Gloria pushed past a startled Jessie to get a better look at the infamous Rite homestead.

"Can I help you, Gloria?"

"I'd say so." Gloria slinked into the living room, making herself comfortable on the overstuffed couch. "I see some things have changed. Didn't like old Glynis's taste in furniture, huh? I always thought it was a little stuffy myself; but what would you expect from a Duchess?"

"Gloria, I'm not sure I know what you are talking about. You wouldn't mind getting to the point, would you?" Jessie said, remaining standing. The last thing she wanted was Gloria thinking this could be a social visit.

"You wouldn't happen to have some coffee in this place, would you?" Gloria asked.

"No."

"So, the fancy hostess, Jessie Rite, doesn't think I'm good enough to step foot in her lovely living room?" Gloria said, beginning to seethe.

"I'm expecting someone, Gloria. Can you get to the reason for this visit?"

"Why, you snotty witch, as if you didn't know the reason for this visit. Just because you got away with killing Roger don't think you are going to get away with cheating us out of what's rightfully ours!"

"You know, Gloria, I think everyone is right; you are crazy. It's time for you to leave," Jessie said, turning to lead Gloria out of the house.

Gloria yelled, "You know I have as much a right to the money Big Roger left as you and Roger. I'm not stupid. I know what you are up to. I got me a great lawyer, and he says I can get part of this ranch. So don't go acting all high and mighty or I'll just have to knock you off your high horse. This time you won't be able to pretend you don't remember." Gloria paused to take a ragged breath. "This time everyone will know this family is no better than the rest of us lowlifes."

"Excuse me for interrupting, but the door was open."

Jessie swung around with a look of joy on her face. Sam almost forgot Gloria's raving at the top of her lungs.

"Oh, it's nothing. Gloria was just leaving," Jessie said, glaring at the garish woman.

"We are not through, Miss Smarty Pants," Gloria threw over her shoulder as she stomped to the front door. "I see you didn't take long finding a new man. Poor old Roger wasn't even cold in his grave before you're taking on anything in pants."

"I think you should leave now," Sam said. He grabbed her arm and pushed her out the front door.

"You highfalutin' people are the same as us. You'll see when I knock you off your tower, you witch." But Sam and Jessie didn't hear the end of Gloria's tirade because Jessie slammed the door before she finished.

Gloria saw red as the door slammed in her face. "Why, you slut," Gloria hollered and stomped back to her car, pulling open the door with such force one of the May Brewery beer bottles in her car fell to the ground.

Wobbling on her high heels, Gloria bent to pick the bottle up, getting a brilliant idea. "You'll be sorry you didn't settle with me, you snotty witch!" With a last retort she heaved the bottle at the house, missing the front door and slamming it against the side of the house.

"You've got some real nice friends," Sam said, trying to lighten the mood. "What did she want?"

"She was raving about getting half the ranch, me and Roger trying to cheat her out of her money, and something about taking us to court. She is nuts!" Jessie said, missing the implications of Gloria's ravings.

Estralita asked, wiping her hands on her ever-present apron, "Why I hear lots of commotions?"

Estralita noticed for the first time the handsome man and turned to Jessie giving a quizzical raise of her eyebrows. Jessie stepped to the small woman, slipping her arm protectively around the older woman's shoulders.

"Nana, this is Sam Ellison, the man I told you about. Sam, this is our Nana, Estralita Mandez."

"Hola Senora. Como esta usted?" Sam said, surprising Jessie with his fluency.

"Muy bien. Gracias," Nana blushed.

Jessie looked back and forth from one to the other as they continued to converse in Spanish like old friends.

Sam turned to Jessie. "You ready to start work?" He grabbed her arm to lead her to the library. She glanced back at Nana, getting a wink and an encouraging wave before shooing them off.

"Don't worry about the house, Jessie. You just go ahead and get your papers straightened out. I'll take care of everything else."

"You know, Jessie, your Nana thinks very highly of you Rites," Sam said as he followed Jessie to the office.

"I know. She has been at the ranch since before Jake and I came. I didn't think I would like her at first. She can be very intimidating when she thinks someone she loves is being threatened."

"Do tell?"

"When Jake and I first moved here, she let him know she was keeping an eye on him." She smiled when she remembered how Jake had puffed up like a fighting cock at the suggestion a little bandy hen like Estralita could keep him in line.

"I think I know how your father must have felt. I got very much the same lecture from her." Sam smiled at the comparison.

Jessie and Sam decided to look over the wills first. Jessie had to find the will Roger had made or the estate would be in probate for several years.

"I haven't written many wills, though none as complicated as your father-in-law's, but there is something wrong with these papers."

What could have possessed this guy to cheat his family, his company and the future security of the next generations of Rites? It never failed these spoiled little boys never grow up. If they don't squander away all their assets they end up trying to cheat everyone around them. Oh well, some day they would realize they were better off with this jerk gone. He would make sure they did.

Sam glanced over the policies; they seemed to be in order. He noticed the file Ames had titled "Rite notes" and was surprised by what he found in the file. The receipt for a safety deposit box, a list of policies Roger had asked about, including a travel policy made out on his father and mother. Scribbled on the policy was a note that the policy on Roger and Jessie was initially to be written on Jessie alone. There was also a list of Roger and Ames's meetings. There had been payoff dates to correlate with the times the policies had been written.

"Sam?" Jessie realized he wasn't listening to her. "Sam."

"Sorry, guess I wandered off for a bit," Sam said, red-faced.

"I said, 'let's knock off for the day.'"

Sam casually looked at the keys, noticing the security key had the same number as the receipt. Sam palmed the security key as he went to put it back in the rusty box. "You don't mind if I take this file home to look at it some more, do you?"

"Have you found anything important in there?"

"No, I just want to get a closer look, and I figured you wanted to get rid of me before the kids got home," Sam remarked.

"I… I," Jessie stuttered nervously.

"I was just kidding, Jessie. I have to get home and check on my new stock," he said, trying to lighten the mood.

"Thanks, Sam," was all Jessie could get out. She seemed to be saying that a lot lately.

Sam stepped onto the porch, turning to wave goodbye to Jessie, when he heard something crunch under his foot. He bent to pick it up and swore under his breath, "Crazy broad." Picking up the shards of glass so the kids wouldn't se them when they got home, he noticed they were the same brand he had found at the crime scene. *Interesting*, he thought.

# Chapter Fifteen

Sam leafed through the file, deciding he was getting more questions than answers. His muscles were stiff from the long hours of reading and rereading the file. "Looks like I'm going to have a little visit with Mr. Ames tomorrow." He found himself talking to the cat again.

Heading to the bedroom, Sam gently pushed the cat away with his foot. "I'm ready to find someone who will talk back once in a while," he said, thinking of the green-eyed woman who occupied most of his thoughts.

Sam took a quick shower and made himself dinner. He had a long day ahead of him tomorrow and figured he would need a good rest. He wondered if he could catch Fred Ames at his office this late. He decided to give him a call.

"Johnsford Mutual, Fred Ames at your service!"

Sam hated these jovial types. They never were sincere and generally avoided the point. "Mr. Ames, I wondered if you are going to be busy tomorrow morning. I have inherited my uncle's ranch, and I need to make some provisions concerning the insurance," Sam drawled slowly.

"I don't know, Mr...." Ames said, already counting the bonus he could get running this one through quickly.

"Mr. Ellison, Sam Ellison." He was right. He was one of those slimy types, the kind to give decent insurance agents a bad name. Sam could almost see Ames rubbing his hands together in glee at the prospect of a new client!

"I don't know, Sam, my calendar is pretty full."

"I would make it worth your while." Sam knew money talked as far as these guys were concerned.

"Well, Sam, I do see an early cancellation say around 9 a.m., my office?"

"That'll be just perfect." Sam grinned.

After dinner he gave Jessie a call. "Hi, Jessie, this is Sam." He felt as nervous as a teenager asking a girl out on a first date.

"Hi, Sam." Jessie flushed at hearing his voice.

"I'm sorry, but I have some plans I forgot about. I'll be busy the whole day and won't be able to come over. I hope that's not a problem." He hated lying to her, but he didn't want anyone there when he talked to Mr. Ames. He knew enough about Jessie to know she wouldn't let him go without her. If his suspicions about Ames and Roger were correct, gentle persuasion probably would not be enough.

The rest of the evening drug by, no matter what Sam turned his attention to his thoughts returned to Jessie. He gave up and headed for bed, knowing he would have to get up early to make his appointment with Ames.

***

Sam turned over as the alarm rang. God, he hated the sound of his stupid alarm. He hadn't used one for a long time, but this was one day he didn't want to oversleep.

Looking through his closet, Sam decided he needed to dress the part of a land baron to get Ames's attention. He was sure Fred Ames would be swayed by the talk of money, but he would use any means necessary to get the information. Jessie needed this information, and his gut told him this security box held plenty.

"Howdy, little lady," Sam boomed jovially. "I'm here to see Mr. Fred Ames."

"Mr. Ames is waiting for you in his office. Let me buzz him," the receptionist said, reaching for the intercom.

"No need to do that, little lady. Fred knows I'm coming. He and I have a lot to talk about." With an exaggerated wink, Sam headed in the direction the receptionist looked, assuming correctly that it was Ames's office. Sam wanted every advantage could get. No need to give Ames advance warning.

"Hey, what are you doing?" Fred Ames said as he slid several stacks of papers into a drawer in surprise.

"Sam Ellison," Sam said, heading toward Fred with his hand outstretched.

"Oh, Mr. Ellison," Ames oozed, changing his posture once he realized the possibility of a profit.

"Sam," he corrected Ames, wiping the moisture from Ames's hand on his pants.

"How can I help, Sam?" Ames smiled, pointing to an overstuffed captain's chair.

*Make them comfortable for the kill*, Sam thought to himself.

"A buddy of mine, Roger Rite, sent me here. I need to get some insurance on my uncle," Sam said, lowering his voice secretly.

"I thought you inherited your uncle's ranch," Ames said. Deciding the fee on this one would raise the more they talked.

"That's just a technicality. I'm his only living relative. The ranch will come to me when the old guy croaks," Sam boasted heartily, hoping to give Ames the go-ahead.

"How is good old Roj?" Ames asked, checking to see just how good of friends they really were.

"Didn't you hear? He finally went to the big bordello in the sky!" Sam said, hooting at the tasteless joke. "Yeah, his old lady caught him one time too many with his pants down; blew him and his latest gal sky high."

"That's too bad," Ames said, chuckling along with Sam. "I met her once. It doesn't surprise me she finally took revenge."

Ames was sizing Sam up as they talked, thinking to himself, *This may be just the one to finally set me up in my own office*. He was counting the thousands he could squeeze out of this cowboy.

"Let's get down to business. I know you are a busy man," Sam said. He leaned an elbow on the desk, a serious look replacing the jocularity of a moment ago.

"I need an accident policy opened on my uncle, and I need it now. The old coot is living on a gold mine, but all he wants to do is run a few head of cattle on it," Sam said disgustedly "The land is worth thousands, and I intend to take full advantage of its worth."

"Well, I need some information before I can tell you how much your policy fee will be," Ames said, winking at Sam. *Boy, do I have a live one here!*

"What policy fees?" Sam asked casually as he reeled in the jerk.

"Well, it takes lots of time and effort to get these policies written correctly. Time is money, if you know what I mean."

"How much did it cost good old Roj?" Sam asked.

"Well, every policy is different. Different problems, different fees." Ames squirmed nervously.

"Well, lets say I wanted to get a safety deposit box, a travel policy on my uncle, and a couple of policies on my wife just in case something should happen to her."

"Hey, wait a minute. What's going on? I don't think we have anything further to talk about. I'm afraid you'll have to leave," Ames said. If this guy was an investigator for the insurance board he could be in real trouble.

Sam saw the look of fear flicker across Ames's face, knowing he had him right where he wanted him. "Let's talk a little bit about Roger Rite."

Ames immediately relaxed. This guy was not going to get any information about Rite from him. With Rite dead he couldn't be implicated in any way. Suddenly he remembered the safety deposit box. *I should have cleaned out the box before now. Why didn't I follow through?* Ames berated himself.

"I don't discuss my other clients with anyone. I realize he is dead, but the families are old friends. I don't feel comfortable talking without their consent." Ames liked the last bit; it should be enough to shut off the questions.

He dismissed Sam. "I think this meeting is over, Mr. Ellison."

Sam stood up, casually leaning on the desk with both hands and said, "No, I don't think so. I have some questions, and you are going to provide the answers."

Ames jumped out of his chair and started around the desk to show Sam out the door. "Look, Mr. Ellison, I don't want to have any trouble here…"

Sam grabbed him by the tie and pulled him closer, saying between clenched teeth, "I don't care if we have trouble or not. I want those answers, and I want them before I lose my temper."

Sam noted Ames was becoming an interesting hue of purple and let go of the tie with enough force to land him back in his chair. "Now, are we going to do this the easy way or not?" Sam took a menacing step toward Ames.

"Okay, okay. What do you want to know?"

Sam congratulated himself on correctly sizing this guy up. "Tell me about the safety deposit box first."

Ames straightened his tie and tried to think of a way to get out of this mess. He quickly reassessed Sam, deciding this was no country bumpkin. He realized he should answer all his questions. He could tell this guy knew how to get them anyway. "Rite had me take out a safety deposit box in my name. I don't know what he put in there. It was none of my business," Ames said, taking a pious stance.

"What about the policies? Who signed them?"

"I might have known she had something to do with this," he said, suddenly realizing Jessie Rite was behind this meeting. "I made up the papers, and he had got the signatures." Ames squirmed in his seat.

"Now, now, Mr. Ames. I think you know more than you are telling me." Sam took a step closer to Ames and eyed his tie threateningly.

"I gave him the name of a guy good with signatures. What he did with it was his business, not mine."

"I think you need to get your coat so we can go get the box."

"I can't. I gave him the key," Ames whined.

"No problem, Freddy. I just happen to have the key we need."

"I'm not going anywhere with you," Ames said stubbornly

"We can do this the easy way. No, wait, maybe I should go to the authorities with the information I got from the file. I think the insurance commission would be interested in your little policy fees."

Glaring fixedly at Sam, Ames picked up the phone. "Mary, I'll be out of the office the rest of the day. Cancel all my appointments. I won't be back until morning." Turning to Sam, he said, "Shall I drive?"

"Why, that's very generous of you, Freddy," Sam answered casually.

Ames tried to signal to his secretary on the way out. Boy, was she dumb! She just smiled, returning to her nails. As soon as he got back he was going to look into replacing her...

***

Sam stood up as Ames approached with the satchel of items from the box. "Didn't you want to close out the vault, Fred?"

Ames glared at Sam. He could have found a good use for the box, seeing how Roger had him pay 10 years in advance. "Thanks for reminding me." Ames glared.

Sam watched Ames close out the account and walked him to his car. "Funny, Ames, I would have figured you to have a fancier car," Sam said casually as he patted him down to make sure nothing got misplaced.

"Do you really think this is necessary, Ellison?"

"Can't be too careful," Sam said. "Go ahead and keep the refund. I figure a hundred bucks is ample payment for your time."

Ames pulled open the door and started to get in when Sam cautioned him. "Don't make me come looking for you, Freddy, I may have some more questions for you."

Sam was happy with this afternoon's work. It felt good to be in the thick of it again. Weasels like Ames deserved to be pushed around. Maybe Sam's way was obvious, but guys like Ames did their pushing more subtly. They bully lonely old people and take advantage of the misery of others.

Sam couldn't decide whether to call Jessie or just stop by. When he looked at his watch and saw it was still early he figured he could beat the school bus home.

Estralita opened the door to find Sam standing with his arms full and a sheepish look on his face. "Hello, Señor Ellison. I'll get Miss Jessie."

Sam stepped into the entryway. He was so nervous at the thought of seeing Jessie. What if he had overstepped his bounds? He could tell she wanted to be involved in all aspects of the investigation.

"Hi, Sam, I thought you were going to be busy all day," Jessie said, noting the satchel in his arms.

"Can we go into the office, Jess?"

Jessie felt uncomfortable the way Sam was behaving. She nodded her head, not trusting her voice, and quickly turned to lead Sam to the office. She closed the door behind them and asked, "What's this all about?" She was still eyeing the satchel.

"I hope you're not going to be angry with me," Sam said timidly. "I got the papers out of the safety deposit box today."

"How did you manage that?" she asked. "Isn't it against the law to go into those boxes without the owner's permission?"

"Oh, Mr. Ames was more than willing to open the box for me. We have an understanding," Sam winked at her.

"I was right. He is a sleaze!" Jessie shivered at the memory of his slimy advances.

"That may be, but he gave me some very interesting information. It seems he and Roger has been associated for quite some time."

Jessie figured as much, but she wasn't sure she was prepared for the information in the satchel. "Well, I guess we may as well look at the papers."

"Do you want me to leave, Jess? I'm sure it's full of personal stuff."

"No, you went to a lot of trouble, and I appreciate it. You want to see what's in here, don't you?" Jessie was nervous, and she didn't mind sharing it with Sam. In fact, she found his presence reassuring.

Jessie cleared off the desk, turned to Sam as she motioned for him to dump the contents on the desk. They looked at each other in shock as bundles of $100 dollar bills fell onto the desk. There was easily a couple of hundred thousand dollars.

Several accordion files and two journals fell on top of the bundles.

"What the heck?" Sam said, looking in awe at the money.

Jessie reached for an old journal, stroking it fondly. "I was just thinking about this journal. In fact, it was what made me look in the hiding place in the first place. Roger's Grandpa Rite gave it to him for his 10th birthday. I remember how proud Roger had been of his journal. His Grandpa Rite told him to keep it with him always and write what was important to him to remember forever," Jessie said sadly.

"It was too bad Big Roger and Glynis ignored Roger's talent. Big Roger said it was sissy stuff and Glynis couldn't find any way to make money out of poetry so between them they discouraged him." Jessie remembered the short stories and poems Roger was always writing, very mature for a little guy. "He was really quite good, you know." It was more statement than question.

Sam listened quietly to Jessie and was able to see another side to her husband. "I didn't think Roger had any redeeming qualities."

Jessie just shrugged her shoulders and picked up one of the files. She leafed through it, realizing it was the file containing insurance policies. The term policies Jake had talked about were here, along with some accident policies and the copies of the policies from Johnsford Mutual.

The accident policies on Big Roger and Glynis had been taken out only months before the plane went down and showed Roger as sole beneficiary. Jessie didn't like it, but there was surely nothing illegal about Roger taking out policies on his parents.

The term policies had been cashed in after Big Roger's death, and Jessie had no idea what happened to the money. Maybe this is where the cash came from.

Putting down the insurance file, she picked up another one marked "Big Roger." There were notes in it from Big Roger, along with a listing of names Jessie didn't recognize and what looked like parts of a will.

"Sam, what do you make of these?" she asked, handing the papers to Sam.

"Trouble, let me see the file."

Jessie held the file to her chest, suddenly afraid to find out anything.

Sam gently eased the file out of Jessie's arms. "This is not going to be bad," Sam said with a tender smile."

"Look at this, Jessie."

Jessie leaned to look at the papers. She brushed against Sam, sending a current through them, making them jump apart in shock. They stared into each other's eyes for what felt like an eternity. She was lost in the ebony darkness of his eyes; he was lost in cool emerald pools.

His eyes drifted to her parted lips and back to her eyes, taking her breath away. She closed her eyes, taking a deep breath to steady her reeling senses.

She knew she had to keep her mind on business, although it wasn't easy. No one had ever made her feel like this. She was afraid she wouldn't be able to keep her feelings to herself much longer.

Sam watched the emotions playing across her face, such a lovely face. He could tell she was steeling herself against the feelings going on inside. He was doing the same. He knew they would have to find the answers to this mystery before they could start any relationship.

"Look at this. One thing bothered me beside the difference in writing style, the difference in stationary."

"What difference could that make?" Jessie couldn't figure out why different stationary was incriminating.

"They could have changed stationary over the years, but it's like a cattle brand, your animals become identified by it." Sam could see Jessie was having a problem equating stationary with cattle brands, but she didn't argue.

"Look at this codicil, dated March 21, 1963. I see why Gloria is so upset." Jessie had a sad little smile on her face. "This says Rob Roy is Roger's half-brother. I can't believe it. How could Roger treat his brother the way he treated Rob Roy? All the time it was fear of losing some stupid possessions." Jessie was disgusted. She flung the codicil on the desk. "Give me the rest of the bad news."

"This page of Roger's father's will makes Jake the executor. It leaves you in control of the businesses until the kids turn 25 years of age. Basically," Sam said, rereading parts of the will, "it looks like he didn't want Roger to have any part of the estate."

"How did Roger get away with being executor and CEO of the corporation?"

"Ames sent Roger to someone able to give him all the signatures he needed to pull it off." Sam set the file down, reaching for another sheaf of paper.

Sam saw why Jessie was having trouble organizing the papers. Here were the missing corporate accounts, a small book of ledgers, and several bank account books. Roger had been a busy little embezzler.

"Didn't you say your father-in-law and Roger had a falling out shortly before their plane was lost?"

"Yes, the same time Jake said Big Roger had made him executor of the will."

"Well, I'm betting the answers are right here. These accounts show large sums of money being siphoned from the corporate accounts to Roger's personal accounts. I think these notes in the ledgers were put there by your father-in-law."

Jessie took the ledgers and scanned them perfunctorily. There were totals circled with question marks beside them; notes referring to different invoice numbers, the totals circled in red; and a list of businesses with the notation "corporate holdings." There was a list of names, including Fred Ames and Johnsford Mutual.

"Big Roger must have found out about Roger's embezzlement, which explains his anger with Roger. I never agreed with Big Roger's handling of Roger, but he was never stingy with his money. I don't understand why Roger would have to embezzle anything. He could spend any amount of money, and Big Roger never would have complained."

"I doubt if it had anything to do with the money. Roger was trying to get even with his father. The one thing Roger figured would hurt his father more than anything was losing his money. Even better if he could ruin a couple of his father's holding companies." Sam had dealt with these spoiled brats often enough in his DEA days. The methods were often different, but the motivations were always the same.

"I still don't understand Roger stealing from his father. He was jeopardizing his children's future." Jessie repudiated the facts before her.

"Some people just never grow up. They spend their whole lives hurting the ones that love them, trying to get even with everyone. Sometimes it's the system, sometimes it's their parents, and sometimes it's themselves. They usually end up the same; pointing fingers everywhere but at themselves."

"I want this settled and my life to gain some kind of normalcy," Jessie sighed. "The kids think I'm letting them down, and Jake has taken over all the responsibilities. I have to find out what happened to Roger and why."

Jessie looked at her watch, realizing it was past time for the bus to drop off the kids. The afternoon had passed quickly as she went through the papers from the safety deposit box.

Jessie waited for the children to appear. Just as she had decided they weren't coming, they stepped through the door in tandem.

"Hello, Mr. Ellison," Cristal said, keeping her eyes glued to the ground.

"Sam found some information that should help us…" Jessie was stopped by the stony glances coming from her children. She decided to save the rest of her announcement until Sam left. "Nana's waiting for you in the kitchen." She dismissed them.

Jordan nodded at Sam. She recognized the stubborn jut to his jaw. Jessie knew it would be useless to get him to open to Sam's friendly overtures.

Cristal and Jordan slowly turned and left the office, but not before sending a searing look Sam's way. They could be heard whispering as they headed down the hall. Muted laughter floated to them from the trio in the kitchen.

Jessie leaned against the door, giving a long sigh of disappointment. When she turned back to Sam she was embarrassed by the obvious interest Sam held for her figure.

"Sorry, Sam. I guess we are just going to have to give them time to get used to our friendship," Jessie said, blushing at the look she was receiving from Sam.

"You give them too little credit, Jessie. They see what's happening between us even if you refuse to."

Jessie ignored Sam's implication. He was right, she wasn't ready to acknowledge their blossoming relationship. "I think we had better get back to the papers, Sam."

Sam shrugged his shoulders; he could wait as long as necessary. When she was ready to come to him, he would be there to welcome her.

"You need to get Roger's will filed with probate court. The entire estate goes to Jordan and Cristal, but I'm sure the court will leave you in charge until they become of age."

"What do you mean the entire estate would go to the kids? I knew Roger held me in contempt, I just never figured his vindictiveness would go so far." Jessie felt a smoldering anger growing in her. She thought for a minute and then added, "Are there reasons a judge wouldn't leave me in charge of the estate?" Jessie knew the answer but still needed to hear his response.

"If someone wanted to contest the will or if there were legal reasons, the judge could appoint an independent person in the interim. I don't see that happening. I do think you need to find an estate specialist. Roger's will may not be valid with so many illegalities involved." Sam shook his head dolefully as he realized the extent of the embezzlement.

"A few months before the plane was lost, Roger and his father had some kind of falling out. Big Roger said there would be major changes after he and Glynis returned."

"Weren't you curious about what was going on?" Sam's image of Jessie didn't fit with a person that would allow so much conflict to surround her.

"Roger and his father were always wrangling about one thing or another. Generally Roger would apologize and tell Big Roger he wouldn't do it again.

Then everything would return to normal as if the fight never happened." Jessie realized how lame her excuse sounded.

"I don't think this would have blown over. Roger embezzled over $4,000,000 from the corporate accounts." It astounded Sam that a loss of this extent could go unnoticed.

Jessie was trying to find where Sam got his figures after only a few minutes of reviewing the accounts. She remained quiet, waiting for the second shoe to fall. One thing she was sure of in all this mess, it wasn't over yet.

Sam handed Jessie a journal similar to Roger's old one. "Do you recognize this?" Sam asked tenderly.

"It is similar to Roger's old journal, but I've never seen this one before." Jessie started flipping through it nonchalantly; but her interest was soon peaked. "I guess old habits do die hard." Roger had kept all his escapades documented. He obviously was quite proud of his "adventures."

"I'm always amazed when people keep an account of their activities. No matter how illegal," Sam said, shaking his head.

"One thing about it, you should have no problem getting Sgt. Garza to start working on the case with this information."

"I'm not turning this over to the police!" Jessie hollered, startling Sam with her vehemence. "My children have surrendered enough. Let them keep the illusion he was honest, at least."

"This is pertinent to the case, Jessie. If the state boys don't get hold of this information, it leaves you open to all kinds of charges."

"I'll give them the journal, but only after we find out its importance," Jessie said stubbornly. "I need your help even more now," Jessie said desperately, close to tears. One thing for sure, she wasn't going to give in on this point.

"Okay, Jessie. This folder has all the information you need to send to your lawyer. The sooner you get it to them the faster the estate will be settled. Let me take the rest home and make some notes. We can go over my notes later."

"I was hoping you would say that. I don't have any idea where to start." Jessie was grateful for the help Sam was giving her.

"Don't worry, Jessie. No one else is going to get this information until you okay it," Sam said, touching one of the stubborn curls of hair always springing out of control.

Jessie nodded her head shyly. Drawing away from Sam slightly and smoothing back her hair self-consciously, Jessie led him to the door with a quiet goodbye.

# Chapter Sixteen

Jessie was holding Roger's journal protectively to her chest when Estralita entered the office. "Is that Roger's old journal?" Estralita asked, sitting opposite Jessie.

"Yes," Jessie said, angrily swiping at the tears spilling down her cheeks. "I had forgotten how sensitive he could be, but it didn't take Big Roger and Glynis long to beat it out of him."

"You know, Jessie, we all do the best we can. Roger could be a handful if he wanted. Roger and Glynis had many problems, and their differences couldn't be overcome. Roger always came between the two of them and there just wasn't enough love to go around. It's just the way things are sometimes."

"I know. I can't help wonder what life would have been like if things had been different between him and his parents."

"Things turned out as the Lord intended them," Estralita said, subconsciously crossing herself. "No one can change them. We just follow his life plan.

Jessie looked at Estralita, wanting to take comfort in the words she heard. Jessie hoped things wouldn't be with her children as they were with Roger and his parents.

Estralita seemed to read Jessie's thoughts. "Maybe the kids will understand when they have a chance to recover from their loss. Give them the summer to recuperate. They are children in adult bodies. They have to make up their own minds."

Estralita rose to go back to the kitchen. "We are having your favorite dessert. You know my rules! No dinner, no dessert. Now you join us." It was a velvet command.

"I'll be there in a minute." Jessie had decided to let the kids make their own decisions about vacation.

Jordan and Cristal acknowledged their mother as she entered the room and returned to their dinners with feigned interest.

"Have you two decided on your summer plans?" Jessie asked as she looked to Estralita for support.

"The advisor at camp called when he heard abut Dad. I told him it wouldn't be changing my plans to spend the summer counseling," Jordan said stiffly. The memories of his summers counseling promised to be the diversion he craved. Helping the handicapped children gave him a satisfaction he found nowhere else.

"The trainer at Greensford needs you to call and let them know I'll be coming after all." Cristal looked her mother straight in the eye as if to let her know she was ready to do battle.

"I'll call them in the morning," Jessie said, trying to keep her tone light. The last thing she wanted was for them to feel guilty about their decision after they were gone.

"I'll drive you both to your camps, and we can stop along the way to do some camping together. We can make a mini-vacation out of it," Jessie said with real enthusiasm.

Jordan looked out of the corner of his eye at his sister to see her response to the idea. "That's all right, Mom, I've already made arrangements to ride with Gilly. He is going to be working at camp Sakawa this year too."

"I've already asked Jake to make arrangements to get to the ranch." Cristal said, not wanting to look at anyone for fear she would start crying.

"I see. Well, maybe it wouldn't be too much to ask for us to spend the weekend before you leave together." Jessie said, hoping to mask the disappointment she felt.

"I'm busy this weekend, Mom. Jake arranged for Jonathan to drive me to the ranch, and he said it would be easier on Silver Belle if we let her rest overnight between here and camp," Cristal said, looking at her plate. She was beginning to regret acting so hastily. Nevertheless, she was determined to go ahead with her plans.

Jordan looked at the hurt on his mother's face and tried to make her feel better. "We can always take Labor Day weekend and go to the state fair like we used to do before..." Jordan stopped immediately, regretting having brought up one of the few things his father managed to attend.

Jessie's eyes brightened at the suggestions. "That's a great idea! Estralita and I will make a great big picnic lunch. Maybe we can talk Jake into entering a couple of the horses in the races." She looked to Cristal and was disappointed that she saw little enthusiasm.

"Yeah, Mom, sounds great," Cristal said, forcing a smile.

"I promise this mess will be cleaned up by the time you kids get back this summer. Then we will really have something to celebrate," Jessie said, going around the table to put an arm around both her kids and give them an encouraging squeeze.

Jordan quickly slid off the chair to escape his mother's affection. "Yeah, Mom, great," he said, quickly putting his dishes in the sink. "I need to look in on Hoppy."

"Hey, Jordan, wait for me," Cristal said, joining her brother as he left the house.

Jessie went to the window to watch her children head for the barn. She felt her heart being wrenched from her chest. She was torn between the attraction she felt for Sam and her children's disapproval.

"Don't worry, Miss Jessie, some time and distance will do everyone good," Estralita said comfortingly.

"I know, but it is so difficult." Jessie promised herself no matter what she would keep the promise she made to her children.

\*\*\*

Going through the paper was becoming tedious. Everyone in this stupid place was boring. They had boring children, boring churches, even the crimes were boring. Jim Marshall was picked up for drunk driving, some hick was stopped for speeding, teenagers were nabbed for shoplifting. The only exciting thing to happen in 20 years was good ol' boy Roger Rite getting his just deserts!

Why isn't there anything about the investigation? The state investigators surely wouldn't let her royal highness get off scot-free, would they? If Momma heard something on the radio maybe she would prove to be usefull for something after all.

*I'm sick of all the bills she costs me; listening to the radio all day costs a lot. She had better have some news for me today.*

"Momma, I want to talk to you…I know you're awake…don't make me come in there!

"That's better. What have you heard about the Rite murder?

"Quit your blubbering. If you would listen to something besides that stupid "Playhouse" you might learn something. I told you to get me some information. Now I guess I'll have to take the radio to work with me.

"If you are going to keep on blubbering, you can just go to your room without dinner!" Looking at the closed door stirred the angry emotions threatenting to boil over onto the surface.

*Stupid old woman, I guess I can't trust anyone to get this taken care of but myself. Let's see, a letter; yes, that's a great idea. If Boatwright can't see she's guilty maybe I need to send a letter to the attorney general.*

Papers started flying as a plan of attack was formulated. Maybe we need everyone to see the commotion it would cause when people know about Miss Jessica Rite losing her necklace at "that place." Giggling at the thought of her royal highness getting arrested lightened the mood.

# Chapter Seventeen

Jessie found it was difficult to sleep with the turmoil in her life. "I suppose I may as well get up and get some work done."

"Hey, Pearlie, what are you doing up at this hour?" Jake asked.

"I couldn't sleep. I thought I would get an early start on the corporate accounts this morning."

"Jessie, have Jordan and Cristal told you their plans yet?" Jake felt sorry for his daughter, but he knew this was something she had to work out for herself.

"We talked about it last night. I just don't see why they are being so stubborn about Sam and me working together."

"Give them some time, Jessie. A little time apart will give everyone the chance to come to terms with what they are feeling."

"What do you mean?" Jessie asked, sitting straight up in her chair in surprise.

"Even if you can't see what's going on between you and Sam, it's pretty obvious there is an attraction. The kids are growing up, and they see something going on between the two of you. They haven't gotten over their father's murder yet. They feel threatened by your closeness with a man who may replace him." Jake wanted to make this easy on his daughter. He felt Sam was good for her. He figured when the kids had a chance to sort out their feelings they would understand it too.

"I think you are jumping to the wrong conclusion. Sam and I are just friends. There is nothing going on between us. I'm going to have a talk with the kids." Jessie's face was beet red from embarrassment at how close her father had come to finding the depth of her feelings for Sam. She was angry because he seemed to be interfering between her and her children.

"Cool down, Jessie, everyone is a little on edge right now. Things just need time to settle down," Jake said, trying to calm his daughter.

"I just want to find who did this thing. That's my main concern right now." Jessie found herself offended by every little thing said lately. She was sure it was the suspicions running rampant in the county. Things like this just don't happen in Delaney County.

Estralita was soon up and making a large breakfast for the children's last day of school. Jessie had trouble keeping her mind from wandering. She was anxious for Sam's report about the journal. She wasn't sure she was ready to find the full extent of Roger's betrayal.

"Good morning, kids. Are you kids ready for the last day of school?" Jessie asked as the two entered the kitchen.

"Yeah," Jordan said unenthusiastically.

"I don't even know why we are going. We haven't done anything all week." Cristal's usually sunny disposition turned irritable.

"Just think of the adventures ahead of you this summer," Jessie said, trying to keep the conversation light.

The kids ate their breakfasts quickly and headed to the barn to check on the fast-growing colt. Jessie watched them head to the door. She was struck by the fact Roger's death had drawn them closer. In fact, lately they seemed like they were joined at the hip.

Jessie stared at her coffee cup, losing all track of time. Soon the two were tearing through the door. Grabbing their bags, they headed to the approaching bus. "Have a good day at school!" she hollered at them. She was presented with a pair of genuine smiles and a quick wave of hands as they sprinted to the bus stop.

Jessie waved long after the kids had turned their attention to other things. "They grow so quickly," she said.

"Yes, but they are good kids. They'll grow to appreciate your young man," Estralita said confidentially.

"My what?" Jessie was appalled at the familiarity Estralita implied. When she spun around to set the matter straight she was greeted by an empty kitchen.

"I think she is getting senile," she said. Everyone had the wrong idea about her and Sam.

The doorbell rang on cue. Jessie heard Estralita greet Sam and send him to the kitchen. She was grateful for the extra seconds she needed to calm her racing heart.

"Good morning, Sam."

"Yes, I think it is going to be a great morning," he said, taking her hand and giving it a comforting squeeze.

Jessie was breathless at the intimacy and also a little nervous at the feelings it evoked.

"I hope you don't take this the wrong way, but your husband was a real son of a bitch."

Jessie paled considerably at the statement; she wasn't sure how to react. In her heart she knew Sam was telling the truth, but he was the father of her children, after all. She had spent practically her entire life involved with him one way or the other. She wasn't sure she liked Sam's characterization of him.

Sam was immediately sorry for having blurted out his feelings on the subject, no matter how truthful. "I'm sorry, Jessie. I should have kept my opinions to myself." Sam hoped to smooth the worry lines springing around Jessie's eyes.

He wanted to take her in his arms and hold her until the shock wore off, to kiss the sadness from her eyes. He could tell she wasn't ready for anything but the solution to her husband's murder.

The silence growing between them was broken by Jake's entrance. "Hi, Sam. How's your filly doing?" Jake asked cheerfully.

"She's doing fine, just fine."

"Hasn't my daughter offered you a cup of coffee?" Jake asked with a robust laugh. "Her manners have gotten a little rusty of late. You'll have to forgive her." Jake knew he needed to shake the lull hanging between them. He knew one thing: his daughter didn't take well with criticism.

"No wonder my manners aren't what they should be. I'm used to living around a bunch of old cowboys!" Jessie retorted. Turning to Sam she said in her almost perfect imitation of Glynis, "Tea anyone?"

The tension was broken. Everyone but Sam caught the imitation. Sam wanted to ask about the joke but decided to leave well enough alone.

"What have you been doing to keep busy, Sam?" Jake asked, already guessing the answer.

Sam shot a quick look at Jake and replied, "Jessie asked me to help her go over some of Roger's papers."

"Good, this needs to be settled and settled soon. While the kids are gone for a couple of months you should be able to get lots of work done."

Sam was surprised by the information Jake had supplied. "Where are the kids going?" he asked, turning to Jessie for an explanation.

"They decided to stay with the plans we had made before Roger's death," she said.

The look she gave Sam told him further discussion about the matter was unwise.

"Well, I'd better head out to the barn," Jake said, noticing no one was interested.

Sam pulled out the journals and the notes he had made. Putting their heads together they were able to make a schedule for the next week.

"Jessie, I know you want to spend the weekend with your kids, so why don't we start work on this next week after they've left? You take the journal and read it. I'm afraid you will not like what you find out."

He handed Jessie the journal, gave her an encouraging smile, and headed out the door. Jessie hugged the book to her chest. She started to stop Sam, but part of her wanted to learn everything to help her understand what had happened to her husband. The other part of her just wanted to remember the vulnerable little boy who came to her crying out for friendship.

"Nana, I'm going into the office, and I don't want to be disturbed by anyone!" Jessie said vehemently, not waiting for an acknowledgment.

Jessie was horrified by what she read, but she was mesmerized by the details. She felt compelled to read, much like the need to look at an accident as you drive by.

She got so involved she missed lunch. The wonderful aroma filling the house caused her empty stomach to growl reproachfully. She had spent the latter part of the afternoon cross-referencing the papers by date and was appalled at the enormity of Roger's criminal activities.

Jessica found the extent of Roger's dishonesty incomprehensible. How could he put his family in such danger? The person she found in this journal was someone she had never known. She would have to try to find a gentle way to introduce this person to his children. She found tears falling down her cheeks. She promised herself she was through shedding tears because of this…viper!

There was a polite knock at her door. She tried to quickly wipe the tears off as she stood to open the door.

"Hey, Pearlie, Estralita says you've been in here since Sam left." Jake was trying to keep his tone light, but he was disturbed. "What's happened?"

"Oh, Dad." She was taking deep breaths to keep from breaking down, but it was too late. "It's worse than anything we had imagined." As she crumpled into his embrace, she said, "How will I ever explain everything to the kids?"

Jake held his distraught daughter, thinking to himself he would be more than happy to kill his son-in-law, if he wasn't already dead! All he could do was coo endearments and hold her until the sobs faded away.

She had quieted down and was making the little hiccupping noises. He realized the last time she had been this destroyed was the time her mother had died. He had no better answers for her now than he did then.

"Don't worry, Pearlie, we'll work everything out. You'll see."

"I don't think this mess can be worked out, ever." Jessie grabbed the handkerchief Jake was offering and blew her nose. "I'm hungry."

Jake smiled sadly at his daughter. Would she be able to put the last 17 years behind her and find the comfort she deserved?

Jessie and Jake walked into the dining room. When the kids noticed the tear-stained cheeks and red nose they looked questioningly at their grandfather. He just looked at each child and shook his head, letting them know that it wasn't the time to go into the problems.

# Chapter Eighteen

Jake watched the colt prance in the warm spring morning. He was encouraged by the resilience of the young animal. He hadn't been sure Hoppy would survive, let alone progress so nicely. He watched the colt circle the exercise pen, stopping occasionally to knicker questioningly. Jake wondered if Hoppy knew the children were gone, not to return for weeks. The proud little colt trotted to where Jake was standing. He looked into the older man's face as if to ask, "Where are Jordan and Cristal?"

Jessie walked to where her father was standing and slipped an arm around his waist. She wondered if Jake was thinking how lonely it would be with the kids gone.

"He is coming along very well, isn't he?" Jessie asked listlessly.

"Yes, it's amazing how resilient young creatures seem to be. Don't worry about the kids. It will do them good to be away from the ranch and the memories it evokes. You and Sam get things settled and when the kids come back you'll see they will be more receptive to the situation." Jake tried to relieve Jessie's anxiety.

Shading the sun from her eyes, she looked into the weathered face of her father. I don't think I like what you are insinuating, Jake." Jessie should have been angry, but she couldn't resist the humor threatening to slip from Jake's twitching lips.

"Look, Pearlie, I always thought you were too good for Roger. I don't like the way things turned out, but Sam is a good man. He is the only person I would trust to straighten this mess. I think you could do a lot worse than fall in love with him."

Jessie was dumbfounded; she sputtered as she watched Jake's retreating back. She was unable to find an answer to his remarks, but she was saved any more thought by the fact Sam's rusty old jeep puffed and smoked into the driveway.

Jake waved a friendly hello as Sam hopped out of the truck and headed to where Jessie was standing. "Hi, Jessie," Sam said tentatively.

"Hi, Sam, come into the house and we can get started," Jessie stated matter-of-factly.

Sam didn't know what to think of Jessie's attitude this morning. He thought she might be full of questions, but he could tell from her stride that she had made some decisions. She didn't seem the least bit nervous about their next moves.

Jessie stopped at the kitchen and asked, "Nana, would you bring some coffee into the office?" Turning to Sam she asked, "Would you like anything else?"

"No, coffee would be fine."

Jessie went directly to the desk and picked up the journal. She began to leaf through it gathering her thoughts.

"Do you want to talk about the journal?" Sam asked, trying to get through Jessie's reverie, but Jessie seemed to have forgotten Sam was in the room.

"What can I tell the kids?" she said, sadly, more to herself than to Sam. "How will they ever get over this? Roger wasn't the greatest father, but this is unbelievable."

"Jessie, right now we have to find out what happened to Roger. Later we can worry about the kids." Sam was talking quietly but firmly.

Jessie finally turned and looked at Sam. "I know you are right. I'm still trying to see Roger for the man I thought he was." Jessie felt like crying, but she had no more tears.

She put the journal down and turned to Sam. "So what do we do first?"

"I think we need to go over the list I've made from the journal. You know all of these people better than I do. I'll need to learn more about them before we start asking them personal questions."

"I'll tell you everything I know about them, but right now I'm not sure I'm the right person to make judgments about anyone."

"I have one question I have to ask before we start. Are you sure you don't want to turn this information over to Sgt. Garza? If we don't, you realize there is no way we can go to Boat for help. He wouldn't like it, but he would have to give any information he gets about the murder to the investigating team."

"We give this information to the police and I may as well turn myself in at the same time. With Roger's reputation and this information who do you think they will find guilty? Obviously a lot of people in town hated Roger, but the facts compiled put me at the top of the list. No, I'm not ready to hand this information over to the police yet," Jessie said emphatically.

Sam looked at Jessie for a long time. The more he knew about her the more he fell in love with her. Noticing she was uncomfortable under his scrutiny caused the most charming blush he had ever seen.

"Well, Sam, where do we start?" Jessie found her mouth dry with nervousness. Why did he have to stare at her as if he was looking into her soul?

"What we have to do is try not to make judgments about these people. All I want from you is the facts about them. Okay?"

Jessie nodded in silent acknowledgment; finally, she was holding her future in her hands.

Sam pulled a small notebook out of his pocket, gave Jessie an encouraging smile, and proceeded to open the notebook.

"I want to ask about the people I'm not familiar with. Tell me about Mildred and Lester Brown."

"Well, Mildred and Lester have been around since time began." Jessie smiled at the memory of everyone in town continually trying to guess the age of the two. All guesses range from 70 to 100 years. "Mildred has always run the post office. She is on top of everything going on in Delaney County. Lester, 'Gramps', has always run the depot. It just about broke his heart when they were talking about tearing down the depot and putting in a parking lot. Mildred headed a fundraiser to buy the property and keep it open. When the bus company agreed to have the ticket office in the depot it made everyone happy."

"It seems funny there would be a central ticket office in a small place like this. Why would the bus company want a station out in the middle of nowhere?" Sam was starting to wonder at the far-reaching tentacles of Roger's power.

"I don't know why they would do it. There is still shipping done occasionally. It's worth our while to ship cattle and some of the horses on the train. It's cheaper than shipping them by truck, and we think they travel better. Between the bus company and the train maybe it paid to keep it running. Gramps has been on Social Security for as long as I can remember. He can afford to work part time and still make a living with his Social Security checks."

"Okay, I think that's enough on them. What about the Billings sisters?"

"Well, after the Jackson's closed the feed store we thought we would have to go out of town for all our ranch supplies. Then Jennifer and Tracy Billings bought the store. They turned it around in a very short time. I'm not sure what they did before they came to Delaney. They made a success of the feed store and got our school system and locals interested in agriculture again."

"No one in town suspected the fact they weren't sisters?"

"Never. They were thought of as a couple of spinster sisters."

The afternoon was spent in this fashion. Sam was asking about someone in town, and Jessie was filling in the holes. Soon they had gone through the entire list of people. Sam made occasional notes here and there. When he felt he needed to know more about someone then what Jessie told him, he would ask several questions to help him understand more about them.

Sam's many years of investigating had left their mark. No matter how sure he was of Jessie's innocence, he couldn't let it color the way he went about investigating the murder. Once he started working, his experience from the DEA kicked in and he seemed to go on automatic drive.

"Well, Sam, what do I do next?" Jessie asked, pulling out her own notebook.

"Jessie, I think this will work better if I do the investigating on my own." Sam was concerned for Jessie's safety. This person had killed two people already and had gone to a lot of trouble to confuse the evidence. He wasn't sure what would happen when word got around about their questions.

"No way," Jessie exploded. "This is my life we are talking about. I am not going to let you sift through my dirty laundry without me being there!"

"Your life is exactly what I am concerned with Jessie. These people Roger was dealing with are not above wiping out all traces of their involvement. If they find out Roger has all this information on their business dealings they will stop at nothing to get rid of it." Sam was becoming agitated, and he was reminded of the dangers of investigation by the twinge of pain in his bad leg.

"Sam, if I have to go about this by myself, I will. After all, I do have the same information you do. It may take me longer to find the answers, but believe me, the answers I will find!" Jessie stood and paced back and forth to calm her anxiety. She stopped when she noticed him rubbing his injured leg. "Sam, I'm sorry. I've kept you here all afternoon and the only thanks you get is my ranting."

"I don't mind helping. I can't give all my concentration to your case if I have to worry about you." Sam stood to stretch his leg and to work out the cramp.

"I'm sure you have my best interest at heart. I have no intention of letting you work this out alone." As she stated this she had walked directly in front of Sam to block his movement. Balancing her weight between both legs, she placed her hands on her hips, ready for combat if necessary.

"Okay, okay." Sam shook his head. I know when I'm beaten." Looking into her eyes, he knew at this moment there was nothing he wouldn't grant her.

Jessie felt as if she was falling into a pool of deliciously cool water as she stared into Sam's eyes. She knew she had to do something to break this spell or she couldn't be held responsible for her actions. She shrugged herself back to rational thinking, wishing Sam would not look at her as if he wanted to gobble her up!

"So what's our next step?" she said, her heart slowly returning to normal. "Sam, shouldn't we make some plan of action?"

Sam looked at Jessie, compelling her to forget this crazy idea. He called Boat yesterday to find out the progress of Garza's investigation. Boat had been close. Garza hadn't closed the files as a double-suicide, but he had put it in the inactive file. Noting, although there was no real evidence, their prime suspect was still Jessie!

"Tomorrow we will start dropping suspects from our list. I think it is best we start out of town. News travels fast enough in this county; we want to keep our investigating under wraps as long as possible. Tonight we shall go out and relax. It will be the last time, until we find out who's responsible, for us to relax."

"That's a great idea.." Jessie decided an intimate dinner with Sam was a little too tempting. She was going to make this a real party. "Let me run and invite Jake and Estralita."

Sam smiled crookedly as she ran out of the room. "Hey, it was worth a try!" he said after her.

# Chapter Nineteen

Jake watched his daughter pace up in front of the kitchen window. "Jessie, if you don't stop pacing you will to wear a hole in the vinyl." Jake was surprised by Jessie's abrupt halt.

She stiffened minutely. She took a deep breath and strode defiantly toward the front door. Yanking the door open before Gloria could ring the bell, she exclaimed harshly, "What can I do for you, Gloria?" This was the last person she was prepared to talk to today.

"Well, well, aren't we socialible?"

Jessie stepped back as if she would be fouled by the mere presence of the person in front of her. "I have an appointment, Gloria. Would you mind getting to the point?"

"I heard you sent the kiddies off for the summer. Makes it easier for you to play house, huh?" Gloria walked over to the fireplace, leaned casually against the mantle, and addressed Jessie as if they were the best of friends. "Miss High and Mighty ready to talk business?"

Jessie wanted to get rid of Gloria, but she knew from previous experience Gloria could be as stubborn as a bull ox when she smelled the scent of money. "Okay, Gloria. You want to talk business maybe I need to give Sgt. Garza a call and together the three of us can straighten this mess out." Jessie smiled politely, nodding Gloria to a chair, and headed toward the phone.

Gloria sat with an ungraceful flop in the chair Jessie had indicated. She turned to Jessie with a "Cat that ate the canary" smile on her garishly painted lips, waiting for Jessie to play out her bluff.

Jessie dialed the phone and hoped she could out-bluff Gloria. Sgt. Garza was the last person she wanted to talk to right now. Gloria's smile slowly turned to a vicious snarl when Jessie asked to speak to Sgt. Garza.

"Put down the phone, you stupid witch," Gloria said as she jumped to her feet.

Jessie raised an eyebrow, acknowledging her victory. Congratulating herself, she thought, *I have a knack for this.*

"No, that's all right, I'll call back later. No message," she said as she hung up the phone.

"Well, I'm glad you decided to be cooperative. So, Gloria, lets talk about this little scam of yours," Jessie said, sitting down opposite Gloria and gracefully crossing her long legs.

"I don't know what you are talking about!" Gloria croaked nervously. "I don't know anything about any scam of Roger's!"

Jessie buffed her fingernails nonchalantly against her linen pants, ignoring Gloria's answers until she heard the one she liked. She hoped Gloria didn't notice the interest she took in the bit of information Gloria knew about Roger's many "scams."

"What do you want from me?" Gloria sniffed dramatically into an old tissue she had found in her purse. "All I ever wanted was to raise my poor baby and make a decent living. You Rites are always trying to ruin my life!" she added as she dropped her face into her hands and sobbed dryly.

Jessie watched detachedly, waiting for Gloria to wind down. She gazed out the bay windows. She found something interesting to focus until Gloria decided to cut the act.

"Okay, Gloria, I think we can be honest with each other with that out of your system. Something I've always wondered, do you even know who Rob Roy's father is?" Jessie was amazed at how quickly Gloria was able to regain her composer.

"I wouldn't be asking any questions unless you are prepared for the answers." Gloria dug through her purse until she found a match for her cigarette.

Jessie hated it when people didn't have the good grace to ask if it was all right to pollute the environment. She started to ask her to put it out; she remembered something about lots of fresh cigarettes around the crime scene.

"Excuse me, Gloria." Jessie stood up to get an ashtray for Gloria's cigarette. "Would you like something to drink?"

"I'd take bourbon if you had one."

Jessie noted Gloria was starting early today. "No problem." Jessie shivered at the thought of liquor this early in the day.

"I just have a couple more questions. How many men were you blackmailing as Rob Roy's daddy?" Jessie watched as Gloria seemed to relax once she had downed her drink. "What made you keep quiet about the fact Big Roger had made a codicil about Rob Roy? I know you knew about it, I have Big Roger's notes."

Gloria eyed Jessie for a minute. Jessie was surprised by the laugh erupting from Gloria. "I think I have been underestimating you all these years! I didn't do anything any other woman wouldn't have done in my circumstances."

Jessie was offended by Gloria's lack of scruples. One thing she was certain of, Gloria was in a class all by herself.

"Oh, don't give me your superior look. You never wanted for anything. Your drunkard of a father must have had something big to hold over Big Roger's head. I'd like to know what would get him to take both of you in and feed you all those years."

"Don't put everyone in your league, Gloria. My father earned every dime he was ever paid." Jessie thought abut throwing Gloria out the door, but she needed her questions answered. "Just answer my questions."

Jessie settled back and gave Gloria a chance to relate her story.

"I never had a Daddy Warbucks to support me, ya know. Half the time we were hungry and the other half everyone pointed their fingers and asked where had we gotten the money for new duds. You know white trash jokes. The one thing I learned at home was there was one easy way to make money. I had all the components needed.

"Mom was worn out, so Fred decided it was time for me to earn my keep. I figured if he was going to make me screw all his old cronies, I may as well go into business for myself."

Gloria raised her glass in an expectant manner. She waited until Jessie refilled it before she went on with her story: "I found out the opposite sex found me very desirable. Old men, young men, rich ones, poor ones, they all liked me. You name it, if they were over 12, they found me irresistible. So I took advantage of my 'charms' and earned enough to break away from Fred and his cronies. Never mind I was only 14, I had everyone convinced I was old enough to take care of myself. It was the 2nd greatest day of my life when I told Fred to take his junk and move out. He couldn't believe I really had bought the house. The look on his face when I showed him the title was worth every beating I ever got."

Gloria drained her drink and seemed to relive some awful moment in her life. "You know, it's funny, I had figured I wasn't able to get pregnant. I mean, you would think as badly as I had been used there would have been more than one baby. Rob Roy was the only one."

Gloria's face seemed to age in front of Jessie's eyes. She caught the look of pity in Jessie's eyes and hardened back into the Gloria everyone knew. "At last I had found the way to get off my back, and I wasn't the least bit sorry to do it. It could have been any one of those old degenerates. They all knew it."

"I only knew about Big Roger. How many of them were you blackmailing?" Jessie asked.

Gloria shrugged and went on with her story: "I had decided to take the money and run, but good old Glynis just had to make me mad. She came to my house all high and mighty, insisting she knew all about Roger and me. She demanded I leave town and give my little 'bastard' away. I got so mad I decided right there and then to keep Rob Roy and send birth announcements to everyone paying me." Gloria laughed mirthlessly, and once again seemed to relive a repugnant memory. "After I had Rob Roy it didn't seem like such a great idea to send out birth announcements."

Jessie was squirming in her seat. She had expected to hate Gloria, but she was starting to feel empathy for her. Gloria wouldn't believe Jessie's life wasn't everything it was cracked up to be. Jessie was gaining a respect for Gloria she wouldn't have believed possible.

"I often thought of telling Big Roger about the other men. He still would have given me money. After Glynis came by giving me ultimatums, I decided to keep it to myself. I know everyone thinks I'm just some dumb bar slut, but I've made enough money to see Rob Roy will always be taken care of. Unlike some people, mine was all on the up and up once I bought the bar!" She gave Jessie a knowing look. Gloria ended with her shoulders squared and a look of pride in her eyes. Jessie realized Gloria had nothing to do with Roger's murder.

"Why did you let Roger get away with hiding the codicil?" Jessie needed to know the answer.

Gloria sighed and smiled ironically. "Good old Roj and I had gone for a little drive one night. Rob was sleeping; I didn't think it would hurt to go for a little while. When we got back I knew there was something wrong. Everyone knows the end of the story."

Gloria took a deep breath and finished, "Roger knew all along Rob was his brother. The night he left us I begged him to help me. I threatened; I even told him Rob Roy was his own baby brother. He just laughed as he left us. He said he hoped the little brat would die. I couldn't believe anyone could be so cruel. The poor little guy was so hot the only thing I could think of was to put him in cold water. Then the seizures started. I was the cause of the seizures. What if they had taken him away? You can believe this or not, but I have always loved Rob Roy, in my own way." Gloria slumped into submission. Jessie was speechless. Finally Gloria gathered her things and headed for the door.

"I'm going to give the codicil to my lawyers. I'll have them make you the trustee. They'll probably be getting in touch with you next week," Jessie said, putting out her hand to shake Gloria's. She had gotten a fresh look at the gaudily made-up woman and hoped to let bygones be bygones.

Gloria looked at Jessie's hand, and you could see she was having a flood of reactions. "Oh, what the hell," she said as she grabbed Jessie's hand and gave it a quick shake.

Jessie watched the retreating back of the woman she had held in contempt for so many years. She thought Gloria was walking a little taller, but maybe it was her imagination.

Jessie went to the office to get her notebook. This was one suspect she could mark off her list. She was thinking about implications of what Gloria had revealed when she heard the doorbell. "I'll get it, Nana."

She opened the door almost breathlessly. She wasn't sure whether it was from the thought of seeing Sam or her excitement at doing so well at her first interrogation.

Sam noticed the brightness in her eyes and a flush to her cheeks that deepened when he said, "I hope I'm the reason for all this good humor!" He was rewarded with the charming deepening of her flush.

"Guess who just left?" Jessie said trying to ignore the devilish look Sam was giving her.

"Aren't you even going to ask me in first?"

"Sorry, come on in. This is great; you know I really think I have a knack for this sort of thing." Jessie stepped back to allow Sam's entrance.

"Have you got any coffee in this place?" Sam said lightly.

Jessie waved Sam to follow her into the kitchen so she could continue with her story. "Gloria Ritter stopped by today. I decided to drill her for some information."

"Drill her for information?" Sam asked.

"Yeah, drill, you know get the information—grab some facts—you know." Jessie supposed maybe that she was acting a little weird. If the circumstances had been different she would have said this morning was fun. When she got him to listen to the entire story, she was sure he would be impressed.

"Go ahead, Jessie, I'm all ears."

Jessie started to tell her story; she could tell Sam was skeptical she could get any useful information. Halfway through, she could tell she was gaining respect. He leaned forward, a look of concentration intensifying on his face. He no longer let every little sound from around the ranch interrupt his concentration. He was really listening! When Jessie told him Gloria confessed to the blackmail without remorse, and she implicated Roger in the illness that had caused Rob Roy's slowness, he realized Jessie wasn't going to be a hindrance, but a real asset in the investigation.

"Well?" Jessie asked triumphantly.

"Good job. But what makes you think this means Gloria had nothing to do with the murder?"

"Don't you see, the only reason she had for wanting Roger dead was to get her hands on the trust fund. If she has a nice little nest egg for Rob Roy, then why would she need the trust fund?"

"Maybe she's greedy."

"No, she doesn't care about the trust fund. She just wanted to rub my nose in Roger's philandering. I thought she might not want Roger to know about Rob Roy's true identity, but he knew all along."

"Well, Mrs. Rite, I bow to your perception," Sam said, standing and giving Jessie a stiff, formal bow.

Jessie was satisfied with her accomplishments of the morning and very pumped and ready to go at it some more.

"Seriously, Jessie, I think you are right on line. We can strike her from our list. You feel up to visiting some people in Silverton?"

"You bet!" Jessie said as she jumped up and threw him the keys to her BMW. "You drive. I want to go over my notes from Gloria's interview to see if there was something I might have missed. Sam congratulated himself for finding such a conscientious partner.

# Chapter Twenty

"John Albert is first on my list."

"Do you really think John Albert could have had anything to do with Roger's death?" Jessie asked as she slipped her small notepad into her purse.

"Not really, but I like to whittle my list as quickly as possible. I can concentrate on the important details more easily," Sam replied.

They drove in silence for a while, each contemplating their own theories. Spring had quickly turned into summer, drying the morning mist from the surrounding mountain peaks, turning the cool morning air quickly arid. Jessie started to roll her window down when Sam asked, "Do you want me to turn on the air conditioning."

"No thanks. I like the smell of the desert air in the early morning. It looks like we have seen the last of spring for this year," Jessie added.

"Yeah, I guess we were lucky to have it as long as we did," Sam replied nervously. Sam conversed more easily with Jessie than anyone he had met in his life. Sam had a semi-anxious feeling at the thought of spending the day alone with her.

"I like the summer around here. When the desert cools off and the coyotes bay at the summer moon, I feel as if I am the first person to live in this land. When Jake first told me we were going to have to move to Colorado I just about died. Now if I had to leave I would die."

"Don't worry, Jessie. Everything will work out. I'll make sure you and the kids never have to move." Sam gave Jessie a look telling her he was someone she could depend on for everything.

Jessie felt luck must have been on her side. They drove up to Albert Motors. John was leaving the office, walking to his car to leave.

Jessie was surprised when her wave wasn't returned. Roger had managed to offend or humiliate just about everyone in the county. Jessie and Sam hurried over to John's car before he could pull out.

"John, can't you wait a minute before you leave?" Jessie pleaded.

"I'm sorry, Jessie, but I don't have anything to say to you. If you are worried about the money Allen and Ernie owe you, don't. I'm making arrangements to pay the bill," John said, putting his car into gear.

"Look, Mr. Albert, Jessie and I have a few questions needing answers. If you want us to go to the sheriff with our information, we can oblige you," Sam said gruffly.

"Jessie, you can tell your paid stooge I don't care. I'm sure Roger told you I wouldn't put up with his bullshit and now I'm telling you." He looked threateningly at Sam. "Now, get out of my way before I'm obliged to run over your feet." He rolled up his window and revved his motor threateningly.

"Boy, has he got an attitude!" Sam said.

"John used to be one of our best friends. When Roger and I first got married, John and his wife came over for barbecues almost every weekend. I thought they quit coming over because our families grew and we just went different ways. It seems once we had kids we drifted apart. We never had time for getting together," Jessie explained, saddened by the memories.

"It'll be straightened once we have all the facts." Sam patted her shoulder. They headed toward the car to finish their day's work. Sam noted by the time that they got in the car; everyone in the dealership had lined the windows. It wouldn't take long for the story to spread.

"How well do you know the owner of the Big Burger?" Sam asked Jessie as they parked in the lot of the busiest burger stop in the county.

"I know her pretty well. When I was growing up there was nowhere else in town for us to gather. We spent just about every Friday night after the games eating and listening to the jukebox. Big Roger thought it would do Roj good to see how it was to work for someone else. He always said Roj took advantage of the fact he was the boss's son," Jessie said. "Big Roger was amazed at how well Roj did working for Mildred. In fact, I think he was jealous of Mildred because she and Roj got along so well." Jessie finished her explanation just as they drove into Millie's Big Burger. Sam opened the door and helped Jessie out of the car. Jessie's reputation had proceeded her, causing a buzz of conversation from everyone encountering them.

Mildred came over to Jessie and Sam's table as soon as they walked into the restaurant. There were bets going on all over the county as to when Mildred would retire. She was long past the age of retirement, but she still kept a close watch on the running of her business. Mildred was expected to have a heart attack over the grill some hot summer day when the burger joint was packed to the rafters.

She still did all the grillwork after 40 years of owning the place. She couldn't find anyone to grill a burger to her liking. The day she couldn't outwork five teenagers was the day she would sell the Big Burger and retire to the Bahamas!

Jessie! How long has it been?" Mildred whooped as she grabbed the younger woman in a bear hug.

"It has been too long. I'm craving one of your Gargantuans, with all the trimmings and double the fries. What are you having, Sam?"

Sam looked at the older woman and shrugged his shoulders. "I guess I'll have the same."

"So, you finally found someone to keep up with your appetite? This girl put many football players under the table in the good old days." The older woman chuckled, then she turned to make the lunches.

"Mildred, do you have time to sit with us while we eat?" Jessie wondered.

"Sure, Mondays are always a little slow after school has let out."

"Thanks."

"Let me make your lunches, and I'll be right back."

Jessie was one of the few people in the county to beat Mildred out of her house special… more than once! She always has a Gargantuan, double fries and a Zombie milk shake.

Jessie dove right in to the lunch, leaving Sam looking at the feast in front of him and asking the few questions necessary.

Mildred was not able to furnish them with much more information than they already had. Roger was one of the few people Mildred trained on the grill. Jessie figured it was because she wasn't overly fond of Big Roger. She finally had to admit Roj had a real talent as a fry cook. He could keep every waitress in the place running and still have time to charm Mildred handily!

Mildred told them openly about how Roj had "talked" the bus company into sharing the depot with the railroad. She wasn't shy about sharing the information. She didn't realize Roj was using the depot as a drop spot for his illegal activities.

When Jessie told her about why Roj got involved, she was visibly shaken, but Mildred had lived long enough and seen enough she wasn't left speechless.

"To think all these years he has been using all of us. I'm glad I didn't find out. I would have blown him to smithereens myself!" Mildred wiped the tears from the corner of her eyes as she stood to go back to work.

"Did you know how Roger made enough money to pay cash for his fancy little car?" Mildred went on, not waiting for an answer. "He worked on anyone's lawn that would pay him. He spent as much time mowing and trimming lawns as he did over the grill in here. If only Big Roger would have laid off him. Well, that's water under the bridge. There are still a few people in this town as fond of Roger as I was. Maybe you need to talk to Agnes Cummings. She was more of a mother to him than Glynis Rite ever could be.

"Even after he quit taking care of her lawn, he made sure it was taken care of. David is a nice boy, but he's a little shortsighted when it comes to things besides the library or his greenhouse. No rest for the wicked!" She smiled and waved to her old customer. "Don't be such a stranger, little girl."

"It's not like we could ever eat again after all of this food. How on earth do you eat so much and stay so slim? If I ate this much all the time I would need a crane to get around." Sam was overwhelmed as he gazed at Jessie's clean plate and empty glass.

"It took practice, Sam, plenty of practice. Jake tells everyone I have a tape worm."

It was still early enough in the afternoon, and they decided to pay one last visit before they headed for home. Driving through the gates at the dirt track, Jessie was reminded of the many summer nights spent here. She could almost smell the fumes of the drag cars even though there were no races during the week until after Memorial Day. She knew Ernie and Allen would be here counting the receipts from the weekend and getting the stadium ready to start daily races.

She picked her way through the pit area strewn with car parts and tools. She was amazed that no matter how things change, they always stay the same. This was exactly the way it was when Roj would come and race his car.

"Hey, you're not supposed to be here!" Al yelled at her and Sam.

"Hi, Al, it's me, Jessie Rite. Mind if we talk to you and Ernie?"

"Well, I'm not sure this is the right time to talk to Ernie," Al said nervously. His brothers weren't very fond of the Rites. He wanted to stay out of the fray. Jessie hadn't done anything to them, except have the bad taste to marry a real weasel!

"This is Sam Ellison. We need to ask a few questions about Roj. We won't take long, I promise."

"Okay, but whatever Ernie says, goes." Al turned and went back to working on the souped-up Chevy.

"I think Al has been working on that Chevy since we were in school!" Jessie said quietly to Sam.

Jessie was about to knock on the door, when Ernie pulled it open and hollered, "Al, can you come to the office?" He blinked his eyes several times as if to clear them. When the recognition hit, he grabbed Jessie into the warm embrace of old friends.

He kept his hands on her shoulders and gave her a through going-over before he said, "How long has it been since the last time I saw you?"

"Too long," Jessie said, trying to keep her voice steady.

"Come in here and sit down," he boomed as he put his arm around her shoulder and pulled her into the office. He turned to close the door, when he noticed Sam for the first time. "Who's your friend, Jessie?" He said, eyeing Sam cautiously.

"I'm Jessie's neighbor, Sam Ellison," Sam said as he put out his hand to shake Ernie's. "We need to ask you some questions about Roger."

"I don't really have much to say." Ernie's previously warm manner cooled considerably.

Sam wanted to get this over as soon as possible. This guy was just another one of Roger's victims. People don't work this hard when easy drug money is as available as Roger made it.

"Roger left a journal of all his dealings, Ernie, isn't it?"

"Yeah, I suppose he would. Had to keep a record of all the flies he caught in his web." You could see the subject was distasteful to him.

"I was desperate to show Dad that Al and I could make a go of this track. It was in a real mess when I bought it. There were lots of repairs needed, some back bills had to be taken care of before we could get anyone to deal with us. When Roger came to me and offered to become a sponsor, I made the mistake of not asking enough questions."

"Just what was it Roger wanted for his money?" Sam asked.

"Nothing too much, just hiring a couple of guys to work the pits. They were good mechanics, so I didn't say anything. Roger was good for business. He got cars here, good cars. Things got exciting around here; the crowds loved all the action. I never asked Roger how or why he was willing to do all this for us. A couple of years ago we had a major crash on the track. Al was parting one of the cars out, and he found why Roger was so willing to get all these great racers here from all over the nation. We were giving him a way to transport his drugs."

"How did you get him to quit?"

"I just told him he was through. Nothing is worth that. I knew Roger would not let me off the hook easily. I told him to do what he could; I wasn't going to keep him and his buddies around."

"He let it go?"

"No, he went to Dad and "offered" to give him the evidence if he would sell the ranch. Dad offered not to kill him if he got out of the dealership. Roger got the hint."

Jessie had sat quietly listening to Ernie's story. "Why is John so angry at me? Does he really believe I would condone what Roger was doing?"

"No, Jessie. Roger handed me a bill for services rendered. Dad has been putting everything we have in hock to pay the bill. He is just a little out of sorts with everyone." Ernie smiled, reminding Jessie of the sweet young man from their high school days.

"There is no bill, Ernie. Thanks for the information." Jessie hurried out the door, leaving Sam to make their goodbyes.

Both were very quiet on the ride home. Jessie was remembering all the times she and Roger had spent at the track the last summer before he went to college. Was he always this evil, this corrupt? She was surprised at the lack of feelings the meeting revealed. It was as if she was watching a bad B movie she felt obliged to sit through to the agonizing end.

Sam had his own thoughts to occupy him. Sam was finding his original assessment of Roger Randal Rite, the III, to be correct. He couldn't understand how a woman of Jessie's caliber could have become so embroiled in his web. He found her to be very intelligent. Not just book-learned, but she had good instincts. He had seen her in action. This guy must have been some charmer to fool her.

"Sam, do you think it is possible Roger had been so accomplished an actor as to fool me all those years?"

Jessie eyed Sam closely as he replied.

Sam thought about lying but instead answered a simple, "Yes."

"You never knew him when we were growing up," she gave as an explanation.

"Jessie, quit blaming yourself. I've known a hundred Rogers. You were lucky; you got two great kids out of the deal. Be grateful."

The rest of the ride was quiet as Jessie thought about what Sam had told her. She was making plans how to explain to the kids about their father.

*****

"I knew it! You would think she would have waited a decent amount of time before she started whoring around! Listen to this: 'What newly widowed socialite was seen gallivanting around Delaney County with her latest lover?'"

Crumpling the paper and angrily throwing it down, I guess I need to lead the stupid police to the right person. "Oh, Momma, did you hear? I made a joke. The 'Rite' person!"

Chuckling while picking up the phone, it spoke into the receiver. "I need to talk to Sgt. Garza." Suddenly realizing they might try to trace this call, it quickly hung up the phone. "A letter is much safer, yes, I can cut up a bunch of Momma's old magazines. How to get the letter to Delaney County? Take the bus to Butte; yes, the bus would be perfect."

It took all afternoon to write the letter. The bus would have to wait till morning. This would get the police headed in the right direction. Another joke, the "rite" direction! How funny!

"See, Momma, I told you I would take care of everything! I'm ready for some dinner, so how about Chinese? My treat!" It was already planning a treat for them, after getting home from Delaney; a little socializing might be just the thing.

Not venturing far from the house since "that day," it decided a little space was needed. With babysitting the decrepit old woman day and night, it felt as if the walls were closing in. Why not go visiting? Yes, Momma would just have to fend for herself

# Chapter Twenty-one

Jessie threw the paper down, disgusted with Theda Ream's article. She forced herself to read the story and, as usual, there were very little facts in the article. It was made of conjecture and accusations. Theda refused to let the facts dictate her writings.

The phone started ringing almost before the rooster crowed; people loved passing rumors. Jessie had never paid any attention to the rumor mill around Silverton but since she had become the main source of rumors, people enjoyed keeping her up with the latest stories.

"Hello," Jessie said shortly.

"Hi, Jessie, it's Boat. How are you doing?" Boat was nervous; he didn't want to make this call, but he had to or Garza would be on his way.

"Boat, what's the problem?" Jessie questioned, unnerved by Boat's tone.

"Jessie, I've got a call from the state boys. They tell me you and Sam have been nosing around. They aren't too happy."

Jessie tried to stay calm. Once again she was riding the roller coaster Roger's death had put her on. "So, why would that bother me? They told me time after time they were doing everything they could. So far they haven't gotten any results."

"I know they don't seem to be doing much. It has only been a few weeks since the murder. It takes time to run down leads. They say it makes it difficult when 'amateurs' get in the way."

"Do you think if Sam and I stay out of the way the detectives will be able to find Roger's murderer?" Jessie asked.

Boat was torn in different directions. He knew if he told her yes, he was more than stretching the truth. If he said no, Sam and Jessie would keep searching. They were surely risking the anger of Garza and his lackeys.

"Look, Jessie, if you have any information to help the investigation I should tell you to turn it over to the state investigators." Boat congratulated himself on an excellent non-answer.

"That is no answer, Boat. When I talked to Sgt. Garza I gave him all the information I had." Jessie thought to herself, *It's not technically a lie. I gave him all the information I had at the time I talked to him.* Jessie and Boat knew they were walking a fine line with each other. They told each other just enough truths to satisfy each other.

"Look, Jessie, I just want to keep you out of trouble." Boat was nervous. He had worked on enough investigations he knew when something was wrong. "I've attended one funeral this month. I don't want to have any more of my friends end up in the family plot."

"Don't worry, Boat, Sam and I are just trying to get some things straightened out for the estate." Jessie was glad she didn't have to look Boat in the eye with that one. He would have seen through the thin screen of truth she was putting between them.

"Jessie, all I want is what's best for you." Boat wanted Jessie to know she could turn to him without fear of reprisal from the state investigators. "I'm here to help."

"I know, Boat. I appreciate you being here for me. I'll keep you posted." Jessie was grateful for the support, but the last thing she wanted was to get Boat into trouble. "If you hear anything you think we should know, give me a call."

The doorbell rang as Jessie hung up the phone. She looked forward to the day's work, but she was afraid if she told Sam about the call from Boat, he would press her to turn over the information from the journal. It was bad enough Roger had trashed their lives; she didn't want to bring any more people into her problems than necessary.

"Mr. Holmes, I presume?" She smiled as she opened the door for Sam.

"Dr. Watson?" Sam retorted. "I'll pass on the tea, but I would kill for a good cup of coffee!" Sam had not realized how awful his own coffee was until he smelled the aromatic brew made at the Rite place.

"Nana just made a fresh pot. Come into the kitchen, and we can talk while we have some. Have you had breakfast yet?" Jessie asked quickly without taking a breath. It seemed the more she saw of this man the harder it was to keep her emotions in rein.

Sam was pleased with Jessie's happy mood. They were no closer to finding the answers to this mystery than they were yesterday. He could tell Jessie's anxieties were eased by focusing on her goal instead of worrying about what could happen.

"Okay, Sam, what is on the agenda today?" Jessie asked, putting a steaming mug of coffee in front of him.

"I have the Markhams and the attorneys on our list. If we have more time today maybe we could talk to Virginia Galley."

"I don't see how Virginia could have had anything to do with this mess. She was just a sweet old lady caught in an awful situation. Can't we leave well enough alone?"

Jessie's heart went out to Virginia. Her marriage was known all over the county. She had lived with Fred for 40 years until his cancer took over. His suicide was talked about, but everyone understood. He wasn't expected to live more than six months, but the pain would be unbearable. He chose to save Virginia the agony of watching him wither away and die in pain.

"I am not saying Virginia had anything to do with Roger and Robyn's deaths. Do you know of anyone in town who knows anymore about the coming and goings of this town than her?" Sam was looking at his coffee so he wouldn't have to see the hurt he knew was in Jessie's eyes.

Jessie needed time to get her anger under control. She knew she was angry with Roger, but more often it was taken out on the people closest to her. "I suppose it wouldn't hurt to talk to her. We don't have to tell her we are aware of Roger's little visit."

Sam nodded and rose to fill their cups again. He could feel Jessie's emotions like static electricity filling the room. He watched her face change as her thoughts ran the gamut from anger to hope to confidence. Every day he grew more and more in love with her. He knew the day would come when they would be together. He just hoped she would feel the same way he did when all of this was settled.

He still had to deal with her children. He didn't know much about children, of any age. He would do whatever he had to do to make them like him. They were part of the woman he loved, and it made him want to get to know them. He wouldn't stop until he had won them over.

"What are you thinking about?" Jessie didn't understand the look on Sam's face. She could tell he was thinking about something, but she didn't think it had to do with the investigation.

"I'm making plans for us when this mess is over and you, I and the children are making a new life." Sam wasn't going to beat around the bush about the way he felt.

"I'm not ready for future plans. I'm not even sure the kids will understand about our feelings, let alone ever get used to them." Jessie nervously rubbed her hand over her forehead. Sam couldn't wait.

"Jessie, look at me." She raised her eyes to meet Sam's and was left breathless by the love in his eyes. Sam took her gently into his arms and held her tightly to his chest.

As the heat from his body warmed her, she began to relax. She could feel his heartbeat through his soft flannel shirt. The masculine smell of leather and soap surrounding him was more sensual than the expensive colognes Roger wore could ever be. Her heart raced as she felt him brush his lips across her forehead ever so slightly…or did she imagine it?

"Jessie, I'm not going to give up. You and I are going to make a life together. Your kids will just have to get use to it. Roger was the only man they associate with you, and it's the way it should be. Can you blame them for worrying about you being hurt again?" Sam felt Jessie beginning to relax.

"This is so fast. I don't think I'm ready for any commitments. The one man I loved, or thought I loved, was a lie. Maybe I'm not any good at love. I just don't know what to think."

Jessie gently pushed herself out of Sam's arms and turned to put their cups in the sink. Sam grabbed her, trapping her against the wall, forcing her to look at him. "I said I am not giving up! I won't let you give up, either."

Sam was studying the emotions playing across Jessie's face. He was intently eyeing the lush red lips that she was nervously chewing on. He decided they were exactly the color of raspberries and wondered if they would taste as sweet.

Jessie had quit struggling and was mesmerized by the intent look he was giving her. She felt like a small animal hypnotized by a cobra, but she wasn't afraid. She felt warmth growing inside her, threatening to consume her.

Sam must have read the need in her eyes. As if in slow motion she watched him inch closer and closer. When their lips met she felt the fire explode. She didn't care about anything but getting closer to him. She craved the feel of his skin. She was falling into a pool of azure blue water, water exactly matching Sam's eyes.

Sam was the first to pull away. He groaned as if the move was painful. Jessie felt her skin blush from the tip of her toes to the roots of her hair. She was more confused than ever. This feeling was alien to her; she had never felt this way about Roger. Perhaps Roger knew and this was the reason he strayed.

"Jessie." Sam forced her to look at him before he finished. "We will finish this when the time is right. We have work to do now and until that's finished I need to keep a clear head." He gave Jessie a slow smile to reassure her.

"Thank you, Sam. I need time to sort my feelings." Her mind was grateful, but her heart craved more and regretted Sam's strength of character.

"Let's take my jeep today; it's not as intimidating as your car. We want people to feel free to talk to us." Jessie got a hurt look in her eyes, making Sam regret the bluntness of his words.

As they drove to town Sam was sorry he hadn't wore a lighter shirt. The sun was already warming the morning air considerably. It was sure to be a scorcher.

"Mind if I roll down my window, Sam? It's getting pretty warm for me." Sam wasn't fooled by Jessie's politeness, but he was too grateful to mention it. "That would be great!"

They pulled up to the Marshall's Rexall Drug store, and Jessie was all business. She was sure Jim and Sharon had nothing to do with the murder, but she saw how important it was to eliminate everyone.

They had enough tragedy in their lives. It shouldn't take long to check them off the list.

The dry heat had made both Jessie and Sam thirsty, and they decided to sit at the soda counter for something to quench their thirst.

"Jessie, it's good to see you," Sharon said as she stepped behind the counter to take their order. "What can I get for you?" Sharon was trying to act nonchalant even though she was nervous. This was the first time she had seen Jessie since the funeral.

Jim noticed Jessie and came to greet the young woman. Jim was saddened; Jessie used to be one of their best friends. "Hey, Jessie, Sam, what can we do for you?" Jim had heard the rumors about their activities and wanted to get to the bottom of their visit.

"Is there somewhere we can talk?" Jessie asked, looking to the back of the store where she knew their office was. "We have a few questions."

Sam was surprised by Jessie's gruffness and tried to calm the feathers she may have ruffled. "We hope you could help us find the answers." Sam drawled, trying to ease over the anger showing in Jim's eyes.

"No problem, we have nothing to hide," Jim said shortly. "Sharon, will you watch the front while I talk to Jessica and Sam?"

Sam whispered into Jessie's ear, "Let me handle this, okay?" then he squeezed her hand to stem any further discussion.

Jim shut the door and walked slowly over to the desk and sat down. "What do you want answered?"

Jessie watched as Sam showed another side to the already complex person she found him to be. He slowly pulled out a notebook and flipped it back and forth as if he couldn't find his questions. It was the perfect imitation of a bumbling sleuth. Jessie was amused at the sorry imitation of Colombo.

Sam smiled an apology to Jim. "Sorry to involve you. We are sure you had nothing to do with this mess, but word around town has it you weren't exactly sorry Roger had this…ah…'mishap'?"

Jessie was surprised at the reaction the question illicit from Jim. He was actually roaring with laughter. Jessie watched Jim laugh until tears rolled down his face. She looked at Sam and shrugged; she wasn't sure why the question had unhinged him.

Jim slowly quit roaring, wiping his face and blowing his nose on the kerchief he pulled out of his hip pocket. "Sorry." His face seemed to age 20 years in the blink of an eye. "I guess I have been holding in too much lately."

"Since Elizabeth's death, Sharon and I have been walking around in a daze." Jim leaned back and made a steeple with his two index fingers to lean his chin on. He seemed to have forgotten Sam and Jessie were in the room for a moment as he relived something painful from the past. "Did you know Beth was nominated as spring queen before she died?" Jessie looked at Sam with tears in her eyes. She was thinking what she would do if this happened to Cristal.

"I remember the day she came into the store when she had found out. I can't remember her ever being happier before in her life. Sharon feels guilty because she didn't believe Beth would win. It was different for me. I knew…she had to win…it was too important to her. I didn't care one way or the other; she would always be a princess to me." Tears filled his eyes and fell slowly down his cheeks, but he didn't seem to mind. He was in another time…another place.

"She was so beautiful that night. She always thought of herself as plain. That night even she knew she was beautiful. She came home and wrote in her diary for hours. That night couldn't be taken away from her."

Jim turned into a different man at the thought of Roger. "I'm sorry, Jessie, but if someone else hadn't killed that sorry excuse for a man, I would have found a way."

Jessie was looking at her hands. She was embarrassed by Roger; he never concerned himself with his actions. That poor young girl was no match for Roger and his deviations. What reason could he have had for wanting her? She wasn't his usual type. She was sweet, quiet and not Roger's usual prey. Roger was attracted to the more sensual type. Beth's beauty glowed from within. Jessie had never known Roger to take the time to notice anything more than a pretty face and a full set of breasts.

"When we found Beth in her bed, she looked so sweet. We thought she was sleeping peacefully. I went to awaken her and then I noticed she was so pale and cold. Sharon found me shaking her and screaming for her to wake up." Jim was pensive for a minute. "I never had any idea Sharon could be so level-headed. She calmly called 911 and went over to cradle our baby until they came and took away her body."

Jessie, by this time, was visibly shaken. She wanted to be away. She didn't think she could take any more. "I'm sorry, Jim," she said quietly, knowing nothing she could say would stop the pain.

Jim dismissed Jessie's apology with a wave of his hand and continued his story. "I didn't think I could go on. Sharon was inconsolable, and she blamed herself. She was sure if she hadn't neglected Beth's education about…you know…sex…she would be alive today. We all know who is really to blame, don't we?" He looked toward Jessie, but she could tell he wasn't seeing her.

"Why didn't she come to us? We loved her more than anything. She could come to us for anything. There was nothing she could have done to make us quit loving her." Jim finally broke down. He put his face in his hands and sobbed…deep, silent sobs.

Jessie went around the desk and put a comforting hand on his shoulder. Jim shrugged her hand off his shoulder as if the touch stung him. "I bet you didn't know Sharon had two miscarriages? The doctors said she wouldn't be able to have children. Beth was our little miracle baby. No, I didn't kill Roger. I would have if someone hadn't beaten me to it. Now, if you don't mind, Jessie, I have work to get to."

Sam took Jessie by the elbow to escort her out to the jeep. They turned together and slowly walked out the door. Jessie turned to see Sharon hugging the shaking figure of her husband, staring into the distance with tears falling freely down her cheeks.

"My god, how could he have been so vile? She was nothing but a baby herself. All he was interested in was another notch on his belt. I'm glad he's gone. I'll never forgive him for all this agony," Jessie spit the words out vehemently.

"Do you feel up to talking to the Weston's?"

"Yes. I want them to tell me why they let Roger get away with all of this."

It was a quick drive to the offices of Weston and Weston, attorneys at law. They owned one of the oldest buildings in Silverton. It had housed Weston attorneys practically since Silverton was founded.

It always reminded Jessie of a Southern mansion. Honeysuckle growing up trellises surrounding the verandah. Flowers bloomed from early spring till late fall. Behind the house was a formal rose garden filled with roses of every color.

Jessie loved the annual Weston holiday party, inviting every client handled by the family. Actually, it was an excuse to show off their magnificent house. There were antique holiday decorations that had been in their family for generations. It was said it took the entire month of November to prepare the house for the kick off of the holiday season.

The house was full of fresh flowers from the greenhouse of David Cummings. His work was renowned in the area. His specialty was exotic flowers of every sort. Not only was it a very profitable hobby, it gave him a reputation as a very knowledgeable horticulturist. He was well known in the state of Colorado, and his reputation was growing in the rest of the country. His knowledge of diseases and parasite detection was growing.

Sam walked into the office and told the receptionist they were here to see Frank Weston and his son. Jessie was amazed by the chameleon-like quality Sam exhibited. She knew him as a rancher, then the bumbling detective, now he was a charming yet insistent client, charming his way into one of the most prominent law firms in the county without an appointment. Jessie was prepared to leave when she heard the tinkle of laughter from the desk and was treated to a warm smile from the receptionist as she asked them to wait while she talked to her boss.

"I can't believe you got Frank to see you without an appointment." Jessie looked at Sam with new respect. "What did you have to promise her to get it?" she said with the smallest hint of jealousy.

"Why, I do believe you are questioning my sincerity," Sam said with mock anger.

"Sam," the receptionist said sweetly, "You and Mrs. Rite can go in now."

Jessie expected the young girl to pat Sam on the behind as he walked by. "Yes, Sam, we don't want to keep Mr. Weston waiting," she said sugar sweet as she looped her arm through Sam's and pulled him unceremoniously through the door.

"Hi, Frank. Thanks for seeing us." Jessie was surprised Sam was on a first name basis with Frank Weston. Frank didn't allow many people that intimacy.

"Sam, Jessie. What a surprise," Weston added.

Jessie could tell by the unaccustomed perspiration on his forehead it probably wasn't a pleasant one. "I was going through Roger's things and found some very interesting information," Jessie said, looking to Sam for encouragement. She saw a barely perceptive nod telling her to go on.

"I want to know why you didn't say anything to me about Big Roger's codicil."

"Well...I...we...young Roger made it perfectly clear our services were no longer necessary." Weston pulled out a silk scarf and wiped the perspiration as it became more pronounced.

"Gee, Frank, isn't it a little hot in here?" Jessie fanned her face, letting Weston know she was aware of his nervousness. "Did he let you know before or after Big Roger's death?"

"Look, I'm a busy man. Maybe you can get to the point here." Frank was starting to get angry, but the only sign was the perspiration beading on his forehead, belying any outward calm.

Jessie looked to Sam for help. "Perhaps if you had Frank Jr. come in here we could straighten some things out."

"Leave Frank Jr. out of this," Weston said, raising his voice.

"Now, Weston, we don't want to get excited here. We just want a few questions answered," Sam drawled, soothing the older man's feelings. "Roger kept a journal," he added quietly.

"What kind of a journal?" Weston was on his feet.

"We have the journal of his less-than-legal business dealings with the citizens of Silverton." Sam was leaning forward, ready to spring if he needed to stop Weston's flight.

"I suppose I shouldn't be surprised." Weston had flopped back into his chair in surrender. "I hoped you weren't aware of Roger's activities."

Jessie was still able to be embarrassed by what Roger was doing all these years. "Maybe we should get Frank Jr. in here," Jessie said, looking toward the office she knew was empty more than it was full.

"He's not in Silverton right now. He is working on getting clean again. This time he insists he can stay that way without Roger around harassing him." Weston looked at Sam, embarrassed by the admission. "We've sent him before, but there was always someone to offer him more drugs. We hoped each time he would stay clean, but every time he got in deeper and deeper."

"Roger said something in his journal about his little surprise for you," Sam added, directing the subject back to their investigations.

"You have to believe I had no idea what Roger and Selma were up to. My wife was out of the country touring Europe. I was lonely, and my mistake was believing in Roger. The same mistake a lot of people made. I suppose you have the pictures, too?" Frank Weston shrank before her very eyes, his mortification obvious.

"No, we don't have any pictures." Jessie tried to hide her embarrassment.

"One night I was lonely and I decided to go to the Charles Hotel for dinner. Selma and Roger were there. I had too much wine with dinner and the next thing I remember I was waking in Selma's bedroom. I wish I could say I don't remember what happened. Instead I'll have to carry that humiliation with me forever."

"I did what Roger wanted and that's when he reminded me about his promise all those years before. It wasn't such a bad thing; all I had to do was to keep quiet about Big Roger's last will and the codicil. I know it was wrong, but my wife shouldn't have to carry the burden of young Frank and my infidelity. She is a good woman. She had to put up with us all these years. Go to Boat if you want, but I'll never be sorry for doing what I did. If I could save her any amount of agony, I'd do it again."

"Okay, Frank. If we need anything else, we'll get in touch." Sam turned to Jessie and motioned her to leave.

Jessie was fuming by the time they had gotten into the old jeep and started toward home. "What do you think he meant by business between Roger and Selma?" Jessie had never liked Chuck's assistant.

She was too rough with the animals. Jessie could tell she had no concern for the animals. All she wanted was to keep in touch with wealthy ranchers. Also, there was the better-than-average salary Chuck was rumored to give her.

Chuck was either so smitten with her he wasn't aware of what she did, or more likely he didn't want to know. Everyone in the county but Selma knew Chuck was head over heels in love with her, and had been for years. Selma was just too busy making eyes at everything in jeans that she never gave Chuck a second thought.

"I think we should go talk to Selma right now," Jessie said firmly. "I think she could add a lot to this story."

"That's fine with me. Selma was on my list anyway!"

"Why? I didn't find anything in the journal that would incriminate her."

"When Boat and I were looking around the accident scene we found remnants of a gas can from the Flying A station. I decided to see if they knew how it got out there. I stopped by the station one day and the last person they remembered lending a can to was Selma."

Sam hadn't put much importance on that fact because gas cans are borrowed and loaned over and over. He didn't think Selma was the type of person to be concerned with returning the loaned can.

"I never did like her. She always seemed too interested in the male population around here. Something about the way she was always rubbing up against anyone over puberty. She reminded me of a cat in heat."

"My, my, aren't we a little touchy this afternoon?"

Jessie turned and gave Sam a growl to show just how she felt about his question. "Very clever!"

"Selma always seemed a little 'overstated' to me. I had the feeling she tolerated her work just to keep close to the big ranchers in the area."

Pulling into Chuck's driveway, Jessie noticed Chuck and Selma were arguing. Their disagreement centered over the truck Dr. Smith kept as spotless as his operating room.

"I told you I didn't put that filthy shovel in your precious truck!" Selma hissed angrily.

"Who else would have? You are the only one ever to touch this vehicle besides me!" Dr. Smith hollered at Selma, waving the shovel for emphasis.

Jessie was dumbstruck. She had never heard Chuck raise his voice, especially at Selma. "Hi, Chuck!" Jessie looked from one to the other, obviously confused.

Selma spun around at the sound of Jessie's voice. She was so angry she wanted to tell Miss Smarty Pants Jessie Rite to mind her own business, when she saw Sam Ellison.

"Mr. Ellison, how are you?" Ignoring Jessie, she couldn't have been sweeter if she had honey oozing from her pores.

"Say, Chuck, you wouldn't mind if Jessie and I had a word with Selma, would you?" Sam said, effectively ignoring the purring sounds coming from Selma.

Chuck gave Selma a questioning look; she shrugged her shoulders in response and turned to give Sam one of her most charming smiles.

"Chuck doesn't mind, do you, sweetie?"

Chuck just gave Sam a nod and dropped the shovel to carry his things into his office. Jessie felt a wave of concern flow over her. She hoped he would get over his involvement with Selma before it was too late.

"Well, I don't have all day, hon. You want to get to the point?" Selma had a way of making the most innocent questions in the world seem sleazy.

"You want to tell us about your relationship with my dead husband?" Jessie asked, seeing all of the reasons why she couldn't like this woman in a million years.

Selma leaned against the truck, opting to play cat and mouse with this pathetic excuse for a woman. "Why, Jessie, I don't know what you are talking about!" She was staring at Jessie through her catlike eyes. "Roger was a client of Chucks…and mine." She got a look on her face of satisfaction, reminding Jessie of the barn cat who got into the warm milk bucket.

"Look, you slimy…"

"Now, Jessie, maybe it would help Selma remember what we were talking about if we let her in on Frank Weston's little confession." Sam's lips were smiling, but his eyes had a look of revulsion while roving Selma head to toe.

Selma's look of contentment quickly evaporated into a look of calculating vengeance. "What did that old fart have to say?" Selma's honey sweetness was quickly turning to vinegar.

Sam and Jessie chose to ignore the question Selma had just asked. They just looked at her, waiting for her to answer their questions.

"Okay, what do I have to lose? Yeah, Roger and I had some fun with Old Frank. Roger and I had great times together. If she," Selma pointed at Jessie with the nod of her head, "would just have given Roger his freedom, he and I could have had greater times."

Sam noticed an angry gleam come to Jessie's eyes that he didn't trust. Jessie stood with her arms crossed over her chest, listening to the bile Selma was spewing. Although several things went through her mind, the idea she liked best was thrashing Selma to a bloody pulp. Just as if Sam had read her mind, he grabbed her elbow to stop her from jumping Selma.

Jessie slowly smiled, realizing the perfect revenge. "Every time Roger and I saw you we would try and figure out what it was about you that repulsed every man in the county. It seems Chuck was the only person who could stand to ride in the same vehicle with you, let alone have any kind of relationship with you."

It wasn't exactly the truth. There were lots of men who found Selma's effects enticing. Still, it felt good to see Selma's ego deflated.

"I don't have to take this from you," Selma said as she pivoted on her heel.

"That's fine, Selma, we'll just get Frank to talk to Boat. Then Boat can figure out the next steps to take." Sam and Jessie headed for the jeep.

"Hey, wait a minute, but I'm not sure she…" Selma nodded her head in Jessie's direction, "wants to hear this. I'm willing to tell you what I know." Selma's defeat was apparent on her face.

Jessie leaned against the jeep suddenly. Her knees turned to Jell-O as the adrenaline drained out of her. "You just tell us what exactly you and Roger had to do with Frank Weston." Jessie was afraid he voice would convey the nerves she was feeling.

"Weston's son had gotten into some trouble with cocaine and gambling. Roger wanted Weston to do some legal maneuvering for him, and Weston told Roger to forget it. Roger threatened to let it get out about Frank Jr.

"I didn't think old man Weston had the balls to turn Roger down. Actually, I found the aggressive side of the old guy sexy. I don't think you have any idea how powerful Roger really was," she said as she turned to Jessie and gave her an irritating Cheshire cat smile, making Jessie want to snatch her bald.

"You wouldn't have a cig, would you?" Selma purred as she batted her eyelashes provocatively at Sam. He just shook his head in answer as he motioned for her to go on.

"Well, Roger cooked up this great idea. He decided to get Frank in some, well, let's say 'compromising positions,'" The cackle of her laughter sent waves of revulsion through Jessie. "It was easier than I had expected. Roger got him to dinner one night while the little wife was on vacation, and BAM!!! Roger got some of the best shots of me he ever took!"

"What did you do with the pictures?" Sam asked.

"Roger kept all of them. Did you know Roger was an avid photographer? Yeah, he just loved taking pictures of us together. I told him to let me keep them. Roger could be such a boor sometimes. He never trusted anyone completely. I did anything he wanted of me, things little Miss Prissy would never have considered." Selma seemed to lose her bravado. "I would have done anything for him; he was the only man I ever loved."

"What did you do with the gas can you borrowed from the Flying A?" Sam asked casually.

It took Selma a minute to focus onto who was talking to her. "The gas can? I don't remember any can." The look of sadness was replaced by a quick flash of fear, "I remember now, I left it at David Cummings' place." She turned her back to Jessie and Sam for a second and spotted the shovel she and Chuck had been arguing about. "Oh my God," she whispered. "He needed gas for his generator or something.

"Look, if you want anymore questions answered I think you had better have Sheriff Boatwright look me up." She turned back around and gave them a look of defiance. "I didn't have to talk to the two of you in the first place."

Sam and Jessie watched her walk away, surprised by her sudden lack of cooperation. "I sure would like to know what that was about." Jessie looked after the woman quickly heading to the barn.

"Do you think we should talk to Chuck while we are here?" Jessie wondered out loud. "I sure would like to know why this shovel is such a big deal. You would think Chuck never handled a shovel before the way they were arguing."

"Hand me the shovel, would you, Jess?" Sam took the shovel and looked at it very carefully from top to bottom. "I just need to talk to Chuck for a few minutes."

As Jessie started to follow him to Chuck's office he motioned for her to stay, the last thing he needed was a "cat fight."

Sam's knock was answered by a defiant Selma. She started to close the door in Sam's face when she was pulled aside by Chuck. "Come on in, Sam." Chuck glared at Selma before he sent her to check on the animals in the infirmary.

"You and Selma seem to be having a hard day." Sam smiled apologetically. "Jessie and I interrupted a disagreement when we arrived, didn't we?"

"Oh, that was nothing. We disagree ever day or so on the proper handling of my equipment." Chuck nervously picked at imaginary lint on his white laboratory jacket.

"It seemed the two of you couldn't agree on exactly whose shovel it was." Sam was looking directly into Chuck's eyes, demanding a truthful answer.

Chuck was quiet for a few minutes, carefully thinking over his response to the question. "Selma insists that she doesn't know anything about the shovel. Sometimes I don't understand her." Chuck collapsed in the nearest chair he could find.

"What do you mean, Chuck?" Sam was sympathetic to Chuck's position. He was positive Chuck had nothing to do with the murder, but with Selma's revelations about her and Roger's relationship he was put right up at the top of Sam's suspect list. Sam knew love relationships made the oldest motive known to man…jealousy.

"Look, I knew all about Roger and Selma's affair. She couldn't resist throwing it up in my face. She loved seeing men grovel at her feet. I know all her bad points, but the funny thing is, it never mattered." Chuck was dry-eyed, but his voice wavered. "I knew some day she would see he was just using her and that I had more to offer her then Roger Rite."

"What do you know about the shovel?" Sam wanted this to be over. There was nothing anyone could say to change Chuck's feelings about Selma. He would just have to learn the hard way, unfortunately.

"What shovel?" Chuck was lost in his own thoughts. It was as if he had come in on the middle of a conversation and had missed the main topic.

"The shovel you and Selma were arguing about when Jessie and I arrived." Sam could see why a fast mover like Selma would become bored with a methodically precise person like Chuck.

"I'm not sure whose shovel it is. I have a problem with Selma keeping the instruments to my standards. She insists she didn't contaminate them with the shovel, but I am sure it wasn't there before she used the truck." Chuck's forehead was creased with worry lines, and Sam wasn't sure about what he had said.

"Do you remember the day Selma used your truck?" Sam knew the answer by his previous questioning of Selma. He wanted to know to what extent Chuck would go to protect her.

"Let's see. Yes, it was the day Roger and Robyn were killed." Chuck finally caught the gist of what Sam was inferring and showed some animation. "Look, Sam, you're a friend of mine, but I won't have you harassing Selma. She had nothing to do with what happened to Roger and Robyn. No one knows Selma the way I do. She isn't capable of what you are thinking." Chuck was angered by Sam's insinuation and ended the conference. "I have to get back to work now. Maybe you should leave."

"I'll take the shovel if you don't mind, Chuck." Sam had gotten enough information from Chuck to confuse the facts. Instead of removing people from his suspect list, he now had two new people to add...great!

Jessie found herself being impatient, as a child would, waiting for Sam to return. She knew she had acted very badly with Selma. After all those years of ignoring the rumors about Roger and Selma, it was more than she could stand having them thrown into her face as if Selma was the injured party!

Jessie was pulled back to reality with the clank of the shovel being dropped into the bed of the jeep. Sam was in a sullen mood as they drove toward Jessie's ranch.

"Mind if we take a quick detour to my place?"

"No, I'm dying to see your filly." Jessie felt as if she should apologize for her behavior at Dr. Smith's, but she wasn't going to apologize.

"I'll meet you at the barn if you want. I just have to run into the house for a minute and get something."

Sam stood at the door of the barn for a minute watching Jessie. He decided she was the strongest woman he had ever met. She was able to put her feelings aside, taking shock after ugly shock without breaking. He didn't know many men able to withstand what she had.

"She's a beauty, isn't she?" Sam said as he approached.

"I guess I got a little out of control back there," Jessie said, watching the filly bound to the rail at the sound of Sam's voice.

"Well, I'd say that's the biggest understatement of the century!"

Jessie remembered the look of disbelief flashing over Sam's face when she wanted to clobber Selma, and broke out laughing. "I bet you thought you were going to have to referee a fight." Her laughter startled the filly, and it started bucking and kicking in the small corral, frightened at the unfamiliar sound.

Sam couldn't resist Jessie's infectious laughter and joined her. "I had visions of bailing you out of the county jail after you were arraigned on assault charges."

"It would have been worth it just to knock that smirk off her overly made-up face!"

"It looked to me like you were getting a little jealous." Sam was the recipient of the look of anger Jessie had given Selma at Chuck's earlier. "I was just kidding!" He nervously backed away from Jessie.

Jessie was rewarded with a mock look of terror on Sam's face as she dusted her hands as if finishing a particularly loathsome job. Jessie turned with her head held high and stalked to the jeep. She didn't wait for Sam to open the door for her, but glared at him with disdain when he tried to beat her to it.

"I thought maybe we might want to stop by David Cummings' house on the way to your place." Sam cautiously tried to start the stubborn jeep. He ground the starter for several minutes and then gave the old jeep an expletive unworthy of ladylike ears. "I think we may have to walk."

"What's the matter, Sam, run out of gas? I thought you would come up with something more original than that!" Jessie felt her irritation growing.

"I guess we will have to think of some way to occupy ourselves!" Sam raised his eyebrows and pulled on his imaginary mustache in a villainous manner.

"I could just call Jake to come and get me. We aren't in the middle of the Gobi desert, you know." Jessie's anger was overcome by the easy repartee.

"Let me make you dinner first, and we can map out our day tomorrow." Sam saw Jessie draw back into her shell ever so slightly.

"Okay, but I'm heading home early, Sam." Jessie blushed deeply at the look Sam was giving her. He seemed to study every inch of her face, finding a particular interest in her mouth. She was reminded of the feeling his kisses evoked, making her insides quiver at the memory.

# Chapter Twenty-two

Jessie sat up in bed and stretched the sleep out of her body. She was remembering a lush dream. One involving Sam and herself doing delicious things, things she would have never considered doing with Roger!

The old Jessie would have been embarrassed at the thoughts she was having. The last few years with Roger had made her feel like a piece of meat. She was only something for Roger to satisfy his occasional needs, not caring if she was satisfied. *I'm through worrying about the past*, Jessie thought as she hopped out of bed and headed for the shower. She slipped out of her cotton nightgown and jumped into the shower, singing one of the new country songs she and Sam had listened to on the way home last night.

"Well, my little girl must be feeling better this morning," Estralita noted as Jessie came into the kitchen still humming the catchy tune.

"Oh, Nana, isn't this the most glorious morning you have ever seen?" Nana was right, Jessie felt like a new woman. Thoughts of Roger no longer threw her into a blue funk. She decided she would take a different tack with the kids when they came home. They would have to accept the relationship between her and Sam.

"Yes, Niña. Mr. Jake was in earlier and wondered if you could stop and see him before you and Sam leave for the day." Estralita was glad Jessie was feeling better. The children needed time to understand, but when they understood they would be happy for their mother.

Jessie gave Estralita a quick hug as she headed toward the barns. Jessie did a happy two-step to the tune she was humming as she made her way to the training barn.

Jake met Jessie coming into the barn and was surprised by her jaunty step. "So, Pearlie, things must be going okay for you this morning?" This was a question he didn't have to ask. He could see by the brightness of her eyes things were going great.

"Nana said you wanted to see me. Is everything okay with the stock?" Jessie was at once concerned by the look on Jake's face.

"Are you being careful, Jessie? Roger and Robyn's killer was clever. I don't want anything to happen to you." Jake's seriousness took a little of the wind out of Jessie's sails. She was determined to see this thing through to the end.

"Sam is with me every step of the way. Don't worry about me, I haven't felt this safe since—" Jessie thought for a minute and added, "you and Big Roger taught me how to take care of myself." she gave him a peck on his cheek and started back into the house.

"Jessie, we need some things picked up at the feed store today. I'll call in an order if you and Sam could pick it up for me," Jake called to the retreating back. Jessie waved an acknowledgment as she heard the old jeep chugging up the driveway.

"I see you got some gas," she said, smiling as she watched him jump from the jeep. Jessie noticed Sam's limp had not bothered him for some time. She was reminded of something Jake had said about Sam's residual limp being mostly physiological. She smiled at the mental picture of Jake flipping stations back and forth between "Oprah and Jessie!"

"You're very funny. I told you I wasn't out of gas. "Old Nelly" is just a little cantankerous sometimes." Sam was ready to get on with the day's work. "Let's get an early start this morning. We have a lot to do today."

"I'm ready, but I think we should take one of our rigs. It looks like "Old Nelly" could use a day off." Jessie patted the fender as she walked away from the touchy old jeep. "Jake needs us to pick up a few things from the feed store anyway."

"Well, if you insist," Sam said, sticking his hand out for the keys. "You don't mind if I drive, do you?"

"You know where we are going, so you may as well drive."

Jessie watched as Sam carefully put the shovel behind the seat. She wondered what he planned to do with it. Jessie watched Sam carefully, trying to decide what made their attraction so strong.

He is intelligent, and she had to admit he was the most attractive man she had met in 20 years. Not attractive in a traditional way, but you could tell he broke many a heart when he was young. His striking blue eyes had the effect of a hypnotist. When she was the object of their perusal, she was captured, unable to think or act rationally.

She realized her first estimate of his age was incorrect. She had been fooled by his silver-streaked hair, his weatherbeaten face, and the fact he was retired. After getting to know him she realized he was younger than the town's estimation.

She felt safe in his presence. He exuded confidence in everything he did. She knew if there was even a hint of trouble, he would take care of her.

"Jess...I said we don't have any choice but to turn this over to Boat." Sam looked at Jessie out of the corner of his eye, trying to guess what thoughts kept her occupied.

"Sorry, Sam, I wasn't listening."

"I said we are going to turn this shovel over to Boat. I have a feeling it is involved in the murder."

"Isn't that a bit of a longshot?"

"Not really. An educated guess is more like it. In two years I have never seen so much as a piece of lint on Dr. Smith's truck."

"So?"

"Selma and Chuck were fighting over who put it on the truck. One of the murder weapons was a blunt object leaving traces of dirt and manure. So, I say let's figure out whose shovel it is."

"I think you have left out something you aren't telling me."

"The only thing left out is my gut feeling, but its right more often than not."

Sam was the investigator, not her. She knew there were lots of things she had to learn. "I thought we were going to Boat's?" she asked, confused.

"David's place is on our way. I thought we would stop there first."

Sam and Jessie's arrival at David's house was greeted with David slamming the back door and stomping to his greenhouse.

"I'd say David's upset." Jessie was surprised by the usually unflappable David Cummings' show of temper.

"Everyone in town seems upset lately," Sam replied.

David was too occupied to notice Jessie and Sam as he entered his greenhouse. Sam whispered into Jessie's ear as he bent to help her out of the car. "Who is that?" He nodded toward the small woman perched on the porch, looking after David's retreating back.

"Jessie, hello!" The small woman beamed. "Agnes, look who has come to visit us!" she called over her shoulder.

Approaching the porch, Jessie noticed David's mother, Agnes, peaking around the solid little woman. "This is Sarah Hart. Sarah, Sam, I don't believe you have met our neighbor Sam Ellison."

Sarah hadn't heard the older woman approach. "Won't you come in?" she said, almost bumping into Agnes as she backed into the house. Sarah exclaimed, flushing brightly, "Agnes, you scared the bajeebees out of me! Maybe Jessica and Mr. Ellison would like some tea and some of my cookies. Did you get the ones I left at your house the other day, Jessie? I didn't receive any word—perhaps someone at your ranch might have taken them—I just left them on the stoop. I guess anyone could have taken them," Sarah muttered breathlessly.

Jessie tried to remember what Sarah was talking about. Sam noticed a twinge of irritation flash across the stocky woman's face as Jessie said, "We needed to talk to David. Maybe we could come back another time."

Agnes smiled, almost too broadly. "No, no, come in. Sarah made a special trip out to bring me some cookies. She knows how lonely I get all by myself. David doesn't seem to find time for me anymore. He is always out in his greenhouse working in dirt and God knows what else. Sarah never forgets about me. Even though I can't eat cookies since my diabetes, you understand, it's the thought that counts."

Sarah ignored the last of what Agnes said; she was already heading out the door. "I'll just run down and get David. He could probably use a break after all the time he puts in on his research. You know how these scientists are. They would forget to eat and sleep if we didn't keep track of them!" Sarah bustled out of the house before anyone could stop her.

"How have you been, Agnes?" Jessie asked. "I don't think you have met Sam Ellison."

"No. I don't get out much, you know. David is usually too busy to take me anywhere except shopping once a week. If it wasn't for Sarah visiting once and a while, I wouldn't see anyone," she added with her usual whine.

"I didn't get a chance to talk to you at the funeral, but I appreciate you and David coming," Jessie said, trying to fill the uncomfortable silence.

"That was a terrible thing to happen to poor Roger. He was such a sweet boy." Agnes remembered when Roger came to mow the lawn, and he would talk to her while she gave him lemonade. "You know Roger took care of my lawn for me when he was a teenager? He loved my lemonade. David was always too busy out in his greenhouse to join us, but Little Roger would always visit." Agnes quieted as she was pulled back to those warm summer days beneath the willow tree, sipping lemonade with Roger and listening to his amusing stories about Glynis and his father's arguments.

"I hadn't heard about Roger's enterprising days." Turning to Sam, Jessie explained, "Roger got angry at his father because he wouldn't buy Roger a car. Big Roger told him if he wanted a car he could just earn the money to buy it. To Big Roger's surprise, he did! I thought Big Roger would swallow his tongue when Roger pulled into the driveway with a 1965 Mustang, the hottest car in Silverton."

"What's so funny?" asked Sarah as she entered the kitchen. Not waiting for an answer, she went right on, "David will be right up. He had to put some things away. You know he is very particular about everything being in its proper place."

"You don't understand. I wasn't like those others. Little Roger came to my house because of me, not any money he was paid. He wouldn't even take my money." Agnes had turned red with emotion.

Sam noted Agnes following Sarah's movements about the small kitchen. He couldn't quite put his finger on the problem, but he knew there was one.

"Sarah, would you please stop puttering around? You are making me nervous!" Agnes snapped irritably.

"I just thought David would like a fresh pot of coffee to go with my cookies. They are his favorite, you know," Sarah said, full of pride. "I won three years in a row at the county fair with these cookies. Oh, look, here comes David!" Sarah hurried over to open the door for him. As Sarah hurried to open the door, she tripped over the small dog, making it yip in pain.

"Agnes, why don't you put that awful animal in the other room? You know I'm allergic to dogs," Sarah said, her usual sweet nature replaced by instant anger.

"I'm sorry, Sarah. I keep forgetting about your problem. He is so sweet I forget he is here." Agnes patted the dog and sent him into the other room. Sarah knew Agnes disliked the dog as much as she did, but she decided to let it go

Sam watched the exchange between the two women with interest. He was starting to see the problem between Agnes and Sarah: jealousy. He wondered if David was sore from being pulled both ways.

While Sarah was fussing over David like a spoiled child, Sam went directly to his questions. "I hope you don't mind answering a few questions about the day Roger and Robyn were killed." Sam made it a statement more than a question.

Jessie noticed Sarah's back stiffen a little at the mention of Robyn. Looking more closely at Agnes, she noticed the older woman had turned very solemn. Agnes was obviously jealous of Sarah's relationship to David. Jessie felt the tension in the room. David was caught in the middle of an emotional wrestling match.

Jessie watched the reactions of Sarah and Agnes while trying to listen to the conversation between David and Sam. "I'm not sure what happened. I spend the days when I'm not running the library working in the greenhouse. Had I known I would have to account for my time I would have kept a diary!" David answered, fidgeting nervously.

"Mr. Ellison isn't accusing you of anything, David." Sarah puffed up like a banty hen protecting her young. "Everyone knows you wouldn't hurt a fly!" she added, giving Sam a haughty glance.

David threw a look of disdain to Sarah, ignoring her comment, and turning his attention to Sam. "I don't know who killed Roger and Robyn. I wouldn't have let anything happen to Robyn. I loved her. I was going to ask her to marry me!" David's usual calm demeanor was sparking with agitation. "Roger Rite ruined everything he touched! We were happy until he decided to ruin it!"

Sarah's pale complexion turned to a green pallor at this admission. Agnes found glee at the remarks David was making. Her wan smile turned to a sneer as she turned to David. "I told you I wouldn't listen to that woman's name mentioned in my presence again."

Agnes snapped her fingers, and her guide dog appeared at her feet. She stood and grasped the halter. She decided to say one more thing. "I will not stand and have a wonderful man like Roger disparaged by my own son."

Sam and Jessie watched her walk stiffly out of the room. When they looked at David they were surprised by the look of scorn he was giving the retreating back.

Tears filled Sarah's eyes as she watched David's reaction to Agnes's exit. Any fool could see she was in love with David. Jessie thought they would make a good pair. They both held books in high regard, Sarah ran the library, and David managed the county bookmobile.

Although she knew part of the problem stemmed from the short leash Agnes kept David on, the other part was Sarah's overwhelming need to impress David.

This was one problem Sarah would have to overcome by herself, but Jessie decided she could give a helping hand. Like hosting a small dinner party. First thing after this mess was all cleaned up, she was going to play matchmaker.

"Selma Billings said she loaned you a gas can the day of the murders." Sam ignored the exit of David's mother as if it hadn't happened.

David got very quiet; he seemed to be mulling something over in his mind, something he either wouldn't or couldn't recall. "I seem to remember something about Selma that day, but a gas can..." He was trying to remember. "No, I don't recall her bringing a gas can."

"I'm sure if David had borrowed a gas can, he would remember it," Sarah said. "He is very careful about things like that."

"She borrowed it from the Flying A. She says you had to get some gas for your generator." Sam was trying to flick a memory.

"No, I do not remember any gas can," David said with conviction. "Selma and I don't talk much. We have different interests," David said with contempt.

"David is getting tired, I think you two should leave," Sarah said, once again pressing her imagined authority. "I'm sure he has told you everything he knows. You act like he is guilty of something."

"Sarah, will you stay out of this?" David said with exasperation. "I think I'm old enough to speak for myself."

A myriad of emotions went over Sarah's face. Jessie was surprised at the depth of feelings Sarah was showing. She went from brokenhearted to angry to sweet tempered within a few seconds.

"I know you are old enough to take care of yourself, David. You just always let everyone walk all over you. It's just like I told you with that slut Robyn." Sarah put her hand over her mouth as if to keep anything else from slipping out.

David looked as if the blood had drained from his body. "Don't you ever say that about her again! This is none of your business. It never will be and if you can't remember that maybe you should leave!"

Sarah stood, straightened her shoulders, and gave David a solemn look. "Tell Agnes I'll see her next week. I know when I've overstayed my welcome. Unlike some people," she said, glaring at Sam and Jessie. She grabbed her sun hat and wicker basket, and stiffly walked to the door. She turned to give them a piece of her mind before leaving, but decided against it.

In her nervousness, Jessie stood and went to the window to watch Sarah walk toward town. "She was just trying to help, David. Weren't you a little harsh with her?"

"She and my mother make a good pair," was all David would say on the subject.

"Maybe we could go back to the day of the murders," Sam said, unwilling to give up on the subject.

"I told you. I don't remember what happened on that day." David jumped up and started pacing the room like a caged lion. He stopped and gave Jessie a look of despair. "Okay, how can I help?"

"Just tell us everything you can."

"Robyn and I were going to be married. She was a wonderful girl; she just needed someone to give her a chance. I started helping her with some of her college papers. She was studying to be a legal secretary. She was very bright. She just needed a little help with some of her papers."

"What about her and Roger?" Jessie hated bringing up the fact that his fiancée had been having an affair with her husband. Jessie was saddened by the look of loneliness that filled David's face. She was one person that understood the pain he was feeling.

"Robyn was a little wild, but I understood her need to have fun. She was only 18. Everyone thought she was older, I know. Can't you see how special she was? She had been on her own since she was 13. Can you imagine…13?" David slumped in the overstuffed chair.

"Everything was fine until Roger decided he needed to have one more conquest. You can't blame her. She wanted the love she had never been given as a child. Who wouldn't be overwhelmed by the great Roger Rite? I would have waited for her. I knew Roger would get tired of her. He always did…she never stood a chance. Someone killed them first."

David was mentally worn out. "I bet you didn't know I'm an epileptic? No grand mal seizures, but sometimes I black out. I never know when or for how long, but that day I had a blackout. Sounds a little more than coincidental, doesn't it? Anyway, I woke up in the greenhouse, but I can't seem to remember anything abut that day." He slumped very low in the chair.

"I had been working on a new strain of orchids. I left the bookmobile at the library and went straight home without checking in at the library. I remember thinking Robyn and I could have dinner. I would try and talk her out of this craziness with Roger. She insisted on telling me every little detail of their "friendship." David had picked up one of the doilies decorating the arms of all the furniture in the room, twisting it unconcernedly. "I hated him. All he wanted was to use her. Oh, the unspeakable things he wanted her to do. I know it scared her, but by the time she leveled with me she was so embroiled in his web—I'm afraid I can't recall anything else."

"I don't think we need anymore, David. You get some rest. You look beat." Jessie wanted to get away from this cramped little house filled with morbid darkness.

David looked up, but he wasn't angry with her for opening up a wound so newly healed. "Thanks, I will," was all he could say.

The small guide dog hurried out to sit by David. Looking up at him with adoring eyes had won a small smile from the sad face. David put a hand on the head of the small dog and was awarded with a ferocious wag of its short tail.

David reached down, unlacing the weathered work boots and heaving them toward the back porch. He vowed to put them away later, lacking the energy to do more then give them a cursory glance.

Agnes crept quietly into the kitchen, stumbling over the boots carelessly deposited. "David, are you trying to kill me?" Agnes said as she barely righted herself. Irritated, she thought to herself, *You could eat off of David's floor in his greenhouse, but in my house he is nothing but a pig. His room is nothing but a garbage dump! It is rank from stale air, it is so messy; I take my life in my hands just opening the door!*

"What do you want now, Momma?" David didn't have to look at his mother to see the look of disdain.

# Chapter Twenty-three

"Talk about a weird group," Sam said as he helped Jessie into the air. "I feel sorry for David. Those two vultures are trying to pull him apart."

"I feel sorry for all of them. They all seem starved for love. It does strange things to people when they need love so desperately." Jessie thought of Roger. It seemed as if all the love in the world wasn't enough. He had always craved more.

"Jessie, all the problems of the world do not belong on your shoulders. You have a right to a little happiness of your own." It was if Sam could read her mind.

"Jake needs us to pick up an order at the feed store." Jessie felt as if she needed a diversion. The upheaval of the Cummings household brought back too many unhappy memories.

"Great, it will give us a chance to talk to the Billings sisters," Sam said. He would have never believed any of the stories circulating about their special relationship if he hadn't read Roger's journal.

He was sympathetic to their situation. It was difficult for homosexuals in large metropolitan areas, let alone in a small rural area like Delaney County.

The two "sisters" had taken a nearly bankrupt business and added hard work and determination, turning it into one of the most successful concerns in town.

"You're being very quiet suddenly." Jessie wondered what was happening in Sam's head.

"I was just thinking about the Billings' feed store. It took a lot of guts for them to summarily dismiss Roger's offer. They took a chance of losing everything they have accomplished in the last few years."

"The two have won the respect of the entire county. I like to think the people of Delaney County have more compassion than they are given credit for." Jessie was thinking of her reaction to the rumors Tracy and Jennifer were not really sisters. She had no experience with homosexuals on a personal basis. She had expected to feel revulsion, but she had been raised to appreciate the rights of others by Jake.

She watched with admiration as Tracy and Jennifer went on as if they weren't the main topic of the county gossip mills. They minded their own business, let the rumors fly, and continued working as if nothing out of the ordinary was happening.

A hard work ethic was the mainstay of farming communities, and the acceptance of the community was soon evident. Business picked up instead of falling off, and they were treated by most of the community as if nothing had changed. Most of the nation thought of this region as filled with redneck hotheads. Jessie was filled with pride at the amount of compassion showed by her neighbors and friends.

"I think you should talk to Tracy and Jennifer. They might feel more like opening up to you." Sam knew it was a fine line between asking a few friendly questions and interrogation with the sensitive situation in which they found themselves.

"I'm not sure I know the right questions to ask." Jessie was nervous at the thought of confronting them with her knowledge.

"You'll do fine. Just go with your feelings. Basically all we want to know is if they had the opportunity to commit the murders. They are not high priority on my list of suspects, but they have a motive, no matter how slight." Sam remembered with revulsion Roger's notations next to their names.

Roger was not a person to take rejection lightly. He had made a notation to ruin them and if he hadn't been killed would probably be working to that objective right now. Sam was curious what type of rejection prompted the vendetta Roger planned.

Sam backed to the loading dock after he dropped Jessie off at the front of the store. He figured they may be more likely to talk to Jessie if she was alone.

Jessie wandered around the store, marveling at the ever-growing array of stock. Jessie was intrigued by the variety of things available since the sisters took over. She wanted to make sure there weren't any other customers when she talked to the sisters. She still thought of them as sisters and figured she would as long as she knew them.

"Interested in adding some birds to your stock?"

Jessie jumped as if she had been stung by a bee. "Tracy, you shouldn't sneak up on a person. You could give them a heart attack!" Jessie said, patting her chest as if she needed CPR.

"Sorry, I didn't realize you were obsessed with birds. Was there any particular type interesting you?" Tracy found Jessie's behavior strange.

"Jessie, it's good to see you," Jennifer said as she entered the storefront with a clipboard in her hand. "Did Jake hire a new hand?" Jennifer asked as she motioned to Sam as he followed her through the door.

"No. Sam's just giving me a hand." Jessie raised her eyebrows in confusion. She hadn't had time to ask any questions. There were customers coming in and out of the store, halting any chance of Jessie bringing the topic around to the night of the murders.

By the time Jennifer had the order filled and logged in Jessie's account, the store was empty except for Jessie and Sam. "How have you been, Jennifer?" Sam asked. "I haven't seen you since the fire at The Lanes." It was a little blunt, but Sam knew they had to get to the point while they had a chance.

"I'm fine. I didn't see you there, but I was pretty busy. I hear you have a new filly at your place." Jennifer had read Theda's article in the paper and figured Sam's presence a little more than a coincidence.

"I didn't see Tracy at The Lanes." Sam found himself becoming a little edgy. Sam wasn't intimidated by many people, but Jennifer had a way of watching you as if she knew your every thought.

"No, she was out of town that week. Her mother was in the hospital and one of us had to stay and take care of business." Jennifer had let slip about their 'mother.' She flushed slightly at the recognition in Sam's eyes but hoped he would let it pass.

She didn't care if everyone in the world knew about their secret relationship, but Tracy was not ready to come out of the closet. It was the reason they had moved to Silverton. Tracy's family wasn't ready to admit the truth about their daughter. They preferred to think it was a strictly business relationship, and Jennifer agreed to keep it that way.

"I appreciate your kindness after the funeral. I just didn't feel up to anything, let alone cooking, and your goodies came in very handy," Jessie said, trying to get to the end of this conversation.

"I remember when Dad died, Mom didn't feel like doing anything but sitting around and staring out the window. I learned how to cook during the year after Dad died. Mom just couldn't make herself do much more than look at old albums and stare into space."

Jessie felt as if she was intruding on a painful memory. "I didn't realize your father was dead," Jessie said as she looked at Jennifer for an answer.

Tracy looked wide-eyed at Jennifer, and Jennifer look sadly at Tracy. She didn't want to go on with this farce any longer, and she knew what Sam and Jessie were hinting at but were too polite to say out loud.

Tracy gave a barely perceptible nod to Jennifer's silent plea. "I don't want to seem rude, Jessie, but do you want to get to the point of this conversation? Perhaps it's just a matter of curiosity. Are you trying to see if the rumors circulating around town are true?" Jennifer felt an anger rising she hadn't felt since coming to Silverton.

Roger was a vile contemptible man. He didn't rate her anger, but Jessie was different. She had treated them no differently after the rumors then before. Jennifer didn't know whether to be sad or angry!

The door tinkled as another customer entered. Tracy went to wait on them while Jennifer remained to answer Jessie's questions.

"Maybe we could go into your office," Jessie asked.

Jennifer looked to the smiling face of her lover and decided discretion was the better part of valor. She nodded and led the way to the office. She offered them a chair but remained standing. Sam smiled at how well Jennifer was taking the offensive stance by such a subtle move. It was one reason why she was a successful businesswoman.

"Let's get this over with. I need to get back to work," Jennifer said civilly.

"Roger left a journal," Jessie stated flatly. "He wasn't very pleased with you for some reason."

Jennifer's anger suddenly flowed out of her as a broad smile broke out on her classic features. "I would say that was an understatement!" Suddenly relaxed, Jennifer walked around the invoice-covered desk and settled comfortably into the large office chair. When she realized the real reason behind Sam and Jessie's visit she relaxed and the anger flowed out of her.

"Why did he want to ruin your business with Tracy?" Jessie couldn't figure why Roger would care if Tracy and Jennifer were sisters or lovers.

"What makes you think he wanted to ruin our business?" Jennifer asked, traces of her smile still remaining around her lips.

"He wrote in his journal, not in the most glowing terms, his feelings about you and Tracy. He promised to ruin the two of you." Jessie felt embarrassment at sharing her husband's intentions.

"He found out about us, 'how' doesn't really matter, and felt we might be able to use our 'specialty,' as he so quaintly put it, to work for him." Jennifer shivered at the memory as if a chill breeze suddenly passed through the office.

"It was as if no one had ever told him no before in his life." Jennifer remembered the day as if it were yesterday. Roger smugly sauntered into the office. When he brought up the topic of Jennifer and Tracy's relationship, Jennifer envisioned him as the sheriff in an old spaghetti western. "Be out of town by sundown!" was often the ultimatum. She was appalled by his proposition.

She wasn't prepared for the temper tantrum that ensued. Roger ranted and raved about the depravity of her relationship and how he would make it his life's goal to ruin her life.

Jennifer laughed at him and told him to do his worst, that she knew how to start over, she had done it more than once in her lifetime. This was when Tracy came in to find out what all the confusion was about. Roger had an uncanny ability to ferret out the soft spot in business negotiations, and he automatically pinpointed Tracy's soft spot, her family.

Pointing to Tracy while he glared at Jennifer, he threatened to make sure everyone knew what kind of life they led; families included.

"I would have gladly killed him if he had made good on his word. I don't know what kind of a poker player your husband was, but I decided to call his bluff. Who knows, maybe he just didn't have time to follow through on his threats or then again maybe he never intended to. I don't care. I'm just glad he won't be able to hurt anyone anymore!" As Jennifer watched Jessie's reaction to her story, there was no remorse in her eyes.

"Thanks, Jennifer. You'll send the bill as usual, won't you?" Jessie wouldn't blame her if she refused to ever do business with them again.

"Sure. By the way, Jessie, I don't blame you or your family for Roger's behavior. Your family has always treated us well. You can't help what your husband was." Jennifer stood up and put her hand out to shake Jessie's.

The two women looked at each other for a few seconds, trying to think of the right thing to say. Each decided enough had already been said.

Jessie was sickened by the deviant her husband was, but one thing she knew, he had been told no in more ways than one! Big Roger's favorite word to Roger had been an emphatic "No!" Glynis silently reinforced Big Roger's behavior by her negative attitude toward everyone that Roger grew close to emotionally.

Jessie met Sam in the truck after talking to Jennifer. He looked at her questioningly. She just shook her head as she jumped into the seat beside Sam.

"I think we can strike their names off of our lists." She wasn't ready to share Jennifer's revelations about her husband with Sam. It was making her wonder if there was anyone in the state of Colorado without a reason to murder Roger.

"Where do we go now, Sam?" Jessie was hoping he would say the day's chores were over.

"We are going to go talk to Boat," Sam said, matter-of-factly.

Jessie thought of objecting, but in her heart she trusted Sam, and she knew he would not do anything to jeopardize her family.

"Sam, I know I'm new at this, but I don't see how listening to the agony Roger spread will help us find the answer." Jessie was saddened and confused after listening to Jennifer's story.

"I look at these mysteries as puzzles. Sometimes some of the pieces look the same, so you keep turning them until you find where they belong.

Driving to Marge and Boat's gave Jessie time to realize she had a lot of things yet to learn about investigation. She tried and tried, but the only persons she could be sure were innocent were Jake, Sam and herself.

She found reasons to find every one of her suspects guilty. One thing she knew, everyone in Roger's journal couldn't have murdered him. As they drove up she noticed the patrol car was gone, probably meaning Boat wasn't home. Marge stepped onto the porch at the sound of the truck pulling up and gave them a friendly wave. Jessie had missed her friend. It seemed like years instead of days since they had seen each other.

Marge watched Jessie and Sam approach the porch, thinking what an attractive pair they made. Boat would be furious if she mentioned it, so she would have to keep her opinion to herself for now!

"Hi, guys! What mischief are you to up to today?" Marge was still congratulating herself on her perception about people. Here was the most attractive couple to hit Silverton since—well, since she and Boat arrived! Smiling to herself, she greeted them. "Come in and let me get you something cold to drink." She noticed Sam looking around for the car. "I expect Boat home at any time. He had to go to the state offices."

"Does it have anything to do with Roger's case?" Jessie asked impatiently.

"He didn't say, but he didn't expect it to take him very long. Come in and get cooled off." Marge tried to keep the subject off Roger's case. "Well, Sam, what have you been up to? We haven't seen you since the funeral. I thought you were going to come over for dinner. I haven't had a good game of gin rummy since I let you beat me last time."

"Like you would let anyone bet you! I was lucky last time. Doesn't Boat get tired of you beating the pants off him?" Marge was known county-wide for her luck at cards.

"We needed to talk to Boat about the investigation." Jessie figured Marge knew everything about the investigation. They were partners in every sense of the word.

"They have pretty much run into a blind alley on it from what Boat tells me. The coroner's report came back, but with very little more than the preliminary report. Boat can tell you about it when he gets home."

"Boat can tell you what?" Boat said as he opened the door on the threesome.

Marge went right to the point, "Jessie and Sam are wondering what news there is about the investigation."

"From what I hear, you two can tell me," Boat said as he hung his hat and coat on the hall tree. "As for the state's investigation, it seems to have come to an end."

"Marge tells us there isn't much news from the coroner," Sam stated bluntly.

"Well, you met the coroner at the scene; did you really expect him to give us any information?"

Sam shrugged his shoulders and stood to leave. "I wish you two would let me in on your investigation," Boat said, mostly to Sam.

Jessie turned white at the mention of sharing their information. She knew if the state got a hold of Roger's journal it would be all over the newspaper in no time. "Please don't ask, Boat," Jessie pleaded.

"Our friendship means a lot to me, Jessie. Perhaps you should consider the fact I might be of help to you." Boat had put his hand on Jessie's shoulder soothingly. "You are going to have to trust me sooner or later."

"Boat, I'm afraid of what the newspapers will do with all of this," Jessie said quietly.

"I'm not going to promise I won't give this information to the state investigators. I can't help it. If they ask me, I'll have to give it to them. But only if they ask," Boat said seriously, with just the hint of a smile. "I'm not sure they would know how to use it anyway."

Jessie looked from Boat to Marge and then to Sam. Sam gave Jessie an encouraging smile and nodded his head to affirm what Jessie wanted to do.

"I think Sam should tell you what we have," Jessie surrendered.

"Jessie and I will make dinner while the two of you talk." Jessie started to argue, but Marge just grabbed her hand and towed her into the kitchen.

"I need to call Jake to let him know we won't be home for dinner," Jessie said, giving up to the ministering of her friend.

Marge quickly added the few things needed to extend the dinner while she and Jessie talked about the activities at the Rite place.

She knew about the kids going to camp; everyone in the county did. She was sad to learn Sam and Jessie's relationship had warranted the change of plans.

"They are good kids, they'll come around. They love you and with a little time and distance they'll accept Sam."

Jessie had heard this common theme enough times she should be tiring of it, but it gave her encouragement to hear it one more time. Marge put Jessie to work setting the table for the four. Jessie found the mindless chore relaxing. The comfort of a familiar kitchen made her feel like things could some day return to normal.

Sam and Boat walked into the kitchen to inquire about our dinner. The smells from the kitchen made their stomachs growl in hunger. Jessie always had a hearty appetite, but everyone was hungry this evening.

\*\*\*

On the way home, Jessie was as content as a newborn babe relaxing in the comfortable seat of the large pickup. "I'm relieved Boat knows what is going on," Jessie sighed.

"Looks like a storm is coming up," he noted. "It seems kind of late for a spring storm."

"Oh, sometimes thunderstorms hit this time of year. I love summer thunderstorms! There is so much pent-up energy breaking loose." Just as Jessie said this, a bolt of lightning crossed the sky, followed by crashing thunder. "That's the way I feel lately."

"I'm glad you didn't ask for a cyclone," Sam said, chuckling.

The wind was blowing by the time they had gotten home, but the rain was holding off.

"Do you want to come in and weather the storm by the fireplace?" Jessie asked, holding her collar up against the wind.

"Yes...but I have to check on the new filly before I go to bed," Sam said. Sam didn't know if he should resent the look of relief flittering across Jessie's face. Once again he told himself to be patient. She was newly widowed!

\*\*\*

Tortured screams woke the restless figure. Shivering, heart racing, the figure realized who the scream belonged to. It's nightclothes damp with perspiration, the memory of the dream was hard to shake. Rushing into the living room, it realized the wind was blowing rain through an open window, causing the chill in the small house.

"Momma, I had that terrible dream again!" Quickly rocking back and forth as if to outrun the memories, it said, "Someone was chasing me and there was nowhere to run."

The starkness of the room reminded the shaking figure of that other time, that other place. The frightening vision was slowly vanishing. The rocking slowed as the heart beats returned to normal amid dry sobs of loneliness.

The sky brightened as the lightening streaked and the thunder crashed causing the lone figure to cringe in horror. Lightening illuminated the figure rocking in the darkened living room. "Momma, make the dreams go away!" the figure begged, looking blankly out of the window at the raging storm.

# Chapter Twenty-four

Jessie watched as the old jeep was lit up by another flash of lightening. She hurried into the house as the first raindrops fell to the dry ground with loud plops that made little puffs of dust in the dry dirt.

Jessie stopped at the porch to watch Sam's old jeep chug down the driveway. The moon peaked through a break in the clouds, suggesting the worst of the storm was yet to appear. The moisture quickly evaporated in the unusual warmth of the spring evening, making Jessie think perhaps the storm would not materialize.

The still heaviness of the air felt as if it could be cut with a knife. The air was so full of electricity that the hair on your arms stood on end; everything Jessie touched made sparks fly like an arc welder working in a dark garage.

Jessie watched the light show put on by the thunder and lightning. As it drew to an end she watched the clouds roll away, leaving the smiling face of the moon winking back at her. She waved happily. "Good night, old man!"

Jessie felt exhausted. She was glad Estralita usually turned in early. Tiptoeing to her room, she pulled off her clothes and slipped under the cool sheets.

Jessie drifted off, remembering how she and the kids would watch the lightning rolling up and down their little valley. The kids would clap in glee as if it were a better show then the Fourth of July fireworks. She hoped the kids had seen the storm. She felt a great deal of comfort thinking they may have been watching the same scene she had just witnessed. She wondered if they were missing her as much as she was missing them. Jessie stretched sleepily and fell into a deep slumber.

Outside, Mother Nature had decided she wasn't finished with the light show, gathering the clouds together to add another act to the already spectacular show. Gathering clouds made Jessie stir restlessly in her sleep, a private storm of her own building.

*** 

Jessie heard the sound of approaching hoof beats. Turning, she glimpsed a galloping steed pounding toward her. She was drawn toward the magnificent animal. A flash of lightning and suddenly she was astride a magnificent winged horse, flying over the green pastures of the homestead. Beneath them were clouds so white they appeared to be giant cotton balls.

She felt free, at ease, bounding from one fluffy cloud to the next. Faster they went and the clouds began to change from white to silver. Immediately they turned to the ominous black of impending storm clouds. Streaking lightning broke around them, the thunder deafening, and fearfully they raced to outrun the storm.

A bright flash of light filled Jessie with fear. The smooth, confident gait of her steed changed as the frightened animal swayed and bucked, terrified of the slashes of light and thunderous crashes of the storm. Jessie felt herself falling out of the sky, slowly tumbling toward the ground. Closer to the ground her attention was drawn to a fiery glow beneath her.

Drawn to the fire, she felt her anguish increase. Her attention was drawn to a figure in front of the fire, dancing and clapping its hands in glee.

At Jessie's scream the figure turned in her direction, no longer a spirit filled with glee, but a demon outlined by the raging of the fire. Jessie strained to recognize the figure as it melted into the raging fire. Its clothing and hair whipped wildly by the raging force of the fire, making identity impossible.

Realizing it had been seen, the figure began to float toward Jessie. Hands, outstretched, grasped Jessie, pulling her into the fire.

Crashing thunder wiped the images from Jessie's mind, shocking her awake.

*** 

Jessie realized she was sitting safely in her bed, grasping the comforter closely in an attempt to dispel the terrifying images that filled her semi-consciousness. The resurgence of the storm cooled the summer night, causing her damp nightclothes to cling uncomfortably to her sweating body. Jessie knew if she could recognize the image in her dreams they would no longer invade her sleep. She was sure she would be one more step closer to finding the answer to Roger's murder.

Jessie waited for her breathing to return to normal. She went over in her mind for the umpteenth time what had happened the night Roger died.

The memory of the nightmare made her claustrophobic. The need for fresh air was so strong she wanted to be away from the walls closing in on her. Exasperated, she reached for the locket she had worn for so many years. How did she lose it so close to the murder scene?

She felt loneliness at the loss; it had been like a talisman to her. In good times she felt it brought her luck, at bad times she felt encompassed in its protective shield. Trying to understand why Sam thought it was a bad idea to wear it, she followed his advice and kept it in her jewelry box, away from prying eyes.

Breathing deeply to relax herself, she pulled the comforter close to her chin, willing herself back to sleep. The next thing she knew it was morning and the birds twittered cheerfully. The day broke with the freshness that follows a summer storm. The morning breeze was fresh and cool; the sun beamed brightly, predicting a warm day.

Jessie stretched enjoying the comfort of her bed. She knew she needed to get up, but the nightmare kept her awake most of the night, and she was still a little groggy from the lack of sleep. Hearing subtle rustlings from the kitchen caught her attention, and the smell of the fresh-brewed coffee sent her an invitation she couldn't resist.

Estralita was surprised to see Jessie come to the kitchen dressed in her robe. Her usual morning ritual was to shower, dress for her day, then have her first cup of coffee.

Observing Jessie's youthful features marred by dark circles under her eyes, she tried to perk up the younger woman. "Good morning, Pearlie," Estralita said cheerfully. "Did you see the letters?"

"Are they from the kids?" Jessie asked, hoping they had finally written. "I was so tired I just went straight to bed without going through the mail."

"Yes," Estralita answered, frowning at the thought of her little girl working so hard. Pulling them from her apron pocket and handing them to Jessie, she explained, "I knew you would want to read them with your coffee."

"Oh, Nana, I'm afraid to read them. What if they are still angry?" Jessie felt like a little child again asking for permission from her Nana.

"Don't worry, Pearlie. They love you and couldn't stay angry long. They just had to get some distance to sort out their feelings," Estralita said, giving Jessie a quick hug of encouragement.

Jessie quickly opened Cristal's letter.

> *Dear Mom,*
>
> *Sorry I haven't written sooner, but we have been so busy with lessons I just haven't had time. Everything is going great, but I still miss everyone like crazy.*
>
> *How is Hoppy doing? I hope he remembers Jordan and me when we get home. My classes are going great. The instructors make us work very hard, but it is worth it. We work very hard every day, and the trainers have done wonders with Silver Belle. I hope you aren't mad I wanted to come to Greensford. I just didn't think I could stay at the ranch this summer without Daddy being there. I'm looking forward to spending the Fourth of July with everyone. Can we still have the barbecue this year?*
>
> *I hope Mr. Ellison can come. I think he is really nice. I'm sorry I acted like such a baby. I've been thinking, and I know you wouldn't like him if he wasn't nice. See you when I get home. I love you and miss you.*
>
> *Your daughter, Cristal*

Jessie turned to Jordan's a little more cautiously. His was a little longer then Cristal's, but a little more antiseptic. He avoided any mention of what had transpired prior to going to camp and any questions about how the investigation was going. He also was curious about how Hoppy was progressing and looked forward to seeing him when he came home for the Fourth of July.

It was full of antidotes about the kids at camp. He was obviously as taken with this year's campers as he had been for the last three years working at Camp Sakawa. He and the other counselors had become friends after working together for several years, and he mentioned they had known about his dad's death, but thankfully didn't do more then offer their condolences.

He sent regards to Sam, hoping his filly was coming along all right. He asked if Sam would be available to come to camp on closing day with Jessie and Jake. Perhaps if he didn't mind he could tell some of the campers about his days in the DEA. The smaller kids had built him into some kind of hero, and Jordan was nervous about asking Sam himself.

Jessie wiped the tears from her eyes as she handed the letters to Estralita. "I am so lucky to have such wonderful kids. I think Jordan has even softened a little. He didn't say so, but it's so like him. He wondered how Sam's little filly was doing; maybe it's his way of apologizing."

"I knew my niños would come around," Estralita said through watery eyes.

"What's the matter?" Jake asked as he entered the kitchen.

"The kids wrote. They want to come home for the Fourth of July!" Jessie still couldn't believe they were coming home. "They want to have the barbecue."

"Well, I better get the boys started on barbecue pits. Do you have time to get things together for a big feed, Estralita?" Jake asked as he started in on the breakfast set in front of him.

"I think we should ask the townspeople this year," Jessie said, starting the guest list in her head. A plan was forming in the back of her mind to get to the bottom of Roger's murder. The more she thought about the idea, the more she like it.

Jessie looked down at her robe. She remembered she and Sam had several places to go today. Gulping down the last of her coffee, she hurried to get ready.

"Mr. Jake, do you think this is such a good idea to have a fiesta this soon after Roger's death?" Estralita asked, an unusually hard expression on her face.

"I think it's a great idea. We have lived under dark clouds for long enough. After Big Roger and Glynis's accident, Roger stopped having the barbecues. I think now is as good a time to start as any. These kids need to have their lives return to normal, and as soon as possible. People will talk no matter what, so we may as well get our lives started," Jake answered, putting a stop to further conversation on the subject.

The doorbell stopped any reply from Estralita, although she had quite a bit to say on the subject. Jake could tell she thought it wasn't proper to have such festivities so close after Roger's death.

"Señor Sam, hello, Jessica is running a little late this morning, but she will be out soon. Jake is having breakfast; can I get some breakfast for you while you wait?"

The little woman's force of personality ended any thought Sam may have had about disagreeing with her. Sam could get used to her cooking very quickly. Even though he had lived on his own most of his life, he never seemed to get the knack of cooking. Too many late night stakeouts; it was easier to grab a burger or stop at a taco bar. Breakfast usually consisted of donuts and coffee.

The marvelous aromas coming from the sizzling pan whetted Sam's appetite, making his mouth literally water. He was soon thinking of nothing but the grumbling of his belly.

Sam's eyes widened at the platter of fried potatoes, eggs and a large slab of ham, followed by a plate of fresh buttermilk biscuits. Sam was getting spoiled rotten. He hoped, no matter what, that these wonderful meals would never end.

Jessie walked into the kitchen and was amused at the vigor with which Sam was attacking his plate. She liked seeing him sit at her table in the mornings. Part of her was saddened by the thought he would not be joining her and Jake anymore.

"Would you like more coffee, Pearlie?" Estralita noticed the affection with which Jessie looked at Sam. She missed the boy she helped raise, but she couldn't begrudge Jessie the happiness she saw shining in her eyes.

"No thanks, Nana, I'll just wait for Sam to finish his food. I can talk to him while he eats. If I can get his attention away from his breakfast!" She smiled.

Sam just smiled and nodded his head at her to let her know he heard, but didn't stop eating long enough to answer.

"I have good news; I got letters from the kids today. They are looking forward to coming home for the Fourth of July. I think they are getting over their anger." Jessie smiled at the look of surprise on Sam's face. "They especially mentioned the fact they were looking forward to seeing "Mr. Ellison."

"You're kidding!" Sam said, finally interested in something besides his food. "I figured they would be happy to never see me again."

"I told you they just needed time to adjust," Jessie said, looking around as Jake and Estralita said in unison, "*You* told him?"

"Okay, so I was a little worried, but at least they are softening up." Jessie smiled.

"We used to have the greatest barbecues! Practically everyone in the county came. It was weeks of hard work to get one ready, but it was always worth it," Jessie said, reminiscing abut the great times.

Sam was watching Estralita's reaction to what Jessie was saying and was confused at the scowl covering the usually cheerful face. He knew it couldn't be the work because Estralita was the hardest worker he had ever known. She was always busy at one thing or the other, and the scowl concerned him.

Jake noted Sam's reaction and commented, "Estralita is from the old school. She thinks the mourning period was a little short. I tried to tell her times and people change, but she doesn't see it that way."

"Whatever Jessie wants, I will do. I know I'm just an old lady with different ways, but I hope we won't regret this." With a derisive sniff she left the room.

"Maybe Nana's right," Jessie said, wondering if it was such a great idea after all.

"You just get the invitations sent. Estralita and I will handle the rest of the festivities." Jake patted Jessie's back as he headed out the door. "Don't worry, I'll take care of Estralita."

Sam got up and cleared the table, rinsing off the dishes and stacking them in the dishwasher. Jessie started to chastise him, but he had told her this was the least he could do to repay the kindness of feeding him. It was just one more way Sam differed from Roger. Her husband had no reason to give thanks; in his mind he deserved everything he ever got.

"I thought the barbecue might be a good time to get our suspects together." Jessie was a little nervous. She wasn't sure Sam would like the idea.

Sam was quiet for several minutes, thinking over the idea. "I like it. We want to be sure that we don't tip our hand. I think this could work very nicely."

She was pleased she had come up with the idea. She started going over her list of guests.

"Well, I guess we should get started on our way," Sam suggested.

Jessie grabbed her purse and her note pad. "I want to stop and talk to Jake before we go." Heading toward the barns, they were greeted by a friendly wave from Jake.

"I thought you two would be on your way already," Jake said.

"I wanted to talk to you before we leave. Do you think we should go pick up the kids or make plans for them to fly home?"

Jake figured the kids would fly home. "I think we should leave that up to them. Cristal only has a few weeks left at the ranch. The drive home takes quite a while. She would just as soon fly, probably. It sounds like the kids miss you. If it was me, I would suggest flying."

"I guess I need to call them." Jessie felt the anxiety growing in her chest.

"I'm sure they would love to hear from you," Jake added softly.

That was the thing Jessie was hoping to hear from her father. She had been insecure around them since they made up their minds to go away for the summer. She missed them and felt guilty when she realized she didn't think of them every minute of the day. Especially when Sam was with her.

"I think I have an old guest list, so it won't be hard to come up with this year's list. Sam and I are going up to Wagon Wheel Gap today. We need to talk to the Sandersons. I don't want to leave anyone out."

Jessie was determined to make this year's barbecue a success, in more ways than one. Both Sam and Jessie were preoccupied with their thoughts on the way up to the old ghost town. Jessie was making plans for the barbecue, and she knew that Sam would like to be there.

Jessie's most difficult plans were the entertainment. She knew there would be people of all ages and interests. She wanted to plan activities for everyone's interest, no matter their age.

She was glad the ranch overlooked the small town of Silverton. The fireworks planned would be enjoyed by everyone, whether they were able to attend or not. She hoped the guest's would enjoy the display and stay to dance long into the night. The floor of the ranch house would be cluttered with the sleeping forms of children waiting for the "old folks" to get tired.

She remembered the first barbecue she ever attended. She had never seen so many people in one place in all her life. It looked like a carnival had come to the ranch...

There were pony rides for the small children. She remembered the squeals of delight as the children picked their favorite pony to spend the day playing with. There were carnie games for the teenagers to practice their skills. Many would try to win a stuffed animal or a Cupid doll for their sweetheart.

The adults enjoyed the portable dance floor and stage with a live band playing throughout the day and late into the night. Everyone got into the mood and kept the dance floor busy. When the band took a break to wet their throats and fill their bellies, young wannabe performers filled in. They weren't professionals, but no one cared as long as there was music to kick up their heels to.

The barbecue pits were filled with everything from whole pigs to slabs of beef to dozens of chickens. Everything was drowned in Estralita's famous barbecue sauce and cooked to perfection under the watchful eye of the small woman.

There were hamburgers and hot dogs galore to fill the empty stomachs growling for substance while everyone awaited the slow-cooking roasts. One pit was saved for fresh corn on the cob and baked potatoes. Tables were heaped with the salads, casseroles and other goodies contributed by the guests. Watermelons cooled in barrels of ice water, waiting to be sliced.

Even Glynis seemed to enjoy the get-togethers. She sat in the shade and was regaled with respect from the citizenry of Delaney County.

Everyone commented on how cleverly she handled the responsibility of such a large gathering. True to Glynis, she took full credit for the smooth running of the barbecue. She never gave any credit to all those who worked hard to make it the gala event.

Thinking of the fun ahead, Jessie shivered in anticipation. Hugging herself, she smiled at the thought of her family being together again.

"You look like the cat that ate the canary. What are you thinking about?" Sam asked.

"I was just remembering the first barbecue I ever attended. We had only been at the ranch for a little while. I was still awed by the servants and the luxury surrounding everyone at the big house.

"The horses lived in better standards than most of the people we knew. Jake was a very successful trainer, but mother was happy living quietly. We had a small, cozy ranch-style home. Most of the money Jake made went into the stables.

"I remember the strength of their love. When they were together the air vibrated with emotion barely held in rein. I was young when my mother died, but I still remember how devastated Jake was by his loss."

"He didn't lose everything. He still has you. When we first met all he ever talked about was you. Jessica this and Jessica that. I assumed you would be spoiled rotten from living in the lap of luxury and having someone like Jake dote on you." Sam regretted the thoughts he had about her.

"Everyone thinks money is everything. Roger was proof that it wasn't. Money never made him happy. Now I see he had plenty more then I knew about." Jessie withdrew into her shell, trying to understand what happened to Roger.

Topping the hill, Wagon Wheel Gap spread out below them. There was a bustling hive of activity. Everyone thought the Sandersons were crazy when they bought the rights to the used-up silver mine, including the rights to the ghost town. All along they were planning to turn it into a tourist attraction.

Jessie was drawn back into the Old West the closer they came to the station. The effectiveness of the town was controlled by the park & ride facility. Every visitor was treated to a stagecoach ride back into the Old West.

It took the Sanderson's five years to get the town in full swing. They had every right to be proud of the job they had done. Now they had a waiting list of employees, mostly gathered from nearby colleges. The hotel was booked a year in advance. They were working on a dude ranch to help with accommodations. Lots of people in Silverton were eating crow on this one!

"It seems perfect. Don Sanderson runs the bank in Wagon Wheel Gap. I know everyone buys their funny money to spend in town, but why would he allow Roger to run dirty money through the town?" Jessie asked.

"Roger has a way of making sure people do what he wants them to do. If he could get Frank Weston ensconced in his dirty work, I'm sure Don Sanderson was easy pickings." Sam tried to soothe Jessie.

Sam parked the car and helped Jessie out of her seat. Before they could get settled on the station bench, the coach pulled up and offered them a ride.

The dust flew as they pulled away from the station. The horses moved at a fast clip on the trip to town. Jessie was thrilled at the thought of getting one more step closer to the end of their search.

They stopped right in front of the bank; Sam took Jessie's elbow as they stepped from the coach and headed into the bank. Don looked up as the door opened and was visibly shaken by their entrance. "Mrs. Rite, what a pleasure to see you," he stuttered.

Jessie could tell by the look on his face the pleasure wasn't his. "Thank you, Don." The smile Jessie had pasted on her face was starting to ache. "Sam and I would like to talk to you, if you don't mind."

"I'm afraid I haven't met your friend," Sanderson said, flushing a bright red trying to change the subject.

"I'm sorry. This is Sam Ellison," Jessie replied. She could tell by the derisive statement that he had probably read Theda Reams gossip column.

"I'm kind of busy right now." Sanderson had a hard time pretending he was busy.

"We can discuss this right here, or we can go into your office. The choice is yours." Sam didn't think Sanderson was guilty of murder, but he could see he was guilty of something.

Sanderson looked cautiously around; people were beginning to stare, the last thing he wanted. He had been able to keep a low profile since Rite's murder and was relieved that no one was trying to take up were Roger Rite had left off.

Jessie watched Sanderson shuffle papers from stack to stack on his desk, unsuccessfully looking occupied. Sam clearing his throat made Sanderson stop his fiddling.

"I don't know what you have come here about." Sanderson's usual pallor was replaced by a flush of embarrassment.

"Do you know something about what happened to my husband?" Jessie blurted out.

"I didn't even know your husband, Mrs. Rite. I heard what happened, and I'm sorry, but I was not involved." Sanderson felt his stomach lurch nervously.

"Look, Don, I don't want to cause any problems for you. I just want to find out what happened to my husband." Jessie felt her pulse quicken slightly.

"What makes you think I know what happened to your husband?"

"We have his journal. We haven't turned it over to the authorities—yet," Jessie said, her temper beginning a slow burn.

"Look, Mr. Sanderson, we just want to know what you know about Roger's murder." Sam could see Jessie's temper was about to erupt.

"What the hell. He can't hurt me now." Sanderson sighed. "I never planned to let things get so out-of-hand. He offered to pay a considerable amount for access to the gaming room after hours."

"What did he use them for?" Jessie knew the answer.

"He had friends needing somewhere to play. I needed some money to tide us over some hard times. I didn't think it would become so involved. The more I complained the more he enjoyed my discomfort."

"What does that have to do with laundering dirty money?" Sam didn't feel like going through a song and dance.

Sanderson jerked to attention. "Don't you see? He would get you so involved you had to do what he wanted; he had no morals. The parties went from a poker game to every kind of action his degenerate friends wanted. By the time I'd had enough, I was so intertwined in his dirty tricks I couldn't get out." Sanderson sat with a wry smile on his face. "Now I suppose I will have to do your dirty work." He looked straight at Jessie.

"I want nothing to do with any of Roger's dirty work. Perhaps you got tired of Roger and decided you had enough?" Jessie knew they had come up against another stonewall.

"You can't pin this on me. I was in Durango getting supplies to open Wagon Wheel Gap for the year. I picked up several of the students to bring back with me, and we didn't get here till midnight. We saw the mess at The Lanes and wondered what was going on. I had nothing to do with it."

Sanderson paused. "I'm not the least bit sorry someone killed him and one of his little tramps, but it wasn't me."

"We will check out what you have told us." Sam knew it wasn't worth the trouble. Here was a familiar theme; it seemed everyone had a reason for wanting Roger dead.

"Go ahead, you'll see it checks out. Look, Mrs. Rite, maybe I was wrong about you and your friend. You can understand how I feel. My wife and I just wanted to bring this town back to its glory. Did you know my wife's family originally started this town? When silver hit they got lost in the rush. We often talked about coming home and when we decided to get away from the stress of our jobs we thought this place would be perfect. What a joke! We have been under more stress than we ever knew working in the city. Now maybe we can get some peace."

"Thank you for your honesty, Mr. Sanderson. I don't think we will be bothering you anymore." Sam stood to leave. "No hard feelings, I hope."

"No hard feelings." Sanderson was willing to let things drop.

They all stood at the same time, and after Jessie and Sam shook hands with Sanderson, he went back to work. Sam and Jessie were curious to see what Roger's money had bought and the progress that had been made in the town

Sam was more interested in checking Mr. Sanderson's alibi, but he enjoyed the floorshow at the Silver Dollar Saloon. The beer was cool and the entertainment was great fun. He wasn't so old he couldn't appreciate a pair of good legs and a friendly smile.

Jessie felt a twinge of jealousy, a feeling she hadn't known in many years. Jessie decided to get the kids a memento to let them know she was thinking of them and told Sam she would meet him at the stage depot. Sam followed her out of the saloon; he didn't appreciate a good pair of legs that much!

When they came out of the general store they were treated to a shoot-out between the sheriff and a "notorious" gunslinger. In the distance they could hear the hoots of encouragement at the small arena that afforded area cowboys a chance to practice for the county fair rodeo. There wasn't a large prize for the winners, but everyone was happy to display their talents in the old ways of the West.

Driving back to the ranch they had to pass the spot where Roger and Robyn were killed. Jessie was surprised how quickly Mother Nature recovered. The tall pines still stood scorched against the setting sun, valiantly sprouting new leaves, and the ground was covered with new shoots of grass and wild flowers smiling toward the sun.

"Sam, would you please pull over. I need to see where it happened." Looking around, Jessie was reassured once again at the resilience of nature. "Nature forgets quickly." Jessie sighed.

"I don't think it is a matter of forgetting. It just gets on with life." Sam thought it sounded corny, but it seemed to soothe Jessie's ragged nerves.

Jessie opened the door and walked quietly over to the scarred tree. She stood looking at it for a minute. She reached out to feel the marred bark. Her thoughts ran to the last time she remembered seeing Roger parked here. She tried to remember who Roger had been with, but all she could recall was the look of contempt she received from Roger. He acted as if he was the one being wronged.

Sam gave her a few minutes alone. He could tell by her rigid stance that emotions were flowing through her. This was something he couldn't help her with.

"Show me where you found my necklace," she stated dryly.

Sam walked over to within five feet of where she was standing and stopped. "The car was here, and I found it on the ground by the driver's door." He watched her reaction and found it to be emotionless. He could tell she was confused, but unwilling to discuss it at any length.

Jessie turned and looked to the horizon. She turned and began walking away from the murder scene. She was surprised at the lack of emotion she felt. She should feel something. After all, she had been married to Roger for more than 18 years.

Sam followed Jessie, letting her dictate what happened. Jessie stopped and looked around. She forgot Sam was along, directed by an unseen finger, pointing her to who knows where. She just felt compelled to follow for reasons she didn't understand.

Suddenly she stopped and looked back toward the murder scene, and then she was unable to move. She felt something familiar about the scene, but she couldn't pin down her feelings.

She closed her eyes and began walking, letting the heat of the setting sun draw her forward. She opened her eyes just as she was about to stumble over a small boulder protruding from the ground.

Sam stepped behind her and grabbed her shoulders. She leaned back against him to absorb comfort and courage from his quiet strength.

"I have ridden over this area my entire life, but it feels like I'm a stranger. Roger changed everything I thought to be true." She saw a glint from the lowering sun. She quickly bent to get a closer look and was excited by what she found.

"Look!" she pointed at her feet.

Sam knelt and scraped away the dirt so he could get a good look at what was partially buried in the silt. "It's just a horse shoe."

"When Jake checked Lil' after she came home he found she had thrown a shoe. She might have lost it here when she threw me. Maybe that is why I keep having these dreams. Maybe I'm trying to remember what happened." Jessie was excited by the prospect. If she could remember maybe she would come up with the answer to who killed Roger.

Sam pulled the horseshoe out of the ground and wrapped it in his handkerchief. The two looked for anything else that could prove this was where Jessie had been thrown. Sam couldn't believe she was this close to the scene and no one had found her.

"If I was knocked out this close to the accident, why didn't someone find me?" Jessie had voiced Sam's question.

"Everyone was pretty busy, Jessie. We may never know the answer. The doctors warned you the memories may never come back." Sam tried to console Jessie as they headed back to the car.

The two sat quietly watching the countryside roll by, each occupied with their own thoughts.

Sam wondered if Jessie could have come so close to the murder scene without detection. If not, she could be in more trouble then he had figured. He was more concerned and determined then ever.

Jessie felt like a dog chewing a bone. She couldn't let go of the fact that Sam skirted any attempt to discuss Chuck's part in the journal. Jessie never questioned Chuck handling their veterinary needs. Although, now she knew about his drugging of racehorses, she was a little leery of working with him.

"Sam, I have a question about Chuck Smith."

"I wondered when you would get around to him," Sam said casually.

"Did you know about his involvement with drugging racehorses?" Jessie was trying to find a delicate way of putting it.

"Jake told me about it. He knew Chuck when he was working at the racetrack. He got into quite a bit of trouble from what Jake tells me." He decided now was the time to tell Jessie about Chuck's involvement. "Did you know he put himself through school?"

"I really don't know much about Chuck. He has always kept pretty much to himself," Jessie confided. "He is the best vet I've ever dealt with. I like the way he treats the animals. His concern for their well being is evident. Too bad I can't say the same for his assistant." Jessie was immediately irritated at the thought of Selma.

"His folks were small farmers; they ran a few head of cattle that they sold locally. Most of their food was grown on the farm, and they sold the extra they grew at the farmers' market at Durango. They would have never been able to send Chuck through school, but he got a good scholarship and worked part time for the extra money he needed." Sam felt like he was invading Chuck's privacy, because Jessie was right, he was a private person.

"What does that have to do with drugging race horses?" Jessie asked flatly.

"This story gets so involved I feel like I'm writing a book. I'll try to make it short. His folks ran into some financial difficulties. He was making just enough to stay in school, but he was desperate to help them. It came down to staying in school or dropping out. Unfortunately, he made the wrong decision." Sam was hoping Jessie would be satisfied with this answer.

"If Jake knew about it, why didn't he say something? I think I had the right to know about his background." Jessie felt her face beginning to flush angrily. She felt as if she was being manipulated, this time by her father.

"Don't get hot under the collar, Jess. Jake and Big Roger knew all about Chuck's background, and they did everything they could to help him out. He wasn't involved directly with drugging the horses. He made the horses available to some other people. Big Roger had a lot of pull. He got the school to let Chuck graduate and helped him get his license in Colorado to give him a fresh start. Chuck has been a straight arrow since his probation ended."

"As far as we know." Jessie wasn't really angry at anyone. She just felt as if she wasn't in control, and Sam was the closest person for her to vent her anger.

"When I got the shovel from Chuck I asked him a few questions. He was very open about it, and I'm satisfied he had nothing to do with what happened to Roger." Sam didn't have anything solid to go on, but his instincts told him Chuck Smith had nothing to do with it. Selma, now there was a different story.

"What do you know about Selma, other than I understand you are not very fond of her?" Sam said, trying to lighten the mood.

"There isn't anything I would put past her!" Jessie knew Sam was trying to get her thinking of something else, but all he did was make her blood pressure rise.

"I think Selma knows more than she is willing to say. I think we need to figure a way to get it out of her." Sam was speaking lightly, but he was very serious.

"Well, then I guess I need to add one more name to the list."

"I think we need to put our heads together and make a plan of attack. How about if we catch an early dinner before I drop you off?" Sam was hoping to spend more time with Jessie.

"I don't think so." Jessie knew there was a lot of work yet to do on the barbecue, and she didn't want to leave it for Jake and Nana. "But I'm sure we can squeeze one more plate at the table. You know how Nana loves to feed people."

Sam didn't believe his good luck! Two great meals in one day! "You won't have to twist my arm. Just let me stop at the ranch and look in on a few things."

Back at the ranch, Sam and Jessie said a quick hello to Estralita and then headed into the office to plan their strategy for the barbecue.

"I know Glynis had a plan for the barbecue. She was always updating the menus and the hired help. Her aim in life was the perfect event." Jessie smiled as she remembered Glynis do her part to make the yearly event a success.

Jessie pulled all the drawers out of the large oak desk one at a time so she could make sure she hadn't hidden the plan under all the papers.

"Maybe it is kept in the files," Sam said, looking over her shoulder at the contents of the drawers. Something kept nagging at the back of Sam's mind. He just couldn't put his finger on what was the matter.

Jessie gave up the search, deciding to go with a simpler plan. "I remember the first barbecue I ever attended. It was the most exciting thing I have ever seen!"

"Well, I think between all of us we can make this one a success." Sam could tell when these people got their heads together exciting things happened.

Jake knocked lightly on the door, announcing dinner was ready. Jessie realized she was ravenous. Unlike most people, nerves peaked her appetite. She realized she hadn't had anything to eat all day. She and Sam had gotten so engrossed at Wagon Wheel Gap they had skipped lunch.

After dinner they returned to the office and finished plans for Fourth of July. Jessie had her guest list prepared and when they compared lists, they found them to be almost exact.

Sam had discounted every clue found at the scene as irrelevant except Jessie's necklace and the horseshoe they'd just found. Sam bid a late-night goodbye, planning to come and help with the last minute chores for the barbecue. He knew there was a lot to be accomplished if the party was to be a success. He would miss Jessie and everyone else at the ranch, but he knew to give her the space she needed.

Jake was drawn to the window at the sound of Sam's old jeep driving away and watched the lights go off at the main house, congratulating himself on being a good judge of character. It didn't take a genius to figure out Sam and Jessie were becoming more than just partners or friends. The children would grow to appreciate the fact Jessie deserved a man to care for her the way she needed.

Jake remembered his wonderful Pearl. Maybe Jessie would be as lucky as him after all. She had really never enjoyed love the way it should be. Glynis and Big Roger were just two people living in the same house. He never understood why they had married. If there had ever been feelings between them it was evident those feelings were long gone by the time he and Jessie had come along.

Jake glanced at the waning moon; the next couple of weeks would be full of activity. There was a lot to do before the Fourth if they were going to get everyone in the county fed and entertained. He needed to get all the rest he could.

# Chapter Twenty-five

While everyone at the Rite place worked at a feverish pace to get ready for the barbecue, the repercussions of the invitation list were being felt around the county.

Betty Sanderson had been arguing with her husband for two days about whether to attend the Rite's Fourth of July barbecue. "I don't care how they treated you. If you don't want them to think you are guilty, don't act guilty," she said, losing the little patience she had left.

"Just what exactly do you mean?" Don Sanderson demanded.

"They are offering to pay us to have the can-can show at the barbecue for entertainment. If you are trying to get them to suspect you, let your pride get in the way and stay holed up here. Everyone else in the county will be attending and asking why we aren't." Betty set his breakfast in front of Don and added, "Chew that over." She didn't mean the food!

Don looked at his food and knew his wife was right. He would be a prize fool if he didn't attend. It was free advertising for Wagon Wheel Gap, something they couldn't afford to pass. The extra money would come in handy, and the troupes were excited about performing. Every important person in the state would be there, and they could use the exposure. Don would have to swallow his pride and call Jessie Rite to accept the invitation.

He swore under his breath. He should never argue with is wife; she was always right! One day he would sidestep all arguments with her. "You win!" he exclaimed while throwing his napkin down. He didn't even touch his plate. He left to give Jessie Rite a call.

215

Betty watched her husband leave the kitchen. One of the things she loved about her husband was the fact he wasn't a prideful person. He would listen to advice from others and wasn't afraid to say when he was wrong.

She cleaned the morning dishes and headed for the cafe. She could tell it was going to be a scorcher. Summer had arrived in full force. Betty whistled "Jeannie with the Light Brown Eyes," one of the songs indelibly etched on her memory. She hoped next year to get some fresh entertainment for the saloon.

\*\*\*

The invitation to the Rite's barbecue had finally arrived. "Momma, look, I told you we would be invited. I don't care if you want to go or not—I wouldn't miss it for the world. Don't start whining! You can stay home if that is what you want, I don't care!"

Heading to leave, the angry figure stopped to grab a hat before going outside. "I'm going to move from this hell hole one day." The thought of two more months of this hated summer heat was more than anyone should have to tolerate. The figure had skin so sensitive it would burn without sun block under clothing. In fact, it could burn while sitting on the porch on a sunny day.

"I hate hats. Why couldn't I have dark skin like an Indian or something? These stupid freckles pop out no matter what I do. I know why they are having this stupid party. With Roger gone she wants to spend everything he and his family worked so long to obtain. I think I'll treat myself to an in-town breakfast this morning. You want to come?

"You can pout all you want, but I'm going out. It's your own fault you don't know anyone anymore," the figure stated, tired of entertaining the crabby old woman.

Stopping at the door, it was unable to resist a parting volley. "If you don't straighten up, I won't tell you the gossip about the party when I get home."

\*\*\*

"Chuck, have you decided if you're going to the party yet?" Selma asked. She was a little nervous she hadn't received her invitation yet. As a last result, she knew she could talk Chuck into taking her.

"I'm not going," Chuck said absently.

"What do you mean you may not go!" Selma had to think quickly. "Jessie and Jake would never forgive you," she said, taking a shot in the dark.

"I said that I'm not going! I think there will be plenty of people there. I won't be missed one little bit." Chuck always felt inferior around a lot of people. He had always preferred the company of animals, which is why he decided to become a vet.

"Of course they will miss you. After everything Jake and Big Roger did for you don't you think it would be a little ungrateful?" Selma gasped as she realized this time she might have gone a little too far.

Chuck stopped what he was doing and gave Selma his full attention. "What are you talking about?" he asked coldly.

Selma had never seen Chuck as angry as he had been lately. In fact, she had never seen any emotion from him. She felt the stirring of excitement at the thought of Chuck showing something more than an adoring puppy love.

"Come on, sweetie," she said with a sensuality reserved for a special few of her friends. She walked close to him and put her hands on his chest, sensually rubbing the taut muscles. "You know how I hate to fight with you."

He put one hand over her two, squeezing them in a viselike grip. He said, "I want to know what you are talking about." He squeezed her fingers until she thought they might be crushed.

"Chuck," she hissed through parted lips, "you're hurting me." She felt a twinge of fear that fueled her excitement. "I only meant all the work they send your way."

Chuck pulled her closer and asked one last time, "What did you mean by that remark?" His eyes held no emotion, finally gaining Selma's attention.

She pulled herself away from him and said with an anger to match his, "All right, I knew about your 'extracurricular' work while you were in college. Do you think those stupid farmers aren't talking about you behind your back? Your precious Jessica Rite, she is just waiting for you to screw up so she can send you packing. Roger always said that you were a sap just waiting to get what you deserved." Selma was breathing hard. She had said everything in one breath while rubbing her aching hands. She was trying to decide what Chuck's reaction would be to this latest lie.

She and Roger had discussed the proper use of the information Roger had uncovered on Chuck. She decided to throw in the last bit about Jessica. She was so sick of all the men in this county sniffing around her as if she was a bitch in heat. She was going to pay her back if it was the last thing she ever did.

To Selma's surprise, Chuck began to laugh. "What a relief to get that out in the open!" Chuck, a person she had seen smile no more than a dozen times in the years she had known him, was actually laughing.

"Oooh!" she screeched as she turned and slammed out of the room. "I hate that bitch!" Selma focused her anger on the one person she held responsible for her circumstances. Walking away, the sound of Chuck's laughter fueled her anger.

She grabbed her straw hat and stomped out the door. "I'm taking the day off, maybe the week!" If it was the last thing she did, she was going to make the Rites pay for what they had done to her.

The last Chuck saw of Selma until the night of the barbecue was her retreating back, walking hurriedly down the road toward town.

***

Frank Weston waved to his son as he strode down the fairway to where he was standing. He was so happy to see his son looking healthy that he couldn't resist giving him a large bear hug. The young man was so surprised by the show of affection it brought tears to his eyes.

Young Frank had been angry when his father had demanded he go into treatment for his addictions. His sulk wore off when he started listening to the other people at the center. He had always thought he was alone in his agony.

Sometimes he felt guilty about the jubilation he felt, knowing he wasn't alone. He had learned to overcome his anger and was set free. The healing started with the realization there was no guilt. They were all human, with human frailties.

Frank had talked his wife into letting him greet their son alone. He didn't want her to hear what they had to discuss. "Well, son, I'm glad to see you looking so good. How are you, really?" "I'm good, Dad. I need to thank you for doing what I didn't have the guts to do. I owe you my life. I'll never be able to repay you," he said, his eyes filling with tears. Lately he was easily brought to tears, but he had learned to accept everything that made him human.

"Come on, son, let's go home." Suddenly nothing mattered. He had his son back, and that is what mattered. They would have to decide what they wanted to tell Marsha, but he would be grateful for the fact he had his son back, whole and alive.

The older man put his arm around the younger man's shoulders and together they started down the final road of recovery. People turned and smiled at the fine-looking pair the two made.

"The Rites are reinstating their annual barbecue. I think that would be a good chance to reintroduce you to our neighbors." Frank felt his son tense at the suggestion. He gave him a quick squeeze of encouragement. "I didn't tell you about the visit I got from Jessica Rite." Frank smiled at the face so like his wife's, hoping he wasn't saying too much to soon. The months of separation had showed him he couldn't protect his son forever, no one could.

*\*\*\**

Gloria passed the young woman briskly walking down the road.

"Well, I wonder where Little Miss Goody Two-Shoes is headed on such a warm afternoon."

"Don't be mean, Mom," Rob Roy lisped.

"Don't be mean, don't be mean! God, Rob Roy, you are such a pain," Gloria replied as she drained the bottle of beer she was sipping. She rolled down her window and heaved the bottle in the direction of the pedestrian.

"Hey!" the woman said, startled by the flying beer bottle.

"You stupid slut!" Gloria felt her anger of the morning growing.

"Mom, why do you do that? We need to keep our land pretty," said Rob Roy, his agitation at his mother's antics showing. "Miss Jessie says we have to work hard to keep everything beautiful."

"'Miss Jessie, Miss Jessie.' You never remember what I tell you!" Gloria said as she lit up one of her cigarillos. "I want to know what is so special about that—" Looking at the anger darkening her son's eyes, she finished, "—person?"

Rob Roy had trouble understanding his mother when she was drinking. When she'd had a few beers she made no sense to him at all. He would be happy to see his friend Jessie, but he didn't understand why Gloria would want to see her.

"She probably thought I would be afraid to come back. Well, she has another think coming. I wasn't afraid of that lowlife husband of hers; I'm sure as hell not afraid of her." Gloria was sorry she didn't bring another beer, the heat was parching her throat.

Rob Roy slumped down into the seat as far as he could. He hated it when his mother drank; she got so mean. It scared him, because he never knew who she would go after when she was drinking. He just hoped she wouldn't be mean to Miss Jessie. He wouldn't let her hurt Miss Jessie. He wouldn't let anyone hurt Miss Jessie ever again.

\*\*\*

"I think this is all I need," Sarah said, looking at her list. "I suppose you and Bill will be at the barbecue?" she asked bluntly.

"Bill and I haven't decided if we are going to go or not." Sharon Marshall liked Sarah well enough. She did consider her a bit of a gossip, often wondering where she got her tidbits. Sharon knew Sarah spent most of her time at the library or at David Cummings's home, the two quietest places in the whole county.

"Everyone in the county has been invited, you know." Sarah made it more of a statement than a question. "David and I are going together, of course. I was able to talk Agnes into going. She doesn't like to go out much. She feels so nervous with her handicap, you see," Sarah prattled on, Sharon only half-listening to what she was saying.

Sharon was surprised when they had received an invitation. Bill had not been very considerate the last time they had seen Jessie. She felt as if she should appreciate Jessie's kindness. She could have gone to Boat with the information she had found in the journal she had…but she didn't.

She knew Bill wouldn't have harmed a fly, but he had said so many things after Elizabeth's death. He hadn't been himself; like Sharon, he had been devastated by the loss of his little girl.

Sharon thought back to the day they had found Elizabeth. The note had said it all.

> *Dear Mommy and Daddy,*
> *Please forgive me. Please don't hate Roger. I know he loved me once. I don't know how to go on without him. You are the greatest parents. Don't blame yourselves; I just can't face the town after what happened.*
> *I love you…*
> *Your daughter, Elizabeth*

"Sharon! What's wrong? You look as if you have seen a ghost!" Sarah was patting her hand to try and bring her around. "Do you want me to call Bill?"

"No…no, I'll be all right. I'm okay. I was just remembering something. What were you saying? What were you saying?"

I said, "I hope you and Bill decide to come to the barbecue." Sarah was losing patience with Sharon. It seemed like everyone was going around in a fog since Roger Rite's death, but it wasn't as if he would be missed. Everyone in town had one reason or the other to hate him. "You two need to get on with your lives. I'm sure Elizabeth's death was devastating…"

Sharon gave Sarah a wan smile, interrupting her, "Yes, I think that is the perfect answer."

Sarah assumed Sharon was talking about the barbecue, but she discounted it to the fact Sharon and Bill hadn't been the same since their daughter had committed suicide. "Will we see you there?" She said a little too exuberantly as she headed for the door.

"Hello, Sarah," Bill said as their paths crossed. "Do you have any big plans for the summer?"

"David and I haven't decided yet." She smiled. "See you at the barbecue," Sarah cooed as she headed out the door.

Bill watched her exit the store and went to where his wife was standing, shaking his head. "She will never give up snaring David, will she?"

Sharon ignored the question and said, "I decided we are going to the Rite's barbecue on the Fourth." Without waiting for a reply, she said, "I need to go find a new outfit." She pulled off her duster coat and laid it on the counter without waiting for a reply from Bill.

Bill wasn't excited about going, but for the first time since Beth's death, his wife had been interested in something. He hoped this would get her out of the shell she had crawled into since Beth's death. He felt a cold shiver go down his back; the urge to kill Roger Rite had been overwhelming at times. *Good riddance*, he thought to himself. Thank God there was his work to make him carry on. *I just hope he suffered before he died*. Bill smiled at the vision conjured up by his imagination.

***

"I don't care what you say, I'm not going to that barbecue!" David jumped out of his chair so quickly it made the dishes on the table threaten to tumble to the ground.

"Quit the theatrics, David," his mother said sternly. "You can pull your act on your little Sarah, but you won't get away with it with me."

"She is not 'my' little Sarah," David said through clenched teeth.

"You forget I see more without my eyes than most people do *with* theirs! I may not have seen all of the commotion, but I did hear a car leave after you went to the greenhouse."

David turned gray at what his mother was saying. "I told you, mother, I don't know what you are talking about." David felt the sweat run down his sides. He didn't know what happened, but he felt queasy at every effort to recall.

"I was sure I heard Selma's voice after lunch. You keep insisting I'm getting old. Well, Sarah doesn't think I'm getting old. She has more confidence in me than my own son has."

"Sarah, Sarah, Sarah! I'm so sick of hearing her name. I swear the next person saying that name in front of me, I'll kill them!" David threw his coffee cup across the room for emphasis.

"Momma, I'm going to Silverton, I've got some plants ordered, and I'm picking them up at J&S. Don't wait dinner for me, I'll be late."

The door slammed before his mother could say a word.

"That's fine, my boy. You win for now. Argue all you want, but you will be escorting Sarah and me to the barbecue." Agnes smiled sweetly as she made her plans for the day. She would make sure there were plenty of fireworks for everyone to enjoy. No one would forget her attendance.

* * *

Winnie took a deep breath before she entered the room. "Andrew, darling, look what came in the mail." She was sure any day now she would get a response from her husband.

"Why, darling, you are still in your pajamas. Don't you know what time it is? They'll be bringing lunch soon, and we don't want to be in our bed clothes, do we?" Winnie chattered on and on, telling her husband all the latest news from Silverton and the congregation.

"Oh, yes, Billy Albers and Ginny Galley refuse to be married by anyone except you. So you are going to have to get well, very soon." Winnie couldn't keep the tears out of her eyes as she combed her husband's hair for him.

"Oh, Andrew, why can't you come back to us? We all miss you so much. If you don't come back I will never be able to forgive myself. I need you to forgive me. I don't know how long I can go on this way." The tears were rolling freely down her cheeks as the day nurse brought in Andrew's lunch.

"Now, Mrs. Conners, we must stay positive. Mr. Conners is just resting, waiting to get his mental strength back. If we can't be positive maybe we should come back when we are feeling perkier!"

Winnie hated this nurse's attitude. She was being as perky as she could given the prognosis for Andrew. Medical double-talk was all she ever got.

"Mr. Conners has had a breakdown; as soon as he feels strong enough he will come back to reality; with medication he could return; we have seen this many times; it is just a matter of rest and recuperation; well, no, we don't have any time frame, but with love and patience"…on and on and on and on!

"Do you have any idea when he will be strong enough?" Winnie asked them at every conference. All they could say was to have patience. If she wasn't a Christian woman she would tell them what they could do with their patience.

"I'm fine, and I want to be alone with my husband," she said, holding the door open for the nurse. "I can help Andrew with his lunch."

"That's better. I'll be back in an hour for his tray. You just hang in there, sweetie." Winnie was sick of the double-talk she was given here in this glorified prison.

Winnie turned to her husband and for a minute she thought she saw a flicker of acknowledgment in his eyes. "Oh, darling, you know who I am!" Winnie ran to embrace her husband and was disappointed to find no response. She slowly withdrew her arms and tried to get eye contact with Andrew, but there was none to be had.

"That's all right, I'll wait. I love you, and I will wait as long as it takes."

Once again Winnie began the inane chatter that rolled off her tongue as she fed him spoonful after spoonful of the drab food offered.

"You'll have to try real hard, Andrew; we got an invitation to the Rite's barbecue. It seems as if everyone in the county will be there. I made us new square dancing outfits. I know how much you love square dancing. I hear Estralita's menu is full of all our favorites. I'm going to make my fruit salad supreme. I know it is one of your favorites."

\*\*\*

The Albert brothers finished their meal in silence. Each had his own thoughts to occupy himself. Billy, the youngest, wondered for the umpteenth time what possessed him to get involved with Roger. If he had just listened to Ernie they wouldn't have this black cloud hovering over them.

Allen was concerned they hadn't heard anything from the police. He knew they all could be held accountable for Billy letting Roger entangle them.

John was trying to think of a way to settle everyone's nerves. He was sure Jessie wouldn't pull them into the fracas. They had nothing to do with

Roger's death. With this knowledge firmly in place, he wasn't worried. If Jessie was brought up on charges there was no telling what she would say or do to get the authorities looking elsewhere.

Ernie, because he was the oldest, worried about everything. He knew none of his brothers were involved. They didn't have what it took to commit murder. Even though he hated Roger for what he did to his family, he wouldn't resort to murder.

Billy broke the silence. "I suppose everyone got an invitation?" He didn't have to explain what invitation. "I'm not sure I want to attend?" It was more of a question than a statement.

"I think it would be best if we all went," Ernie stated flatly.

"We don't have anything to hide. If we stay away we will look guilty even though we aren't." John, the eternal optimist, agreed.

"I say we all go. Enjoy the party and forget Jessie ever came to see us. There is no reason to think there is anything going on except a celebration of the Fourth of July." Allen was the thinker of the family. Therefore, the boys usually turned to him with their problems.

"Well, then, I guess that settles it. We are all going to the barbecue. The last thing I want is to try and explain to Linda and the kids why we are the only family in Delaney County not attending," Ernie said, grabbing the bill and rising to pay.

The boys silently agreed as they rose to get their separate ways. Each was trying to assure themselves no one in their family was responsible for what happened to Roger.

***

David surveyed the crowded dining room. He acknowledged the Albert brothers as they waited for Ernie to pay the bill. He wasn't in any mood to talk to anyone. He wasn't even hungry, but the thought of sitting through another uncomfortable meal with his mother was abhorrent to him.

Charlie greeted his young friend. "David, long time, no see!" He whacked the thin man jubilantly on the back fairly knocking him down. Charlie liked the young man, but like everyone else in town, found him to be on the dour side. Not that he blamed him, between his incapacitated mother and the cloying Sarah Hart, anyone would have a hard time finding any reason to be gleeful.

"Hello, Charlie. Can you find me a table? I need to get dinner before heading home." David was annoyed to find Sarah waiting for her meal. The last thing he needed was a confrontation with her.

Charlie spotted Sarah and a wave of sympathy overcame him. He could tell by the color draining from the already peaked young man that the last person he needed to spot him was casually watching the other diners.

"Why don't you join me in the office?" Charlie wasn't really hungry, but he enjoyed the solemn young man's company. He enjoyed the animation, which was usually missing, when David talked about working in his greenhouse.

"I'd like that," David said, turning quickly to evade the watchful eye of the librarian.

"David, oh, David!" Sarah stood and waved her hands to assure gaining David's attention. "Yoo-hoo!" She wasn't about to give up easily.

The diners stopped eating and turned their attention in the direction Sarah was looking. David didn't want to cause more of a scene than was already taking place; he listlessly waved a returned acknowledgment to Sarah's greetings.

"Thanks, Charlie, but I guess I'll join Sarah. I've changed my mind; maybe I'll just have a cup of coffee." David was trying to decide the lesser of two evils, his mother or Sarah?

"David, I'm so glad we ran into each other. It must be kismet," she said as she looked adoringly into his face.

She noticed a blush growing around his hairline and assumed it to be a flush of joy instead of the glow of irritation it truly was. "I just stopped in for a cup of coffee, Sarah." David shivered at the look of adoration gleaming in her eyes.

"Now, David, you know it's not good to skip dinner. All that caffeine isn't good for you. Why don't you let me order something light for you?" Sarah was excited to at last have a chance to speak privately with David, away from work, that is!

"I said I just wanted coffee." David's slammed his hat onto the bench seat beside him, irritation barely below the surface.

"Well, this is my dinner. At least have some pie with your coffee. I'll feel so much better not eating in front of you." Sarah didn't give up easily.

"All right!" David was too tired to argue any further.

"Did you and Agnes get your invitations to the barbecue?" Sarah waited to begin her dinner until David's pie arrived.

"Is Agnes interested in attending?" Sarah held her breath, hoping Agnes wouldn't want to go.

David feigned interest in his pie on the hope of deterring conversation. "Huh?" he asked, pretending he missed her question.

"Now, David, don't gobble your pie. You know it will just give you indigestion." Sarah just loved looking out for her "sweetheart."

"Look, one mother is more then enough, thank you."

The hurt in Sarah's eyes made David regret his harshness. Since Robyn's death he had been unable to suppress his anger. His mother was continually harping on his luck, and Sarah was smothering him with kindness. If they would just leave him alone for 10 minutes!

"I'm sorry. I just want what's best for you, David," Sarah said, folding her napkin and reaching for her handbag. "I didn't realize I was such a burden." She sniffed.

"Sit down, for Pete's sake," David said more gruffly then he intended. "Please stay," he added more gently.

Sarah's pleasure returned at his change of heart. She knew he would realize some day that she was the woman for him. Lucky for her Roger Rite got a yen for Robyn. That little piece of fluff wouldn't be missed for long.

"If we went to the barbecue together I could help look out for Agnes. I know how you worry about her..." Sarah rattled on, secure in the fact she would indeed be escorted to the Rites by her love...David.

*** 

Jennifer watched as Tracy helped David put the fertilizers and plants in the back of the converted van. David was becoming one of their best customers.

His horticultural sideline was becoming more profitable to them then some of their oldest customers. His reputation as a grower and problem solver was gaining statewide acclaim.

In the last two years his exotic plants sold out even before the garden started. People from surrounding counties called to reserve some of their favorites even before they were set out in the spring.

"Jen...what are you daydreaming about?" Tracy placed a reassuring hand on Jennifer's.

"Just what a sweet guy David is." Jennifer sighed sadly. "I feel sorry for him. He was really hung up on Robyn. He just hasn't been the same since she died."

"Do I have a reason to be jealous here?" Tracy winked conspiratorially.

Jennifer looked around the store, hoping no one had heard Tracy's remark. She was aware of the rumors going around about her and Tracy, but she wasn't ready to confirm them yet.

Tracy was irritated by the look of horror glued to Jennifer's face. Everything was going fine until that damned Roger Rite came into the scene. Too bad he couldn't have been killed just a few weeks earlier. She and Jennifer would still just be the Billings sisters and that evil so and so would be in hell where he belonged!

"Forget it, Jen. I was just kidding." Tracy took a step back to give Jennifer much needed space. "Are you interested in going to the barbecue?" She didn't really have to ask. Tracy was happy to stay home and enjoy Jennifer's company. It was the only time Jennifer seemed truly relaxed. Tracy knew Jennifer would be happier if she just "came out," but experience had taught her this was a private lesson to be learned.

"Should we?" Happiness was beaming on her face.

"Beats staying home and eating your cooking!" Tracy was touched by the childish glee Jennifer took in the smallest joys. "I'm ready to go kick up my heels." Tracy looked forward to a firsthand experience at the legendary "Rite Fourth of July Barbecue."

# Chapter Twenty-six

Jessie and Estralita were going over the last of the arrangements for the barbecue when Jake pulled into the driveway with the kids. Jessie gazed anxiously out the window; she brightened at the sound of the beeping of the horn, visualizing the kids before she saw the truck.

"Nana, the kids are home!" Jessie yelled as she ran out of the kitchen to greet them. The two children barreled out of the truck and ran to greet their mother.

"Mom, how have you been?" they cried in unison. All remnants of their anger missing, they hugged their mother as if they had been gone for years instead of weeks.

"Cristal, Jordan, I've missed you so much. I'm so happy to have you home." She wanted to ask about their summer, but could tell by looking at them they were having a great summer. They were both brown as berries and seemed to have grown a foot.

Jordan was the first to comment. "Camp has been great. The kids are so swell time seems to fly by."

Cristal broke in, "Greensford's great, I've learned a lot. Silver's training is going great. They want me to enter all the jumping competitions I can this year. I thought…"

"Jeez, Cristal, can you cut it short?" Jordan said with exasperation. "Maybe Mom wants to get a word in! How is Hoppy doing? I bet he doesn't even remember me."

Jake and Jessie smiled at each other, glad to have the kids back.

Jordan looked first to Jessie and then to Jake, "What?"

"Talk about a blabbermouth!" Cristal glared at Jordan. Jessie was happy to see some things never change. She didn't think she would ever be happy to hear their bickering again; it was music to her ears.

"I say we go get a look at how much Hoppy has grown," Jake broke in to stop the bickering.

Cristal broke into a run so she would have a chance to get first claim on Hoppy. Jordan tried to be mature, but the memory of the small, trusting colt made him rush after her.

Jake put his arm around Jessie's shoulder to give her a squeeze. "I'm glad to have them back. I knew they would be back to their old selves if we gave them a chance. You raised them right, Jessie, and that's what counts."

Jessie just smiled up at her father with her eyes glistening with tears. She didn't have to say anything; he could read the agreement on her face.

The kids watched the colt with anticipation. They both felt as if they had been gone forever, uncertain as to whether he would remember them. Jordan gave Hoppy a welcoming whistle. The colt stood for a moment as if trying to regain a forgotten memory. Giving the air a swift kick, the colt cantered over to greet his two friends.

Jake and Jessie left them alone to get reacquainted. "Don't be long. Estralita has made all of your favorites as a homecoming treat," Jessie informed the two kids.

The two broke into the kitchen filled with savory smells, hoping they wouldn't have to wait too long for dinner. Clamoring into the kitchen, Jordan grabbed Estralita and swung her around as if she was nothing more than a sack of potatoes.

"Come on, Jordan, put her down." Cristal felt like it had been years since she had seen her Nana instead of weeks. "She missed me too you know."

"I missed both my little niños; I spent the whole day making all your favorites." Estralita wiped her eyes on her ever-present apron.

"What's this tempting smell?" Jake boomed, lifting one of the lids on the stove. "Are we ever going to eat all this great food or are we just going to stand around hugging each other all night?"

"As soon as I set the table we will eat." The little woman began skittering around the kitchen like a whirlwind, making sure everything was done to perfection.

"I'll set the table," Cristal piped up.

"Let me help." Jordan's mouth was watering at the thought of real food after four weeks of camp food. He would do anything if it meant eating quickly!

"I know you two wouldn't come in without seeing your colt. You get cleaned up, and I'll take care of the table."

Sitting with family around the table, Jessie realized she wouldn't have her children with her much longer. She bowed her head and said a quiet blessing from her heart.

There was a loud "Amen" and Jessie watched as her family dove into the wonderful food set before them. As the utensils clinked and the food disappeared she felt as if her life might have meaning again.

Everyone emptied their plates and groaned in delicious agony. Estralita jumped out of her seat and got the triple chocolate cake, everyone's favorite dessert.

"No more. I'll burst if I eat another morsel," Jessie complained, rubbing her full stomach.

"Not me," the two kids chimed in unison.

Jake smiled at the familiar sight his family made. Even before Roger had been killed they were used to eating without Roger in attendance. He could see the tension Roger's absence caused would one day be gone, and it would be replaced with easy camaraderie of people who enjoyed each other's company.

Gobbling up their cake, the kids cajoled Estralita into letting them clean up the dishes. Jessie was full and content with her children around her again. She felt as if nothing in the world could ruin their renewed happiness.

Jessie, Jake and Estralita found themselves gently shepherded into the living room while the kids cleaned up the kitchen. Estralita picked up her ever-present mending and smiled to herself. Once again her family was together and happy.

Jake turned on the TV to catch his favorite sitcom while Jessie settled herself into an overstuffed armchair. Gatsby, her fluffy angora cat, jumped onto her lap excited to have her companionship back after what seemed a long absence. Jessie's eyelids grew heavy and a smile of satisfaction came over her lips as she slipped into a fog of apprehension.

The hum of the television gave way to whispering sighs of a slight breeze; Jessie felt anticipation growing as she floated toward the crackling of a growing fire. Huddling into the comfort of the overstuffed armchair, she felt the heat of the fire increasing the closer she came to the fire.

Jessie fought against the beckoning of the flames. Her agitation was growing because of an unidentifiable form. The flames jumped around her, and she found her attention drawn to the ever-illusive figure. As always the figure started out as a small forest sprite, growing with the intensity of the flames. The flames licked at the ground around Jessie's feet, causing her to jump away in defense. Jessie tried to turn from the sight, but she felt as if she was mired in mud, glued to the spot.

The visage came closer, grasping, always grasping at her. To block the vision, she flung her arm over her eyes. The growing specter continued to grab at Jessie, causing her to writhe in fear.

Jessie's struggles to escape the terrifying vision of her dream caused Gatsby's purring to change into an irritated rumble. When he jumped to escape the thrashing of his owner, Jessie was startled awake. She looked around, still in the foggy edges of her dream, to find her family watching her.

"What's the matter, Mom?" Cristal asked, looking at Jessie's startled look.

"I didn't mean to fall asleep," Jessie said, not wanting to ruin her children's homecoming with the revelations of her dream.

Jake was aware of his daughter's irregular sleep. "Estralita fed us so well today we all could use a catnap," he said, winking at Estralita.

Jordan wasn't so easily fooled by the attempted humor from his grandfather. "Have you been okay while we have been away?" Jordan was sorry for his viewpoint as soon as he settled in at camp.

He had the time to look back at the life his mother was living and realized she lived through years of agony. It wasn't the greatest life, his father treating them as strangers. Ellison wasn't such a bad guy. He and Cristal wouldn't be around forever and then what was she to do with the rest of her life?

"Oh, I've been fine. Just a little tired." She didn't want to start them worrying when they would be home for such a short time. "You know how difficult it can be getting ready for the Fourth."

"We are home, and we can help, can't we, Jordan?" Cristal gave him a look that would shrivel Medusa if he didn't agree. Jake didn't want any quarrels this evening, and as he started to get in between the two teenagers, the phone ran.

"Saved by the bell!" Jake exclaimed.

Jordan just shrugged his shoulders as Cristal ran to answer the phone. He knew it wasn't for him; all of his friends were either on vacation or at camp.

"I think I'll go see how Hoppy is doing." Jordan had missed the companionship the colt had given him.

"Hello, Mr. Ellison." Cristal was embarrassed about the way she had treated Sam. She had decided to be nicer to him for her mother's sake. Her dad was gone and no amount of anger toward Sam or her mother would bring him back.

"Mom, its Sam." As she laid the phone down she looked at the retreating back of Jordan. She knew he was heading out to see Hoppy, and she wondered what he thought of Mr. Ellison. She decided to follow him to the barns.

"Hi, Sam, they're just great." Jessie was glad she didn't have to lie to Sam. The kids really seemed to accept that she and Sam were friends.

"Could you use a hand getting ready for the party?" Sam needed to fill Jessie in on his idea.

"Sure, we can use all the help we can get," Jessie said, looking forward to seeing Sam again. It seemed like ages since she had seen him. "Why don't you come over for breakfast? Believe me, you will need the fortification."

"That sounds like a great idea. See you at 7:00."

"Okay, goodnight." Jessie felt a familiar glow at the thought of seeing Sam. She wasn't sure what the kid's reaction to Sam would be, but she was too happy to worry about it tonight. She decided to join the kids at the barn.

Jessie noticed how tall Cristal had gotten since she had left. She and Jordan were almost shoulder to shoulder, watching the antics of the frisky colt. Her heart melted at the sound of muffled laughter coming from the pair.

"You two look wonderful. I can't tell you how much I have missed you." Jessie wiggled in between the two and put her arms around their shoulders, giving them a bone-crushing squeeze.

"Jeez, Mom, don't break my neck!" Jordan was still teenager enough to be embarrassed by the embrace. "Hoppy still remembers me; he comes right up to me when I call him."

"He remembers me, too!" Cristal didn't want to be left out of the conversation.

The kids looked so grown-up, Jessie forgot they were still children. "Of course he remembers both of you. You're his mother as far as he's concerned."

"Jeez, Mom," Jordan turned purple at the thought of being the small colt's mother.

"You know what I mean." Jessie was having trouble keeping a straight face, but Cristal didn't even try. She was literally rolling in the hay, holding her sides.

"Keep it up, Cristal, and I'll knock your block off." Jordan didn't find any humor in the situation.

"Sorry, Jordan." Cristal sat up, trying to keep a straight face, with straw poking out of her hair and a rosy flush to her cheeks. Jess didn't want to ruin such a happy moment, but she felt she should let the children know Sam was beginning to fit into her plans for the future.

The kids noticed something was bothering their mother. "Is something bothering you, Mom?" Cristal asked suddenly serious.

"I just don't know how to say what I need to." The courage she had found earlier suddenly evaporated now that she was eye to eye with her children.

"You're not sick or anything, are you, Mom?" Jordan jumped in front of his mother so she couldn't evade the question in his eyes.

"No, it's nothing like that. I know you and Cristal were upset about Sam's friendship with me before you left."

"I want the two of you to know that I love you very much. You were my life when I had no reason to go on. When you were little you didn't realize the problems that your father and I went through." She felt her eyes begin to water and the last thing she wanted now was tears.

Jordan looked at Cristal, interrupting his mother. "Look, Mom, Cristal and I have had time to think things over. It's true we didn't like Mr. Ellison coming around, but we decided if Mr. Ellison is going to be your friend as far as we are concerned, he is welcome."

Jessica felt the tears fill her eyes again. The only thing she could find to say was, "Thanks." She noticed it was well after dark and they had an early day. "I think it's time we called it a day. We have a big tomorrow, so let's turn in."

Jessie knew there was a lot of work to be done if they were to be ready for hundreds of people swamping the ranch. She couldn't believe how quickly time passed. In two days people would be teeming throughout the property. She hugged herself at the thought; many things could happen.

She was sure some people would come to see the "merry widow," but she wouldn't let them ruin the homecoming of her children.

# Chapter Twenty-seven

"Okay, sleepy heads, time to get up!" Jessie called the two kids. She felt as if nothing had ever come between them. They were up and at the kitchen table before she could get their dishes filled. "I guess you kids missed Nana's breakfasts?"

"You bet. Food at camp is okay, but nobody cooks like Nana," Jordan said, looking forward to his favorite breakfast.

"They have lousy food at Greensford. I'm surprised I haven't lost a ton. I can hardly keep their swill down." Cristal was literally licking her lips in anticipation of the steaming stack of pancakes she knew Nana would make for her first day home.

"Well, you must have been able to keep something down," Jordan quipped. "It looks to me like you have gained a ton!"

Cristal had a mouth full of food, or Jordan would have regretted the cutting remark. The look she gave him told him what she thought of his opinion. She decided she was above the ramblings of her stupid brother and continued to eat her breakfast.

"Jordan!" Jessie wasn't ready to return to the usual digs between brother and sister. "Eat your breakfast!"

The clinking of forks was heard as the kids turned with fervor to their plates. Jessie watched her children eat with gusto that has been absent after the death of her husband. She knew it was too much to hope they had recovered totally from the loss of their father.

Jessie's attention was drawn to the door as she noticed Sam eyeing her intently. She felt the hair on her arms raise as her skin turned to goose flesh. He was waiting for her to ask him in; his anxiety was evident on his face. He did not know if the kids were ready to accept him in their realm.

Jessie was so intent on Sam she didn't realize everyone was looking at her. Trying to be nonchalant, she turned to Estralita and said, "Nana, will you let Sam in?"

Estralita smiled broadly as she led him to the table. "You sit here, Mr. Sam. I'll have your breakfast ready in a moment."

"Hi, Mr. Ellison, how's your filly doing?" Jordan asked.

"Well, she's doing just great, Jordan." Sam tried to keep the amazement out of his voice.

"Have you decided what to name her?" Cristal wanted to know.

"Well," he said, looking to Jessie for support. "Your mother and I have been pretty busy. I'm not even sure I can name her."

"Jordan and I are really good at figuring out names, right Grandpa?"

"Jeez, Cristal, why do you always have to stick your nose in everyone's business. Mr. Ellison doesn't need our help." Jordan was losing his patience with his little sister.

"Oh, Jordan, you're so mean. I just wanted to help." Cristal's eyes filled with water and were threatening to overflow.

Sam was surprised by the feelings of protectiveness overwhelming him. He was used to taking care of no one but himself. The feelings he had since he had become involved with this family were alien to him.

"Well, Cristal, I think you hit the nail on the head. I have no idea where to begin. I can use all the help I can get. Maybe you two can think about it when you get back to camp and come up with some good suggestions." Sam was rewarded with a look of pride from each one of the kids.

"That would be great, Mr. Ellison." Cristal had the look of hero-worship in her eyes. Jordan practically swelled with pride at being handed the responsibility of naming the filly.

Jordan remembered the day he was handed the responsibility of naming his first horse. He had asked his grandpa if he could join them at the birth of the newest member of the Rite herd.

He felt a growing nervousness, but was rewarded with a barely perceptible nod from his Granddad Roger. A look of confirmation greeted with the usual twinkle of an eye granted him permission from his Grandpa Jake.

He remembered the long walk down to the barns. Standing between the two older men, he was more awed than comforted by the twin towers of strength. He was very solemn when they entered the foaling barn. For some reason he didn't understand, this was to be a very special day. After several hours of waiting they were rewarded with the birth of a new filly.

"Well, son," Big Roger began, giving Jake a quick wink, "what do you think of her?"

Jordan was speechless for the first time in his short life. He looked at the tiny replica of the mare and was mystified by the miracle made possible by nature. "She looks exactly like Quick Silver." What's her name going to be?"

"Jake and I have decided to let you name her." Big Roger surprised him.

"I don't know what to call her." Jordan felt terror at the awesome responsibility. He had heard Jake and Roger argue for days over the naming of one of their animals.

"Your grandfather and I feel the importance of a name is second only to the breeding," he said, smiling at his old friend. "Jake and I feel you are up to the responsibility."

Jordan could tell by the tone of his Grandfather's voice that there was no choice. "How do I find a name?" he asked.

He remembered feeling as if he was going to be sick, or cry, or God forbid, wet his pants. He knew the importance of the name of an animal. It could follow for generations. The overwhelming enormity of it was enough to scare the youngster out of two year's growth!

"You don't have to name her this minute, Jordan." Jake tried to soothe the young boy's concerns. "Big Roger and I will help you any way we can. Make a list of names and when you think you're ready, let us know." He gave the youngster a pat on the back and headed off to do more urgent chores.

"Thanks." Jordan wasn't sure what to feel. He let it sink into his head that he really got to name her. He leaned on the railing and said out loud, "Don't worry, little girl. I'm going to make sure your name is perfect."

The filly was startled by the unfamiliar sight and let Jordan know she wasn't easy to charm. She ran at the boy, turning just in time to kick her heels at him. She let him know who would be the boss.

Jordan laughed at the filly. "You'll see that I'm not easily put off." The filly pranced behind her mother and looked curiously at the strange image that appeared above the railing.

"Jordan?" Jessie wondered where the young man's mind was. "Earth to Jordan."

"Yeah, sorry, Mom, I was just remembering something." Jordan didn't want to be bothered by any more questions. "I think I'll go see if I can help the boys with anything." He hurried out the door before anyone could guess how proud he was Sam had asked for his help.

"Teenagers!" was the only thing necessary to say on that subject.

"Cristal, do you want to go to town with me? I have some last minute items to get for Nana." Jessie wanted to stay as far away from Sam as possible. She knew she was in love with him, but didn't feel free to express her feelings until she was well out of the mess that Roger's murder had placed her in.

Just as Cristal and Jessie were heading out the door, the kitchen crew Nana had hired was arriving. "Are you sure you don't need any help, Nana?"

"My helpers are here, Pearlie, you just hurry back. I will need my supplies."

Jessie knew it would be useless to argue with the older woman. She gave her a quick hug and motioned for Cristal to follow. She was grateful to see the three most important men in her life huddled together, obviously setting their plans in the proper order.

Sam turned and waved at the pair as they moved slowly down the quickly filling driveway. He hadn't been prepared for the enormity of the job ahead of them until he met the trucks filling the road ahead of him.

"Well, it looks as if the girls are escaping while they have the chance!" Sam said with a chuckle.

"Give me setting up the grounds any day. Estralita is a slave driver. We had to go out of state to escape her reputation and find kitchen workers!" Jake said with just a modicum of humor.

"Well, with what I've had of Estralita's cooking, any amount of slaving is worth it," Sam replied, his mouth watering at the memory of the breakfasts he has enjoyed.

"We'll put you on her list of slave labor next year," Jordan retorted.

Sam didn't miss the implication he would be around next year. It was the best thing he could have heard. He set off to do his work, whistling, with a jaunt to his step missing since he learned of the kids return. He was pleased, to say the least, that the children had decided to accept him.

Jake's idea of a small rodeo seemed a stroke of genius to Sam. he wanted to make sure the Sanderson's attended and it gave the perfect excuse to ask for their assistance. Sam whistled as he nailed the stands together at the outdoor arena.

He was able to consider the teenagers who had returned from camp and realized he was genuinely fond of each of them. Cristal was sweet and gentle, but with an iron will that brooked no argument once her mind was made set. She gave him a vision of what Jessie had been like as a child.

Jordan, well, now he was a different story. He had heard of the happy-go-lucky youngster full of practical jokes and irresponsibility as only teenage boys can be, but he had only seen a nervous, withdrawn young man.

The story of the Rite's prize stallion escaping when Jordan forgot to secure the pasture gate was told to Sam by just about everyone in the county. Sam had not found the story humorous. He remembered the dejected young man following in Roger's wake the day Roger came to retrieve the stallion. Jake pointed out Roger had missed the humor, humiliating Jordan in front of the entire crew. Then, with the death of his father, Jordan's happy-go-lucky personality was replaced by the insecure, sullen attitude of a teenager.

Sam promised himself he would make it his personal responsibility to see the previously renowned jokester was back before the year was out! Cristal would not be ignored by him. He would see she had the support of an adult male besides her grandfather so she wouldn't feel the insecurities by which Jordan had been plagued.

# Chapter Twenty-eight

The morning of the party broke with a glory seen in few places besides the high desert of Colorado. The bustling generated by the last minute details of the party made it difficult to visit with anyone for more than a minute. Estralita was cracking the whip, making sure her orders were carried out to a tee.

The party was coming together and as the carnival rides were set up and the barbecue pits full of apple wood and mesquite giving off a glorious scent, things were in the ready for the party. Soon the spits were filled with whole pigs and impressive chunks of beef. The tables were covered and ready for the contributions of the guests.

Jessie found the morning quickly slipping away. She needed to get away for a few minutes to ready herself for the party. Jessie was still finishing the last minute details when their first guest arrived. She looked at her watch and wondered where the time had gone.

She was awake before the sun's rays peaked through her window. She figured she was the first to rise, but the aroma of coffee told her Nana was already in the kitchen.

As she grabbed a quick cup of coffee she was greeted by the band making last minute adjustments to the stage. She inhaled the acrid scent of mesquite as slabs of beef cooked in the barbecue pits.

She grabbed her list of last-minute chores to make sure every detail was completed. Estralita would be coordinating the serving of the feast, making room for the goodies added by the arriving guests.

Nana had a gentle flush to her cheeks, the only sign she was anxious about her workmanship. The bubbles of excited laughter announced the entrance of the two teenagers. They were dressed casually, ready at a moment's notice to jump into their party clothes. Impatiently they waited for the party hour to arrive.

Jake, dressed in his usual Levi's, country shirt and ever-present weatherbeaten hat stained with years of use, stood ready to oversee any last-minute crisis.

"Jeez, Grandpa, you're not going to wear those old clothes, are you?" Jordan asked, hoping he wouldn't have to watch his grandfather spend this of all days working.

"Why wouldn't I?" Jake asked, winking at Estralita. "I'm just an old cowboy working for his keep," he said, solemnly holding his hat over his heart for effect.

"Oh, Grandpa," Cristal laughed at his routine. He said the same thing every time they made him dress for an occasion.

"Jake, are you harassing these poor children?" Jessie asked as she looked up from her list, amazed at the controlled chaos.

"Do you need any help, Nana?" Cristal already knew the answer but wanted to make sure everything came off without a hitch.

"Everyone has been kind enough to make their own breakfast, and my helpers are due to arrive any moment. Everything is prepared." The small woman was organized enough to feed a small army at the drop of a hat…for her this was a cakewalk!

"Well, then, I'll leave you to your work and get my own work finished."

The next thing Jessie knew her list was completed and the early birds were arriving; hoping to get a front row seat for the ensuing excitement.

Jessie let in the hired servers, directing them where to put on their uniforms and excused herself to change for the party. She was so occupied with the last minute details she had missed Sam's arrival. He watched her work diligently amazed at how casually she greeted both workers and early guests.

She was working with a fervor that put everything else out of her mind. He noted her grin of satisfaction as she closed the book. He began to approach her, but changed his mind and decided to give her an opportunity to dress for the occasion. He could wait. He knew from experience the wait would be worth it. He looked forward to seeing her for what he considered their first real date.

Jessie had chosen her outfit carefully. She wanted to look perfect for the day. She felt she could finally admit to falling in love with an extraordinary man. She looked at herself in the mirror as her bath filled. She had been too busy with the excitement of the last couple of months to get a haircut. She put her hand to her usually short-cropped hair. It had quickly grown out of control. The natural curl not evident in its standard cut framed her face in a halo of curls, drawing attention to her deep emerald green eyes.

The summer sun had turned her skin a coppery gold, contrasting attractively with the mint green summer dress she had chosen. Jessie took an extra few minutes in her bath to claim her nerves. Jessie knew she should hurry, but she was too relaxed to move. Roger's murderer would probably be present, and she was sure the day would hold plenty of intrigue.

Jessie heard the band tuning up. She had lingered longer than anticipated. As she stood up to step out of the bath there was a knock on her door. "Mom, you better shake a leg. Everyone is starting to arrive, and you don't want to miss any of the fun!" Cristal said excitedly.

"Okay, I'll be down in a few minutes." Taking a deep breath, she stepped out of her bath. Jessie threw her towel on the bed after quickly toweling off. She felt the cool softness of the mint green silk dress as it slid over her skin. Clasping her locket around her neck, she hoped Sam was right and the necklace would spark interest in the right person. Jessie didn't know why, but every time she thought of the necklace she had a rush of terrifying emotions. The vision, although becoming second nature, was as illusive as ever. She shrugged off the edginess the thoughts of that night elicited. She planned to make today her first day of freedom.

She turned to the mirror and took one last look; she felt a flutter of excitement in the pit of her stomach at the prospect of seeing Sam. The golden locket winked brightly on her chest. Sam figured Roger's murderer would be in their midst and this may be the one thing to bring him or her into the open.

Sam stepped impatiently onto the porch, realizing he couldn't wait any longer to see Jessie. They had been together every day for weeks, and it was agony these last few days not seeing her.

Jessie opened the door, causing Sam to take a deep breath. She was a vision in mint green. Her silk summer dress provocatively hugged her body. She looked like a teenager, wide-eyed and a little shy. He wanted to grab her and never let go. His eyes amply conveyed this message.

"Sam," was all she was able to say. She was attracted to Sam's virile looks, but today she saw he was more than attractive, he was beautiful! He was dressed in a sky blue shirt with dark blue ribbing that matched his eyes exactly. His custom-cut jeans hugged the sinewy length of his legs compellingly. She blushed at the inviting look in his eyes.

The embrace began as a welcoming hug, quickly turning into more as Jessie felt herself lifted onto a cloud of emotion. Her legs seemed to lose their will. All she wanted was to fall into the languorous feelings evoked by the taut strength of Sam's body.

"We should join the party," Sam whispered in her ear painfully, when all he wanted was to breathe in the wildflower scent surrounding her, carry her to her bedroom, and take her completely, branding her with his love.

Jessie sighed as she returned to the present. She knew Sam was right, but she wanted to melt in the safely of his arms. "Yes," was all she could murmur over the lump in her throat.

Sam knew the slightest suggestion and they wouldn't join the party, not yet anyway. It wasn't enough for him. He had waited his entire life for her, and he didn't want anything to stand in the way of her complete surrender.

"God, you are so beautiful." Sighing in resignation, Sam set her away from him while he still could. "This isn't finished by a long shot!"

Jessie was struck speechless by the look of hunger in his eyes and knew he wanted her but would wait until she was ready. "Thank you, Sam." Nothing else needed to be said between them.

# Chapter Twenty-nine

"Well, here comes our hostess, finally," Sarah whispered into Agnes's ear. "And on the arm of her new beau, I might add."

Agnes had always held ill feelings for Jessie, especially after she snagged Roger. Roger had been more like a son to her than David had ever been. If that little snip hadn't lured Roger away she would have been invited to live at Rite place after the disappearance of Big Roger and Glynis. She would have been the one to comfort Roger in his hour of need, though in her eyes they never deserved the exceptional young man as their son.

Sarah saw the play of emotions over Agnes's face and wished she could read minds. She knew hatred when she saw it, and Agnes hated Jessie. Sarah would get to the bottom of this if it was the last thing she did.

"Tell me what she is wearing." Agnes smiled with her lips, but behind her dark glasses her lifeless eyes held no emotion.

Agnes didn't care what she was wearing, but it would keep Sarah from prattling about useless gossip. "Sarah, will you take me over to the pool. It's cooler over there, and I can listen to the children laughing and having fun." Agnes thought, *At least I can keep her away from David by running errands for me.*

"What a fine idea, Agnes." Sarah was glad to get away from the demanding old ninny. "I can bring you some cool lemonade to sip until lunch is ready." Sarah wanted to spend as much time alone with David as she could. This would be the day when he realized she was the woman he needed.

"Not necessary, dear, just sit with me for awhile. You know how nervous

I get at these functions." Agnes smiled at the effect her plan was having. The battle lines were drawn, and she wasn't about to lose another son to a conniving woman.

Sarah was getting tired of these power plays with Agnes. She was as patient as the next person, but Sarah felt her time was running out. She had to ensnare David today, or it could be months before she could get another chance.

"You will never guess who just arrived, Dr. Chuck Smith, and he has Selma Billings on his arm!" Sarah was amazed at the audacity of the woman.

"Now, Sarah, you know Chuck has been in love with her since before she started working for him." Agnes wanted to keep Sarah thinking about anyone but David. She had allowed her knowledge of Roger and Selma's affairs to be untold. She knew Roger had no lasting feelings for the silly woman. He just used her as he used every other woman he knew. Agnes's was the opinion he respected.

"That may be true, but she is just using him. Everyone in the county knows it." Sarah didn't want to waste time discussing the biggest whore in town since Robyn got what was coming to her. Sarah got a smile of satisfaction on her face at the thought of the demise of Robyn.

"Chuck, honey, aren't we going to say hello to our hostess?" Selma cooed in Chuck's ear. She had plans for today, and she was in a hurry to get started on them.

"You promised me no funny stuff if I brought you along today," Chuck replied stiffly.

"I just wanted to apologize to Jessie for the way I acted." Selma placed a pout on her lips she knew Chuck couldn't resist. She gave Chuck a seductive look that made him putty in her hands and cemented his acquiescence.

"Fine, but no funny stuff," Chuck said soberly.

"Hi, Jessie, looks like a great party." Chuck was beaming bright red, remembering the embarrassment over the last conflict between Jessie and Selma.

"Chuck, I'm happy you were able to make it." Jessie smiled broadly at Chuck. All enthusiasm was lost as she turned to greet Selma. "Selma," was the only greeting she was able to spit out.

"Why, that's very gracious of you, Jessie." Selma ignored the fact that Jessie's comments were directed to Chuck and not her. "I need to apologize for our last meeting. I was very upset and didn't think before I opened my mouth." The words sounded sincere enough, but the look in Selma's eyes belied the fact.

244

"No problem, Selma. I understand perfectly," Jessie replied, always the perfect hostess.

"Well, that's very sociable of you, Jessie. I wonder if maybe you might have a swimsuit I could borrow. The pool looks inviting, and I forgot to bring mine. I don't think it would be *too* big." Selma couldn't resist the parting shot as she batted her eyes innocently.

"Yes, I'm sure I can find something large enough to fit you." Jessie wanted to tear out her hair but decided it wasn't worth the effort.

"Come on, Selma, you look like you could use some cooling off." Chuck grabbed Selma by the elbow and headed her toward the bar.

*I hate that woman!* Jessie thought, shaking her head to get rid of the irritation she was feeling, and headed to the next guest. She was still waiting for a reaction to the locket she was wearing. She was disappointed Selma wasn't the one to leave the necklace as evidence, but Selma hadn't even blinked an eye when she saw it.

Jessie was both surprised and anxious by the turnout of the community. She worried the day could turn into a circus if the press got it into their mind to make more of the day than it was. She hadn't seen "Old Beagle Nose." She was probably sniffing out any little piece of information she could turn into dirt.

Jessie surveyed the turnout. Everyone was having a great time. Time after time old friends came up to her to tell her they were glad to see her. Maybe with time she would lose the humiliation of the newspaper stories around the country: "The now young, rich widow of one of the largest independently owned working ranches left in America"— Blah, blah, blah! She could still see the headlines. She would put the past behind her and look to the future.

Jessie took a deep breath and caught a wave from Rob Roy as he and Gloria walked into the party. Gloria headed to the bar, twirling a large, gaudy parasol. People split like the parting of the red sea in her quake, afraid of mortal injury by the unsafe paring of her parasol.

Rob Roy headed to where Jessie was standing and looked down on the tall woman. Jessie saw the similarity between the two half brothers now that she was aware of the relationship. She felt heaviness in her heart. He was a young man who at one time had so much potential. If only Big Roger had taken responsibility for his actions, so many things could be different.

"Miss Jessie, here I am!" He presented himself with much pride. He was proud of the new clothes he had talked Gloria into purchasing for the party.

"Why, Rob Roy, this must be a new outfit." Jessie smiled sweetly at the overgrown boy. She knew he would be pleased she noticed, although it would be difficult not to. Rob Roy's usual attire, summer or winter, was a pair of tattered old overalls, complimented by a t-shirt or wool hunting shirt, depending on the season.

"Yeah, my Mom brings them to me," he beamed. "She told me 'You aren't looking like something the cat dragged in.'"

"Well, you look very nice," Jessie said, unable to resist giving the young man a swift hug.

"Miss Jessie?" he asked, shyly digging the toe of his highly polished boot into the soft grass. "Mom thinks I'm too big for the ponies." The confusion was evident in his eyes. His ancestor's love of horses evidently flowed through his veins, even with his limited capacity to show it.

"Yes, Rob Roy, I'm afraid you are." Jessie noted the tears surfacing at this admission. "But later Jordan and Cristal are going for a ride. I'm sure they would like you to go. Have you seen the new colt, yet?"

Excitement replaced the previously sad face. "There is a baby horse?" Rob Roy asked, rubbing his hands together in excitement at the thought.

"Yes, I think Jordan and Cristal are down at the barn showing him off. Why don't you join them?" Jessie wasn't surprised when Rob Roy forgot to say goodbye at the thought of the colt. She watched his clumsy gate as he hurried to join the teenagers at the barn.

"Where is that dope going?" Gloria had stepped behind Jessie as she watched Rob Roy head in the direction of the foaling barns.

Jessie was startled as the women spoke from behind her.

"Why, Gloria, isn't it nice to see you concerned for the welfare of your boy?" Jessie knew she was being pious, but it irritated her when Gloria treated the young man with such contempt.

"Cut the sweet stuff, Jessie. You know we understand each other perfectly. You think you can get a hold of his money, too, just as you did his brother's. Well, I'm here to see it doesn't happen." Gloria teetered on 4-inch spike heels, swaying dangerously.

"Why don't you find someplace to sit? Lunch is about to be served. You look like you could use something to eat."

On cue the large dinner gong sounded, announcing the serving of the banquet.

To Jessie's surprise, Gloria wasn't argumentative as she headed to a spot by the pool. Plopping herself down, she grabbed two drinks from a passing server. She thought to herself how enjoyable it was to drink someone else's alcohol for a change.

While Jessie watched Gloria wobble over to a table, she searched out someone to take her a plate of food. Gloria irritated her, but after listening to her tale of abuse she felt compelled to tolerate her.

The reverberations of the gong created a stampede of young children. Their appetites were aroused by the bounty of the long tables of foods and the aromas emanating from the barbecue pits. Everyone settled down to fill their aching stomachs with the food piled on table after table. Jessie's family had saved a seat for her and Sam with them, but did not stand on ceremony; Jessie noticed they were in line! Jessie smiled at the wonderful sight of her family together, happy for now!

While everyone was eating, Jake took the opportunity to make his annual announcement. Sounding the gong to attract everyone's attention, Jake began.

"Everyone attention! I would like to take this time to give a round of thanks to a little woman without who we wouldn't be enjoying this feast. Estralita!"

The round of applause wouldn't stop until Estralita stood and took a small bow.

"Mr. Jake, I will make you pay for this!" Estralita said through gritted teeth, just loud enough for him to hear.

Everyone raised their glasses and toasted her. "To Estralita!

After filling their stomachs the band tuned up their instruments and began to play. Everyone loosened their belts to enjoy the festivities. The band's music soon had everyone's toes tapping. The guests paired up to enjoy the dance music, which promised to last late into the night.

The band was made up of many different people, some professional and some just in love with entertaining. They all took turns suggesting songs, creating a wide variety of music.

Everyone clapped as Hank Lemmings grabbed the microphone to announce a rousing set of square dancing to add to the entertainment. The band began the merry notes of "Turkey in the Straw," an old-time favorite to start the square dancing.

The dance floor quickly filled, causing squares to be formed on the grass surrounding the stage. Soon even the audience was tapping their feet in time with the opening beats.

Hank boomed, "Bow to your partner, bow to your corner, grand allemande right and left," starting the dancing that would continue till the last couple surrendered.

There were squares on the stage used for the can-can, and squares overflowing onto the surrounding yard following the calls. The dancers were dressed in every kind of attire. Some women were dressed in thickly petticoat square dance costumes, others in tight wranglers with bright colored shirts of differing designs and high-heeled cowboy boots. Wives and husbands were in brightly colored matching outfits, some shining with sequins and others with hand embroidery embellishing them.

Jessie sensed the time flying by. The day was quickly changing to an evening shade. Jessie watched her children laughing and enjoying all the fun. Her neighbors had settled into an easy camaraderie, enjoying each other's company. She felt at ease with the world!

Jessie had halted some conversations as she walked by. She knew she was the topic of the day, but she chose to ignore the indiscretions. She wasn't going to let a few loose tongues ruin her day.

Sam closely watched the reaction of each suspect to the locket Jessie was wearing. Unfortunately, he saw nothing out of the ordinary. He hoped it would be as simple as seen on TV. The murderer was caught because 10 people turned him in. But in the real world it was seldom as simple as that!

Jessie's attention was drawn to Chuck standing alone. She was touched by the look of isolation surrounding Chuck. He seemed at ease only when he was working with animals, as an afterthought she wondered where Selma was. She is probably skulking around somewhere, hunting new game! Jessie thought disgustedly.

"Hi, Chuck." Jessie realized this was one person who needed a friend. "Having a good time?"

Chuck, as usual, seemed at a loss for words. "Yeah, a great time, everything was good," he finally said. Chuck glanced furtively around, hoping to find a quick exit. Even though there was a cool, early evening breeze starting to stir, something caused the sweat to break out on Chuck's forehead.

"It seems like you have lost you date." Jessie took no pleasure in the cause of Chuck's discomfort, but she could tell by the look on Chuck's face that Selma was up to no good!

"She...a...she was looking for somewhere to change into her bathing suit," Chuck stuttered, showing he was a really lousy liar.

Jessie wanted to let him off the hook. She didn't trust Selma as far as she could throw her. Selma would use any means to get what she wanted, and Jessie was afraid to find out what that was. She knew it wasn't good.

Sam noticed anxiety increasing in Jessie's manner and decided now was a perfect time to let his "hostess" know what a great party this was.

"Jessie, great party, do you have time to spare me a dance?" Sam asked, grabbing her before she could decline. The couple slid not unnoticed among the milling dancers. Jessie and Sam acknowledged their friends and neighbors as they passed them on the dance floor.

"Sam, I've been talking to everyone, and I haven't notice anything out of the ordinary." Jessie was trying to smile, but her disappointment was evident.

"I know I've been keeping an eye on you all day. The results have been less than satisfactory." Sam tried to keep his voice casual so Jessie wouldn't become discouraged.

"Have you seen Selma?" Jessie asked as Chuck bounced by, being led to the slaughter, so to say, by Theda Reams. Jessie had done a great job of avoiding the newspaperwoman all day. Poor Chuck hadn't been so lucky!

She hoped the food and all the excitement would keep Theda occupied. She didn't want to read any "juicy" news items in the newspaper this week. She smiled with sympathy for the poor man.

"No. Selma's kept a low profile all day. I'm surprised she's kept her roving to a minimum. There are lots of available men here today."

Jessie could tell by the curl of distaste around Sam's mouth that he wasn't available. "I think she has lost a bit of allure as far as Chuck is concerned. She's not about to press her luck."

The music took a lively turn. As Sam led Jessie off the dance floor she said, "I'm getting a little chilly, Sam. I think I'll get a shawl."

"Do you want me to come with you?"

"No, I'll be right back. You just save me some more dances." Jessie smiled as she pointed out the fact Theda was on her way over to capture Sam for a quick "turn" around the floor.

Jessie gave Sam a smile of encouragement as he was led off on his jaunt. Jessie stopped at her front door to survey the party. Everyone was having a great time. Jessie was proud of the hard work they had all done to bring the party together in a short amount of time.

Jessie opened the hall closet to get her wrap when she noticed the light at the office door. She moved to listen at the door, intrigued by the sound of movement from inside.

Jessie opened the door a crack to see who was in the room. "Maybe I could help you find what you are looking for."

Selma dropped the folder she was holding. Swinging around in surprise, she tried to think of a believable lie, but she settled for the truth.

"You have some pictures belonging to me," Selma said as she settled into the office chair.

"I think you must be mistaken." Jessie tried to keep the resentment out of her voice. "Who gave you permission to be in here?" Jessie asked, although she knew the answer.

"I didn't think I would get permission. You and I both know the last things you want are those pictures to come out in the open." Selma settled into a comfortable overstuffed chair and crossed her legs nonchalantly.

"I think it's time for you to leave, or perhaps I could get Sheriff Boatwright to escort you." Jessie felt her face redden with anger.

"That's up to you. Won't this make a great cover story for Theda's paper?" Selma brightened up at the thought she finally had the high and mighty Jessica Rite just where she wanted her.

"No better than the story where you were arrested for breaking and entering." Jessie realized how empty the bluff sounded.

"Actually, I didn't have to break in, the door was open," Selma said, the satisfaction showing on her face. "Like they say in Hollywood, 'Any publicity is good as long as they get my name right'!"

Jessie held herself in check; she wanted to wipe the smirk off of Selma's face. "Oh, they'll get your name right when they arrest you for the murder of my husband and Robyn." Jessie was grasping at straws, but she enjoyed how quickly the smirk disappeared. "Hit a soft spot, did I?"

"Look, all I want are the pictures, and I'll be saying goodbye." Selma was leaning on the desk, gripping it, her knuckles turning white.

"I'm afraid I don't know what you are talking about," Jessie said truthfully. "Even if I did, you would be the last person I would give anything to."

"I swear if you don't give me those pictures—" Selma was interrupted by Sam.

"You'll what?" Sam had never liked Selma. Her angry glare had transformed the normally attractive features to a strained, ugly mask. He had always figured beneath the surface lay the angry shrew now evident.

"Selma and I were discussing inviting Boat to join our little party." Jessie was relieved to have Sam joining forces with her. "We are trying to out guess each other as to the next headline in the *Silverton Gazette*."

Selma decided to take a different tack. "You two lovebirds look like you want to be alone."

Jessie grabbed Selma by the arm as she tried to slide out the door. "I'm not through with you yet. I want the answers to my questions, and I want them now."

Selma shook her arm loose from Jessie's tight grasp. "I don't owe you any explanations." She tried to squeeze past the two guarding the door.

"Just what do you want with the pictures you're so sure I have?" Jessie asked.

For the first time since opening the door Jessie saw what she knew was surrender in the other woman's eyes. Unfortunately she was sure the love Selma felt for her husband was true. She realized Selma was capable of many things, but she wasn't sure she was capable of murdering Roger. Selma wanted the pictures as mementos, but Jessie didn't have them.

"Why don't you just go home? There is nothing here for you." Jessie stepped out of the way so Selma could leave.

Jessie felt herself being engulfed in a warm embrace. "She isn't the one, just another dead end." It was all she could do not to break down.

"We just have to keep going. We'll get the one responsible." Sam knew the longer the investigation went on, the less the chance was of solving it.

Jessie trusted Sam, but she knew all the statistics. This was their last chance to catch the killer; with darkness nearing, the chance was soon coming to an end.

"Let's go join the fun. We don't want to let Selma ruin what's left of this wonderful day," Sam murmured in Jessie's ear.

She pulled back to look squarely into Sam's eyes. Revived by the knowledge she was protected, she found warmth and comfort in the love she found in his eyes.

"I'm ready for that dance you promised me." She stepped out of the embrace but grabbed Sam's hand, unwilling to break the physical bond she needed.

The automatic outdoor lights went on around the pool, confirming the setting sun. The bandstand was lit by the spotlights directed on the band. The melody from the rented carousel filled the gap as the band took rest in-between sets.

Jake sought out his daughter to tell her it was time to begin the fireworks. He spotted Jessie and Sam leaving the house hand in hand. He watched them walk proudly through the crowd. He was pleased Jessie had a friend she could count on. Here was a man deserving of the exceptional woman his daughter had grown into.

He figured the fireworks could wait a while longer. There were still plenty of dances left in the band, and plenty of people still enjoying Estralita's feast.

The children talked their parents into making s'mores by the dozen at the still-glowing barbecue pits. Children enjoyed this day when bedtimes were forgotten. Today was a day to be remembered forever. Puppy love bloomed between the teenagers as everyone was free to celebrate the nation's birthday.

Cristal decided to take a quick dip in the pool. She shivered as she poised to dive into the pool; she was chilled by a quick gust of wind blowing down from the mountains. As she broke the water she was enveloped in its warmth. She glided under water to the shallow end of the pool to be greeted by Jordan and some of their friends sitting in the warm water.

"Is anyone ready for some no-rules polo?" This had always been one of Jordan's favorites. He came out the winner most of the time by sheer dominance of size. Cristal had already talked all of his football buddies into being on her team. This was her night for revenge!

The teenagers divided into teams and began the game. Jordan's team was filled with teenage girls and Cristal's team was mostly boys. "Sorry, girls, but this is my night for revenge!" Cristal beamed.

"We can beat you guys with one hand tied behind us, right girls?" Jordan retorted.

The teenage girls looked from one to another then, as if prearranged, jumped in unison to dunk Jordan.

As he came up for air he was stunned. "I thought you were my team!" he said, sputtering.

"No rules, remember, Jordan?" Cristal laughed at the look of amazement on Jordan's face. "They are all on *my* team!"

"No problem, I can beat all of you!" Jordan boasted.

It took only a few minutes for Jordan to give up. He was not about to be beaten and ruin his long-standing reign as no-rules polo champion. He had to give Cristal her dues. This was a great plan, getting everyone to be on her side, but he still plotted to keep his title.

"I give, Cris. Great idea getting everyone on your team, but let's play keep away. You can choose the teams if you want." Jordan was ready for anything but losing his crown.

Cristal knew what her brother was doing, but she was having too much fun to be upset. She didn't care if they won the polo championship. It was enough that she was able to pull one over on her brother.

"That's a great idea. Everyone that wants to be on my team over here, and everyone that wants to be on Jordan's over there." Cristal roared in laughter as everyone came to her side of the pool.

"Hey!" Jordan yelled.

All of the kids in the pool roared at the dejected look on Jordan's face. He was always a favorite around school because of his good-natured jokes. It was fun for everyone to get a change to tease him. The kids broke into two teams and were soon splashing and having a good time.

Agnes listened to the good-natured splashing in the pool with a slight smile of indulgence, her thoughts far away from the swimming pool. She hated Jessica for stopping her move to the Rite place. She was convinced Roger would have asked her to replace Glynis. She knew she would have made a wonderful surrogate grandmother for the children. Roger wanted the move, needed her to assume the role she deserved. If only David could be the man Roger had been, maybe she wouldn't find so much disappointment in her son.

No one noticed the range of emotions that traveled over Agnes's face in the evening light. Many times Roger had discussed how he wished Glynis wasn't his mother. It should have been Agnes; she was the one woman in his life who truly understood how he felt. She would give him free rein to anything in her grasp. Many a time when David was gone she would let Roger visit the greenhouse. He seemed to enjoy the work David did. So what if he brought women there occasionally? She didn't mind. She would have done anything he wanted, if only he hadn't brought that whore…

\*\*\*

Sarah sat by David, contentedly watching the people dance around them. She knew David wasn't interested in dancing. She didn't mind. She had been too busy to be interested in music or dancing. She could carry a tune, in fact, at church they said she sang like an angel. Singing got you nowhere, though; she had better things to do with her time.

"Look, David, the group from Wagon Wheel Gap is getting ready to put on their show." Sarah took the opportunity to lean close and grasp David's arm.

David had spent the entire day avoiding Sarah and her attentions. Why couldn't she just leave him alone? He was emotionally exhausted. If he could only ignore the way she looked at him and tried to manipulate him. He wrestled his arm away from Sarah and turned his attention to the act without replying.

Everyone present was transported to the Wild West as the cast members of Wagon Wheel Gap showed their specialties. The music announced the advance of dancers; they gave a whoop and began a time-honored can-can. The dancers were full of energy and did amazing tumbling routines, setting everyone clapping to encourage the dancers to do more and more difficult steps. The applause was endless as they finished their acts.

Lights beamed brightly around the arena where galloping horses raced at breakneck speed while their riders did fantastic stunts as the horses raced faster and faster!

Soon the middle of the arena was filled with cowboys and cowgirls twirling their lariats to the rhythm of the racing horses. The grand finale was a greased pig contest where the kids scurried to out-do each other for the sheer joy of being known as the champion for the year!

Jessie was more entranced by the spectators than the entertainers. Looking from face to face she wondered if the guilty person was present. Every face showed contentment. Couples were sitting in the shadows thrown by the footlights, heads together, arms clasping each other. Children kneeled at the bottom of the stage, eyes wide in wonder, transported to a more exciting time. These are the times that inspired active imaginations.

Her attention was drawn to a lone figure sitting in the dim light emitted by the glow of the pool. Agnes Cummings was sitting on the fringes of the excitement, as usual.

Jessie scanned the crowd, wondering how David escaped Agnes's grip for an entire evening. She was surprised Agnes allowed him any space of his own. Jessie smiled to see David and Sarah sitting together. She was aware of the feelings Sarah had for David. Perhaps the enchantment of the evening would work its spell on David.

Sarah turned as if she read Jessie's mind, causing shivers to run down Jessie's spine. Jessie felt herself wracked with shivers, bringing to memory the old saying, "Someone walked across my grave." Jessie, drawn back to the present by the resounding applause given the contestants, hugged herself to shake off the eerie feelings.

Jake bounded to the stage to announce the advent of the "greatest fireworks west of the Mississippi!" Sam slipped his arm around Jessie's shoulder as he felt her shiver. "What's the matter? Are you still cold?" he asked, pulling her close, encircling her in the warmth of his body.

"A little, I guess," She lied, grateful for the warmth his body gave her. As if on cue a chill wind blew through the crowd, making couples huddle closer to each other and children search out their parents to watch the promised show. The fireworks began with a splendor reminiscent of years past.

***

Sarah knew she should be chilled, but the excitement of her nearness to David gave her a warm glow from inside. She scooted her chair closer to David, grasping his arm and snuggling closer to the emotionally distant young man.

Sarah whispered something in David's ear, making him recoil in disgust and stand as if to leave. Sarah clung desperately to David's arm. "Let go of me, you viper! Everything mother said is right. I want it to stop—now!" David slung his arm, breaking the stranglehold Sarah had on him.

"What do you mean?" Sarah asked, the anger darkening her large eyes. "Your mother and I are friends. She wants our relationship as much as I do." Sarah scanned the area, looking for an outlet for her growing anger. "She told me many times..."

"Mother warned me if I was too nice you would make more of it than necessary. I always thought she was wrong, and I told her many times. You're the same, always clinging and always bossing. Well, I've had it with you—both of you. Get away from me—and stay away from me. One person smothering me is more than enough!" David missed the murderous look in Sarah's eyes as he turned and angrily strode away.

"After all I did for you, Robyn never deserved you! All she ever did was cheat on you behind your back with Roger Rite. I'll get even...you wait and see!" Sarah's attention was drawn to the lone figure illuminated by the soft glow emanating from the pool.

Jessie found herself mesmerized by the interaction between Sarah and David. Sarah's usual placid features seemed to sharpen at what David was saying. Sarah turned, searching for someone in the crowd. She glowered in Jessie's directions. The silhouette of Sarah against the bright sky rooted Jessie to the spot. She felt her world tilt dangerously as if struck by a severe case of vertigo.

"Jessie?" Sam asked as he felt her lean against him.

"Oh my God!" was all she could say. Immediately she realized she had found the answer to her dream.

Sarah looked from side to side for a quick exit, as if she could read Jessie's mind. She berated herself. Coming to the party had been a terrible mistake!

Before she left she had one small job to finish…she was going to take care of that meddling old bitty once and for all!

Agnes had whined ever since receiving the invitation, complaining about the crowds of people, the children roughhousing, and that she had no real friends in Silverton. Sarah was convinced Agnes wouldn't come, or she never would have suggested she come with her and David!

Sarah was sure when she and David were alone and could enjoy an evening together he would see how perfectly matched they were. Then Agnes decided, "Maybe it would be good to get out after all." It was all Agnes's fault; she always got David upset. Well, not anymore!

"I'd like to kill that old bitch," Sarah said dryly as she headed toward the pool. As she approached the blind woman from behind, Sarah said, "I could ring your neck, you old hag!"

"Sarah, dear, is that you?" Agnes was confused by what she had heard.

"If you don't keep your mouth shut you'll get what's been coming to you for years." Sarah had stopped and turned to confront the blind woman—she was so angry she could spit fire! David had spurned her feelings. Was any other person in the world going to give him a second look?

"Sarah, what has come over you? Have you lost your mind?" Agnes's usual exasperation for the silly woman was replaced by fear. Sarah stood rooted to the spot by dark emotions spewing from deep inside of her. Sitting in front of her was the focal point of her anger.

Agnes stood in confusion, facing the younger woman. The two women stood toe to toe; the older woman towered slightly over the younger woman. Sarah held her chin high in defiance.

Jessie had thrown off Sam's protective arm and was hurrying to where the two women stood, squared off for battle. Jessie pushed people out of her way as she ran to stop what she realized was about to happen. Her head throbbed. Inside her head whirled the vision of Sarah outlined by a raging fire.

"Don't talk down to me! You are all alike! You think you can run everyone's lives! Well, I'll show you what I think of you!"

"Sarah, stop!" Jessie screamed as she approached the two women. Jessie slowly worked her way around Sarah, placing herself between the two women.

Agnes, terrified of the menacing woman, took the opportunity Jessie afforded her to step away to a safer distance. When she was out of Sarah's reach she started screaming, "Help!" Slowly she teetered from table to table, stumbling. She retreated to what she figured was a safe distance from the mad woman.

"You—you are nothing but a meddling slut!" Sarah turned and flung her pent up anger toward Jessie. Sarah's eyes, usually the color of an overcast winter sky, had turned coal black. The force of Sarah's anger hit Jessie as surely as a slap across the face.

All of Sarah's attention was at once on the necklace adorning Jessie's neck. "I knew it was you!" Jessie said. Suddenly the elusive vision plaguing Jessie's dreams was crystal clear, as clear as the night Roger was murdered. "Sarah," Jessie whispered, finally aware who had been at the site of Roger's murder. She backed away from Sarah, at the same time repulsed and frightened by the lack of emotion overtaking the simmering anger in Sarah's eyes.

"Give me that," Sarah commanded blandly.

"I don't know what you want." Jessie tried to pacify her while she backed away, hoping to keep a safe distance from the stranger in front of her.

"All of this is your fault. *You* should have died! Then everything would have been perfect." Sarah's lips turned to a snarl of scorn. "I got rid of her. David would have been mine if only you would have left him alone."

"No, Sarah, please don't." Jessie felt her heels hit the molded edge of the pool, afraid she would be pushed into the shallow water.

"I knew you were the one who got the necklace. It had to be you or the police would have known you were the one who killed them. You have ruined all my plans!"

Sarah hunched, ready to spring, but she was grabbed by Sam. Sam's touch turned Sarah into a screaming, scratching banshee! Sam, surprised by the strength of the portly little woman, let his guard down for just a second, allowing Sarah to break loose.

Her attention, still focused on the locket around Jessie's neck, drew her like a magnet. Jessie instinctively sidestepped the ensuing attack, pushing Sarah away from her in the process.

There was a look of total disbelief as Sarah flew into the pool. She plunged headlong into the shallow end, striking her head on the submerged steps of the pool.

Jessie watched in morbid fascination as Sarah's blood mingled with the reflection of the fireworks in the glimmering pool, making a kaleidoscope of color that faded to nothing as Jessie lost consciousness.

# Chapter Thirty

Jessie sat impatiently awaiting her ride to town, her thoughts centered on the last time she and Sam had gone to the Boatwright's for dinner. They had been looking for help, determined to find the person guilty of killing her husband.

She was not sure she would do it again if she knew the outcome. She was dropped as the suspect, but the misery they uncovered had been so far-reaching. She should be grateful to learn the truth, but all she felt was sadness.

The sweet young boy turned into a monster. Most of the lives in the small down of Silverton had been soiled by him. Someday she hoped she could forgive him and forget all the pain he had caused and remember the good times.

With the wrapping up of the investigation it seemed as if a lifetime had gone by instead of a month. The kids were home. School was nearing, and she knew she would have to do all the normal things associated with this time of year. She just wasn't sure she had the energy.

Jessie thought once the mystery had been solved her life would return to normal. Why was it she felt so guilty? It wasn't as if she had asked Roger to turn from his family. It wasn't her fault Sarah was Looney Toons. Still, she couldn't get over the feeling she could have done something. She should have paid more attention to what he was doing. Why she let things get so far out of hand she would never understand. *It had just been easier to turn a deaf ear to the things that were being spread around town for the sake of the kids*, she thought.

The doorbell rang, pulling her out of her reverie. She looked up as she heard the familiar greeting Sam always gave Estralita. She felt her heart flutter at the thought of him.

They had decided to give their relationship a little space, but it was a decision she had quickly learned to regret. She had known after a couple of days it had been a mistake, but could she be sure Sam felt the same?

She stood, eyes the size of saucers in her small face, afraid of what he had to say. All she wanted was to run into Sam's arms and never leave, but the insecurities held her glued to the floor, unable to move.

Sam held his well-worn hat in his hands, twisting it unconsciously. He had missed Jessie, but he didn't want to rush her. A lot had happened to her in the last three months, more than anyone should have to deal with in a lifetime.

First she had lost her husband in a grisly double murder, then to find he had been involved in the death of his parents. Last but not least, she found him firmly ensconced in a crime syndicate.

She was one heck of a woman, and he wasn't going to let her get away from him. She could hide out in her big fancy house for as long as she wanted. He would wait for the day when she found she couldn't live without him either.

"Hi, Sam, how have you been?" Jessie asked cautiously.

"Lonely," was all he said, but his eyes spoke volumes.

Jessie felt all of her inhibitions disappear as she saw the look of love in Sam's eyes. She ran to embrace him. "I'll never let you go again." This was one promise she knew would be easy to keep. She was swept away on a tide of emotion.

Sam's embrace tightened as he claimed her lips. Jessie returned his kiss with fervor unlike any he had ever known. The passion which was reined all summer broke loose.

The two were alone in the world, the only people alive. Sam reluctantly pulled himself away. They were expected at the Boatwrights, and he was not going to let anything spoil the first time he expressed his love for Jessie. He wanted to love her the way she deserved being loved.

Jessie moaned in denial. She felt isolated as Sam released her from his warm embrace. She looked into his eyes questioningly. She could tell a dueling of wills was going on inside Sam by the way he looked at her.

"What's the matter, Sam?" Jessie whispered.

"Nothing is the matter. In fact, everything is perfect." Sam fought to keep his distance. "The Boatwrights are waiting for us at home."

Jessie groaned at the memory. She wanted to call Marge and cancel the invitation. She had a hunger no one but Sam could stave.

"It's time we left," Sam said regretfully. "We will finish this when we can take the time we deserve. Sam grabbed Jessie and kissed her with a slow-burning kiss that seared his intention on Jessie's brain.

Jessie felt as if she would swoon. Her heart was pounding and leaving her so lightheaded that when Sam released his embrace she felt she was walking on air. "You are right, Sam!" Jessie planned to make it an early evening. For the first time in her life Jessie's appetite was missing.

All she wanted was to feel Sam's hard body against hers. She glanced at his strong hands as he drove to Boat and Marge's, shivering at the thought of them playing over her body. She smiled in anticipation of the idea. She couldn't stand the distance separating them in the cab of the old jeep. As she slid over, Sam automatically lifted his arm, encircling her in his embrace. He said quietly, "I say we make this an early evening." It was as if he read Jessie's mind.

Boat was sitting on the porch swing going over the easiest way to tell Jessie what he had found out about "Sarah Hart." His reverie was halted by the sound of Sam's jeep. He wasn't surprised by the sight of Jessie and Sam's quick embrace before exiting the vehicle. His face broke into a broad smile! He would probably have to listen all night to Maggie's "I told you so." A very enticing idea, at that!

"Jessie, you look great!" Boat felt like a fool blurting it out, but it was so obvious something about Jessie had changed! He almost felt sorry for Marge; all her plans and conniving for the evening were unnecessary, for the two needed no help. They were madly in love; any fool could see that.

Marge, putting the finishing touches to dinner, thought to herself, *I won't let my two favorite people in the world pine away for each other.* She promised Boat she wouldn't interfere. It would be just a small dinner party to celebrate the resolution of Roger and Robyn's murder, as if Boat didn't know what she was really planning.

Marge remembered watching the two while they danced at the picnic. They could have been alone in the entire world; she could tell they *were* alone, in their minds anyway. Drying her hands, she was ready to put all her plans into action. She heard the commotion as her three favorite people in the world came banging into the house.

The four friends sat around the table, making small talk. No one was willing to open the subject that brought them together. Marge and Boat looked from one to the other in amazement as Jessie pushed her food around her plate, missing her world-famous appetite.

Waiting for the coffee to percolate in the kitchen gave Marge and Jessie a chance to clear the table. The coffee and dessert would keep the loathsome topic at bay for a while longer.

Jessie was used to attacking things head on, but this was one time she wasn't even sure she wanted to know the answers. "Well, Boat. I guess I'm ready to hear all of it."

Boat solemnly began his narrative.

"Sarah Hart, alias Dorothy 'Dot' Wilson, was born April 1, 1952, in Detroit, Michigan. Dot's mother was mauled and killed by a dog when she was four years old. She never recovered from the incident. Her father remarried when she was six years old.

"Two days after her 12th birthday, Dot was found at the house in a bloodied nightgown. Her father and stepmother were found hacked to death in their bed. Dot was in a catatonic state, and as a minor her records were sealed.

"After the investigation it was decided there was no need for a trial. The neighbors were shocked by the actions of the young child. She was not a typical adolescent; she was extremely bright and precocious. No one could understand what had made her commit such atrocities. She was a minor, and she obviously needed the help of a psychiatric facility. She was remanded to a state facility until she was 18, at which time the doctors felt she was able to return to society.

"When she was 18 she was sent to live in a halfway house. Her parole officer found her to be an excellent worker. She kept all her appointments with her psychiatrist. At the end of her parole she left her job and disappeared. There was no sign of her until she turned up here as 'Sarah Hart.'"

"Was Sarah Hart just a name she made up?" Jessie wondered.

"No. There was a real Sarah Hart. She had a degree in teaching from Oregon State University. She was on her way to a new position in Salem when she disappeared. Her parents have been waiting 17 years to find her. They never gave up hope that they would one day find out what had happened to their daughter. She was probably just in the wrong place at the wrong time."

"Sarah, I mean Dot, worked for the school system. Why didn't they find out about her stealing Sarah Hart's transcripts?" Jessie was terrified at the thought of such a lunatic being in control of children's minds in their formative years.

"There are no laws mandating a criminal background in this state. It just doesn't have a high priority on our legislator's agenda." Marge was a long-standing member of the citizen's advisory committee to the school board and this was just one of her many crusades. "Well, what happens to Sarah now?"

"She has recovered from her physical injuries although she is still in a catatonic state. The district attorney has chosen to not prosecute her because of her mental state." Boat watched as Jessie turned a deep hue of red. "Even if she was to come out of the cationic state she is in, because of her prior record, it's a pretty safe bet she'll spend the rest of her life institutionalized."

"Why did she do it?" was all Jessie could find to say.

Sam looked at Boat and then related what little information they had. "Agnes Cummings helped fill in some of the details, but we probably will never know the entire story. Agnes knew Roger and Robyn met at the Greenhouse. Roger found perverse pleasure in using David's girlfriend in his Greenhouse. Agnes was happy to let it go unheeded; she was filled with anger at David. She felt he had abandoned her and taken up with a slut on top of it." Sam was trying to keep his voice neutral, but the disdain was obvious.

"Agnes heard a commotion from the greenhouse but was afraid to discover what had happened. She assumed David had committed the crimes and was afraid to say anything. Agnes, ever the realist, knew if David was found guilty of the murders, she would be left alone. This was her mortal fear, being left alone.

"We assume Sarah found them and took the opportunity to get rid of her competition. She tried to place the blame away from David in case somehow the police found they had been killed at his Greenhouse.

"Roger gave her more cover by leaving a journal of his various activities. Just about everyone in the county had a reason to wish him dead at one time or another. It's just a coincidence he was with Robyn when Sarah killed her. Roger's bad luck was to be with Robyn. Sarah's obsession with David started the whole mess."

Jessie felt as if it was happening to someone else. She figured she should feel relief that Roger wasn't the prime victim, but there was no comfort in that fact. Roger was still dead. He was still a horrible person, and she would have to find a way to tell the children.

"Did Sam give you the journals?" she asked.

"I don't know what journals you are talking abut. Any pertinent information would have to be turned over to the state police, and at this point I don't see they would be of any help in the final resolution of this case." Boat was trying to sound like a county sheriff, but Jessie only heard the sound of a friend.

"You know Glynis gave Roger a journal to write in when he was little. He wrote the most beautiful poems." Jessie sighed.

Boat jumped on the chance to end the conversation. "Well, I don't see how a journal full of poems could help close this case."

Jessie gave Boat a grateful smile, turned to Sam and said, "I'm awfully tired. I'm ready to head home." Jessie felt as if her energy had been drained and replaced by a lethargic sadness.

They said their goodbyes at the door. They planned to get all of their friends together for their monthly "Bible Studies" as usual.

Jessie looked at Sam as he and Boat were discussing the mundane chores of running a small ranch. Life returns to normal. It's the one thing keeping her going. Perhaps this was the start of a new life for all of them.

# Epilogue

## Colorado State Hospital for the Insane

A small woman sat rocking in her bed, minute traces of a smile on her lips. The usually blank look was replaced by a stormy glare, darkening her pale grey eyes as she stared at the bare walls.

She had to keep her thoughts to herself. No one but Momma ever loved her; she alone would understand her torment. Her mind returned to a time long ago...

\*\*\*

"Dottie, it's time to go!" the dark haired, petite woman called into the back yard. Surrounding her feet was a menagerie of animals ranging from cats rubbing against her legs lovingly to small puppies wagging their tails fiercely, each patiently awaiting his turn to be noticed by its sweet-tempered mistress.

"Coming, Momma!" the toddler called. The small child wrinkled its forehead, irritated to be taken from her game. She loved collecting bugs, the fear it evoked from her mother gave her pleasure, but her real joy came from the various experiments she performed on them. She liked to see what would happen when she pulled off different body parts.

"She makes me so angry I could just spit!" The small girl spat in the dirt just to emphasize her point.

"Dottie, if you don't hurry we won't get back in time to get Daddy's dinner ready!" The small woman loved her daughter beyond reason, but she never understood her moods.

At the sound of her voice a large, lumbering dog came running to greet the woman. The dog sat at the feet of the woman, solemnly awaiting her notice.

"I'm afraid you can't go today, Duke." It was as if the dog could understand what his mistress said. He dropped dejectedly to a lying position and put his huge head on his front paws.

The little girl glared angrily at the large dog. She hated the fact her mother could find anything worthwhile in all these mangy animals. She had learned the large dog was impossible to intimidate, so she vented her anger on the small puppy, stomping on its tail as she headed to the bathroom.

The yelping puppy drew the attention of her mother, and she immediately turned to the puppy. "Are you all right, Skippy?" The concern was evident in her voice, although not in her eyes.

"What happened, Dottie?"

"Oh, Momma, poor Skippy ran under my feet. Do you think I hurt him?" Her face was screwing into a small knot but any sign of tears were missing.

"Oh, baby, don't cry. I'm sure Skippy will be fine." The small woman was teary-eyed at the thought of anything being hurt. She wiped the tears from her eyes and took her daughter by the hand. She made a little game out of their walk to the neighborhood grocer. Along the way the neighbor's dog ran to get a pat and a word of praise from the small woman. She could never resist even the ugliest mutt in the world and always had a comforting pat or calming word for them.

Walking through the parking lot of the grocery store, she passed a pickup, not noticing a formidable-looking crossbreed dog. As she passed the dog, Dottie threw a rock and by sheer luck hit the dog in its eye. The enraged dog lunged at the small girl, but was blocked by her mother.

Witnesses said the small woman was thrown around like a rag doll by the immense animal. Before anyone could stop the enraged animal the poor woman had been mauled to death. The little girl was unable to take her eyes off the spectacle. She rejected any try at comfort, mesmerized by the violent act in front of her.

As the authorities tried to help her mother, the crowds of people were on one hand amazed and on the other revolted. The small child acted as if nothing out of the ordinary had happened. She chirped gaily on about the happenings of the day, ignoring the fact she had just seen her mother lying in a pool of blood after being mauled to death.

Upon reflection she couldn't understand why everyone was so upset. Her mother asked for what happened to her. If she wouldn't have kept all those stupid animals around she wouldn't have gotten in trouble.

It's just like all the stupid housekeepers her father hired after her mother died. She made a game of finding the easiest way to get rid of them. It was amazingly simple. No one would have believed a little girl could manage to get rid of adults so handily.

When her father married "Simply Pat" as she always thought of her, she had drawn the line. Pat surprised Dottie by her resilience; no matter what Dottie tried, Pat seemed to ambush her at every turn.

Pat tried to be a good stepmother to Dottie, but every overture of affection was spurned by Dottie. Every gift was rejected, the toys relegated to the garbage bin. The small animals each ended up in a more grisly form. The parakeet, it's a featherless body lying in the bottom of the cage; the kitten, its neck twisted at an odd angle, lying on the back stairs; the sweet little gerbil, stuffed in a jar, the lid secured to insure suffocation.

Pat said to her husband, "I'm sure Dottie is innocent. Her mother loved animals so." But to her best friend she confessed, "I'm afraid for our well being. She can be so isolated that there is no way to touch her emotionally."

When Dottie was awakened on her 12th birthday by a puppy lovingly licking her face, she was angered beyond belief. The small ball of fur yelped in pain as she threw the small animal against the wall. The small animal cowered in pain and confusion, terrified by the unexpected cruelty.

The party went without a hitch; Dottie was calm and collected, even showing enthusiasm for the gift of a puppy. Pat relaxed, thinking perhaps she had been wrong about Dottie's attitude toward animals. When later walking past Dottie's room she heard the muffled sounds of an animal in pain, her worst fears realized. When she opened the door she found Dottie with her hand holding the puppy's face in the pillow to muffle its cries, while she beat the poor dog with her other.

Pat wrestled the puppy from Dottie and kept it with her for the rest of the day. Upon her husband's arrival, she informed him of Dottie's behavior, sending him in a rage to confront the young girl. All she would say was, "It wet on my floor," dispassionately.

The next day when Pat's best friend, Ellen, arrived, she was greeted at the door by a grisly sight. Standing in a blood-soaked nightgown was Dottie.

Ellen, horrified at the memory of Pat's confidences, slipped past the strange visage in front of her. Ellen was not ready for the carnage confronting her, she was sickened by the sight of Pat and John hacked to death, mutilated beyond recognition.

When the police arrived they found the almost hysterical woman ranting about a demon-child and the sight of a blood-filled room with two mutilated bodies. In the living room sat a small blood-covered child staring blankly at the cartoons on the television screen, mumbling, "Stop screaming at me."

***

She had lived through this once before and she could do it again. She knew how to handle the testing. She had learned as a little girl. The know-it-all doctors, so full of themselves, were the easiest to trick. She had fooled them once, she would do it again.

"Don't worry, Momma. I'll get us out of here," she whispered. The smile disappeared and the blandness returned at the sound of the key turning in the lock.

The nurse entered with her breakfast. "Good morning, Dottie," the ultra cheerful nurse greeted the silent woman. "How are we doing today?"

The young nurse knew what the woman had done; she just couldn't believe this little woman could be responsible for the deaths of at least five people.

Freshly out of school, she was determined to make her mark in the psychiatric field. In her heart she knew this was the first step on her journey. "Come on, sweetie. We must keep up our strength."

The nurse felt sorry for Dorothy. She knew Dorothy would spend the rest of her adult years behind these walls if she didn't help. If she did recover she would have to take responsibility for her actions, but what if she didn't recover? The young nurse still promised herself she would help the sad creature on her road to recovery.

Dorothy was silently plotting her miracle breakthrough. "Yes, Momma. We'll be out of here one day soon." She would utilize every opportunity afforded her. Upon meeting the spineless ninny attending her, Dorothy realized she could manipulate her into doing whatever she wanted.

When she had all of her plans formulated, then they would start over. She had the time, she could wait; she had waited for the perfect opportunity before. She had always wanted to see the Northwest. Yes, the coast promised to be spectacular—one day soon, Momma. Yes, one day—soon!